Rave Reviews for A KILLING PACE!

"SIZZLING" — *Publishers Weekly*

"CAPTIVATING" — *The Chicago Tribune*

"GOOD FUN" — *The Washington Post*

"TERRIFIC suspense plot. It's moving, exciting and insightful." — John Ehrlichman

"GRIPPING good read." — Nancy Dickerson

A KILLING PACE

by Les Whitten

ZEBRA BOOKS
KENSINGTON PUBLISHING CORP.

ZEBRA BOOKS

are published by

Kensington Publishing Corp.
475 Park Avenue South
New York, N.Y. 10016

First Zebra Books printing: August 1984

Printed in the United States of America

To my father
Leslie H. Whitten (1889–1959)
and to Leslie H. Farber (1912–81)

I am grateful to my sons Leslie and Andrew for their editorial help.

. . . One morning we depart, our brain pans
    squirting fire;
Our hearts are fat with hate and longings' acrid lees.
We go, all following the ocean's rhythmic choir
To lull our infinites upon the finite seas.

One leaves an ill-famed land. How glad his farewell cry!
Another flees the fears sucked in his mother's milk.
Some seem astrologers, drowned in a woman's eye,
A cruel Circe with scents as treacherous as silk.

To keep from being swine, they quaff off cups that brim
With light's intoxicants, with blazing skies and space;
The ice that mangles and the sun that coppers them
In time dry up the stigmas left by her embrace . . .

Strange, spinning Wheel of Fate, how can we ever cope?
Your goals are never fixed; you may be anyplace;
And foolish man, although he never loses hope,
Runs on in search of rest, a crazy, killing pace!

—from "The Voyage" by Charles Baudelaire
TRANSLATION BY LES WHITTEN

CONTENTS

I.
PHILADELPHIA
INTERNATIONAL
AIRPORT

The M-16s lay in the wooden crates as neatly as perfectly stacked cordwood. The thin film of dry lubricant on their ebony flanks made them look dull, even harmless, under the fluorescent warehouse lights. I counted the guns in the top row aloud. Six across. My client had ordered 105 rifles. I did not want to send him only 104, because the distributor had inadvertently shorted me and I had failed to catch it.

The counting done, I picked up each carbine, examined the fourteen-inch barrel, the collapsible stock, the other visible parts, snapped the receiver, and gave the weapon to Hector, my assistant.

He wrapped each of the automatic weapons in heavy, flexible plastic. Then he handed the gun in its translucent sheath back to me. I cloaked it in crinkly brown paper before I slipped it into a cardboard box and put it atop the other boxes in a high-impact polyethylene air carton. We had to repack the guns well. They were going a long way.

The documents from the State Department's Office of Munitions Control authorized me to ship the M-16s from Philadelphia to Monrovia, Liberia. A Liberian government contracting officer was paying me $130,000 for them.

Hector and I fastened down the final air-carton cover. We bound the cartons with steel straps and clamped on lead merchandise seals imprinted with my company name, Frazer, Inc.

I thought for a moment about the automatic weapons dormant in their boxes. They were clean, naked things, designed and manufactured to do precisely what they were supposed to do. Unlike electric shavers and cars and TVs, they were not built to break down after a certain time. Colt had to make their weapons well or international sales would go to Fabrique Nationale or Heckler & Koch. Or to the Russians.

With the rented warehouse's liftloader, we stacked the crates in the truck, also rented, and drove it to the Air Capricorn plane on the cargo ramp at the far end of the airport. I used Air Capricorn because it would cut the necessary corners. Its pilot would not make a report to the State Department if a disguised transport plane was waiting at Monrovia to onload the guns for their true purchaser.

Hector and I watched from the dark apron as the loading team hefted the crates into the converted 707, with its peeling paint and its chipped

12

zodiac symbol on the cabin. When the loading was done, the pilot walked over from the freight terminal and introduced himself. His copilot was already waiting in the cockpit.

I had seen the plane's manifest. Also on board was a shipment of "china" for Conakry. I wanted to make sure my guns went to Liberia before the "china" went to Guinea. That was why I was here: to handle details in person, as in the packing of the rifles. People made mistakes or defrauded the customer slightly less easily after looking into his eyes.

"Monrovia is first," I stated to the pilot.

"Yes, Mr. Fraser," he said, young, respectful.

I dipped in my pocket and brought out a sheaf of twenty-five twenties.

"This is a bonus in advance for good work." He did not take the money. "Don't worry," I told him. "When Freddy"—the president of Capricorn—"was a pilot, he understood the need for performance bonuses." I laughed lightly. I could have bought into Air Capricorn back then. I was glad I had not. It was in shaky health.

The pilot took the money and glanced up at the cab toward his copilot.

"Give him what you want," I said. "Your ass is on the line, not his."

He climbed up the ladder and in moments the engines revved and the specks of grit from the apron struck Hector and me. In the 707's instrument lights, I saw the pilot's face dimly. He gave us a thumbs-up. They all dreamed they were still in the air force, where things were simpler, flying

13

gallant missions against latter-day Richthofens instead of running guns to seedy African and Middle Eastern countries. Hector and I raised our thumbs in response.

On his way to return the truck, Hector dropped me off at the terminal building. I called my contact in Liberia from a pay phone, wondering whether it was a sign of efficiency or of nervousness that he was standing by for the call. I told him the cargo should be there in nine hours. He began to thank me effusively. More experienced crooks said thanks once and pocketed the profits.

The deal had taken us a total of seven days. We had netted $30,000 on it. For some years, I had been making that kind of money with that expenditure of time. Now I was getting sick of it, not the money, but the way I was making it.

In the parking lot, the late spring air still was cool to the lungs. I opened the door of my car, a Cadillac. I had needed the big car to impress my clients. In Philadelphia, at a consulate, or in Washington, at an embassy, there was nothing like a black limo for picking up a military attache for lunch. For pleasure, I drove an antique Morgan I had bought recently.

I called my wife on the car's telephone to let her know I was heading home. It would have been just as easy to call from the airport pay phone, but the call from the car was a tradition. Twenty-one years ago, when we were dating, I had always called her from the car telephone to tell her I was en route. Then the phone had been evidence that we were on the move to something exciting, uncommon: big money, big adventure, big deals.

"Hello," my wife said in those peppy, business-like accents that people from outside Philadelphia call Main Line even when they originate in other toney places. There was not a trace of hardness or brusqueness in her voice, only confidence. And why not confidence? Her firm, Fraser and Brockman, had the best tax practice in the city.

"Hi, Anne," I said, trying to sound easy. It was difficult. Our marriage was almost moribund. We hung on, both of us hoping the long habits of liking each other would generate a miracle that would make bearable all the things that had now gone wrong. "I'm done," I said. "On the way home."

Now the M-16s were passing beneath the stars toward Liberia. I had asked the Liberian contact man when we met in Monrovia whether he wanted the rifles individually packed in watertight containers. His buyers might want to stash them in the ground or the sea for a bit. "No," he had said, unable to avoid looking at me meaningfully. "Not necessary." I knew that meant they would be going into action on delivery; soon there would be a lot of dead people someplace.

Two weeks later, I found out how many: one Italian minister of justice, one Italian judge, two policemen, four adult bystanders (two men, two women), a one-year-old baby in arms, and two presumed Red Brigadists.

On the front page of the *Inquirer* was the picture of a young cop standing before a public building in Rome. His cap was ludicrously askew and his face was anguished, as if one of the dead might be a brother officer, or a brother, or his own child.

In his outstretched arm, he held up in outrage, as if it were some awful poisonous syringe, an M-16. Behind him were the bodies of the dead jumbled in slaughter, one by an open car door.

The Red Brigade, whose operations were generally carried out like precision surgery, had bungled, gotten into a gun battle. Now, instead of a high official and a judge and a couple of cops who could have been written off as members of the oppressor class, there were all these dead.

I read the story, my intuition telling me the M-16s were the ones I had shipped even before I came on the evidence: a wounded and captured (and tortured, I was sure) Brigadist had told the police the weapons were part of a recent shipment from Liberia. The police had found twenty more M-16s in a run-down apartment house just north of the Vatican. The serial numbers had been filed off and the merchandise seals had been snipped from the high-impact plastic containers in which they were packed.

Eventually they would be traced to me and I would explain to the FBI and the Commerce and State departments that my papers were in order. I would express horror—genuinely—that they had found their way from Liberia to Italy. I knew how to cover my ass.

And in the process, I would cover Danny Surrett's. He was a lawyer who had set up the deal. He was also my oldest friend, more my surrogate elder brother. And by not telling me where the guns were eventually headed, he had betrayed me.

I tried to sort out my responsibility.

If one sells guns, people get killed with the guns. That kind of rationalization had held up well for many years — twenty, thirty, maybe all my life, forty-six years.

I stopped cold in mid-self-excuse. As a queasy man may suddenly be clutched by paroxysms of uncontrolled vomiting, I gagged with revulsion, confronted fully with what I had done.

Oh, sure, I had set some standards. An underdog myself, I had sold by preference to underdogs. Through legal but shady middlemen, I had sold to the Kurds fighting Khomeini and to anti-Duvalier rebels and to the democratic faction in Angola. I had not sold to murderers merely because they were underdogs, like the Irish terrorists or right-wing Arab extremists. But I had taken a fine profit. And I had winked, oh, how I had winked. Now my eyes were propped open. It was my guns, my cunning, my contriving that had killed those people in Rome. There was no way to wink at that.

I called Surrett, who, out of caution, didn't want to talk about it on the telephone. We arranged to meet after work. For the rest of the day, I thought about those dead people, particularly the bystanders and the baby. They might have been me or mine.

If I had kept exclusively to private investigations, the work I had loved with an addict's love, these people would be alive. For I had been the very model of a modern private gumshoe. I had been president of the National Association of Private Investigators and during my tenure I had pushed through some good reforms. I had done lecturing stints at the FBI Academy in Quantico and at Temple and Penn and a few others. My cases had made the networks and national newspapers and magazines.

But the big money had been, initially, in selling bugging and antibugging gear. From there, while I never gave up investigations, it was easy to move into even bigger money in small-arms sales. The same customers who wanted to bug other people wanted to shoot them.

In the last few months, I had lost my stomach for it all: investigations, electronic sales, small-arms peddling, the way a lawyer or journalist or anybody gets tired of doing what he does even when he does it well. And with me, there was the added factor of a slow late-blooming morality. But the work-weariness and the morality had not come on soon enough or strongly enough to save those dead innocents in Rome.

At the end of that terrible day, before I left to see Surrett, I walked into Hector's office. He was bent over his desk, studying the litter of papers from which he was able to find in seconds the ones he needed. His was a strong personality, and he resented his man-Friday role with me. Still, we trusted each other, and we had made a lot of money because of that and because of other traits we had in common, like enterprise and guts and shrewdness. In the long run, that similarity between us had worked out better than actually liking each other.

I could sell out to Hector. He would like that. On the edge of my lips were the words — "I'm quitting" — that would launch me into the unknown. But I did not say them. Although I was more ready than I had ever been, I knew quitting would push Anne and me even closer to divorce. Better therefore that job, like marriage, remain in limbo.

"See you tomorrow," I said.

"That's upsetting about Rome, hunh?" he said, but I knew it was more out of sympathy with what I felt than anything Hector felt yet himself. It'll come, Hector, I thought. Just wait a little.

"Yeah," I said.

Danny Surrett, who thirty years ago had operated out of a nearly bare ten-by-twelve room, now had a half dozen associates and a small platoon of office staff, most young, female, pretty, and available to Danny.

Along with more savory clients, Danny represented many of the city's top mobsters, mainly in corporate litigation, but sometimes on criminal cases. They paid well. All his clients did. He had accumulated apartment houses, a bakery, a miniconglomerate of Philadelphia real property, goods, and services.

In place of the two gooey landscapes in that

long-ago Broad Street office, modern abstract prints adorned his anteroom. The ones in his huge corner office were signed and numbered by the artists.

It was already dark outside when I got there, and we could see people in overcoats hurrying under the lights of Washington Square. It was hard to believe Surrett was sixty-one. His suits were perfectly cut, his hands manicured, his specs gold rimmed. He still had the handsome looks of a movie cop. The good living had told only in the broken veins on his nose.

"I saw the picture in the paper," he said. "I'm sorry."

"You should have told me. I wouldn't have shipped them."

"I know. I needed them shipped," he said.

I shut up and waited. He was better with words than I was and I had learned a long time ago that the best way for me to express displeasure and force him to talk with me was for me to be silent.

"I had to do something for them," he said.

"For a bunch of fucking terrorists? Red Brigades?"

"Them. But for my clients mainly."

I knew instantly what he meant. He meant the mob.

"For some cheap hood? You did that to me?"

"For Bernie," he said.

A hood, he was saying, but not a cheap hood. Bernie Magliorocco, in the Philadelphia Mafia, was number one. One of the last of the old *caporegimi* in the country. But what did that have to do with left-wing Italian terrorists?

"Why?" I asked.

Surrett took off his glasses and rubbed his eyes.

"I'd rather you didn't know."

"My God, Danny. It was a Roman My Lai for me."

"Okay, okay, spare me the analogies. . ."

But I was in my groove.

"Haven't I got enough problems? Me and Anne? Me trying to find a reason to stay in the goddamned business? So you come along and shit on my head, give me one final, flaming reason to get the hell out?"

"Bernie is in trouble with his Young Turks. They think he's too old to run the outfit. So he has to do something to show he's still all in there. Something to make big, big money. It's going to work this way: the terrorists get the guns; he'll get cheap prices on the merchandise they have to offer."

"Merchandise?" What the hell did the Red Brigades, or any other terrorists, have to sell except other people's blood? Then I understood. Some of the Latin American terrorists, I had learned, were paying for guns with cocaine.

"Dope," I said.

Danny shrugged.

"I don't ask Bernie about merchandise. I just set up the arms stuff."

"But that's what it is."

He shrugged again, this time in assent.

"You roped me into that?" I asked incredulously.

21

Now his coolness was gone. He understood how upset I was, how badly he had wronged me. I would get the whole truth.

"Georgie, I had to. Bernie's got his hooks into me. You know how it happens. You've been smart enough to stay away from the mob. But I — and the stakes for Bernie are everything. I had to do it."

"The Red Brigades. Shit, they aren't that big. Those one hundred and five M-Sixteens would arm everyone of them twice."

"It isn't just the Red Brigades," Surrett said.

Then it hit me. Magliorocco was planning something that was going to make him, and Danny, and everyone else on their side very, very rich. Or very, very dead. If he could corner the market on guns-for-drugs around the terrorist world, then he could match the income of all but the biggest New York families.

"You mean for all of them?"

"Not all of them. Lots of them. The ones who aren't too ape-shit to do business with. If it works with the Red Brigade, he's thinking about some of the PLO factions and the Tupamaros and that Golden Triangle KMT bunch in Asia."

"And you were going to use me. . ."

"Just this one batch was all," he said. "I needed to be sure the first gun deal went through perfect." He smiled, knowing the compliment would not pacify me. "After all, I trained you."

"Not for this. And it didn't go through perfectly. There were —"

"A lot of people killed," he interrupted, irri-

22

tated now because he had tried to be frank. "But it worked perfectly for Bernie and for the Red Brigade leadership. It's their foot soldiers who screwed up. It worked perfectly."

"And if the rest of it works, then you've got cheap dope all over town. All over the East Coast. And guns, brand-new guns, in the hands of maniacs all over the world. You're crazy to be in on this."

"Christ, Georgie," he said, defensive again, "you act like I *want* to be." He paused and I saw the depth of his worries. Even the enormous amount of money he would make could not cover up for the fact that if it didn't come off, the rebels in Bernie's mob might snuff him along with Bernie. In fact, Danny would be an easy target. He didn't have a structure of triggermen among his next of kin to revenge him if he were killed.

"We could be caught in the middle of this," I said.

"You've taken chances before."

Suddenly, uncharacteristically, I wanted to cry. I wanted to explain that it was not cowardice, not even selfishness, that made me not want to take these kinds of chances anymore. A thing in me had been growing; I wanted time for it to flower. If it would.

"Danny," I said, choked up but tearless. "I know this is going to sound nuts to you. But I am trying in some way to become a better human being. It doesn't show yet, but. . ."

He looked at me as if I were on the verge of some sort of breakdown. Deciding I wasn't, at least not yet, he went back to safe practicalities.

"I'm going to make sure I only handle the legal aspects of this thing," he said.

"Are there any?"

"There always are," he said with the emphysematous sigh of a man who had smoked too much and too long.

II.
GEORGIE

I don't say my friendship with Surrett was inevitable. That's the kind of word that implies destiny, fatalism. But it was likely. He was a beat cop on the streets near where I lived in South Philly and I was a street kid, my home a nightmare from which I awoke only when I was out of the house.

My father, a godly man, had been a bricklayer until he was crippled by polio shortly before I was born in 1935. A good mason, he had wanted me to follow his aborted trade. Even disabled, he had sought some physical labor he could do in Philly's factories with his powerful hands.

But in those depression days, he was lucky to have even a candy, soft drink, and newspaper stand. It was outside the Philadelphia Saving Fund Society, five blocks from our home.

Pop was Scotch-Irish, an oddity in South Philly, but no more so than my mother. Although Italian, she had been converted to a Pentecostal church and thenceforth shunned both her family church and her parents' language. She never let pop or my brother Ricky or me forget how poorly pop had prepared himself for the polio, which she made us all feel was somehow both foreseeable and my father's fault.

At the best of times, our family had the structure of a neurotic feudal court. Mother was the ruling duchess, my father chamberlain, and Ricky and I the vassals, constantly interrogated as to our loyalty, constantly, and in my case falsely, swearing fealty to her. It was a situation made for madness, and the virus took.

I can remember Ricky as a one- or two-year-old holding his breath until he almost passed out, can remember him banging his head on the floor while mother, her wasp's-sting tongue sheathed briefly, held him close, rubbed his purpled forehead, and begged him to surrender, to breathe.

When I was thirteen, after I had given her some lip, she swung at me. I was stocky, beginning to muscle out. I grabbed at her arm but missed it, and she caught me a good one across the face. My anger flashed, but I contained it. I took both her arms in my hands and held on. Finally she stopped struggling.

"Don't ever hit me again," I said. "If you do, I'll hurt you." She knew I could. I probably wouldn't. But I could. That had brought into our relations an armistice without love, but an armistice.

I met Danny Surrett about that time because my best friend, Mark Smolen, was a thief. Mark, another half-Italian kid—he was half-Polish—was adept at sneaking into houses through unlocked doors and windows. He stole portable radios, shavers, mixers, anything small that could be easily disposed of.

When he asked me to help, I had brains enough at first to say no. But he persisted. Loyalty in that place and at that time were important. And I was not that much of an angel anyway.

Because Mark pulled most of the burglaries, I had the job of selling the stuff. Through other young thieves, I found a sixteen-year-old, a school principal's son, who did the fencing for the area. I should have known never to trust anyone in a job like that who didn't really need money.

When the educator's son was caught in his adult fence's pawn shop during a raid, the boy set me up. He would have pigeoned on Mark, too, if he had had any idea I had a partner.

I was arrested by Surrett and another uniformed man. I shoved the electric drill, radio, and porcelain tufted titmouse that I had planned to fence into a trash can before they grabbed me. They wrote in their report that the goods were in my arms, making their case easier. But perhaps I am putting too fine a point on literal honesty.

They released me to my parents' custody. In the next few days, thanks to the principal's son's memory, Surrett came to my house to question me about dozens of burglaries.

He was a tall man with a clean-cut brash look, a smooth police con man. He let drop, when he was talking to me about one of our heists, that it had happened near his old home on Hoffman Street, four blocks from Snyder.

"Georgie, I want you to call me Danny," he said

27

when he came by my house the first time. "We are going to be stuck together for a long time whether we like it or not."

I didn't call him Danny. I clammed up on everything he asked me or, when it appeared safe, lied. Still, I knew he was certain I had mainly carried the goods, not made the entries.

"You can save your ass," he said once with what sounded like real concern. "All you have to do is tell me who did the burgling. We're going to make an example of somebody for all this shit. And, right now, it's going to be you."

I was steadfast if frightened. My obstinacy got me a three months' sentence at the children's reformatory outside town. Because my "cottage" was for under-fourteens, still presumed to be novices at sexual brutality, I was not raped. But I was everything else. My arm was slashed by a switchblade; I survived several partial stranglings and a skin burning by several patriots who assumed from my name I was a Hitler youth. Fraser sounded German to one of them.

At that, I was lucky. One boy was fatally zip-gunned and another was gut-stabbed, though not lethally. Only people who forget how it is to be children are foolish enough to think that children are childlike.

When I got out, I was tougher than most adults, and perhaps more bitter. I felt, rightly or wrongly, that I had been punished not just for my crime, but for the honorable act of not squealing on my friend.

Surrett stopped me on the street about a week after I came home.

"Whyn't you get a paper route next time?" he asked.

"There aren't any." I didn't want to squabble. Nor did I want to talk, fearing he would question me about some burglary he had forgotten on the earlier go-round.

"You know what IQ means?" he persisted. "A test you took in school?"

"How smart you are."

"Yeah. Yours is one hundred fifty-one. Remember that. You're a smart little shithead. Some smart kids make money without going to jail."

So even then, I knew he wanted to do something for me. Perhaps like most big-brother-little-brother or father-son things, he saw something of himself in me. Vain about his own brains, and with that elitist element in him, he did not want to see a bright kid go into the scuppers. It got too close to home.

Then, too, I didn't understand in those days how desperately he wanted out of South Philly, not the area so much as the mode. He saw that being a cop would get him out with less risk, less hassle than the alternatives of the mob or minor crime—or hard, respectable work.

Did he see in me then how desperately I, too, wanted to get away? From my mother, from the fate of my weak, well-meaning pop, whom I loved and did not want to be like? From the pinched, mean streets of South Philly?

Whatever the case, Surrett made an exception for me in his all-embracing selfishness. It was he who put me on the road to Chestnut Hill.

Just as Surrett predicted, I made money. And strictly speaking, I did not go back to jail. Now, instead, I lived in a fancy home in Chestnut Hill with a fancy wife who no longer thought she loved me, and a fine daughter who, I was sure, did.

Driving home on the night I recognized my guilt in the Roman massacre, I pushed my mind to think about Anne instead of those dead people. My marriage, at least, was a familiar kind of mess. Unlike the thing that assaulted me from the front page, taking me by surprise, the anguish with Anne had grown slowly.

We ate that night as two civil strangers might with a mutual friend, in this case our daughter, Alexandra. When Alexa, as we called her, went upstairs to study, I told Anne briefly that the guns I had sent to Monrovia had been the guns used in Rome.

"Oh, God," she said, decently shocked at the murders and at my role in them. There was in her another reaction. She knew the deaths would pull me still further from my work. But she was not so cruel as to probe that sore now.

"I know how awful you feel," she said sympathetically.

"Yes," I said gloomily. "Shitty, very shitty. About the kid, the two women particularly."

That night, she gave me a backrub, a luxury that in other days we had extended to each other routinely when one of us was depressed.

She rubbed my tense calves and back with alcohol as I lay naked on the bed. Her small, strong hands kneaded the flesh that had never ballooned into fat, though it was not what it once had been.

"You have such a good body," she chaffed. "If I had not been so taken with your mind, I might have fallen in love with your body." It was an old, good marital joke. Physical magnetism had been the first bridge across the gulf that separated Radnor and South Philly. Later, for other good reasons, we had come to like each other. And over the years, despite the mores of the times, we had been — and I was as certain of her as I was of myself — faithful to each other.

"If you hadn't had such a beautiful body, I would never have fallen in love with your mind," I spoofed her harmlessly, my first lightness since I had seen the paper.

She was in her nightgown and when I rolled over, my arm touched her breasts through the sheer cloth. Her body had always enraptured me, her arms slender, like a ballerina's a little muscular. Her deep-valleyed back tapered then flared out to small perfect buttocks and athletic legs. Her face was equally beautiful to me: nougat brown eyes whose slightly beetled brows set off her thin, facile mouth.

She had found in my mix of Celtic and Sicilian, light blue eyes and black hair with darkish skin, what she wanted physically. On my back, I drew her body to me, thinking of its aesthetic, its grace, and hoped. But when we tried to make love, I could not arouse. For the last few months, I had been unpredictable, sometimes impotent.

Even before the Roman deaths, she had felt

threatened by my gradual recoiling from my work — and I felt threatened by her threatened feeling, a classic sexual cycle. Unfairly, I related my impotency to her; at my worst, I saw it as a parallel to my mother's unmanning of pop.

Yet, contrary to all reason, she wanted more out of me sexually, as if that might bind me to our old way of life. She had her hair cut, tried to dress more alluringly. I was both touched and upset.

I could joke of Falstaff, in whom desire had so long outlived performance. I could hope my condition was temporary. At any rate, I knew it was common. I had learned that from my gumshoe days. But men did not talk about it except with their psychiatrists or the private eyes they hired to spy on their wives. I had neither.

Unable to be open with Anne about the sexual swamp in our marriage, I turned to its analogue, my decision to phase out of my business.

"I want to sell out to Hector," I said. "The thing in Rome. . ."

Anne was ready for it.

"I feel terrible about what happened there. I don't argue how painful it is to you." She withdrew her body from mine, where it had been consolingly pressed. "But if you give up work, you give up part of our last structure. You'd just be dropping out."

The job had its romance, along with its scruffy elements, and Anne, for good and bad reasons, had been attracted to both the romance and the scruffiness. She liked being married to a South Philly Rhett Butler. But I didn't want to be Rhett Butler any longer.

I also wasn't all that positive about her job. Basically, what she and her partner, Maurice Brockman, Jr., did was to sell loopholes to corporations that could afford to pay taxes. Until recently, I had been as enthusiastic about discussing her cases as she was in handling them. Now, they had come to bore, even offend me.

As long as I was selling guns whose only purpose was to kill, I was in no posture to criticize her, even had I wanted to. But now my guns seemed wrong. And, for her, her infighting with the IRS to fleece the Treasury still seemed right.

Then, too, although she made every effort to be attractive while she was with me, she was with me less. More of her energies seemed to go into her firm. There were no longer companionable lunches, were few afternoons at the theater or beside our pool, the occasions we had made a point to build into our lives.

So, although we clung together, unwilling to admit failure, we had gotten to that season when partners face each other alone and ask themselves, "Is this the person I want for the long, long haul?" For me the answer was a circumspect "I think so." For her, it was "Not the way things are now."

In the darkness that night, I said to her:

"Maybe, in the very beginning, you bought the wrong horse."

"No. that's a cop-out," she said. "I've known hundreds of men in my practice, maybe dozens of them well enough to judge what they're like, and I know that up to a few months ago we had a good marriage, that I had the best of husbands."

Her hand slipped familiarly to my hip, as if to assert our contact. "And although probably sometimes you don't believe me, I don't want to lose you. In all this, *all* of it"—and here I realized she was even talking about a life with me as an erratic lover—"there's something inside me that says, 'Keep him. You won't find anyone half as good again.'" I knew what she was going to say next and I pulled her close as if to deny her words with my faulted body. "But, George. . ." and her voice wavered, "if you want us to last, then you've got to think whether there isn't some way you can stay in the kind of world we've had."

I didn't try to respond. I knew that if it hadn't been Rome, it would have been somewhere else, Yemen or Indonesia or Colombia. As if I were considering her ultimatum, I held her gently until drowsiness took us our soft, separate ways.

Perhaps my answer to her was that instead of going into the office the next day, I spent it in the garden. The tomato plants were tangles of healthy pregnant vines. I set out the wire cages, tenderly twisting the plants' wayward runners into the cages, pinching off the suckers. There was going to be one helluva tomato crop around here. For somebody. The warm air, the buzz of the insects, the caw of the jays, and the trickles of sweat as I worked on this unseasonably hot spring day seemed to heal some of my self-revulsion.

Late that afternoon, as I gardened, I heard a sound behind me and started like a rabbit caught in the carrots. Anne had come home early. I looked back at the smooth, nylon-clad legs, the expensive patent-leather pumps, then up her body, straight and slim in its tailored seersucker.

"Why are you so goddamned beautiful?" I asked from my knees. "It would be so easy for me if I didn't love you so." I did not rise and she knelt beside me, a little awkward, the way women are when they bend their knees while wearing high heels and a straight skirt. Her eyes were on a level with mine. Her nose narrowed an instant, smelling, I knew, the reek of my sweating body.

"I love you, too," she said. Her lips drew back from her teeth in a smile: sadness and warmth, but no amusement. "And just when I can begin to express it, everything goes to hell for us." Strained from the kneeling she rose, I with her, the two of us holding hands to support each other. But she dropped my hand as she looked in my eyes. "You've made up your mind, haven't you?"

"Made it up enough," I said. "I can't go back. I have to be me, this me, before I can find out what I'm going to be." The sun was hot. On her upper lip, just in the few minutes she had been out of her air-conditioned Mercedes, a fine dew had formed.

"Oh, God," she murmured, no louder than a breath suspiring, but as concrete acknowledgment that at last she knew that I could not go back.

"I'm sorry," I said. Taking her in my arms wasn't going to do anything for us now.

"Oh, God," she repeated. "What are we going to do?"

"I don't know. Plough along awhile? Hope something will happen. That you will change. Or I will."

"Getting somebody to mediate. . ."

A marriage counselor? But our battle lines were drawn as classically as if they were diagrams in a military textbook. We didn't need sorting out. We needed concessions, huge ones.

"There's no way you can take me this way?" I asked. "On the face of it, it wouldn't seem so bad."

She laughed, but again without amusement.

"That's the dopey thing. Nine women out of ten would love to have a sort of teddy bear with money and good looks and brains who just wants to putter around the house."

"Maybe not," I said.

"It doesn't matter though," she said, "does it?" She took my hand again to give her support for what she said next: "It doesn't matter because, George, I'm that tenth one."

"Maybe," I said, the desperation rising in me, "the teddy bear will find something to throw himself into."

"When?" she asked, an edge in her voice.

"I don't know."

"George, maybe you'll just stay this way." She was pleading now. "If I were sure you'd do something, establish an investigating school, set up an electronics firm, something, maybe educational gadgets for disabled kids. God, I've thought of so many things. If you'd do anything. But you may never!"

It was true. I might just remain the ahimsa kid of Chestnut Hill. I was not dishonest enough to try to refinance my marriage with a promissory note I might not be able to pay.

Surrett called me later that week and asked if I would come by. We crossed the late-afternoon streets to the Top of the Square. We ordered Virgin Mary's. Surrett was off the booze, as happened periodically, and I didn't want to drink when he was trying so hard.

"Anne feeling any better about things?" he asked when we were settled in. He, like Anne, had invested a lot of himself in my life.

"Nope. Worse."

"Armed truce? Open warfare?"

"Neither. To hear each other talk, we both think the other is the greatest. Just not as a marriage. She says our paths are no longer parallel. She's right. Another way of putting it is that it just burned out."

"*You* just burned out," he said without kindness. "You're a perambulatory stiff. I smell the stink every time I see you. Shit, you ought to unburn. Maybe you are finished as a private eye, a gun hustler. But if you were hot for anything, *anything*, pacifism, or prison reform, or, for Christ's sake, saving the harp seals even, she'd buy that. She might not like it at first, but if you'd go at it like a zealot, like you went at investigating. . ."

He was right. If the me who had gone at almost everything in life so enthusiastically was still me, then Anne and I might have worked out something. But that me didn't exist anymore.

"You didn't have me over for marriage counseling," I said curtly, closing him off.

37

"No," he said. "Now sit tight when I ask you this. I know you don't want to have anything more to do on this thing with Bernie, but—"

I began to blow. All my life Surrett had tried to manipulate me. Sometimes I resented him doing it so much I wanted to break free from him entirely.

"I told you. . ." I began hotly. "Even you said—"

He held up his hand.

"I'm asking you to help me get out of it, goddamn it," he said. "Just listen."

He told me that the Red Brigade's liaison man would soon be on the way to Philadelphia to open negotiations with Bernie Magliorocco. This would be Bernie's first personal contact in the narcotics aspect of his grandiose scheme. Bernie had ordered Surrett to check out the emissary—one Ernesto Calvacadi. If Surrett found evidence from the FBI, which could squeeze it out of the CIA, that Calvacadi was slippery, that the Red Brigades were sending an untrustworthy emissary, then it might scare the cautious Bernie into junking the plan with the Red Brigades, maybe with the rest of the terrorists. After all, most mobsters shunned, even feared them.

The Mafia was conservative, religious, and even patriotic. Free Enterprise, God and Country meant there would be plenty of businessmen on whom they could batten, and plenty of businesses, legal and illegal, that they could run.

Terrorists, on the other hand, represented unsettling anarchism in which corporations, unions, and governments became too destabilized for underworld manipulation and exploitation. Under anarchy, bribes did not stand up, shylock loans went into default, police got out of hand. The fabric of the underworld was always violently and unpredictably disrupted when political terror was rampant.

In addition to the FBI checks, Surrett wanted to do some checking on his own, with my help. He wanted me to bug a meeting he would have with Calvacadi and run him secretly on a voice lie detector machine. He also wanted me to get some still photos and film of him so if he got cute later, the mob would at least have some pictures a tracker could use to find him. Surrett promised that Magliorocco would know nothing of my role, that he would say only he had "gotten someone in from Chicago" to do the jobs.

"If we make a case against Calvacadi," he said plausibly, "maybe the whole thing will just collapse. Peacefully."

"If you don't make a case, I'll have been a party to the goddamned thing."

"Georgie," he shot back angrily, "what the hell can I do? Just what in the hell can I do?"

"Yeah, I know. You made love to cancer and now you've got it."

"Shitty way of putting it."

I refused to do it, but Surrett pleaded and cajoled.

"Why can't Bernie's boys take the pictures?" I asked.

"They're too stupid," he said, feeling me weakening. "They know how to take bribes. They don't know how to take pictures."

"How about somebody else?"

39

"You kidding? Who can I trust?"

"When does this guy get here?" I said, reluctantly agreeing.

"I'll let you know," said Surrett, relieved.

I loved my daughter Alexa for her dark Italo-Hibernian looks, so like my own, and for all the other reasons that fathers find it easy to love daughters. She wanted to be a lawyer. And although she might not be a better lawyer than her mother, she would be a different kind. Alexa liked people better. She was less afraid of liking them.

A few evenings after the Red Brigade killings, Alexa pounded down the stairs to my study.

"Daddy, a murderer, a pervert. . ." she said, bursting into tears. I bowled up out of my chair and ran to her, all the old juices flowing, gripped her arm, then headed to the drawer for my pistol. Instant rage! My daughter! I would kill the man, pump six bullets into him without a thought!

"No," she said. "On the phone. He's hung up. I got him on a recorder."

Frustrated that I could not shoot the caller, I stood dizzily at the foot of the steps, trying to get control of myself. It was more than a minute before I could speak.

"You recorded him," I said at last. Her father's daughter. Still shaking, but rational, and worried now that she might have goofed, I said, "Let's make sure you got it!" As we ran up the stairs, I said, "What do you mean, murderer, Alexa?" Pervert callers were an endemic sickness of the times, but they weren't the killing kind.

She tried to explain in an orderly way, telling me the voice on the telephone had first asked politely whether this was the Fraser residence. She began to cry again.

"It was so awful," she whimpered.

Again, I felt murderous. To harass me was one thing. I had gotten hundreds of crank calls over the years. But my gentle daughter!

The Sony was on her bed by the phone. I quickly pushed, "rewind," then "play." Tinny rock'n'roll came out, made tinnier by the small recorder. I listened impatiently. On a downbeat, the music finally switched to a voice with a slight South Philly accent, muffled to thwart identification.

I had known such bully voices from my youth, but this one had the gloss of education on it. It would be one of Bernie's enemies within the mob, letting me know that they knew I was behind the M-16 shipment to the Red Brigades, and that I would be regarded henceforth as one of Bernie's allies.

". . . and cut off your titties, little girl—" Even knowing it would be like that, I gasped in fury. Again I thought of the sick, vicious caller. I saw myself firing into his face, or in his gut, where he would not die so rapidly. When I had steadied, I gave her shoulders a quick hug.

"Alexa," I said, "people who call and make threats like that don't carry them out. They're slimy cowards. Besides, they know that if they warn us, we'll be ready for them. If someone really wanted to hurt us, they wouldn't call first."

She nodded, not as reassured as I'd hoped she

41

would be. I turned on the machine again, listening hard to the accent.

". . . and your mother, like I told you, we're going to tear out her tongue and take a railroad spike—" I cut it again, and turned my anger on Alexa.

"You know I've told you the best thing with these people is to hang up on them." Alexa bridled and looked as if she might cry again.

"I kept him on for the voice. I thought it might help us catch him," she said.

"I'm not thinking straight," I apologized. "I'm so damned mad that I'm talking stupidities." Mollified, she pushed the "play" button herself this time, all investigator now.

". . . and jam it up—"

On the tape, Alexa interrupted, full of outrage.

"You, you filthy bastard—"

". . . her pussy. And your father," and now the hate was really in this guy's voice, ". . . that evil, evil man"—the word *evil* said with such peculiar sincerity that it was almost funny amidst this offal—". . . we are going to. . ." The man seemed to have a genital fixation. He was going to tie wire around my testicles and pull them off. That was the younger mobsters, all right. The old-timers talked of meat hooks in the anus or freeway cement.

When the recording ended, I jotted the date and time on the cassette, got Alexa to initial it, counterinitialed it, and slipped it into my pocket. Fat chance of this case ever reaching court. But from old custom, I did what was supposed to be done.

First I called an old friend at the Philadelphia office of the FBI. I told him I thought it might be the mob but didn't tell him why. He listened politely as I played the tape over the phone.

"It's a needle in a haystack," he said. "You going to rig anything up?"

"Yep."

"Let me know if you come up with anything more," he said. The FBI could take jurisdiction on telephone obscenity cases and it shared jurisdiction with the Philadelphia cops on telephone threats.

A lieutenant friend at Philadelphia police headquarters wasn't much more helpful.

"Could be anybody; everybody hates you," he said with cordial graveyard humor. "Shame they bothered your little girl."

"She's the one that put the recorder on him," I said with pride.

"Tell her to join the cops when she's old enough. We're short again this year on the women's quota." Everybody has problems, I told him.

I began rigging lines from my telephone and the three extensions of the family phone. I would buy an automatic dialing device and hook up a recorded message to it. If the phone creep called, whoever answered would only have to push a button connected to the dialing device, and the recorded message would alert the phone company to trace the call to the caller. I'd have to pull some fancy strings at the telephone company to get them to cooperate. They didn't like to do things that didn't add to their profits.

Anne came home from work while I was under her desk putting in a junction box. I crawled out, told her what had happened, and played the tape.

She was more upset than Alexa. Of all the phone threats, this was the first one that had been explicit about how her person would be violated.

"The pig," was all she could gasp when the thing was done. Then, after breathing hard, trying to get herself together, she said disgustedly, "How dare he."

"He dares," I said. But my mind was more on the danger to Alexa. Only in retrospect did I realize that Anne's finely tuned antennas had picked up the inequality of my concern. And that it had hurt her.

Surrett played the tape for Magliorocco, who was as eager to identify his enemy as I was. The deaf old man did not recognize the voice. Neither did his son — who was a bit short on natural talent, Surrett said, but the only member of his entourage that Magliorocco trusted.

Three days later, Surrett got his own warning. In a neatly wrapped parcel post package was an out-dated volume of Title 18 — the federal criminal code statute book. When his secretary opened it curiously, she saw the middle had been hollowed out. In the concavity was the gory snout of an animal.

Surrett had run into the anteroom at her scream. It was a sheep's nose, cleavered off, with the lips intact: a relevant gift for a go-along mouthpiece.

"Jesus, who?" I asked.

"Don't know. Bernie's got some ideas. But no proof."

"They should have picked a goat," I said.

"Goats are harder to find than sheep," he said

44

glumly.

It used to be piglets garroted with wire, a warning for squealers. The younger generation had gotten imaginative.

"They've seen *The Godfather* too many times," I said.

"Yeah," he said, too frightened to let me lift his mood.

"Can't you get out of it?"

"No. Now less than ever. Bernie knows this is a test for him. If he buckles, he'll be the next sheep." He paused. "You want out, I guess? I need you, but if you. . ."

I had been unmanned enough by my failures with Anne. I couldn't chicken out now on Surrett.

"When is this guy coming?" I said, as morose now as Surrett.

"Next week. Thanks," he added.

III.
THE RED BRIGADIST

Surrett became Bernie Magliorocco's lawyer in the first place because he was so intelligent, so inventive, so thorough, and so malleable, particularly when the price was right. Before the terrorist, Ernesto Calvacadi, got to Philadelphia, Surrett had done his homework. He had pulled strings with the police, the FBI, and, through them, the CIA and State Department to get background material. The Red Brigade leader came out as doctrinaire, fanatic, and honest to a fault.

Danny told me with solemn pride, "When this Calvacadi says somebody is a target, you can be sure that guy will be counting his kneecaps pretty soon."

For my part in the terrorist's visit, I spent hours studying a huge map of the airport, where I would get my movies and some of the stills of Calvacadi. I installed a "super-mini" videocamera in the receptacle behind one of Surrett's recessed ceiling lights, cutting out enough metal just behind the light for the videolens to protrude.

I pulled out the medicine cabinet from Surrett's private bathroom and bolted in a second videocamera and a Hasselblad with an electric remote shutter release. Then I covered the aperture snugly with see-through mirror. The full light in the bathroom would give me my best shots.

In Surrett's office, I put two microphone bugs under an easy chair and his desk. Then I swept the whole office, something I did for him twice a year anyway. I was fearful his queries might have stimulated some government agency to get electronically inquisitive about what was up with Calvacadi.

Aside from a chitter of radiation from his clock and his air conditioner, the place was clean as the Liberty Bell. That done, I set up my video and voice polygraph consoles in Surrett's supply closet. Cramped atop a box of Xerox paper, I tested the rig and found all my systems were go.

I wore green coveralls like those of the airport maintenance squads over my slacks and shirt. A shady photographer friend had forged me an identification badge. My picture on it looked woebegone. With good reason.

In the wheeled trash can where I planned to dump butts and candy wrappers gathered up from airport ashtrays, I had cut a hole for the lens of the little Super Eight I had mounted inside. I had film in it so fast it would photograph anything but crows laying black eggs in a closet.

47

The on-off switch and a zoomer ratchet extension were rigged on the brim of the basket. I had to aim the entire trash can but had practiced and could zoom in on a face at thirty yards. Inside my shirt, I had a holstered .38.

Calvacadi, for good and sufficient cause, wasn't flying in from an Italian airport, where his own cops might spot him. He came in from Frankfurt on Lufthansa. I had a blurry mug shot Surrett had wangled from the FBI. I dawdled by the incoming gate, worried that the terrorist would be disguised and that I would miss him.

The first-class passengers cleared. Then I spotted him in a clump of tourist arrivals. His hair and beard were brick red, his face pocked and sharp, his eyes suspicious and alert as a wild animal's. He was slender and about five ten. In his conservative ready-made clothes, he looked like the poorly paid assistant manager of a small bank.

I aimed my trash can dolly and got him. His gaze swept past me. He was looking, I was sure, for cop or Mafioso types, not cleaning-man types.

As he swung toward Customs, I shot a few more feet of his receding back. He had a distinctive bounding walk that would make him easy to spot.

Unhurriedly, I wheeled the can around Customs, cleaning up a floor butt from a no-smoking area. Calvacadi would be waiting impatiently in line. I was ready for him when he came through the Customs gate on the way to the exit.

There, I saw a thirtyish brown-haired man in a sharp corduroy suit move toward him. A mod FBI agent, I thought. But no, I — and the camera — saw the two men exchange a brief greeting, then shake hands. The mob was changing its image.

Next day, from my stuffy audition booth, I saw on my videomonitor Calvacadi enter Surrett's office. The wide-angle lens made him bulge like a barrel at hip, then shrink at feet and head. I flicked on the audio switches and watched the meters and the graph needle on the voice polygraph — known as a PSE, for "psychological stress evaluator."

Smooth as grease, Surrett showed him to the easy chair with the mike under it. I heard the springs creak minutely in the earphone. Calvacadi looked directly at the videocamera in the ceiling but did not see the lens.

"I will be talking about your, um, background if that is okay," Surrett began. "My friends tell me that you have been in this profession for five, six years? My client, of course, does not want to be dealing with a novice."

"Six years," Calvacadi replied, his English so heavily accented it was difficult to understand. "You are not dealing with a novice."

"And you come, I believe, originally from Milan, or Turin."

The one thing we were sure of from the background check was that he had been born and raised in Venice.

"Yes," he said. "Milano or Torino." An overt lie. But the PSE made no telltale response. It acted like it was hearing gospel. I gave it a nasty rap.

Surrett had arranged for them to lunch in his office. When the secretary brought in their avocado and fresh shrimp, and a pint of sherbet in a little ice bucket, I saw Calvacadi's eyelids flicker. He quickly studied her buttocks and legs as she left to get the bread, wine, and other fixings. At least we would have one personal fact about him indisputably on the record: he liked women.

Before they began eating, Surrett suavely asked him whether he would like to wash up, almost as if it would be an insult to Surrett if he did not. I flicked on the second videocamera and a new picture popped up on my number-two monitor: the bathroom.

Calvacadi locked the door, then took out a prescription vial and plucked out a pill. He washed it down with a handful of water, disdaining the glass to avoid leaving too convenient a set of prints behind. I wished I could see the vial. If it was a hefty tranquilizer, that would help account for the voice polygraph's mindless refusal to register falsity — or truth.

Calvacadi washed his hands, dried them, then moved close to the mirror and gingerly pinched a pimple between his two forefingers. I pushed the plunger to advance the Hasselblad film. I would have close color shots with every shade and contour of Calvacadi's ruddy face. They would show me whether the brick red beard was darker

50

or lighter at the roots. How often did these birds changes plumage? Damned often, I was sure.

During and after lunch, they sparred some more, chary of each other as an old bull elephant and his young rogue challenger. About all Surrett got out of him was an assurance that he spoke for his leadership and that embarrassments like the Roman misfires would not happen again.

"Those on the mission who escaped will not be part of our work in the future," said Calvacadi. I was sure he meant that the leadership had found them and killed them.

For my part, all I got out of it was some good shots of the Italian squeezing a pimple and further evidence that voice lie detector machines weren't worth the current it took to turn them on.

Nevertheless, when Calvacadi left the office, Surrett asked me to "put him on the plane" next evening. Bernie's own gumshoes would cover him up to then. Surrett wanted to be sure he took the TWA flight to London he said he was taking and met no one at the airport—in a word, Surrett wanted to make certain he was straight.

In coveralls again, I watched through the doors as Calvacadi bid his Mafia driver a perfunctory good-bye under the purplish lights. Too modern to buss cheeks, they merely shook hands. The terrorist went past me, again without a glance, but he guardedly surveyed the area

51

leading to Customs.

I had all the movies I needed. This time my only equipment was a flat little Minox taped to my wrist in case Calvacadi met anyone, the .38, and a butt shovel for nipping up debris. I checked Calvacadi in and out of Customs-Immigration and trailed far behind as he boarded the shuttle bus to TWA in the main terminal.

My car was unticketed so far. I followed the bus, parked illegally again, and picked up Calvacadi as he went down the corridor toward the TWA international flight area.

As I trudged behind, stopping at each cigarette receptacle, I became aware of a third man. Newspaper under his arm, he strolled halfway between Calvacadi and me. His walk brought me up with a jolt. Do men carrying pistols walk differently from other men? The thought had never occurred to me before. The answer, I realized, was yes. My badge had gotten me through the security by-pass gate with my concealed .38. How had he gotten his pistol through?

The third man wore gray, cuffed trousers, an old dark green sports coat, an open dull blue shirt, and glasses. He was the kind of Mr. Anybody I would be if I wanted to be hard to remember later.

I was not sure he was tailing Calvacadi until I saw Calvacadi stop and glance into a gift shop and witnessed almost simultaneously the third man break stride and pause by a window. My chest tingled where the .38 pressed.

I hoped vehemently that it was either one of

Magliorocco's men, sent by him out of an excess of caution, or some kind of cop: from Philadelphia intelligence, or the FBI, or maybe the CIA. If it wasn't one of those, then the son-of-a-bitch was one of the Mafia dissidents, come to queer Bernie's big deal.

Wrecking the deal meant killing Calvacadi right here at the airport, where the whole mob, in Philadelphia and around the country, along with the terrorists now talking with Bernie, would understand one thing: doing this kind of business with Bernie meant dying.

Calvacadi bought a candy bar and continued toward the departure lounge. The third man renewed his stroll, nonchalantly unfolding his newspaper. Far behind them, I stopped where I could see them but not be noticed. If this guy was going to kill Calvacadi, I didn't want to be in the way. The mob's most frequent victims were other mobsters. The second most frequent victims were innocents who got in the way.

Then I thought again. If the third man was one of Bernie's opponents, then he was from the faction who had threatened Alexa and Anne, had invaded my home. I felt an emotional replay of my fury that day.

I started up the corridor briskly, not entirely sure what I planned to do, but sure I was going to do something. Calvacadi was seated in the waiting area, staring out into the evening. The runway lights and the glaring eyes of the planes blotted out the subtle colors of the fading sunset. I looked at the arrival-departure screen. There'd be about ten minutes before Calvacadi boarded.

The third man had sauntered up to within forty yards of where Calvacadi sat. He carefully touched his own chest. He's a hit man, I thought, not a doubt of it. Calvacadi, all unawares, rose and walked across the corridor toward the rest room. Now I knew that whatever else, I wasn't going to see the terrorist shot down in cold blood. Calvacadi's rising had destroyed some timing the hit man had fixed in his head. I felt his tension, or was it only my own?

Attaché case in hand, Calvacadi entered the rest room. The man lurched across the corridor and moved toward the closed door. What better place than in a stall to shoot a man? There would be no or few witnesses. The gunshot would be deadened. I moved fast toward the door, the two of us converging. At the door I cut in front of him, my butt shovel at port arms.

The man's face, younger than I had thought it would be, twisted in surprise and anger.

"I gotta clean this place," I said. "The next one is just down the hall, sir." He sensed there was something phony but made an effort at charade while he collected himself.

"I gotta pee," he said.

"Down the hall," I said.

"I'm gonna pee in there," he said ominously.

We were in the alcoved doorway of the rest room. His right hand moved toward his coat. I dropped the butt shovel and gripped his right wrist with my left hand. I saw the shock in his eyes. He was stocky, shorter than I was, and maybe less sure.

"No, fucker," I said. "You are not going to pee in there." I whisked my .38 out of the holster, fast as a snake, and pushed it into his groin at testicle level. "You may be going to pee in your pants, fucker. But you are not going to pee in there."

Fear of the gun paralyzed him, but he was resourceful. Knowing that my main purpose was to keep him from the door, he slapped the gun away and bolted down the corridor.

I holstered the gun, picked up the ash shovel, and jogged after him. Panic must have gotten to him. He would sense I was from Bernie's camp. He would know that if I caught him, his role as a fifth columnist would doom him to a terrible death. Better than anyone, he would visualize just what torture would be applied to him to make him give the names of his fellow rebels.

I knew I would kill him if he tried to shoot me, but I would prefer to capture him and turn him over to Surrett and Magliorocco. That would be more than enough vengeance for the call to Alexa which he or an accomplice had made.

As he ran, he dodged those who did not make way for him. The last passengers for the TWA flight stared at us as they scurried along in the opposite direction.

Because he was, in effect, my blocking back, I was able to gain on him. He looked back and I saw he was frightened. But he did not draw his pistol. Was it that he was a bad shot at a distance, fit only to kill at six feet or less? Or, not recognizing me, did he think Bernie had imported me from

New York or Chicago, the Olympuses of hit men, a Mars against his mere humanity?

Far down the corridor, I saw another man break from a crowd of passengers around a gate station. Instantly, I knew it was a confederate, the torpedo's driver, probably. He was better dressed, a lean, stylish-looking man with his hand pressed to his topcoat pocket, perhaps to keep a pistol there from flapping against him.

"Tatto," he called at the gunman I was chasing. "Tatto!" The voice, shouted though it was, had a familiar resonance to it. Wasn't it the same voice that had growled those hideous words to Alexa? The suspicion that it was fired my blood with murderousness. I pounded on faster.

An electric cart driven by an airport employee was picking its way steadily up the corridor, just in front of the new assailant. On its back seat was a bent old lady. The man in the topcoat, lithe as a cornerback, drew up on the cart. The driver braked suddenly in alarm. The man grabbed him, flung him from the seat, and wheeled the cart just as my quarry came up to them. With a lurch, the would-be assassin jumped in beside his getaway man. The old lady screamed but held tight.

The cart with its three occupants accelerated down the corridor. It just missed a second one, loaded with baggage. As the second cart stopped, I ran toward it, pulled out my gun, and waved the driver out of the seat.

"Police," I shouted at him. At the sight of the pistol, the driver bailed out sideways, fell heavily onto the floor, and crawled to the wall. "Police," shouted everyone within voice shot, an incantation that seemed to promise somehow I was going to take care of everything.

As I trod on the accelerator, I holstered the gun and shoved the baggage off the back. Thus unencumbered, the little vehicle shot off in pursuit of the torpedoes. The old lady was scrunched down in the back seat, her white hair flying in the wind, terrified into silence, staring at me with unbelieving eyes.

My adversaries rushed on. Clearly, they did not dare abandon the cart for fear of being apprehended by airport personnel. We ripped past dumbfounded travelers toward the security gates, where I was sure we would be stopped by armed police on duty.

At the security portals, one of the uniformed policemen drew his pistol and stood gunfighter style in the exit lane. Could he be fool enough to fire with the old lady in the seat and in a crowded airport, where ricochets could kill?

The fleeing mobsters hunched low at sight of the cop but ploughed on. The woman looked around, saw the potential for horror, and shrieked.

"Don't shoot, for Christ's sake!" I screamed above the whirr of the electric carts. My airport coveralls gave me a cloak of authority. But there was no need for me to cry out. The cop was just a gutsy man trying to bluff. As the electric cart streaked toward him, he dodged back in a clumsy veronica and the cart, with mine close behind now, shot by.

"Get 'em," the cop called encouragingly. "Good man!"

The drama had become cops and robbers, cowboys and Indians. My overalls conferred on me the right and duty to pursue. The gunsels' muftis and kidnapped victim made them the skunks.

As we rolled into a main corridor, travelers fell to each side, giving us an alleyway. Like bumperless Dodgems, we tore along at top speed. A young ticket agent at an Eastern station ahead leaped the counter and grabbed a gigantic valise from an amazed patron. He was going to try to throw a roadblock into the path of the gangsters.

The hit man in the topcoat drew his pistol, aimed it at the straining ticket agent. I saw the little burst of flame, heard the enormous blam echo in the vast enclosure, and gasped as the airline worker pitched to the ground. The valise he had shuffleboarded slammed into the cart, deflecting it momentarily, throwing my quarries off balance.

Two men dashed out to assist the fallen clerk. Now I was truly on the side of the angels. The men I pursued were at best attempted murderers. We rushed out of the main terminal and into a new corridor. A temporary ramp had been built down toward the apron so that building materials could be brought in for repairs.

The work day done, the ramp was railed off. The mob renegades saw an escape. Disregarding his frail passenger, the driver swerved into the barrier, smashing it aside. The old lady bailed out directly into my path. I screeched to a stop. My little vehicle spun for a moment out of control. The woman crawled toward the wall, agile as a mouse, her thin legs moving like pistons.

I wheeled the cart and zipped down the steep ramp. In the airport lights, I saw far ahead my targets' cart tearing across the runways toward the fence that marked the airport's boundary.

Did they know the terrain from some former duty as hijackers of goods? Willy-nilly I raced under the garish lights in pursuit.

An American Airlines jet was pulling from its bay. The tiny cart ahead rushed straight for it. For a moment, I thought the cart would ram the plane's gigantic wheels, but it brushed just in front of them and out to safety on the other side.

I took no such risk, but rounded the rear of the plane, feeling the hot blush of the engine heat. The jets fouled me with smoky exhaust.

Out on the clear runway now, I saw the cart again. Once more the driver took a reckless chance, roaring directly into the path of a DC-10. The ponderous craft lifted off just as he reached it. The gunmen must have ducked to avoid its wheels.

The runway lights and the erratic spotlights of the plane lights let me see the cart only fitfully now. But I had a clear shot at it. And they at me. I saw the passenger look back, then forward again, then back, this time with his arm extended. He was shooting! The full-throated jets coughed out the trifling hack of the pistol shot.

I pulled out the .38. As best I could, I aimed it

and squeezed off three quick shots. They could not have hit, for the cart bore on. But the distraction of the gunfire had made the driver lose concentration.

Above them, floating in gracefully for a landing, was a two-engined commuter aircraft. Its pilot clearly had not seen the wayward vehicle. The prop plane dipped and, for an instant, I saw the cart brilliantly illuminated. The pilot saw it, too, for within feet of the runway the plane's motors wildly roared and the aircraft leapt upward crazily, saved from crashing into the cart only by a navigational miracle.

My eyes, caught by the plane, did not see the cart for a moment. Then I saw it flip over on its side and spill two dark bundles to the runway. I was sure the gunmen would get up and escape over the fence and perhaps down to the river, where I would never find them.

Wary of more landing planes, I made for the edge of the runway and then cut back toward the overturned cart. Its wheels, the accelerator jammed, still spun with an automaton hum.

Gun drawn, I crouched behind my own cart, then sprinted to the crashed vehicle. Just beyond it, I saw a man. It was the first mobster. He lay crumpled in a posture of frozen violence. I waited a moment to see whether he moved. Then I raced to him. The arms were outstretched, the hands empty. I need not worry about a gun. Nor anything else: where his head had been there was a bloody torn stump. The prop plane, seeking a landing place, had chewed off his skull.

I looked back and saw the headlights of motor vehicles headed my way. One, from the looks of its rotating lights, was a fire engine. The tower had obviously waved off all air traffic temporarily.

Soon they would be on me. To stay was to invite explanations that I could not give without compromising myself. It was to bring on a stormfire of publicity.

Besides, now I wanted the fleeing man. From that quick turn of the first gunman's head as they sped across the runway, I knew this man had ordered him to shoot at me, to try to kill me. He was the leader of this operation. In my mind, I heard his voice on the Sony, threatening to sever the breasts of Alexa, rip the genitals of Anne with an iron spike, tear off mine with wire.

This was the monster who had spewed his horrid poison into my home. Oh yes, I could kill him now, perhaps not in cold blood, but with the slightest excuse: a hint of resistance, or flight. I would welcome the chance.

But I dared not pursue him on foot. He would hear me crushing the skeletons of dead underbrush as I ran and would bushwhack me.

I gunned my cart along the fence bordering the airport and found two tracks: a little-used jeep path that began near its western boundary. The cart's soft tires muted the sounds as I bumped along the path until it degenerated into a foot trail. There I abandoned the vehicle. My quarry would be heading for the road to town, of that I was certain.

In my mouth as I jogged along the path, I tasted the foul, oily air of the jet engines. Where the trail met the road ahead there was the glow of a street-light. A mile away was a filling station, I knew. If I were the gunman, I would push along the road, ducking off when cars passed, and summon help from the station's phone. To return to the airport for a taxi was to ask for trouble. My circumnavigation would have given him a chance to be half-way to the station by now.

Gun drawn, too out of breath to run, I half jog-ged, half walked along the road. The phone booth was near the road. I could not see whether it was occupied. Cautiously, I crept through the shadows, eyes on the booth. As I approached, I saw the dark vent of its door. Open. It was empty. Still, my theory was my only hope. Perhaps he was behind me someplace. Perhaps he had made his call and was waiting somewhere off the road for a pick-up from another of his rebel confeder-ates.

Where would he be if he were waiting? Obvi-ously, on my side of the station. He would not needlessly expose himself with a walk past the bright pump lights. He would have called and slunk back up the road in the direction he—and I—had come. I eased deeper into the shade, put a tree between me and the road, and waited, breath-ing through my mouth to silence my panting, pis-tol in hand.

I knew I had guessed right when I saw a brown Chevrolet slow as it passed the filling station and stop a hundred yards from me, too far for me to see its tags well. Even before I glimpsed the shadow moving from amid the trees, I was running, stumbling under the branches to get close enough to spot the numbers. It was my only hope, and a good one, of chasing down the man who had tried to kill me tonight and who, I was certain, had verbally assaulted my daughter with sick, vicious threats.

The man climbed into the car, which moved away even before he slammed the door. "Four seven five," I panted aloud, picking up the first three numbers. And the last number had been a four. Or was it a one? As the Chevy disappeared, I stopped, gasping, clutching my chest from the unaccustomed sprint.

My head cleared, I thought: how many cars in Pennsylvania have 475 as their first three numbers and one or four as the last? A thousand? Two thousand? And how many of these would be new or year-old Chevrolet sedans? Not very damned many.

Excited at the prospect of nailing the fugitive, I ditched the coveralls, bent and buried the identification badge, put a heavy stone over its grave, and walked to the pay phone. As unobtrusively as I could, I sawed off the wire to the receiver with my penknife and dropped the amputated phone in my pocket.

Then I walked briskly to the airport. Ah, Commerce: the huge airport had closed in over the recent excitement as if nothing had happened. I called Surrett and told him what had transpired. When I had finished, he asked with forced jauntiness:

"Either of those guys have on a sheepskin coat?"

The gory animal head! Only then did it fully hit me how vital to me was this man who had escaped. Caught up in the chase, in my hatred over the obscene call, in the shots at me that night, I had not had time to think what it all meant.

This guy could kill me and my family. He knew of my role in the gun deal, as his threats indicated, even if he did not, at least yet, know I was his pursuer. He knew of my closeness to Surrett, and by extension he would assume my fidelity to Bernie Magliorocco. When he had the power to move against Bernie, I, and perhaps Alexa and Anne, would be on his "hit" list.

Catching him, therefore, was no mere matter of revenge. Catching him was everything, the most important case I had ever had. Starting now, I must make no mistakes. None.

Next morning, the story in the *Inquirer* was on page one, but somewhat less prominently than I, as a participant, had expected. The dead man had been identified as a minor Philadelphia hoodlum. The brave Eastern employee had been hit in the hip, possibly crippled. There was, nevertheless, a brief hospital interview with him. The escaped man was being sought for attempted murder, larceny of the cart, technical assault on the old lady, and use of a gun in commission of a felony. The pursuer was mentioned only as "an unidentified airport employee."

Surrett explained to Magliorocco that this same

"employee" was, in fact, the 'Chicagoan" he had hired. Bernie's only sorrow was that the second dissident had not been captured or that the dead man had not survived with head intact so names of would-be insurgents could have been extracted from it.

That day, I took the telephone receiver to the retired identification cop who did my fingerprint work for me. Then I drove in the Morgan to Harrisburg, where the main motor vehicle files were and where a police lieutenant friend had paved the way for me.

The motor vehicle department's computers saved me hours, maybe days. A cantankerous old computer buff in the department estimated my three sure and two probable numbers worked out to well over two thousand cars, assuming no information on make and model.

His eyes narrow behind his bifocals, his fingers flashing on the mystic keys, he came up with long lists of Chevies, rejected coupes and those from the western part of the state, rejected all but this and last year's models, still had a slew, and began whittling away those outside a hundred-mile radius of Philadelphia.

It was three hours before he sat back and smugly pushed a button, summoning up four sedans. He pushed his printout key and out came their vital statistics on paper.

One was a rental car. I was sure it was the right one. The man my target had called had rented the car and that was why it had taken so long for him to get to the airport.

The old civil servant gruffly shook off my offer of a bonus. From Harrisburg, I called my lieutenant friend. He would not be so punctilious. He agreed to find out whether any of the four cars were stolen and to check who had signed for the rental car. I drove back to Philadelphia and called him. None were stolen.

The rent-a-car had been picked up by one Vivian Lambeth. Son-of-a-bitch, I thought. Bonnie and Clyde. But she had an address in Bryn Mawr. No Bonnie. The car had been turned in this morning with fifty-seven miles on it.

Without going home, I went to the airport car rental counter. The young woman remembered the classy blonde in her late thirties or early forties who had nervously rushed her for "whatever car I could have fastest."

I asked her where the car was now. It was out, and when I inquired whether I could rent it as soon as it got back, she became suspicious. It took a call to Surrett, who I was sure knew somebody who could get a high-up in the rental company. While I waited at the counter, the call came through and the girl sullenly gave me the name of the renter, a man from Phoenix. I located his home number there, got his wife on the phone, and quieted her fears with an honest story about an investigation of the car's previous renter. But I learned from her only that he was staying at the Holiday Inn nearest the airport and was making sales calls in metropolitan Philadelphia on behalf of his graphite products firm. I found where he was registered — it was a Sheraton, not a Holiday, with whatever ramifications that had for what he was telling his wife—left work, and got back to work on Vivian.

A reporter for the *Inquirer* to whom I had fed a few stories over the years checked the paper's morgue and turned up for me a Vivian Lambeth who three years ago had been mentioned in a two-paragraph story as chairwoman of an effort in Bryn Mawr to raise money for epileptic kids. Bored society lady plugs in to plausible thug, I thought. Where the hell did she meet him? The paper identified her as the wife of Merrian Lambeth and something in me went click-click.

Chestnut Hill, while socially coequal, was in a different part of the forest from Bryn Mawr. We did not know all of them. But there was a certain crossover. A picture of a vaguely etiolated man came to me, a man like a well-bred—but not first-rate—racehorse who is plagued with a wasting disease and is too weak to run anymore. I called Surrett.

Ah, Danny. What a cop he would have been if he'd stayed with it. In an hour, he had discovered the name of the guy's lawyer and that Lambeth and his wife didn't get on, or at least that at a recent society soirée they had had one of those glacial little in-the-wings talks and left separately.

I hustled over to Danny's office. With a Puckish finger wiggle that seemed sadly boyish on a man over sixty, Surrett signaled the current beauty who was his secretary that he didn't want any calls.

While I sat there, he telephoned Lambeth's lawyer. Surrett, despite his clients, was a bigshot in law circles. The ritzy lawyers didn't want to be seen with him in the Union League bar, but they didn't snub him either. He could throw them fat corporate clients in the kind of contract, labor, and merger cases he didn't handle. And when a Main Line client wanted a down-and-dirty investigation done of a business foe, or a wife, or an ex-lover, it was important for the Philadelphia and Rittenhouse clubs bunch to know who could accomplish it discreetly (if expensively).

Lambeth's lawyer was out. I watched Surrett, listened to him as he flirted with the lawyer's secretary to impress on her the importance of a callback the instant her boss returned, wooing her into helping him should he make a future call.

"I want you in this full time," he said, turning to me.

"I'll chase down this guy for us," I said, emphasis on the *us*. As long as he was out there, he was as much a danger to me as to Danny. I did not want my own head arriving at Danny's as the entrée to the sheep's head appetizer. "Then I'm done."

Danny sighed. He started to make a case, then stopped, filed it away. I knew he would come back to it, as he always did, pushing everything he did to the limit. For Surrett was a beautiful lawyering machine. I had found that out many years ago.

IV.
DANNY SURRETT

For quite awhile after my time in the reformatory, I stayed out of serious trouble. I went to school with considerable regularity, got Bs — even an occasional A — in English because, like my father, I loved to read, and As in freehand drawing, which also was fun. For the rest, because of my inattention, I got Cs, Ds, an infrequent F, except when a rare teacher of, say, history or science invigorated my mind.

Only in the gang fights of those days did I risk further brushes with the police. It was long before *West Side Story* made gangs as romantic as Capulets and Montagues. In the Verona between Passyunk and Moyamensing, the gangs from Ritner or Johnston or Tasker streets fought bloodily in woods near the naval hospital.

Sometimes I fought on the side of the Italians in the neighborhood, sometimes as a sort of janissary for Greeks, Ukrainians, and other South Philly minorities more numerous than Scots.

From these affrays I remember the taste of

blood in my mouth, the feel of a fist shaking my brain through my cheekbone, the odd rasp of a broken finger. For when I was hurt..., it was badly. I had a reputation for doing the same to my enemies.

It was from one such vicious fight that I reencountered Danny Surrett. I had injured a comrade of a renowned tough in an Italian principality some five blocks away. The tough, Bassio di Lessandro, unknown to me except by reputation, caught Ricky on a trip to the library for pop. He robbed Ricky of his allowance and cuffed his ear so viciously that Ricky was partly deaf for life.

There was nothing to do but fight the bully. I caught him late one evening as he came home,

"You beat up my kid brother. You took his money. You hurt his ear," I challenged.

"Fuck ya," di Lessandro said. "Now it's your turn."

We fought, without weapons, but with fists, knees, feet. Finally, our clothes ripped, our lips bloodied, he was on top of me and pounding my head on the hard dirt around a sidewalk treebox.

I limited the impact by grabbing his sinewy arms, but I knew that he was crazy, that he could kill me if I did not stop him. With desperate strength, I bucked him forward and off-balance, wrenching his arm upward involuntarily as I did.

The leverage of his fall against my twist of his arm popped it as obviously and neatly out of its socket as a cork out of a bottle. He screamed with pain. Head dulled by his effort to brain me, I fled.

70

That night I heard a motor die outside our house, then two doors slam: Bam! Bam! I was sure it was di Lessandro's allies or his older brother. I rushed to the window. It was two men, plainclothes cops by the Bobbsey twin looks of them.

My mother pushed past me to open the door and I heard a familiar voice whose evocations unnerved me:

"Sorry to bother you and Mr. Fraser, but we got a complaint. . ."

It was Danny Surrett, a Juvenile Squad detective now, looking faintly amused.

On the way to headquarters, Surrett told me that the injured tough's father was a Democratic ward organizer who wanted me in jail or worse for sending his son to the hospital. It did no good for me to protest I was discharging a debt of honor, or that young di Lessandro had been irrationally intent on cracking my skull.

In the Juvenile Squad cubicle, Surrett pulled out a file folder, found a piece of paper in it, handed it to me, and said, "read."

Even then the sociologists were abroad in the land, and I knew this typed memo must have come from one of the numerous interviews I had undergone with well-meaning nonteachers at school.

"George's home and free-time environments appear to be causative of his compulsiveness and hostility. The result is pronounced antisocial behavior. However, he has the high sensitivity associated with level-one Stanford-Binet scores. With encouragement, this sensitivity may be a building block to mitigate George's antisocial acting-out. . ."

"Do you understand that?" Surrett asked.

"Yes." I did more or less.

Surrett sat back and looked at me speculatively.

"Well, if I was you, I'd use some of my god-damned sensitivity and call up the old man and tell him the whole story and offer to work in his dry goods store to pay for the medical bills." He paused. "It's not just you that this guy can screw over. He can push your old man off that street corner."

I sat there uneasily, thinking.

"Be smart, kid," Surrett repeated.

I looked at him, saw only earnestness, and, for the first time, took a chance a cop was straight. Surrett dialed and went all syrupy when di Lessandro senior came on the line. Surrett cajoled, scraped, joked deferentially until I could hear the voice on the other end of the line modulating its wrath.

"Oh, yes, sir," Surrett purred. "It will be a part of his permanent juvenile record. One more offense and—" The voice from the receiver interrupted for one more harangue.

"Yes, sir. I'll bring the little bastard over right now. If you want, we'll go to the hospital. He is very ready to eat eight kinds of shit. What's your son's favorite flavor? Total Humiliation?" Chuckles from the Democratic presence. "Sure, if you'd rather, he'll do it over the phone. To you? Right now?" Surrett handed the phone to me with a stern look. With repugnance, but with sensitivity, I ate eight kinds of shit. Ending with Total Humiliation.

Surrett drove me home, past Independence Hall, lighted up for the tourists, a world as irrelevant to South Philly as Uranus.

"People do serious things by mistake," he said. "A kid punches another kid and the kid goes down and cracks his head and poof, manslaughter. They try him as an adult. It's maybe Moco" — Moyamensing prison, the hideous old fortress held up to us almost from birth as the end station for bad kids. "Some animals over there catch the kid alone and he's raped a half-dozen times. If he's lucky, they soap him up first. And if he isn't, they get to him dry, like you'd stick in a broomstick." Surrett was talking with mildly sadistic pleasure, but now his voice turned grim with disgust engendered by his own graphics. "Or even *with* a broomstick. Think you'd like that, Georgie?"

"Jesus, no," I said, impressed.

We drove in silence, the image of savage men in my mind, until I succeeded in pushing out the thoughts.

"When'd you go into Juvenile?" I said, trying to be conversational.

"Year and a half ago," he said. "At Juvenile I get night hours." He said he was working on a law degree at Temple, then smiled at me. "So I can make some money defending little hoods like you. By the time I quit the police, you'll be rich enough to afford me, Georgie."

73

"Very funny," I said. "But I'm not a little hood. And I'm not going to need you."

I almost didn't. I hung on at school while others, including my old friend Mark Smolen, were quitting. I pulled away from gang fighting. (Young di Lessandro, the only adversary I had truly feared, moved far north to Fisher Park. Presumably, his father's organizational genius was needed to whip some upstart Republicans and recalcitrant Democrats into line.)

Also unlike Mark, I kept my drinking to beers, stayed clear of the drug hustlers who were beginning to show up along Broad Street, and resisted the lure to shoplift, unless such minor and rare pilferage as walking out on a fountain check or snipping up a toothbrush or candy bar is shoplifting.

And unlike Mark, too, I had a part-time job, at a filling station on Morris Street. It was ironic, therefore, that except for Mark, I might have been permanently quits with Danny Surrett.

One night in May when I was sixteen, Mark, whom I had not seen for months, called and asked if I wanted to cruise. I was bored, in bad often with my parents although on balance not feeling badly about myself, restless, ready to leave home but too confused and, job notwithstanding, too broke to do it.

When I saw Mark's car, I knew why he had said he would pick me up at Broad instead of my house. It was an unfamiliar, middle-aged Ford, stolen, I was sure.

"Don't touch anything," he said. I glanced in and saw he had gloves on. I felt a mix of dread and excitement. Mark's face, already thin whiskered, had gone venal in the years since the reformatory.

He flung open the door. For an instant, I heard the alarms go off. Then, gingerly, I got into the car, knowing it was trouble and doing it anyway.

As Mark explained it, on three consecutive Saturday nights he had staked out a drugstore in Narberth, a rich suburb. He had seen the manager leave at nine-thirty, walk a block to the bank, and put a bag in the night depository.

By the time he had laid it all out, we had crossed the Schuylkill and I was kicking myself for even having listened.

"Stop the car, Mark," I said. "I want out."

"I got to have somebody. Just to start the car after I grab the bag," he said fiercely. "One time, Georgie! You can have a third."

"It's not the money," I said, although that did have an allure. "Turn this heap around. Or just drop me. Right here."

"You can shut your eyes. You won't even know it's happened." I was beginning to listen again.

"Suppose he fights?"

"He ain't gonna fight."

"You can never. . ." I began.

Delicately, as a man might lift a pearl necklace from a velvetlined case, Mark leaned across as he drove, opened the glove compartment, and took out a heavy old revolver.

"No," I said. "No. Stop. I want out. Now."

He considered a moment, then put the pistol on the back-seat floor. It was a concession, enough at least to keep me in the car. And that was all he needed.

We waited across the street from the drugstore until the last customers straggled out. Finally, a man in a tan suit emerged with a paper sack in his left hand.

"It's him," whispered Mark. He slipped out the door, grabbed up the pistol from the floor, and began jaywalking toward the man. I froze. He had betrayed me. But he had read me right. I would not betray him.

Mark caught up with the slight man in front of the dark show windows of a pastry shop. The man spun: I saw the black mass of the big pistol as Mark quickly backed him into the shop's doorway.

Suddenly, the two figures joined in a confusion of violent movement. There was a downward flash of an arm and then Mark was running toward me, clutching the bag.

We said nothing until we approached Philadelphia.

"It was better than shooting the bastard," said Mark. "He wouldn't let go of the goddamned bag."

He tried to get me to take a share of the money. Glumly, I refused. There was a short write-up of the robbery next afternoon in the *Bulletin*. Mark had fractured the manager's skull with the gun barrel. He was on the critical list.

When Mark was shot by a shopkeeper three months later, he was identified by the victims of eight robberies who filed by his hospital bed. I knew he had looped me in when his brother caught me outside the house and slipped an envelope into my pocket. Inside was $500. This time, I took it. It was all that could save me from jail. I did not hold it against Mark that he had eaten cheese on me. With eighty years facing me, maybe I would have turned pigeon, too.

Street wisdom dictated that I try to get probation. I didn't want to dodge fugitive warrants all my life, and this was, after all, my first real felony. I stashed the $500 in our attic crawl space under dirty insulation. I'd have climbed on the roof and lashed it to the chimney in a can if I hadn't • been scared to death of heights: an acrophobic. My father, looking for good in everything, once said wryly but not entirely unseriously that at least my fear of heights kept me from ever becoming a cat burglar.

The police picked me up at home, handcuffed me, though outside after I had said good-bye to my parents, and took me to the detention center. The dormitory, with its GI-blanketed cots, stank of urine and the yeasty smell of sperm-stiffened mattress covers.

Next morning, my parents arrived with the sad, graying hack of a lawyer my father had dredged up from some court-of-quarter-sessions mourners' bench. We sat around a table in the interview room, that foyer of lost souls.

The lawyer's eyes were watery from perpetual

cycles of drunk-hangover-drunk. His ginny breath, at ten-thirty in the morning, reeked through the cheap after-shave on his thin, old cheeks. The man was Defeat. Yet my parents sat by helplessly as he slurred questions about who might provide an alibi, or whether I was agreeable to his working to cop me a cheap plea.

I looked at my father. So totally within the law himself, how inadequate he was in such matters! But I wanted to fight, not give up. I asked the lawyer to let me talk alone with my parents. I begged them to get rid of this guy.

"Promise him fifty and tell him to get lost. Find Surrett."

At last they acceded. My mother did the dirty work. The lawyer's sallow face reddened, and he gave me a venomous look.

"I hope you burn, you little prick," he said as he drifted off to invest his fifty dollars in his bane.

Danny Surrett showed up that evening. He had the bold, brave look of the successfully dishonest cop. He wore an ersatz Ivy League suit, moccasins, and a new haircut. As a proffer of his skill as a fixer, he had an order from the juvenile court in Montgomery County, where Narberth was located, releasing me to the joint custody of himself and my parents. Here was someone I could do business with: a man on the make.

The drive home from the hideous gray Gothic detention building in Surrett's Dodge, smelling of newness, further lifted my spirits. His air, as much as my freedom, made me hopeful. Surrett got down to first things first.

"Your family has come up with two hundred. If I get you out of this without you getting put away, it's going to be five hundred flat. That's unless you want to plead to some chamberpot offense and get off with six months or so." He looked at me with his piratical blue eyes, testing my willingness to fight.

"I want to get off the hook," I said.

"If we go to trial, it'll be another two hundred, but I don't anticipate—"

"I don't have the money," I said, taken aback at the change in him from gratuitous juvenile counselor to paid judicial counselor.

"How much do you have?"

"One-fifty," I lied.

"You want me or don't you?" he said, a little angrily. "I know goddamned well you squirrel stuff away. Who the hell do you think you're dealing with, Georgie?"

"I got two-fifty now. If you got to have more, I'll find it."

Still not believing me, he went on, "Okay, get me that by this afternoon."

"My God," I said, still shaken by his switch from giver to taker, "Can't you give me a little time?"

"Georgie, the police department isn't giving me that old rain-or-shine check anymore. I got rent to pay, car payments to make."

"How long you been a lawyer?" I ventured.

"Four months," he said. "Why?"

I thought of saying I could get somebody with some experience for $500, but I took a different tack.

"Look, I'm a first offender." If I went to adult court, this would technically be my first criminal charge. "Why can't you just con your old friends into dropping it?"

"First offender," he scoffed. "A gun robbery? A guy in the hospital with a crater in his head like the moon. An accomplice for a guy with eight armed robberies? Plus those old juvenile offenses." He quickly got down to facts. With no alibi and with Mark's testimony against me, I was cooked on the merits.

"Suppose I can work a deal to get the case dropped if you join the marines or the army?" he asked.

I knew kids in the neighborhood who had struck bargains like that with the courts. I had gassed about it last night with two older boys at the detention center. But that would mean three, four years out of my life, and maybe the Korean War in the bargain.

"What's the most I'd do if they convict me?"

Surrett whistled and thought a moment.

"Maybe a year. If you're unlucky, two, three. There's the gun. And can you imagine the judge and jury staring at the guy's head the whole time he's testifying, thinking he could have died?"

My parents were all for military service. My mother thought it would straighten me out and save the family name, what was left of it. Pop just didn't want to see me animalized in jail. I slept on it and told Surrett yes.

I was awed at the pace Surrett worked. He took

me to Narberth, where I promised the drugstore manager that I would make restitution for his medical bills and for my share of the loot. Surrett solicited supportive notes from three of my old teachers, two English, one history.

He spoke with the cops concerned and got a reluctant prosecutor to agree to drop the case if the judge approved and if I went forthwith into the service. His coup was to get the case transferred from a retributive juvenile judge to an adult court presided over by a friend of his uncle's. Surrett's uncle spoke feelingly to the judge. I signed up on my seventeenth birthday with the United States Army.

V.
VIVIAN'S LOVER

When Merrian Lambeth's lawyer called, Surrett used his distinguished-advocate voice. He told the man that in the course of one of his investigations, he had come across Vivian in a compromising situation.

"As an old acquaintance, I'd have been remiss—" Surrett began, and then I saw his face go shrewd and intense as if it had suddenly been ignited from behind.

"Son of a gun," he said. "Son of a gun."

He listened some more.

"No, no," he said. "Not a dime. It may work out for us both. I hope it does. But not a dime. Not a dime." It was the expansive tone of a man who has just won big and can afford largesse.

The intensity in his face turned to open joy as he cradled the receiver.

"Son of a cocksucker!" he said to me. "Hot shit! Lambeth is in the middle of cranking up a divorce suit against the bitch." I wasn't all that surprised. When there's straying, the marriage is likely to be lousy. Therefore, divorce cases. Hadn't I begun as a private eye on that premise? But Surrett was way ahead of me.

"Lambeth thought his wife was up to something, but was too much of a piss ant to do anything about it. This guy, this lawyer, is the corporate guy for Lambeth's company. They have Charley Saylor" — a fancy but able divorce lawyer — "doing the divorce stuff."

Now I saw; we would piggyback on the divorce case.

"Can you get us into it?"

"Can we get in?" Surrett beamed at me. "Can we? Who the hell wouldn't want the services of George Christian Fraser for nothing in a divorce case." I laughed.

"Gratis? You promised me to him gratis?"

"Sure. I'll say we'll share the information we develop on the man in question, who we have reason to think figures prominently in a case already under investigation by us. They cooperate — "

"By letting us wire the goddamned house."

"Now you see it. I thought the old IQ was — "

"Spare me that," I said, sobering. "This is the last one. When I find this guy, if I do, then — "

"Sufficient unto the day," he cut me off. I had forgotten he was raised a Catholic.

That evening I talked the man from Phoenix into returning the brown Chevy so I could rent it. Fearing the Mafia man might flee the city or the country, I worked all night with my ex-fingerprint cop. We lifted dozens of latent prints off the car and the phone. But when he used his pull to get the FBI to process them the next day, not a damn one of them looked promising. The only one with a real record was a Richmond insurance man who had been busted in 1948 for forgery. Our quarry, perhaps a South Philly boy himself, had learned what Mark Smolen and I had known all those years ago about fingers and crimes.

Merrian Lambeth, his divorce lawyer, Surrett, and I all met in Surrett's office next day. Lambeth was thirty-nine, his wife thirty-six, and after twelve years of marriage they were sick and tired of each other.

Lambeth's money had come from his father, a big coal-and-fuel-oil distributor, and Lambeth didn't want to give up a penny he didn't have to. He also wanted the two kids. In an ordinary incompatibility settlement after twelve years of marriage, Vivian could probably count on close to a million, plus alimony. If Lambeth could catch her in adultery with a hood, she'd get peanuts and, in addition, Lambeth would get the kids.

Merrian, however, had his own vulnerabilities. His lawyer, as a matter of precautionary necessity, had told Surrett that Lambeth was into mild masochism with prostitutes. The lawyer had warned Lambeth to limit his sex play to himself and Mrs. Lambeth, at least during the legal battling.

Lambeth looked about what you'd expect of a switches-and-belts enthusiast. He had a mousy pale moustache to match his receding hair and rosebud mouth. It was odd to meet a pervert who looked like one. Most I'd known looked like fullbacks or welterweight boxers.

Mainly our talk was about how to place the bugs. Finally, we decided that Hector, posing as a property evaluator, and I, as his assistant, would visit the house one day when Vivian was out. It would be natural enough for Lambeth to call in the evaluators with a property settlement in the offing.

"Can you carry it off if your wife comes back?" I asked Lambeth.

Lambeth looked worried.

"Probably."

"Probably isn't good enough, Mr. Lambeth," I said.

"I did drama at Princeton," said Lambeth seriously.

"This'll be your greatest role," interjected Surrett with no sign of humor. "Straight out of Shakespeare."

On Thursday, Lambeth called to let us know that Vivian was out. It was the maid's regular day off and Lambeth said he would have the second servant, a handyman, Simonizing the cars.

Hector and I, both dressed in cheap conservative suits, presented ourselves at the mansion, carrying briefcases in which we had copies of the county's fire, building, and electrical codes and three books on assessing. We had studied them for the past two days. Inside my case, also, were the bugs and taps.

Unfortunately, it was not Lambeth, but Vivian Lambeth who came to the door. She had arrived home while we were on the way over. I could see what her boyfriend saw in her. She wore a white cardigan over her dark flowered blouse and modest chest. There was no gut pushing out the tan tailored slacks. She was an attractive woman, from the clean tennis shoes to the youthfully dark blonde hair. She had an open, likable face.

Then, at second glance, I saw something selfish beneath the prettiness. Or was it just the guarded look of a woman married to half a man, a woman who wanted a little loving before her late forties and fifties made it more difficult to find?

She ushered us in, with the society woman's knack of setting visitors at ease. I felt sweat on the handle of my briefcase. Hector inspected the hallway ceiling with the critical, impertinent eye of the veteran assessor.

Lambeth was terrific: he urged his wife to show Hector the laundry, recreation, and other basement rooms while he gave me a preliminary look at the first floor.

They were no sooner down the steps than I installed a tap on the phone in her study and a bug beneath her desk. I quickly tapped the kitchen phone and plastered a bug under the coffee table in the living room. The wood underneath the table was rough as concrete. Worriedly, I added another strip of thick industrial tape and rushed up the stairs.

There I tapped her bedroom phone and put a bug under the nightstand. The bed itself was verboten. Years ago I had learned that energetic intercourse could jar loose a device or, at best, clutter its transmission with squeaks and blams from springs and slats.

Time was running. I dashed down the stairs, decided to double-check the coffee table, and gasped as I reached in and felt the bug. A corner of the tape was loose. I rolled on my back and pressed it hard. No stickum. A week, ten days, and the tape would dry, the device dangle or fall. It would alert her, ruin the entire investigation, destroy my chance of catching the man who was my family scourge. My underarms ran sweat.

I pulled loose the bug, planning to attach it to the sofa's understrutting. But at that instant, Hector's and Mrs. Lambeth's voices sounded at the top of the cellar steps. Above me, I saw pure horror in Lambeth's face. I thrust the bug under my back, and lay outstretched on the floor, hands nervously at my sides.

Hector and Mrs. Lambeth stared at me with shock, but Hector recovered first.

"The ceiling?" he asked, as conversationally as if he were asking for a match. He turned to Lambeth. "You had any trouble with the ceiling?" I caught on.

"Right there," I pointed up to a spot on the smooth, creamy plaster. "About three feet from the chandelier fixture. See it?" All three heads bobbed up toward the ceiling. I could feel the hard edges of the bug beneath me.

"That slight bulge?" asked Lambeth, also triggering. Princeton dramatic club be praised!

"Water damage?" asked Hector.

"I don't recall any. Dear?" asked Lambeth

"Never." she said. "I don't see it."

"You can bet a better look if you lie on your back like he's doing," said Hector. "A long perspective."

"No thanks," she said. "I'll take your word for it. Is it?. . ."

"Nothing serious," Hector assured her. "A little fault in the false ceiling." He made a graceful, rolling motion with his hand. "The untrained eye. . ." he murmured soothingly.

"You guys do a thorough job," said Lambeth.

"We try," said Hector.

We kept the rented bakery van in which we had installed our receivers parked in a nearby shopping center behind a delicatessen owned by an old acquaintance. Nobody in the deli asked us any questions. But I was sure they knew something wasn't kosher.

Three or four times a day, I dropped by the van to check what the bugs and taps had fed into the voice-actuated recorders. I felt slightly guilty when I found Mrs. Lambeth spent a fair amount of time on the phone doing things for good causes: soliciting friends for donations to cerebral palsy relief, setting up a lunch benefit for the Red Cross, other conventional charities.

She was an innocent in all this. Married to someone like Merrian Lambeth, why wouldn't she want a lover? But, I thought, using her as the bait is the only way to the Norway rat who could kill my family. Sure, if I succeeded, she might be humiliated. But she wouldn't be dead.

While the lady of the house was away, the servants took over the telephone. The handyman had a boyfriend in New York with whom he twittered interminably—on the New Yorker's phone bill.

When Dolores, the maid, and the manservant

weren't snarling and snapping at each other, she was purring invitations to her lovers. If she had been our target instead of Mrs. Lambeth, our job would have been an easy as falling off a bed.

Dolores was a groaner and, at climax, a shouter. Once with the dry-cleaning-truck driver, her passionate outcry rang not only through the living room bug but, in echo in the microtransmitter in Mrs. Lambeth's office, all the way across the first floor.

It was Dolores's fun and games that gave us the first real hope that Vivian Lambeth might lead us to the Mafia renegade. The maid's regular boyfriend was a noncom at Fort Dix. One Wednesday afternoon, Dolores explained to him that she could not leave early the next day to meet him because Mrs. Lambeth, who usually fixed Thursday supper, was going into town and wanted everything ready to put on the stove when she got home in the afternoon.

The gruff voice from Fort Dix said, "Hell, that shoots a big hunk of our day. I might as well stay on base."

"No, honey," said Dolores piteously. "Please. I can't help it." Then, determined to amuse him, she said, "She's go to get a little, too. You know, if she had to depend on Mr. . . ."

Guffaws from the military stallion: Sergeant Neverfail laughing at Mr. Everlimp. In other years, I would have thought it funnier.

"I'd give her a little," he went on.

"You give me a lot," Dolores chirruped.

When I called Surrett after monitoring the tape, he said with relief: "At goddamn last." I decided to stay in the van all night in case there were anything of further use, any hint on the morrow's rendezvous.

A night with the Lambeths began at 7:00 P.M. on the FM receiver. The two of them chatted coolly and politely over drinks in the living room. The bug was doing beautifully; I could hear the ice clink. After the small talk, she turned the subject a little tensely to why he wasn't pushing his lawyer to get a settlement proposal to her lawyer. Jesus, I thought, the whole world's in divorce court.

One of the kids came in.

"Mummy," came the voice of, I assumed, the seven-year-old boy, "Punky won't let me get my Superdumper out of his room. He won't. . ." And the Lambeths' talk degenerated — or was uplifted — into settling their kids' dispute.

At ten-thirty, I clocked her into bed on the bedroom bug. I heard her sniffle quietly and there was a long pause. I thought she had gone to sleep. Then I heard a regular, accelerating movement in the springs and the quiet squeak of the wood. She was masturbating, unable to wait until the next day gave her a more dangerous relief.

Hector and I used a rented Ford to follow her into town, rather than my Cadillac with its radiotelephone aerial. She pulled her Chrysler into a parking garage near City Hall. I jammed my car into a no-parking space. We tailed her down the long stairs into the City Hall subway station, boarded the subway in cars bracketing hers, but lost her when, just before the train left, she stepped back outside.

By failing to prepare for her cautious tactics, we had blown the case, I was sure. I was disgusted. Hector tried to put the best face on it:

"You'd be careful too if you were gambling a million dollars every time you got a piece of ass."

During the next few days, I became a walking zombie. I worked in the office and spent the rest of the time in the van. Hector spelled me from time to time, but he was impatient with the lack of results. Besides, I had not confided to him about the Mafia angle and he felt uneasy because he sensed that I had not leveled with him. He had always preferred the arms and electronics aspects of the business anyway.

The van smelled like a flophouse from the unhappy sweat we shed. Old sandwich wrappers, newspapers, Coke bottles, Hector's cigarette stubs cluttered the floor.

To make matters worse, the case began to go bad. The living room bug went dead. I had to go in again as an assessor wanting one last look at the water-heating system and the ceiling in order to replace the bug's battery. Then Dolores dropped the kitchen phone and the tap inside stopped sending. I couldn't venture there again. We had to pray that if Mr. Mystery called, Vivian wouldn't take it on the kitchen phone.

On the eighth day after our subway misadventure, at 9:30 A.M., when Vivian was bustling about her room, singing 'Dancing in the Dark" to the bedroom bug, the phone rang and she picked it up on the first ring. I turned up the volume knob of my monitor.

"I'm delayed an hour," said the strong masculine voice in a whisper, and I gagged a moment on my swallow. There was no doubt, not a moment's, that the voice was that of the caller who had threatened to mutilate Alexa, Anne, and me, the man I had chased at the airport.

"Fine," Vivian said, disappointed. That was all.

We gambled everything this time. Hector drove in behind her with his Mercury, I with the van. When, true to form, she popped out of the subway train at the last moment, I was waiting outside to pick her up as the train rattled off with Hector inside.

While she looked for a cab, I popped into the illegally parked Mercury. I followed her cab twelve blocks to the Gordon House, a medium-sized, medium-priced hotel on Delancy, quickstepped past the desk clerk as she ascended in the elevator, and saw the floor light stop at ten.

As I left, the acidulous old clerk asked whether he could help. "Wrong address," I said. Back in the Mercury, the radiotelephone was buzzing. It was Hector, calling from Walnut, the stop past City Hall. I hurriedly told him where I had the lovers at bay.

"Great, great," he said, as excited now as I was.

When he arrived and parked the van, we double-checked the suitcase and duffle bag in which we had stored our assault equipment. Before he could pick up the suitcase I gripped him by the wrist and he looked at me with a start.

I handed him a .38, holding it by the muzzle. He stared at the gun.

"Who is this guy?" Hector asked angrily, suspecting already.

"A mob guy."

"Ah," Hector said, incensed. "You fucker."

"I'm sorry," I said.

"The M-Sixteens? The Rome thing?"

"Indirectly."

His Latin face, generally so impassive, had been writhing with dislike for me. Now he brought it under control. He took the pistol, automatically checked the chamber and safety, then looked in my eyes, his brown eyes hiding fury.

"When this is over, we got to talk."

I knew he meant he was going to leave me if he couldn't talk me into leaving myself. I felt sick that it should come this way. Still, I would have felt worse if he had been surprised by the man inside and had not had a gun to defend himself.

Without another word, he picked up the suitcase and disappeared toward the hotel's service entrance.

I fiddled with the frequencies of the two devices he would be using. One was a contact microphone: it worked like the mikes that World War II pilots pinched on their throats to talk with their crews. Once taped to a wall and wired into an amplifier-transmitter, it had surprising pickup power. The other was a spike mike, a tiny ball on a slender wand, like an ear on a stalk. To insert it, a hole was bored with an awl almost into the interior of the next room. Then the "ear" on its stalk could be thrust in to listen through the thin layer of remaining wall.

Thirty minutes passed. I unloaded the .38,

looked at the one choked ashtray, put the six bullets on the table by the console, and nervously swabbed the pistol for the second time in twenty-four hours.

Suddenly I got a staticy signal on the contact-mike channel. That meant Hector had listened from door to door on the tenth floor until he heard Vivian Lambeth's familiar voice. He would then have listened at the adjacent rooms, prayed the one he chose was empty, picked the lock, and let himself in. There, he would be setting up the mikes on the common wall.

I turned the delicate dial and heard the murmur of voices, too low to make out words. Then, on the dial for the spike mike, I began to get static. Through the static, as I tuned both dials more finely, I was able to distinguish words. I turned on the recorders.

". . .darling," the man's voice was saying, ". . .so beautiful, so beautiful. . ." Words of love, I thought, damned different from the murderous obscenities I had heard in this same voice.

"Ummm," she said, ". . .you, too . . . umm . . . feel good?"

"Ummm," he said.

". . .have to rush," she said, and I felt sick. Or was she saying *don't* have to rush. It was nerve-wracking. God, I hoped this Mafia stud was the long-lasting variety.

Static crackled out their talk for a minute or two. I tuned studiously. I prayed they hadn't hurried it, like a couple of dogs.

"No," she said, ". . .no . . . it doesn't, not at all."

94

"You're sure," he murmured.

"Yes, darling."

The tone was too conversational for me to think we would catch them at this point flagrante delicto, the moment when I knew it would be safest for us to enter the room.

What then? If I were certain he would do time eternal in prison for the attempted homicide of the airline agent and related charges, with a year or two thrown in for his mayhem threats against me and my family, I would turn him over to the police.

But that was not the way things happened with powerful men in Philadelphia. Or anyplace else. I would turn him over to whomever Surrett sent for him. Or if he fought when I tried to capture him, I would kill him myself. For him, it would be an easy way out compared to what Bernie Magliorocco would do to him.

"Now the other," the thug was saying, gentle as a nannie. By now, I knew, Hector would be outside in the hall, sweating, waiting for me to get a cue and to rush up and join him.

"Yes," I heard Vivian sigh. "Yes."

"and the other. . ." I wondered what the hell they were doing.

"Umm-humm, so sweet." There was a pause and when they talked again, I could hear a little more urgency in the tones.

"Oh, yes," he was affirming. "Yes."

There was a groan or two. Well, if I were wrong, I could dish the whole thing. But to me it seemed like the time to move. I patted the gun, returned now to my shoulder holster.

I picked up the duffle bag from the bottom of the van and rushed through the service entrance. The elevator took forever coming down. It stopped at the lobby floor while my blood seemed to run into my shoes. Three guests boarded and stared at me, but blessedly only one stayed until the tenth floor — and she went on up after I disembarked.

Hector was trying to look nonchalant, reading a paper by the elevator door. We double-timed down the hall, silent as assassins.

"You're sure they're?. . ." he formed with his lips.

"I hope so," I formed back.

I stumbled as we came up short in front of 1009. Hector assessed me quickly. I opened the bag and carefully took out the camera and a short crowbar whose claws I had machine-sharpened. Hector put the camera strap around his neck and held the camera in his hands.

A picture of my nemesis would be necessary if I killed him. Then Surrett would need it so Bernie could identify his rival. If we took him alive, Lambeth would want pictures of them both for his divorce case. Such photos could be useful to us, too, if we needed to pressure information from Vivian about her boyfriend.

I inserted the crowbar in the doorjamb as adroitly and silently as a surgeon making the first incision. We did not dare pick the lock: it would take too long and if the lovers heard it, my quarry would be waiting on the other side of it with a pistol. The crowbar's tines went into the jamb only three-eights of an inch. I hoped it would be enough to pop the door at first wrench.

"Crack!" went the door as I put my muscle into the crowbar. With a shriek of offended metal, the door gave most of the way. Instantly, we slammed into it. Our shoulders burst what was left of the lock's tongue from the groove and snapped the futile safety chain.

Gun in hand, I bulged through the tiny foyer, Hector behind me, camera chest high.

At the arch into the room, a sinewy man of about forty, naked except for a Burt Reynolds moustache, ripped at the pocket of his suit pants where they hung over a chair. His pistol had stuck inopportunely in the pocket. His penis hung limp as if in the first panel of an obscene photo sequence.

Now I could do it! Here was the man who had threatened to butcher me and my family, who had tried to kill me: the murderously swinging sword over my head as long as he lived.

And it would be self-defense. I waited a split instant for him to get his fingers on the pistol grip, still in the pants pocket, so I would always know I had to kill him. He wheeled, his dark face contorted with numerous emotions, all of them violent.

As the pistol, hidden in the crumpled pants like an animal in a magician's great handkerchief, came up, I steadied my .38 at his left chest. "Die," I either said or thought I said, as full of hate as he. I pre-saw him hurled backward from the force of the slug even as I heard the unthinkable.

My pistol merely clicked. Even as I dove, hearing his gun go off — muffled by the pants — I saw the six

97

cartridges standing by the side of the console. My head cracked against his bare knees.

Hector blazed the flash. I whipped upward with the .38 and caught him on the elbow of his gun arm, grabbing desperately for the pants with my left hand. With all my might, I pulled down on a pant leg, tipped him over, and wrested gun and trousers both from his hand, which must still have tingled from my pistol blow.

We came to our feet simultaneously. His face, a mask of raw ferocity, tried to form some oath of surprise. I swung at him with the pistol and missed. But Hector blasted again. Christ, I thought frenziedly, don't photograph him, shoot him!

My combatant, blinded and perhaps panicked, flung his arms outward. His left hand grazed my pistol arm. He knew now where I was and his right hand flickered out quick as a lizard's tongue and caught me on the cheekbone. I staggered against the wall.

From the bed around the corner of the L-shaped room, Mrs. Lambeth began to scream, her paralysis finally broken. But there was not time for damsels in distress.

The tall adulterer grabbed at my gun wrist as Hector bashed into him with his shoulder. The collision sent us all into a heap on the floor like so many tag wrestlers. Our assailant, more frantic than we were, kicked and squirmed. His sweaty, naked body was difficult to seize.

With a manic lunge, he got to his knees and began to crawl toward the door. Although I was half on my back, my gun arm was free. With a powerful sweep, I brought the pistol around and slashed it into the flesh of his cheek.

He screamed like a huge wounded feline beast. Bare tail bouncing, he bounded through the door, hand clutching his bloody face. My wrist ached from the smash I had given him with the pistol. I rushed after him but tripped on the door. Behind me, Mrs. Lambeth was shouting. As I righted myself and dashed into the hall, the nude Mafia man reached the floor's exit door and flung it open.

I reached it on the run, with Hector pounding up behind me. Flecks of blood led upward. We heard the quarry's thudding feet.

Taking stairs two at a time, I leapt after him.

"Gimme the gun," I screamed at Hector without turning, but he was already too far behind. I followed the bloody trail to a bedroom and tried to stanch my staccato breathing as Hector ran up, the pistol proffered in his outstretched hand.

Without giving him a moment to catch his breath, I sent him down for the crowbar. Yet even as I waited for his return, I knew we had lost the mobster. My incredible stupidity had let him get away. This time, Hector worked the crowbar while I stood back, gun in hand. There was a momentary rush of anxiety as I edged into the room, but it was empty, as I had feared.

A sheet was gone from the bed. The Mafia rebel had wrapped himself in it and fled. I grabbed up the telephone. The operator was forever coming on. I shouted into the phone that a rapist, perhaps in a sheet, but with a bloody face, was fleeing down the stairs and for her to alert the police.

"Get the desk to block him," I cried.

Down two floors, while Hector pulled the bugging stuff from our eavesdropping room, I went into the disrupted love nest. Vivian Lambeth would be long gone, I was sure. But from the bedroom alcove I heard sobbing. When I saw her, I understood why she had not left. I understood, too, the meaning of her and her lover's words.

Vivian Lambeth was tied to the four corners of the bed with what looked like clothesline. Open and pink as a veal cutlet, she writhed to free herself from the bonds that her lover had so gently but capably attached to her arms and legs for their mutual pleasure. He had hoist her with her own petard.

Gutlessly, I asked Hector to take the picture, but from the side. Gutlessly, and perhaps only because he had let me down in refusing to shoot the mobster, he took it. Then we untied her.

The lobby was a bedlam of bellboys and other hotel people, but no cops. We strolled out, stashed our gear in the van, and took up posts as casually as possible at the front of the hotel and at the service entrance.

But it was no go, nothing. After three hours, we broke off the surveillance. I went back that evening, this time openly as a private eye "representing a party in the case." The garage attendant was eager enough to tell me what I wanted to know: a man with a sheet around his shoulders had gunned up the ramp an hour or so after we left and burst right through the wooden parking-ramp arm. By next day, the cops had found the stolen car, abandoned in a seedy warehouse district by the river.

"Freud could build a theory on why you left those bullets in the van," said Surrett when we met for lunch at La Fonda, a new Mexican restaurant. He chose it because the mob ate in Italian restaurants, the criminal bar in French, the prosecutors in steak houses, and the cops in Chinese. We needed dimness and privacy.

"I wanted to fail," I said, more depressed than I would admit even to him. "And I failed."

"You don't know the half of it," he said, but not cruelly.

"Who was the guy?"

Bernie had identified him from our pictures, Surrett said, as Baxter Dylis, a trusted lieutenant. I vaguely recalled the name. He had been on the lam in Athens from a federal bankruptcy charge.

"That's some mob name, Baxter."

"He wasn't born with it."

Surrett pulled from his briefcase the blowup we had made of Dylis's face and put beside it an old police mug shot. It was of a kid of about sixteen. I knew a slightly younger face like that kid's and felt a jab of ancient fear without remembering the name that went with it.

" 'Bassio di Lessandro' in the original," said Surrett, savoring it. "You didn't make him, did you? From Tree Street. You kicked his ass in your gang wars and I had to save yours. . ."

"Holy shit," I murmured. "No." I had been inches from him and hadn't recognized him. "It was dark," I explained almost in a trance. "In winter it gets dark early—so long ago. And this one had a moustache." My mouth was open. Surrett's hard chuckle brought me out of it.

"Why'd he change it?" I asked.

"His old man got indicted years ago, some vote fraud. Bassio went to Lehigh. I guess he didn't want to sound like the son of a hood and he didn't want to sound Italian."

But I still remembered that evening, the insanity in di Lessandro as he banged my head on the hardened dirt, the pop of his upper arm.

Surrett was going on. Dylis—di Lessandro, he said, was the last man Bernie had suspected. Bernie had set him up as head of a real estate outfit called Hellas-Penn Real Holdings. Bernie had taken the company over by shylocking and extortion from a local Greek businessman down on his luck.

The company had owned some run-down but lucrative warehouses and garden apartments in Philadelphia and New Jersey. The businessman had also been forced by Bernie to turn over a second company called Hellabilt in Athens, Greece, which owned some handsome apartment houses there.

On Bernie's orders, Dylis had milked the American properties with excessive second mortgages, ballooned salaries, and wild expenses, thus sticking creditors with several small fortunes in business losses. It was this that had led Dylis into the federal bankruptcy-fraud charges.

Dylis skipped the country for Athens and was living fat on the unmilked Greek properties, sending a handsome tithe to Bernie at home. Dylis's degree was in business administration and he was a classy type. Prior to the bankruptcy-fraud charges, Bernie, Surrett thought, had considered him as a possible heir.

"Bernie was heartbroken," said Surrett. "Dylis was over there and Bernie had no idea he'd slip into the country and try to do this to him. He thought Dylis was twice the man his own son is."

"Sad," I said sarcastically. "Where'd he meet Vivian?"

"Lambeth had talked to him once about renting a warehouse before the fraud stuff got him, and Vivian met him at Lambeth's office coming out and they had a few words."

"He worked fast."

"Well, he was very polite and he called her later and that was that. At that point in her life, she was ready. And he was there."

"Love story. How'd you find out?"

"Vivian's told Lambeth she's ready to settle. She blubbered and said Dylis had never told her his real name—"

"Likely story."

"And that she thought his car had broken down out there at the airport. And she begged—"

"Lambeth not to let the picture out or any word that could get to her society friends about Dylis being her boyfriend."

"She didn't care so much about the affair getting out, but not that it was Mafia."

"Not even college-educated, *Lehigh*-educated Mafia?"

Two Temple graduates, we laughed in spite of our distress. Then all the breeziness left Surrett and he sighed unhappily.

"Four other guys scooted out overnight. Bernie's sure they and Dylis are on the way to Athens. These guys were serious about taking over the mob here."

"What'll Bernie do?"

"Send somebody over."

"To kill him."

Surrett shrugged in affirmation, then added:

"The truth is he hasn't got anybody in Athens." He leered at me. "You want the job?"

So it had come to that. Well, it was true that in addition to everything else, this was the thug who had deafened poor Ricky. And painful as it was to accept, it was my incompetence that let him escape.

Still, I was not going to be Bernie's, or even my and Surrett's hit man. Let Bernie send his own torpedo. Besides, there was the possibility Dylis would stay put in Athens. Surrett read the drift of my thoughts.

"Dylis'll be scheming right now how to get rid of those criminal charges, buy some judge maybe, and come back over here and eat up old Bernie."

I didn't have to be told what that meant. If Dylis got control of the Philadelphia mob, I had better think about taking out a PI license in Outer Mongolia and bringing Alexa—and Anne, even if it was my final act of consortium—with me.

Because even if Dylis hadn't recognized me during the doorbust, it wouldn't take him long to conclude who it was: the same kid who had dislocated his arm, the same man who had helped with Bernie's gun deal and then queered the assassination of Calvacadi.

"Tell Bernie's candidate to shoot straight," I said, not needing to. Danny Surrett would be as dead as I if Dylis found a way to move his power back home.

VI.
PARTY BOY

For the first five or six years of our marriage, my trade kept Anne and me outside the pale of Philadelphia society, and not unreasonably.

If I had been invited to the good parties, there was a chance I might meet some black-tie aristocrat whose last encounter with me had been on the other end of a flash camera as he whipped, fellated, or otherwise sexually enjoyed some woman, boy, or animal in a Rittenhouse Square love nest.

On the other hand, Anne had always been a hostess's catch: descendant of pre-Revolutionary WASP landholders, promising tax lawyer, and the best kind of liberal. She was always good for free tax advice for the Opera Society and other responsible civic causes. But she'd also take a down-and-outer for the American Civil Liberties Union if the abuse was flagrant enough.

That kind of decent lawyerly behavior, plus our new and handsome house in Chestnut Hill, and my gradual switch from doorbusts to more acceptable corporate private-eyeing — whose very exotica made something of an attractive freak of me — eventually coalesced to get us invited to all but the best of the social gatherings.

Anne had always liked the parties. It wasn't just that they reflected her own feeling of self worth. She saw them, although she would not have put it this way, as a means of influencing the mighty she met at them, of seeding the powerful with her ideas on law, on social issues. They gave her a sense of her own powers.

When I was honest about it, I liked the parties, too. My interest in them, however, had dwindled along with my ardor for my job. It was one more point of friction between Anne and me. And what attrition wasn't doing to our social life, my ties with the mob and the Rome murders would. For there is a kind of osmosis in Philadelphia, perhaps in other cities as well, that passes secrets through membranes without much explicit being said.

As I put on my tux for the party we were going to a few days after Dylis's escape, I gloomily thought that the osmosis would be working at its most efficient that night.

Our host was to be Senator Ambrose Crawfield. He had been a Pulitzer Prize-winning historian on Colonial America before he became an election-winning Republican conservative.

We drove in Anne's Mercedes — not that she would have wanted to go in the Morgan anyway. It was a symbol of all the undesirable things I had become. We traveled toward Crawfield's home in Saint Davids through suburbs with woods, parks, open land. The houses, smug and sprawling on fine plots, were screened by stone walls or squared-off hedges.

The big houses made me think, as I often did then, of how we would split up the goods if we split up the marriage. We had put money into land in Montgomery and Delaware counties, a barge, a coal mine . . . It was odd that both of us had made so much for ourselves. In the last ten years, she had made three and a half million, I two. And yet with the losses, the cars, the house, the luxurious trips, we were cash-short enough so there'd be squabbles about money if we broke up. I thought of Merrian and Vivian Lambeth, their greed. We would never be as bad as they became. Or so I hoped.

Crawfield's house was like Anne's parents' had been, one of those old three-full-story jobs built for more than the three acres it was on now. It was large enough so that its four two-story columns didn't look forced. As we walked up, I saw the uniformed local cops and the state plainclothesmen in their cheap dark readymades. But there were some others there in quality blazers or well-fitted suits and different lapel pins. I glanced at the walkie-talkies. They were not state-cop equipment.

"Somebody hot," I said to Anne. The state cops would be there for the governor. These other guys with the bugs in their ears were for a significant import.

"This'll be one where they've got congressmen serving hors d'oeuvres just to get in the door," I joked, and she smiled. We were, at least for the time, at truce.

I helped Anne out of her black lace capelet and

handed it to a maid. We looked around for The Notable.

A group of people surrounded a short man whose reedy Main Line tones were as distinctive as the gutturals of his predecessor several times removed, Henry Kissinger. It was Schuyler Matthews, the secretary of state, Pennsylvania's big cheese in Washington, lured here by God knows what leverage from Crawfield. Short of the president, he was the ultimate catch, and I was impressed.

"My God, no," he was saying with assurance to his circle. "We won't intervene in Brazil. Not now, not in ten years. Not ever. . ."

Anne and I gave our orders to a black waiter, one of several blacks, all waiters, at the party. Crawfield, a conservative, did not believe in tokenism. His votes came from outside Philadelphia.

Anne's sherry and my bourbon and water came like magic. I drank nervously. Who, I wondered, would hit me first with the Roman connection?

The party reached critical temperature quickly. Besides the governor and Matthews, the publisher of the *Inquirer* and the resident chiefs of the network TV channels were there, each flanked by his editor or station manager, the First Amendment mammons and their subordinate gods. The president of the University of Pennsylvania and a couple of bank chairmen were there and Pennsylvania's only Metropolitan Opera diva, Betty Jane Tarnowska.

Anne and I were drawn into different groups. I talked with a federal judge, Murtagh Leary, a sweet guy before whom I had testified about five years ago. He was afflicted with hootch, "Irish cancer" he called it. We were joined by Pierce Bouts, an associate FBI director who once had been special agent in charge of Philadelphia. Bouts came from Kensington, a Philadelphia neighborhood not unlike my own. We both knew a little more than was proper about some of our fellow guests. Pierce put the first knife in me.

"Murtagh, George here is tired of just meeting us at parties," he said, putting his arm around my shoulder.

Poor Leary looked confused.

"He wants to see more of us," said Bouts with a suggestion of derision for the florid-faced judge. "He wants to begin seeing us under oath." Bouts chuckled at his nasty little joke.

"In trouble? Nothing serious?" Honest Leary was constantly afraid of conflicts of interest. He was torn between his curiosity, his desire to keep sanitized from any case that might come before him, and his genuine liking for me. He looked unhappily at Bouts, then me.

"I took a case through Danny for the outfit," I told Leary. "That's what shithead here is talking about. It was a one-time shot," I told Leary. He would have asked Bouts about it later anyway, I was sure.

"Confession is good for the soul," said Bouts.

"You *are* a shithead," observed Leary softly of Bouts, as if he were saying something as obvious as that it was night. Bouts was slightly taken aback. He was one of those people who never understood that weak people sometimes bit back. That's why he would never be FBI director. Someone unexpected was sure to nail him at his confirmation hearings.

I left them, more heartened by Leary than angry at Bouts, and looked across the room at Anne.

The oval face had no sags. She shaped the beetled brows, but not very much, for they balanced the even mouth, the white teeth. While some women had bent with childbearing and children, she was as slender and erect as when I had first encountered her by chance in the Bar Association Library.

Beneath the sheer black chiffon of her dress, her shoulders and breasts were as young to me as when we had made love on our honeymoon beside the sea, her belly as smooth and fresh, her thighs—well, almost—as supple. Men of any age, I had seen, found her lovely, magnetizing.

Her small fingers, fingers that had been mine to touch all these years, held the sherry-glass stem with confident grace. The severe, paired platinum rings set with small rubies gave her hand the dash and hint of flirtation the rest of her seemed to deny.

A mannikin could make herself up to be beautiful. But Anne's beauty was not cosmetic. It was a meld of intelligence, of —though it was seldom now directed at me—goodness and decency. And ability and strength. On merit, she surpassed all but a tiny number of her male rivals. Even now, she chatted, with deference only to his age, with the state chief justice, who frequently had cited her briefs in his opinions.

Was this not the best evidence of her attractiveness: the caliber of men she mesmerized, the wise old justice—and now, drifting from his own entourage toward her, the secretary of state himself, his brilliant blue eyes fixed on her from his small, parchment face? As if I were in a theater, I saw her smile at him. She took his hand as they were introduced, without a hint of inequality, for if anything it weighed the other way. I saw the veiled lechery in that diplomatic Princeton face. I felt a start at this Susanna and the Elders spectacle. A start of what? Pride? Or jealousy?

I sniggered bitterly. When men spoke to me of Anne, they commented on her courage, her intelligence. Her class. But they were thinking of the primitive male question: How is she in bed?

As if indirectly to articulate that question, Leary said from behind me, "You are a very lucky man." He had loyally returned to talk with me, but he was already half adrift. "Thanks," I said. I swigged on my own bourbon and looked for another. Leary was always the last to know—whether his friends were getting into bed with criminals or getting out of bed with their wives.

When we went in to supper, it did not surprise me that Matthews, leading his wife, a mineral heiress he had married after his long-ago divorce, joined six of us already seated at a table for ten.

I caught the overt, quick look Matthews gave first Anne then me, and the equally quick look Matthew's wife shot Anne. I had been well paid for years to recognize the language of looks. I smiled, perhaps a little foolishly from the bourbon. I drank hard liquor so seldom that two or three drinks affected me. Anne glanced at me with a suggestion of concern. Then again she was all vivacity.

I ate cautiously, afraid I might do something stupid under the influence; I munched on my endive salad, chewed the tender chops from racks of lamb, and listened, genuinely fascinated, to the charismatic little secretary of state.

Matthews's smile showed slightly overlapping incisors: they gave him the look of an albino crossbill. He moved his attention stingingly, brilliantly, from one guest at the table to the next like a pale, cheery vampire, sucking from each a little substance, leaving with each a little poison. He did it all with élan and a pretense of good humor.

Flatteringly, if a little sarcastically, he called me the "Lafayette of Haiti," then when attention was briefly diverted elsewhere, he added so that only Crawfield and I would hear, "and I gather the Alfred Krupp of Roma if I read my dispatches aright." I felt like he had slapped me in the face. Crawfield would ask him after we got up what he meant; Matthews would tell him; Crawfield, privy to hot gossip, would spread it around the guests.

Those in the gathering who knew me would soon see me as a defector — lock, stock, and barrel — to the Mafia. With a surly sniff, I thought about this bunch: they had been bought and sold by other entities no more savory, merely less notorious.

Matthews, the little shit, had been responsible for the death of several hundred Americans and no end of Guatemalans in a recent policy misadventure there; Bouts, in vainly clawing toward the FBI directorship, had acquiesced in blackmail and housebreaking and perjury; Crawfield? God, what corporate behemoth had not bought his vote? Oil, the pharmaceutical industry, investor-owned utilities.

Anne, to my vague irritation, was still listening to the secretary. And she was loving it. The pallid little man's great azure eyes were dancing for her:

"The multinationals, in the best of all possible worlds, would answer to an international tax court with the power to prorate taxes to the countries where they take their profits. . ." he was telling her. As I listened, he seemed to be hinting that she would be the ideal judge. She'd been given a crack at a U.S. tax court judgeship six years ago. That job had neither much prestige nor pay. But an international judgeship ". . .we would set it up in The Hague. . ." Matthews was saying.

Now, drunk as I was, or maybe because I was so drunk, I saw suddenly and clearly what was happening. Anne was giving off some kind of scent: the smell of a woman whose marriage was no longer working right. And Matthews, subtle as a wine taster, had picked it up. I wanted to run into their group and smash him. And then, with a choked sob, I felt a fuller fury.

He had diminished me, shamed me at this party, the better to distance her from me. By such means, he would try to set her up for himself. And the ultimate outrage was that he was doing it casually, as one might reserve a new novel at a library without any definite intention of picking it up. If one happened by, then . . . but otherwise.

For the rest of the evening, I was withdrawn, my speech slurring, a classic party drunk as embarrassing to Anne as if I had been at the other extreme, the exhibitionist.

I was sure she bowed us out early because of my condition, but once we were outside, the free, fresh air sobered me somewhat. On the way home, I fumed about how I hated Matthews, how he had spread the word on my ugly commerce.

And she let me have it, cold and mean, about my drinking.

As we neared home, I suddenly got a strong distaste for humble pie.

"I had a thoroughly shitty time. If it takes getting tipsy to get through one of those things—"

"Getting drunk," she corrected me. "And making me pay for it."

"I pay every time I go to one of those things. I'm sick of them. The hypocrisy. And this crap about influencing the high and mighty. You get something besides intellectual jollies there. Matthews—"

"Oh, my God, that creepy white little body. Are you crazy?"

"No, you weren't overtly seducing anybody. You flirt with them all, the same way. With your mind. That way you don't have to deliver."

"That's psychoanalytical bull," she said. "You made a fool of yourself and now you're calling me . . . a cockteaser." Her uncharacteristic vulgarism startled me. It sounded like something she picked up from Brockman junior, her law partner.

"Psychoanalytical, you're damned right. Bull, no. A shrink could draw such a parallel with your flirting at those damn parties and your flirting with your old man, it would make—"

"I don't need any instant diagnoses from you,"

she said, cold razors in her voice. She slowed, and looked at me frigidly, assessing how much she wanted to injure me. She must have decided plenty. "Have you ever thought how much your dropping out had to do with your pop? If you want to do a little psychoanalysis, consider the genetics of weak wills."

She must have seen the stunned hurt on my face and she was sorry. When we got home, I went directly upstairs. In bed, I lay there thinking about what she had said. As I slowly ran it through my mind, all her anger sloughed off of it and I wondered why I hadn't thought of what she said myself.

By the time she came to bed, I was, in truth, about like pop would have been after an attack by my mother: passive, nonrecriminating. Anne, however, was nothing like mother would have been: She was feeling terrible about it.

"I'm sorry," she said. "You're not like pop. Not that I don't love him, but. . ." We were both in full sprint away from the chasm's edge.

"Oh, there's an argument to be made on that," I said. "Outside, I was always the Man Called Intrepid, tough, aggressive. But around the house, I've been more like"—I smiled at the absurdity of the image on my lips, and so said it—"Gunga Din worshipping Victor McLaglen."

Glad to be able to laugh at last, she did. But we both knew that the fight represented a new phase in our marriage, or more accurately, our estrangement. We had never said things like that to each other before. Nor was it one of those cathartic spats that leads to understanding.

It was, we knew, a harbinger of more anger, more frustration. And at the worst of it, I had felt something new toward her, a desire to hurt, a desire, almost, for the kind of violence I had left ten miles and thirty years behind on Snyder Avenue.

Pop was in a nursing home two miles from our house. It was a fine place — as it should have been for the cost — staffed by well-educated, caring people. I visited him there weekly. On this glorious July day, the windows of most rooms were open. Other patients, susceptible to even warm drafts, lived in rooms forever closed. In the hallway to pop's room, I smelt the exotic but vaguely familiar smell of marijuana. The nursing home was very hip: some of the old folks were allowed to use it, to pacify them, make the pain of age easier. I'd given them permission to let pop have it if it seemed to please him.

In his private room, I held the senile old man's hand, and kissed his newly shaved cheek that smelled of the Tabac I had brought him, a smell that implied to me what I had wanted for him: success, thoughtfulness.

I said, "Hi, pop," and looked into his unfathomable blue eyes. They were all that seemed to live in that clean caved-in body. Pop lay in a fetal position, because that was the way his back rested best.

He looked at me affectionately. I liked to think it was the reflection of his residual love for me rather than merely random warmth transmitted from his brain as it worked away in some far galaxy. For he

117

had loved me as a minor hoodlum, as a soldier, as a success. And these four years since he had slipped into peaceful muteness had not, I was sure, changed that.

He had loved Anne, too. That was one more reason why our marriage problems were so desolating to me. It betrayed pop, although he would never know it.

Together, Anne and I had fixed up his room with oversized photos, blowups of Anne and me and Alexa, an old black and white of the Philadelphia Saving Fund building with his newsstand at its classic base. We took some new shots of houses he had once wheeled by on his way to work. They were sunny, with front-porch planters and kids on tricycles.

I had an enlargement made of picture of pop when he was in the mason's local. He stood, big shouldered and cocky, with the other men, a man on the way up. I looked at his heavy construction man's hands in the photos and then the same oversized hands so fragile now on the coverlet.

Even the wheelchair calluses had softened and whitened away.

I had omitted any picture of mother from the room. It was not out of meanness — she, like Anne's parents, were dead and Anne and I had largely made our peace with their memories. But I feared my mother's likeness might be the one memory that could disturb pop on his distant planet.

Unable to reach pop, I sat alone with my thoughts as on all my past visits, hoping my presence might give him some feeling of being loved.

Today, all my worries came rushing at me: the Mafia and the Red Brigades, Anne, my work. Most of all, what upset me was my failure on Dylis. What I had said to Surrett the day after seemed all the more true now. I had wanted to fail.

Looking at it coldly, I had every reason to shoot Baxter Dylis. He had been a split second away from firing his gun at me and, in fact, if the trousers hadn't made him aim clumsily, I would now be dead. Moreover, if I had killed him I would never have been blamed for it. The cops would have taken it for a mob feud. Vivian Lambeth was in the alcove and would not have seen us. Besides, on learning Dylis was a mobster and on thinking another mob faction had killed him, her fright would have infected her with instant lockjaw.

I was distracted by pop's hand trembling ever so slightly on the sheet. I put my hand gently over his. If he could hear me, I could explain that it wasn't just forgetting to reload the bullets that disturbed me; I could have prepared Hector better so we might have trapped Dylis. I could even have taken along a third man.

"I wish you could talk," I whispered to pop. "I need somebody who loves me to talk with." I looked into his eyes. They were not so much vacant as pensive: as if he were in touch with gods behind the empty skies.

But what would he have told me? To go back into the business with determination to redeem my self-esteem with another case. To return to the kind of life Anne wanted.

And that I could not do any more than I could

become an Eskimo or a midget or a hermaphrodite or anything else good or bad that I was not. The me that could go back to what I had been had died, finally, along with those people in Rome.

A few days later, Surrett called. From the hint of hysteria in his voice I knew it was serious. For both of us. We met again at La Fonda.

"They killed the hit man," he said.

"How do you know?"

Surrett looked like he was falling apart.

"They sent Bernie his finger, his trigger finger with his wedding ring taken off his ring finger and slipped on the top of it. God knows what they did first with the rest of him."

I was horrified and simply stared at him. When he had gotten control of himself, he went on:

"In one of those little wooden cigar boxes. Packed in salt."

"Oh shit," I moaned. Things were rapidly headed for the bottom. "What now?"

"This guy's got a mania for mutilation," shuddered Surrett, not yet able to deal with practical matters. He sat thinking for a few more seconds. Then he took a bite of nachos.

"I'm telling you, Georgie, we've got to find some way of keeping him in Greece or we'll have to steel-plate our nuts every time we start our cars."

Over the steamy entrées, we came up with a plan of sorts:

Surrett would contact a prosecutor friend and make him a proposition. The unsolved shooting of the airline agent, who had been crippled, did not look good on the records of the police and prosecutors. Surrett would offer evidence that would allow a warrant to be issued against Dylis, supplementing the earlier one for bankruptcy fraud.

He would say that on behalf of a client, whose name would be protected by the client-lawyer privilege, I had been retained to check out a case involving Dylis. For purposes of the warrant, I would agree to testify that my investigation had led me to Dylis and a confederate at the airport.

The chase had ensued after I approached the confederate. The airline clerk had been shot by Dylis's accomplice while Dylis drove the baggage cart. Under Pennsylvania law, that made Dylis equally subject to an attempted murder charge.

"If they want to stretch it, they can charge Dylis with stealing the cart and involuntary manslaughter of the guy that got his head chewed off by the plane," said Surrett, warming to the legal possibilities. "Not to mention technical assault on the old lady, and attempted assault with a dangerous weapon, to wit, the cart on the cop at the gate, another felony."

I felt sick.

"It's going to open up the whole can of worms," I said.

"No, it'd be no deal unless we could limit it to just that much. Christ, Georgie, it's even true."

"In a way," I said. "But it confirms to Dylis that I'm the prize prick in all this."

"He'd know it by now anyway."

Maybe, even probably, so, I thought.

"It'd let Magliorocco know I was your Chicago guy."

"You can't have everything," Surrett said sternly.

He was right. If we didn't pull our strings, Dylis'd pull his. With the kind of money he'd be making from the Greek properties, particularly now that he didn't have to tithe to Bernie anymore, he could buy whomever he needed. He wouldn't be the first exile allowed home in exchange for copping a plea to a couple of nonjailworthy misdemeanors.

"It's only a stopgap," I said. "His magic still may be better than ours."

"Any better idea?"

"I'll do what we have to do," I assented, feeling in my guts that this whole goddamned thing was going to come unraveled in some horrible way.

VII.
SOUTH PHILLY BOY

It was in the army that I first learned to do what I had to do. Acutely aware of the alternatives if I busted out, I put up uncomplainingly with the six o'clock rising, the useless drill, the standing in line for everything: mess, washbasin, PX beer, aspirin. How not bear it? I faced three years of it.

Some things I loved: the rifle ranges particularly. I felt an almost sexual satisfaction with the Browning Automatic Rifle—the BAR—which climbed and snorted as it burped out its bullets—in the thudding shock of the .45 caliber automatic, the clipped zap of the M-1. I scored expert with every weapon.

When I got to the "Iron Triangle" in Korea, my platoon was depleted by the brief, bloody skirmishes of a dying war. The Browning Automatic Rifle man had just been wounded and I drew the most dangerous detail in the worst kind of unit in the army.

The rain drummed down day and night. Lugging the heavy BAR like a cross, I patrolled the checkerboarded fields when it was light. After dark, I warmed myself in my "hootch" with whiskey, or sometimes at one of the wood-and-plasterboard huts that did at the front for bars, with their one-or two-girl brothel shed attached.

Whatever else the army did for me, it made me realize that Danny was right. I was different, at least from the rest of the lower class, of which I was obviously a part. I was cursed—or blessed—with a sensitivity, crude and embryonic as it might be, that made me turn away from things that seemed perfectly acceptable to most of my comrades.

In combat, I killed. But I was revolted when my company mates dragged Chinese or North Korean corpses back within our perimeter, propped them against a tree, and used eyes and teeth as bull's eyes for target practice. Yet these same sick, brutish men who practiced shooting at dead men's heads were often the ones I found most brave and dependable in vicious swaps of automatic fire with the enemy. At such times, it came down not to who was most intelligent or most humane, but who I could trust most. The camaraderie of the platoon made me feel good about myself. I was damned proud, proud enough to send a cable to my parents when, after our platoon corporal was sent home, I got my two stripes. I could have shucked off the heavy BAR then on someone else. I kept it. Way back inside, beyond articulation, I liked to compare myself with a BAR: steely, solid, reliable—and a little old-fash-ioned.

Shortly before my enlistment ran out, my C.O. promised me sergeant if I reupped. He could have promised me general. I had had enough.

I came home in my uniform with my combat infantry badge, my battle stars, and my corporal's stripes. My father, straining to embrace me from his wheelchair, looked far less vigorous than I had remembered him.

On my first meal with them, all of our distrusts washed clean in the clear happiness of reunion. We were like I imagined an ordinary family should be, my mother awkward and yet not without pride, my father very much the patriarch, if only by consent, and Ricky bright-eyed with joy at the sight of his big brother. Yet, even in his excitement, he seemed frail, the weak pup of the litter.

I stayed home only three days. Even without the former strife, the house was a museum of old tensions and failures. I found myself a cheap room on Manning Street. With Danny Surrett's help and my calls to the few of my old pals who were not in jail or on their way to an early failure, I looked for work. Danny came through first. He got me apprenticed to a doorbuster, a private detective of no great scruples.

One day Surrett, his part-time clerk and his secretary out, borrowed me from my employer and dispatched me to the Bar Association Library in City Hall. He gave me two pages of legal-size paper with citations of state, federal, and tax court cases, law review articles, IRS rulings—they all figured in some client's urgent problem. I was too cocky to tell him I had no idea how to find most of them, although he should have known. But he was desperate.

In the venerable, high-ceilinged Bar Association

Library in City Hall, I groped from one book, one shelf to the next. By late afternoon, I had only a pathetically small stack of Thermofaxes in front of me. I felt the despair of the interloper in this vast old room with its dark, dignified portraits and magnificent gold chandeliers.

Across from me, a young woman worked head down, meticulously checking off items she had finished. From time to time she popped up from the walnut trestle table and returned in a minute or two, a book in hand, efficiently marked with a rectangular piece of paper. Here was someone, obviously at least a law student, who, unlike me, knew what she was doing.

Another few minutes passed and I was finally stymied.

"Jesus," I sighed.

She looked up with annoyance. I flinched at the frown in her brown eyes. She had unplucked brows, cool, clear skin, and the haughty stare of a Philadelphia snob. I took her to be about two years younger than I was.

"I'm sorry," I said. "I need some help." She gave me a pinched look, weighing whether to put me off or do the ladylike thing.

"If you can be quick, I can give you some advice."

I handed her the two pages of yellow paper and she held them up in her swift small-fingered hands and peered at them with the assured glance of a cockatoo looking at sunflower seeds.

"Aren't you a law clerk?" she asked.

"No."

"Well, what are you?"

"A private detective." She looked shocked, even outraged. I quickly added, "And one out of his depth." Her outrage turned to noncommittal curiosity. She shook the two yellow sheets.

"You sure are," she said. "What's a private detective doing with *Winrow* versus *IRS?* I thought all you did was break down doors."

I smiled as winningly as I could.

"I do that, too."

The brown eyes focused. The nose crinkled slightly as if to sniff out any subterfuge in this creature from another forest.

"Well," she said, "I'll give you a few minutes."

I followed her into the stacks. List in hand, she consulted indexes and pulled out the books I needed. In ten minutes, she had decreased my list by four items on which I had spent the last hour and a half.

Pleased with herself, she stood by the desk, gathering up her own notes, putting her pencils in her pocketbook, pushing a stray hair up from her cheek. I whispered my thanks.

"No trouble," she said antiseptically. Still, did I imagine a germ of interest in her gaze, even of humor at my situation?

"I'm starting on this stuff again tomorrow at nine"—the library's opening time—I said. "Is there any chance. . . I saw her hesitate, "you could just point me in the right direction?"

"I have a class at eight," she said.

"Nine-thirty?" There was something heady about being helped by a pretty young woman from a world I knew only through keyholes.

"I have to be here anyway," she said.

As promised, she showed up at nine-thirty. Dressed neatly in a belted summer dress, she swept up to where her books were stacked and took my list from me. In quick march time, she showed me how to use the "key" system to find cases, led me to two of the most elusive IRS rulings, and told me in a pleasant upbeat voice that a case on my list, 42 B.T.A. 1314, had been superseded by 348 U.S. 426.

I got hard to work now on my own, with some hope of success, and said nothing to her as she burrowed away in her research. For a moment or two at a time, I glanced at her neat brown no-nonsense hair. And when she went to the stacks, I ventured a look at her thin, straight back and swinging skirt. At noon, she gathered up her papers to go.

"Leaving already?" I asked.

"I'm finished. Are you doing okay?"

"Yes," I said. At last I looked boldly into her eyes and saw in them reciprocal curiosity and something else. I smiled inadvertently. "Will you be back this afternoon?" was all I could summon to hold her.

"No," she said, hesitating, not saying, "I don't want to see you again." And suddenly, it was overwhelmingly important that I know her. In her eyes, still fixed to mine, I saw a hint of adventure as exciting as any of my cases. I sensed in her intelligence, grace, humor. I also sensed the dampener of our differences, which could smother the spark in her for me.

"Could I buy you a cup of coffee?"

"No," she said, hastily rather than rudely. Whether she would have done the same to anyone under the circumstances or whether it was my reek of South Philly, I could not be sure. But I was hurt. I had dared to hope because I had perceived in her eyes that she was attracted to me.

She saw the destructive power of her rejection, yet her mind was made up.

"I'm sorry," she said. "I don't think I want to. And I'm sorry that you do."

The snub rankled for months. But it was a busy time. I could not afford much romantic mooning. I set up my own one-room office on Broad with money borrowed from Surrett. I kept the desk drawer open and a snubby .38 there where I could get to it quickly if some grief- and anger-stricken victim of my investigations opted for revenge. It lucked into a quick "make" on my first case, a routine marital doorbust, and my share from the husband was $1500, big money in those days.

I went to my father's stand the morning I got the check. When he protested my branching out on my own, I told him the size of the fee. I left him drop-jawed, but he still shook his head.

"It's dirty work. I'd have stuck with the army."

"I'm not sticking with what I don't want," I said quietly. "If I get tired of this, I'll leave it, too." But how impossible that seemed!

Pop smiled, liking the sound of my confidence even if he didn't like the words. He had always seen me as a winner, even when mother and the rest of

Snyder Avenue judged me jail fodder. I reached over the papers and touched a patch on his face he had missed with his razor.

"You feel like a goddamned walrus. How about an electric razor?" I had wanted to buy him a wheelchair with my new wealth, but the one he had was like an extension of his body.

"I don't know," he said, rubbing his cheek. "Maybe I ought to stick with the old strop."

But I bought it and he loved it. For mother, I bought a dozen red roses. For Ricky, I got a leather briefcase. He was starting at West Chester State. I saw too little of him and knew I ought to see more. He had become withdrawn, and when I tried to reach him, there was an odd walling off that hid something deep and scary.

For myself, I got an efficiency apartment near Logan Circle. I traded my broken-down Ford for an almost-new Dodge, not the red Mercury convertible I craved, but a car better suited for surveillance. I had a new apartment, a good car, lots of work, and lots of debt: I was part of the American dream.

Danny Surrett called me one day in his serious tone of voice. I went to his new office. He was moving up so fast I figured he couldn't have his stationery printed in batches of more than a few hundred. He had two secretaries, both pretty, and a clerk who was a law student at the University of Pennsylvania.

Even his clients were getting big league. Rich but

cornercutting businessmen were coming to him with high-fee cases. He had taken a few "bust-outs" — Mafia bankruptcy cases in which legitimate companies are bled dry, then put in bankruptcy. I was doing much of his gumshoeing for him, but he kept me clear of the Mafia stuff.

In his hand when I came in that day was my report on a surveillance. I had typed it with exemplary neatness. He smiled and said, "It's got just the right mix of sanctimoniousness and fact. When you going to get a high school diploma?"

I had thought of it. But I didn't want to waste the time. The money was coming in. The cases were building up. I was doing fine with my nine years of school.

"What for?"

"Hell, you're only . . ." He tried to calculate.

" Twenty-two. Almost twenty-three."

"Twenty-two. You ought to be thinking of college, too."

"Jesus," I said, disconcerted. "College is four years."

"It's not that you *need* to know any more. High school, college, they make you respectable. It'd help me if I could say my investigator has a B.A. from Temple and a batch of prelaw and criminology courses." He leered. "We could up the fee."

"I don't need a B.A. to break down doors," I said.

"You want to do that all your life?" he asked.

"It's not bad. The money—"

"The money is in corporate gumshoe work," he said, "where they want a degree to let you in the

131

door. The money is in making and selling this new electronic shit." Now he was getting irritated at me. "Maybe you're too dumb to do anything but shoot beavers."

Once into studies, I found it inordinately easy. I had never left off the reading that had lured me as a young boy. In Korea, I had devoured everything from sleazy sex novels to Chekhov plays. It wasn't that hard to substitute high school equivalency biology books. The math, physics, and chemistry came harder, but when I passed the achievement exams, still goaded by Surrett, I got the Temple catalogue. When I figured up a B.A. in night school at twenty credits a year, counting summers, it wasn't impossible.

During those years, I saw much of Surrett. It was a comfortable but peculiar friendship. What confiding there was was my confiding in him. As to his personal life, I knew it mainly by indirect reference and by occasional visits on business to his series of new apartments, each a bit bigger than the last. He needed no family, as families are generally understood. When he wanted sex, he took it casually from his women employees, from other women he dated, all of them pretty, none of them with either real intelligence or class. He invested little of himself in anyone.

I was a handy adoption for him, the son and younger brother he never had, and he was proud of me. He helped me in every way, throwing me cases, advising me against this or that lawyer, counseling me on how to handle cases where his knowledge could be useful.

He showed me concern without taking responsibility, did me favors and got a great deal of self-gratification out of my gratitude. I felt for him the love and caution that a son might feel for a slightly distant father or much older brother who is not quite right with the law. In that final respect, it was an ironic reversal of the roles we had when I was on the streets of South Philly.

By the time I was twenty-five, I was buying, at wholesale, electronic surveillance and antibugging equipment and reselling it at an honest markup to cops in the small towns around Philly and to other private eyes. With Surrett, I had talked about marketing handguns in bulk to some of his Latin American clients. I looked on myself as very much the investigative hotshot.

So I was not all that surprised to get a call from Maurice Brockman, a partner in Liggett and Canterbury, one of the oldest and largest of the city's law firms, and one that coined money from the world's wealthiest and basest entities.

Liggett and Canterbury would represent a bank in a regulatory hearing, but not a bank president in a divorce case; the sugar growers of the Dominican Republic, but not its malevolent rulers; a crooked lawyer with a civil tax problem, but not in his disbarment proceedings for some felonious sex offense. Liggett and Canterbury knew where to draw its lines.

In their boardroom two middle-aged men and a young woman waited for me, all expensively and carefully dressed, and bunched at the end of the long table like two uncles and their niece in some

English baronial movie. The men were Maurice Brockman, Sr., and Frederick Tabard, another partner in the firm. The young woman, trying not to look ill at ease, was the same one who had snubbed me in the Bar Association Library years before. Her name was Anne Bouchard.

Like the men, I had on a three-piece suit (I had bought it from Jacob Reed's Sons without Surrett's having to tell me) and a white shirt. By now, I knew South Philly lads on the make wore protective coloration—charcoal gray. My only manifest rebelliousness was a fine silk tie with tiny handcuffs on it.

Everybody shook hands. Anne Bouchard gave me a strong grip.

"You've probably forgotten," I said. "We met in the Bar Association Library some years ago."

"Of course I haven't forgotten," she said a little too heartily.

The case was a beauty, made for me. Brockman, the older of the two men—bald, plump, with a ringing alto voice—outlined it.

Their client was Mid-National Gas and Pipeline, a gigantic Pittsburgh company. It was contesting another gas transmission giant, Purpose-Richman Natural Gas, for the right to provide gas to customers in large parts of Pennsylvania, New York, and Ohio. Whoever got the nod from the Federal Power Commission in Washington would get a monopoly worth billions over the long term.

Mid-National, thanks to Liggett and Canterbury, was winning the case and Purpose-Richman was desperate. So desperate, said Brockman, that they had apparently bugged the suite of Mid-National's president, Raymond Kuhling, while he was at the Bellevue talking legal tactics with Brockman and Tabard.

"Apparently?" I asked. In fact, it wasn't the usual paranoia. A maid had seen someone leaving Kuhling's suite after Kuhling checked out; the hotel security man had found a trace of stickiness under the coffee table, perhaps residue from an adhesive. And Purpose-Richman's filings three days later had been awesomely accurate in rebutting Mid-National's best arguments-to-come as prepared in the strategy meeting in the hotel room.

We batted it back and forth and at the end, Brockman, a man with a common touch despite the Phi Beta Kappa key on his belly, looked at Tabard, but not at Anne, to see if there were any objections and said, "You're on."

"Who do I report to?" I asked.

"On the major things or anything that might reflect on the firm, me." I knew he meant that if I broke down any doors, he would want to know about it so he could be prepared to swear he didn't know about it. We understood each other and were going to get along fine. On the minor things, Anne Bouchard would serve as liaison and I was to give her a brief daily report. I felt a sweet start of dizziness.

The daily reports took me through two months of dogged work and brought me close to Anne Bouchard. The first nonformal word we spoke was when I took her to the courthouse one afternoon moments before closing to file a paper. She leapt

135

from the car, and straight skirt held above her knees with one hand, ran on her high heels to make the filing deadline.

Flushed and pretty when she returned, she thanked me and I risked:

"You must have been the star sprinter at Vassar or wherever."

"Bryn Mawr."

"I'm on the high-speed night commuting team at Temple," I said. We made small talk about what I was studying. I asked her where she'd gone to law school. Yale, she said, with summer classes at Penn. It was intimidating. But I had broken the ice.

I dropped by her office one day when I was back in Philadelphia to take care of several other cases that I did not dare neglect. After I reported my most recent dead ends on Mid-National, our business done, she went over the prospectuses of the two pre-law courses I was taking next semester.

When I called in after that, we gossiped a bit about ourselves. I talked a little about my family, mostly pop, and she about hers.

She had grown up in Radnor, a place of large lots and incomes. Her father had been a vice-president of a railroad, often out of town in Washington, where he lobbied against Roosevelt's railroad regulation. I sensed, without her being explicit, that he was a charming, authoritative type, a freebooter, perhaps a philanderer. As a railroad lobbyist in those days, he was also very likely a crook.

I also gathered he had invested their money poorly. He had died of a heart attack in 1957 and she and her mother still rattled around, a bit at odds with each other, in a white elephant of a house in Radnor.

There was not the slightest doubt in my mind that she had a kind of hots for me, and my dry throat when I talked with her, if I had needed any other signs, let me know how strongly I felt the same about her.

But her no at the library had set in her mind. We were colleagues in this case, and she was too ambitious to make a fool of herself by trifling with her firm's hired gun. As we became friends, however, I saw the South Philly in me was no barrier. Her father was also no aristocrat and the buccaneer quality in him, I came to feel, was something she had admired.

The one time I suggested she might like to go to supper with me, she turned me aside nervously with ". . . another appointment." I took it stoically. This case would end one day and I would have my hour. Meanwhile, I wondered who she was dating, whether she had ever been in love, hoping that by my strong, gaudy lights she would find her other suitors pale and attenuated.

For weeks, my daily reports were all negative. I checked out private eye after private eye, queried makers of electronic equipment, ran mug shots of investigators past the maid. But nothing broke for me. Discouraged, almost hopeless, I complained to Anne, confiding that I was even feeling guilty over taking my fee.

"Well, that's absurd," she countered. "You're earning it."

More often we talked of the technical aspects of

the case—how she could produce enough case law to get the FBI into the picture, for example. Or she pushed me for vouchers to keep me current with expenses. I loved these business encounters and could not bring myself to bill Liggett and Canterbury for time I talked with Anne, even when it was on the case.

I finally broke the case in San Diego, where I found the bugger. Surrett had helped me by pulling some strings with an old FBI contact. Brockman and Tabard were elated. Anne was excited, barely hiding her personal pride in me from the two older attorneys. They quickly threatened the bugger with a ruinous civil suit and, using pull, got Philadelphia prosecutors to hold criminal housebreaking and illegal bugging charges over his head. Under this pressure he first bent, then confessed his client was a subsidiary of Purpose-Richman.

That was all we needed. Even the Federal Power Commission couldn't be fixed to award a monopoly to a company that we could prove was guilty of gross industrial spying—and in a case that was before the Commission.

Surrett, when I called him to tell him of my success and to thank him for his crucial help, was congratulatory but pointed:

"I'm amassing a lot of your blue chips, Georgie. One day I might ask you to pay off on them." He sounded a little like Rumplestiltskin.

"Sorry I had to push you so hard. I wanted to make this case like crazy."

"You wanted to make the fair lady. Better you should look for some upwardly mobile South Philly girl. Some of them are lawyers, too, you know. And they don't piss on your feelings."

I had seen Anne often for more than two months. I had lost my temper with her, cursed her, if mildly, sneered at her for her ignorance of gumshoeing, been sneered at by her for my ignorance of the law—all the interchanges of an intense business relationship.

In the course of our daily contacts, we had come to respect each other, and without even anything as intimate as a premeditated touch, to know each other. We had snacked together from time to time, but never eaten out. Nevertheless, I knew that she would not refuse me now.

I took her to Shroyer's, a place of sound food, pictures of landscapes, and dignified paneling, but not overly romantic. Over the old-fashioneds before supper, how easily we fell into a comfortable mode. "Now, honestly," I asked her, "wasn't that case more fun than tax law?"

"Not for me," she answered, never one to bend her views for the convenience of others. "Just different."

"But you can see why—"

"You're in it? Sure. And I loved seeing you in it. It's almost . . . awesome. The intensity you put in it. But it wouldn't work as a job for me. I'm fascinated by Tarzan movies. But that doesn't mean I'd want to live in the jungle. No matter how attractive Tarzan is."

"But when Tarzan comes to London in his society clothes as Lord Whosit?. . ."

"Oh," she said, still flirting. "Is Tarzan going to

139

put on society clothes and become Lord Whosit?" I blushed, suddenly inept.

"Tarzan is not much on society clothes," I said lamely. "But he is a fast learner."

Despite her attitude about criminal law for herself, there was much that our work had in common: the paper skills like accounting, contracts, grantee-grantors. When she talked about her cases, I understood, and vice versa. We never lacked for conversation.

But though I loved to listen to her talk, more deeply I loved merely watching her, talking or silent.

On that first date, in the muted country-club air of the fine old restaurant, when she put her drink to her lips, the soft light cast streaks of rose and yellow through the glass onto her amused face. In her feminine tweed suit and jonquil blouse, her hair swept back, she seemed first beautiful to me, then, all of a sudden, wondrous.

That winter I worked to exhaustion at my office and in my classes. I lightened and let my spirits blossom only when I saw Anne. I knew she dated other men, but I also knew I profited by comparison, that she saw in me a different sort of man. She could trust me not to push her. I did not threaten her. As she understood that I would not hurt her and did not want to play deceptive games, she came to need me. In a sense, I became mildly addictive for her.

I saw my first real play with her, Ibsen's *A Doll's House*. Afterwards we discussed it passionately, drawing on the play to talk of our own lives. Her father, son of a Venango County oil baron, had married upward in wedding her mother, Alexandra Stanford Dindley, whose family had helped settle the Lackawanna Valley before moving into iron and coal.

It was her father's streak of nonconforming cussedness — and her ability with numbers — that led her, I was sure, into tax law, not your usual Radnor debutante's métier.

Once, over after-work drinks, I introduced her to Surrett. He was engaging, manifestly on the make, as he was with all goodlooking women, not caring that it upset me, not caring that it did not take at all on Anne. When she and I were alone at supper, she said:

"Surrett is like my father, dashing. A pirate really, but an agreeable one. His feelings are in his hands, you can tell. He wants something, okay, he grabs it." Then realizing she had been pretty harsh on her old man, she added, "He's probably worse than my father."

"Well," I said. "He's got his faults. But he's what got me where I am."

"He needs you more than you need him."

I looked at her curiously. She started to explain, "You are the only thing he's got he can be proud of. I don't mean you *do* things for him. You just *are* for him."

"He *is* for me, too," I interrupted. I thought of my weak, crippled father, my mother, a burned-out — well, nearly burned-out — scorpion, my poor fractured brother. "Surrett is also all I've got," I

141

said, not daring to add, "until you came along."

My brother, Ricky, had been doing miserably at West Chester State. Pop had gotten me to force myself on him for a visit. Ricky was withdrawn and anxious. After that, I tried to get him to come into town for supper several times, but he put me off. A few weeks later, Pop told me that he got two Ds and three Fs on his report card. I called him and raised hell with him, irritated that he was doing poorly, irritated that he wouldn't let me help.

One night, while I was out with Anne, I called my answering service to see whether a surveillance I had contracted out to two moonlighting Trenton cops had paid off. There was an urgent message from my father. I phoned him from the restaurant. Ricky had hanged himself in his dorm room.

Anne, uncomfortable but generous, came to the funeral. I wept and wept as I looked at Ricky, cosmetized and waxen in the coffin. When we were children and when mother's scolding and arm grabbing seemed to be mastering me, pop had sometimes risen from his wheelchair, supported by one brawny arm, and shouted at her, "Enough, goddamn it!"

I could recall no such intervention for Ricky. It was as if they had reached an unspoken compromise. Mother, I thought with a shiver, had agreed she would abate her manipulation of me in exchange for Ricky's soul.

Ricky's death cut into my heart. For years, thoughts of it came on me by surprise, momentarily

142

stopping my words in the midst of conversations, eliciting at other times a grunt of pain when I believed I was thinking absorbedly of something else. Yet my own life was running open-tapped: I grieved for Ricky, but I grieved on the fly.

The business was booming and Surrett incorporated me when my sales of electronic gear rose above $100,000 a year. It was then that I bought the telephone-equipped Cadillac. It impressed the local consular officials and it was an Italian commercial consul in Philadelphia who got me my first big foreign contact.

I flew to Rome, then to Tripoli to cinch the deal. It was amazing how my street Italian helped. I began to see how the Rome-Tripoli-Philadelphia axis might create a *mare nostrum* of money for Fraser, Inc. in the coming years.

I dropped out of Temple, determined, however, to go back for my B.A. But I could not continue classes without giving up my dates with Anne. She and the business were everything to me. Sometimes they overlapped.

At eleven one evening, for instance, dead tired, I called her at home to ask:

"How smart would I be to do the Arab stuff through a Swiss or Lichtenstein subsidiary?"

"Don't."

"Why not? The tax advantages —"

"Are marvelous," she said. "We have a client right now we are advising to do exactly that, George. But he has been in business a long time. He has his lines straight with the IRS and the Commerce Department. Don't fool with it until you are solid."

"*Business Week* said —"

"Then damn it, get your tax advice from the circulation department at *Business Week*. My God, it's eleven at night and I'm not even billing you . . ."

I knew Anne was serious about me not so much from our increasingly heavy necking, but when she invited me to meet her mother one evening before we went out to supper. Mrs. Bouchard, a small woman with a fixed expression of being slightly put upon, did her genteel best to show her disapproval of me without an explicit word. For my part, I was polite yet stubborn. Anne complained I had been sullen, even rude.

But however unpleasant that evening, the long-term consequences of my lese majesty worked in my favor. For a few days later, Anne called me at home. She and her mother had had a set-to. I was sure it would have been low voltage compared with those chez Fraser. Still, it had shaken Anne enough for her to call her pal-confidant-suitor at 10:00 P.M.

"I'm moving out," she said. "In a week." I wondered how I figured in this. She answered without my worming it out of her. "It began to come to a head when she gave you the old-Colonial-family treatment. Sweet Melissa mustn't get serious about the overseer even if they've dallied a little."

When we had moved her in her new apartment and sat, dirty and in old clothes, drinking beer from cans, I looked at Anne and knew she liked me as

144

well as she ever had any man.

As the months went by, we bicycled, camped, took long hikes, walked in the parks, and gardened in the tiny plot behind her first-floor apartment. By preference, we generally went out alone: to movies, to Robin Hood Dell for outdoor concerts, to the Art Museum.

If there was anything in her that I thought might endanger us, it was an aura of rigidity that let me know I must adapt to her ways. They were *her* friends we met with, *her* kind of Philadelphia that we would live in. I had no objection. There *was* no *my* entertainment, friends, or milieu for me to hold out for.

But beyond these things, in a partnership with her, I would also bind myself to live her kind of life. It would be a life structured on hard work, achievement of social and economic position; it would be a life set in the ways of Radnor, without much reflection and frivolity.

We were married in July 1962 at Saint Martin's Episcopal Church in Radnor. My father, in his wheelchair, was my best man. Surrett was my only usher.

VIII.
THE DROPOUT

As long as I had some hope that Magliorocco's henchman would take out Dylis, my own failure did not assail me full force. I was depressed about the seemingly deliberate way I had disarmed myself, and about my poor planning, but I was not shell-shocked. When the finger came back in the cigar box, however, it pointed at me, paralyzingly.

The fact that I knew it was psychologically sound for a man not to feel completely guilty until he was caught did not make it any easier for me. Who had said that to understand everything is to forgive everything? I didn't forgive myself. I had never felt lower in my whole life.

I talked to Anne about Dylis. She had a right to know that the security I had hoped we would have from him wasn't going to develop. I thought of voluntarily leaving the house. In terms of safety it was a toss-up. On the one hand, Dylis might seek revenge solely on me, making it safer if I moved. On the other, if he acted against my family, they were safer with me around.

Anne dealt with it all not just encouragingly, but sympathetically.

"Poor George," she said. "God, I'm so sorry."

"I feel awful," I said.

"Nobody else would have gotten the case far enough along to where something like this could happen."

"I know, but I never thought of myself as 'nobody else.' " Moved by her support, I offered her the very thing I had feared she would suggest. "Maybe I ought to clear out." She hardly paused to think of it.

"No, you can't do that." Then, shooting a little self-deprecatory humor into the mess, she added drolly:

"When I get my chance to be the kind of monster you sometimes think I am, I don't seem able to rise to the occasion."

I chuckled emptily.

Next morning, Surrett and I met at the prosecutor's office. He was a tough little Italian, the kind whom, as a kid, I had fought for and against in South Philly. Well, I thought, looking at the gray metal desk and the framed map of the Philadelphia metropolitan area, this guy went his way and Bassio di Lessandro went his and Surrett and I went ours.

At another time, I might have thought that Surrett and I, in our expensive suits, with our fancy houses and cars, had made it and that this prosecutor hadn't. But today he seemed clean and we didn't.

When the bargain was struck, he called for a secretary from the office pool to take my affidavit, the main grounds for a warrant against Dylis. He planned to pick up ancillary statements from the crippled airline agent and others at the airport that night. He had photographs from the files of the federal bankruptcy case against Dylis and hoped somebody besides me would identify him as the man in the cart. Surrett and I said nothing about our own photo.

The three of us waited silently for the secretary to arrive. I brooded about the publicity: when the warrant was issued, the papers would pick it up and mention my affidavit. If Dylis didn't know now I was the skunk who had interrupted his various fun and games, he would know when the newspaper clips reached Athens.

The secretary buzzed that she was on her way and the prosecutor looked up humorlessly from Surrett to me with his intense, impersonal dark eyes.

"When you guys want to talk about your clients, Danny, don't forget where to come," he said. Implicit in his words and look was that anyone sleazy enough to work for the mob was sleazy enough to turn on them. His assessment of me didn't make me feel any better about myself.

Two days later, I was still morose. I turned down some idealistic Darby Creek landholders who were fighting polluting industries upriver and wanted someone to find out if the companies were criminally conspiring to keep it up. If I'd wanted anything at this stage, it would have been that one.

Time passed, but I moped on, unable to drag myself from despair. I obsessively replayed the case hundreds of times, often fantasizing different and happy endings. These pipe dreams, as if they were drugs, gave me a brief but illusory respite from pain.

Lingering over supper five days after the disaster, Anne and Alexa made a family council of it.

"You know," Anne said, "you ought to be pulling out of it a little. I'm not trying to badger you, just making an observation. It's not the end of the world."

"Dad," said Alexa, "this is just one case. Look at all the others. . ."

But in this one so much was at stake.

"Alexa," it was easier nowadays to address her than Anne, "I prided myself on not making mistakes. And I made them."

I could no longer put off facing Hector. I went into his office. Papers were scattered even more widely on his desk than usual. For more than a week, he had been doing my work, too. He looked up, his eyes veiled.

"You still want to buy me out?" I asked.

"Yeah, I do," he said rising excitedly. "Just the guns and electronics," he added cautiously. "You know I never wanted the investigations."

"We'll figure out a way," I said.

There was more of a cleanup operation at Fraser, Inc., than I had thought there would be. We began when I came in next day. On the small walnut conference table Hector had stacks of paper ready for me.

His questions were an abstract of my old world. Had I promised a 10 percent rebate, read it kickback, to an Omani minister? Yes, I recalled. Did I have notes on my initial talks with Fabrique Nationale on a big order of FN-LAR assault rifles? Our middleman was claiming an inflation adjustment. No, only mental notes. Hector looked upset. He always kept notes of such talks. Our contact man in Indonesia had moved from defense to foreign affairs. Did I know a good substitute in defense? I agreed to consult my files at home and come up with names. Hector again looked uncomfortable. I knew he felt I should leave all noninvestigative files at the office. After all, he was buying me out.

When we had concluded, Hector cleared his throat and fell into the conditional interrogative tenses he used when he was uneasy.

"What would you think if I?. . ." Hector began. He wanted to change the name to Fraser-Fernandez. It was courteous of him to ask. He was buying the company name with the company and could do anything he wanted with either.

"That's fine, Hector," I said.

"Do you think it sounds funny?"

"No. It sounds fine. I'm proud you want to keep me on there." Part of me meant it.

One day, I drove to the Art Museum. With the FM playing "An American in Paris" and no cloud in the blue sky, I purred along the parkway past lush woods and on down to where boatmen tacked their sailboats on the Schuylkill.

Given my druthers, I would not have gone to the museum alone. But I had remained a loner. Except for Anne and Surrett, I had never had any real friends. I wasn't in a mood to be with anyone less.

The paintings reminded me of my courting days with Anne; it had been one of the things she'd gotten me to do—ah, how willingly—in hopes of getting South Philly out of me, as I had, by then, gotten out of South Philly.

Now I found peace among them without feeling they made any intellectual demands on me. I wandered past the blank, undeveloped faces of the Italian Byzantines, then past the frozen clashes of armored steeds and men-at-arms and into the sumptuous colors of the cinquecento.

I stopped before the museum's voluptuous prize, a Flemish *Leda and the Swan*. The portrait gave me an uncharacteristic feeling of being vulnerable to sensuality. Leda's harvest body turned lushly from the satiated bird, her chubby breasts and haired mount flushed from the caresses of white wings.

Might there not be some lover of galleries someday who carried that succulent form beneath skirt and sweater? If I were to risk an affair, it would be with such a woman, pensive of countenance, reckless of body.

I looked at the painting again, at Leda's body, the brazen cleft, the candid thighs. Not bad, I let myself think: that wouldn't be bad at all. At least I felt a stirring of life.

That day at Arthur's Steak House, where I had been lunching for more than twenty years, I allowed myself an old-fashioned. And with the shrimp cocktail, filet, and perfectly crisp conventional salad, a half-bottle of red Burgundy.

I pondered my enervation in this room of steak smells and old wood. I doodled on a paper cocktail

151

napkin, sketching the wine bottle, the solid, efficient salt and pepper shakers, the coffee cup. Once I had been as these men eating here, a businessman with nothing more on his mind than getting back to close a deal.

Most days I spent puttering around the house, to Anne's aggravation. For her part, she put ever more time into the law firm, as if to blot me — us — out of her life. Fraser and Brockman waxed while Fraser and Fraser waned.

From the beginning, she had run her firm with an efficient but a light touch, an acquired rather than a natural skill. She knew the Philadelphia law establishment would watch the firm to see if it looked like Russia under Catherine. To the contrary, it began as and remained a happy, parochial shop.

She had stayed with Liggett and Canterbury for fourteen years. During that time, Brockman junior had joined his father at the firm. He and Anne had worked some cases together with mutual respect. Shortly after Anne left to form her own firm, Brockman senior had retired and his son shifted to Anne's fledgling firm. The two of them had gradually taken on a clutch of young lawyers, mostly non-Ivy League. The criteria were law journal staff or articles, toughness, compulsive industriousness. In the days when I picked Anne up late on the way home, there were always two or three lawyers settling in for a long night.

Brockman junior, at thirty-seven, lacked her breadth, her grasp of the tax considerations down the road, the political effects. He might recommend that a multinational copper client take the maximum tax write-off for its overseas investments, royalties, and fees. Anne would hold back a little, aware that too much greed would arouse the IRS, the competition, and the public. But on balance he was a talented tax lawyer.

Despite his lesser rank, Brockman took no nonsense from Anne, not that she gave him much. He was pudgy but energetic, and curt where his father had been suave. Anne called him "Brock" to his face, a nickname he liked, but "Brockman" to me. He had been married to the daughter of a Liggett and Canterbury partner. That had fallen apart four years ago and now he was working his way through the distaff side of the junior bar.

Brockman and I kept our distance from each other. I think he feared that if he tangled with me, I would put a bug under his bed and record his pleadings with his juridical teenyboppers. For my part, I thought he was a slob, and besides, I didn't fully trust him, although obviously Anne and his clients did.

Meanwhile, Anne and I hung together in the house, neither quite willing to take the first step, neither of us really having that much of an alternative life in mind. What was left of our liking for each other began to peel away like cheap lacquer rubbed with paint remover. When we squabbled, it was over minutiae because we feared the centrifugal forces of fighting on a big issue.

But even on the little things, we knew each other's Achilles' heels with precision. Sometimes I found myself planning during the day how I could give her little cuts in the evening. When I discovered it, I detested my pettiness, hated what I saw happening to two people with decent instincts. But I was quickly back into it, wondering if she did not plan her sallies against me during the day, too.

We had repetition after repetition of the kind of flash fire we had put out after the Crawfield party. Only now we did not put them out. They smoldered under our superficial politenesses.

At night, we still slept together, finding in the warmth of each other's bodies something familiar and peaceful. At times, if we had spent supper without arguing, if she had a little wine, she was amorous. And I gamely tried to give her pleasure without coitus. But sex, if not perfect in the past, had been too good for either of us to settle for that. And gradually even those feeble efforts at intimacy lapsed by silent, mutual agreement.

IX.
BLOODLETTING

Neither Bernie nor Danny had gotten any intelligence from Athens on what Dylis was up to. All of us were uneasy. The money from Hellabilt would be building up, becoming a bank deposit for whatever venture Dylis might direct at us. I wondered where his hatred was focused, and my hands sweated when I thought of the jagged wound I had put on that vain, handsome face.

Although it wasn't the kind of break in my stagnation that Anne had in mind, one day I shaved, got casually and smartly dressed, and drove into town — to register for a freehand drawing course at the Academy of the Fine Arts.

I was feeling almost chipper. I had taken the Cadillac into town instead of the Morgan to keep the motor turned and, with all its windows open, purred toward home.

My headlights caught the boxy girderwork of the old Falls Bridge. It looked like a series of scaffolds. Gloomy subject, I thought, but the kind of thing I might try to sketch the next day, might take into class with me. Faintly on the hot air, there was the summer smell of cooking skunk cabbage, steamed leafage, dead vegetation. I was annoyed with myself. There is too much to living to coast on like this, I thought.

At the turnoff to Chestnut Hill, I was aware a car was following me. I looked back as I turned into my street, saw nothing, sighed, and then was unnerved again: the car had rounded the corner.

I slipped the .38 from the glove compartment, checked the cylinder, and put it on the seat. At my driveway, from the car's sudden acceleration, I knew it was after me. The men inside, I knew, would try to kill me or kidnap me. I did not want it to happen near the house and swerved away from the driveway entrance. I stopped parallel to our stone wall, which was topped beneath the ivy with barbed wire.

My blood was pounding. These men were here to drink my substance and had come to the world of my home to do so. If they had wanted to strike me down, it should have been in the city where I had done the deeds they sought to kill me for, not here where I was a family man, an innocent. But, of course, it was their reach into the heart of Chestnut Hill from Athens that would have the most impact on Bernie and his cohort mobsters, equally ensconced outside the dirty city in their own placid suburbs.

Alexa! Anne! Ah, these monstrous animals! The drab lassitude of the past months sloughed off me like the camouflage canvas from a Sherman tank.

I bailed out and squirmed behind the left rear

tire, where the thick rim would give me some protection. The wall was to my back. The onrushing car, a dark four-door sedan, screeched as it braked on my asphalt driveway, then bumped to a stop twenty feet from the Cadillac. Its lights remained on to blind me and shield them.

But the stupid bastards hadn't bothered to disconnect the interior light. It blinked on as two of them sprung from the doors on the right side of the car. I saw their vague shimmering outlines for a moment before they slammed the doors. Their right arms were extended by objects I was sure were small automatic weapons, Uzis or some such.

Running in a crouch, one of them veered toward the wall, a dazzling silhouette, insubstantial as a flashing figure in a shooting gallery. I fired and he dropped into the dark grass, leaden and solid looking now that he was out of the headlight's scintillation. I was sure I had hit him.

I potted out one headlight, then rolled under the Cadillac, knowing the shot would reveal my whereabouts. The heat of the muffler pipe scorched my back. I wriggled free of it, silently cursing myself for not bringing with me the box of cartridges in the glove compartment.

In the dull red glow of the rear lights I thought I saw a demonic figure and fired. Lucky shot; he dropped into the grass out of sight. I was sure I had hit him, too.

I could not have been more wrong. From the front of the car where the second man had crept, a burst of submachine-gun fire raked the Cadillac. I hugged the ground, praying the bullets would not ignite the gas tank above me and broil me in my own front yard. I inched backward, but suddenly felt scalding liquid on my feet. His shots had burst the radiator. I edged out from under the car and huddled by the front wheel. Steam from the ruined radiator whistled up in a spume and rained mistily on the back of my neck.

Momentarily, in the backglow from the Cyclops light, I saw a flicker of darkness. The man was by the hood, trying to figure out where I was behind my fortress vehicle. If I could hold out a little longer, the cops would be here. The automatic-weapon fire would have interjected itself even into the loudest TV show. My family or some neighbor would have called the police.

My assailant must have realized that, too. On the dark side of the car, he ran for the weeds at the foot of my wall, firing a burst to cover himself. This time, I used the staccato flame-spit to shoot him. His gun flew up in the air. He lay still, making no effort to retrieve the little submachine gun.

Two down. The driver was still in the car. He would know the interior light would go on if he tried to get out. Scared shitless, he would be planning simply how to escape with his life.

Knowing the terrain, I snaked toward the wall. In a moment the inside light blinked on and I aimed through the front window, hoping to get a shot at the top of his head even if he crouched. But the driver had squirmed over the seat back and dropped out of the back door. From my unsuspected vantage point, I would have a clean shot at him as soon as he cleared the shadows of the car. He darted around the rear of it, keeping it between himself and the Cadillac, where he thought I hid.

As he came into the open, I saw with astonishment how tiny he was. Like an elf, he flitted gingerly across the grass toward security on the other side of my driveway. I shot him before he made it to the sanctuary. But he was up and away again at a fast limp. This time, I took aim and got him in the back. Down he went.

I had no more shells in my chamber. I could not be sure any of the gunmen were dead, but the police surely would arrive soon. Did I want that right now, though? Resolved, I slipped my hand through my car's window and into the glove compartment. I reloaded the chamber and wormed up to the nearest of the fallen men. There was no need to worry about him. Face up, he had the special stillness of the heads I had seen in Korea.

The second man lay face down in the grass twelve feet away. Faking? Waiting to bushwhack me? I did not take a chance. Sighting with the pistol, I shot off the back of his head.

The driver was on his back in the driveway, where he had crawled. He still moaned, clutching the right side of his chest. Both his hands pushed at the wound where the bullet must have come out, as if to press back the pieces of lung that had come out with the slug. The submachine gun was beside him.

My pistol directed at him, I ran up and kicked the submachine gun farther away. In the floodlights, I could see the glistening whiteness of his teeth. Fear and pain had drawn his lips back in a hideous smile.

The shock had taken all the expression from his

eyes. I knew I had not hit him a fatal shot. The bullet had come out the upper part of his chest and there was no great gush of arterial blood. He was helpless. If I tried, I might save him. Yet he was an assassin, even if not a very good one.

Now, at last, I could hear the cop sirens. Once they arrived, my neighbors, my family would venture from their houses. The small man on the ground was staring at me, moaning more softly, sensing perhaps, even in his shock, what was going through my mind.

If I let him live, there would be his trial, the publicity, maybe another effort on me, perhaps by someone else with a grievance. If I killed him, I would be done with it after a spasm or two of publicity. And it would be a lesson of sorts to Dylis to leave me alone.

I carefully pointed the pistol at his forehead. As I did, his eyes bulged and he began to squawk wildly. I shot him and quickly turned toward my house so I would not have to see what I had done.

Fortunately, the gore was deep enough and the Philadelphia media bad enough so that the full story behind the assassins' attack on me stayed buried. I simply parried questions by saying I didn't want to talk about it while the police were investigating.

What did come out, probably from some blabbermouth on the outer fringes of Magliorocco's bunch, was that I had taken a brief look into the Dylis bankruptcy scandal on behalf of minority stockholders in Dylis's Athens-based company, Hellabilt. The papers speculated that "allies of Dylis" had taken it upon themselves to warn me away from further probing. It was a story I could live with. The papers, I suspected, would not even have come up with that much if one of the gunmen, the first one I shot, had not proven to be a Greek citizen. The other two were dissidents from the New Jersey lodge of Magliorocco's mob who had skipped off to Greece some weeks ago to join Dylis.

The feeling of our neighbors and social friends was more positive than not. After all, I was a man defending his home—and thus by extension, property values in Chestnut Hill—from three murderous and presumptuous (Italian and Greek) assassins.

Anne had hugged me and wept when she found out what had happened. And in that instant, I had realized that whatever became of us, however great the distances became between us, in substantial ways we were permanently bonded. In our depths, when we were not possessed with the immediate anger, each of us wanted the other to live and to prosper. Each of us wanted happiness for the other.

It was an eerie recognition, coming when it did. For it did not necessarily mean we would stay married. Indeed, we were soon back in the mode of piffling disagreements, of daily irritations.

They minimized our problems, defused the greater eruptions. For increasingly, our flare-ups had in them the elements of fury. Both of us knew we were pregnant with a major blowup.

Alexa had a serious boyfriend. Gary Prasilza was a freshman at Temple on scholarship. His family was poor Slovakian Catholic from Easton. He was a pot-smoking, eccentric libertarian, one of those latter-day naifs so far into laissez-faire they sounded like anarchists.

Alexa had met him when a group from Shipley had gone to Temple to support some student First Amendment demonstration. Alexa's plump intensity and the dedication of the skinny, brilliant Prasilza had set up some kind of chemistry that defied my understanding.

On his first visit to pick up Alexa, he came in a car that matched him for shabbiness. His long hair smelled defiantly of the divine weed. When I found a chance a few nights later at the table, I said moderately to Alexa that I hoped Gary didn't smoke pot while he drove.

Alexa, equally reasonable, said, "I'm trying to get him to leave it alone. He's got so much going for him, he doesn't need it," the immemorial voice of the good woman trying to reform the town rake.

Both Anne and I saw Alexa as a successful lawyer, marrying — after she was established — a professor, a doctor, an economist — but not a boy like this. I recognized the hypocrisy of this view in a South Philly dropout like me, but it didn't lessen my apprehensions.

In better times, Anne and I might have worked out a mutual plan to deliver Alexa from the enemy before he delivered her from us. Now it was just the kind of issue over which we argued: she adamantly against the kid, me (doubly hypocritical) defending

162

him on the basis of we Underdogs versus you Main Liners.

On his and Alexa's eighth date, we watched from the front window as they drove off in his rattletrap. Anne, a bad day behind her, observed with uncharacteristic asperity:

"Alexa would never have gone out with a person like that a year ago." It was code language for "you changed, she changed." The battlefield was unoccupied. Almost inevitably, I marched my forces in:

"What's that supposed to mean? That my fall from the ranks of the employed is turning our daughter into the profligate mistress of a dope fiend or something?"

"Well, what, I mean existentially" — God, I hated that word and she knew it — "Does she see at home?"

"A man with an abusive wife," I said.

Almost immediately, I was sorry. But it was too late.

"A man whose wife has been driven to become something that she'd rather not be."

Now I flamed out at her, "I don't see you the way I used to either. Actually, I see myself as a person changing for the better."

"I've been just what I was," she countered. "And if you'd be honest, you'd see your change has been to a grotesque of what you were. Oh, you're brave enough when bullets are flying. I grant you that. But in the job of living your life, you've become a wimp." Again, it was the kind of silly, cutting insult Brockman junior would have used.

"Wimp? Anne, you should be so lucky to change

the way I have. Change so you don't become the kind of person your clients are: corporate usurers, polluters, shysters of every kind. You—"

"Oh, it's into the Saint George role again, right?"

"—wanted me right in the crap with you, peddling guns or taking more cases for criminals like those Mafia scum," knowing I was being both sanctimonious and unfair, knowing to my sorrow heart deep that this was the explosion we had both tried to dodge. And still I went on. "Well, Anne, I'm not doing that anymore. You stay with your bankers. Dear Jesus, you can line up thirty bankers and thirty bank robbers and you've got fifty-eight criminals. And you figure out ways these crooks can chisel the government, can put the tax load on some poor bastard living on an eighth of an acre in Levittown. Meanwhile, they charge the same poor bastard twenty percent interest. You help them screw people both ways—"

"Ah, I see it, you blow your cool and take it out on me. Well, I don't need this. I won't take it!"

Alas, I was in full rage, no less agitated than when I fought for my life that day with the young di Lessandro. "Oh, you pay your little kiss-ass to the ACLU and the women's movement and then chew the heart out of the poor and out of poor women in particular with what you do for bankers and other corporate shitheads. Look at yourself! You're the good German!"

"George, you're walking on thin ice. You're saying things we aren't going to be able to live with." She wasn't goading the witness anymore. She was sounding a warning, putting the witness on notice.

But the witness was too far gone into anger now.

"We've never really talked about how we made our livings. What bloodsuckers we were, what a bloodsucker you still are. Well, I'm talking now. I'm out of the sewer. I feel clean at last and that's what you can't stand. Because you're in love with the filth you live in."

"Hypocrite!" she, who so seldom ever raised her voice, now shouted. "Shoddy, shameful tactics! You did a million things I never criticized you for, never would have thought to. We went into this . . . time of alienation saying we wouldn't be judgmental. You've lied. You've broken the contract, George."

She was right. Implicitly we had agreed that if we broke up, it would be in a civilized way. But the acid in me had eaten off the silver plate of the last twenty-five years, right down to the base copper. I was reverting to a streetfighter, and Anne was swept along with me.

"Maybe we were wrong not to judge ourselves," I said with the sneer of the converted zealot toward the unconverted. "Maybe we should have gone into other work in the beginning. Maybe you should have been using your mind to do something *for* people instead of against them."

"I . . . I," she stammered, bludgeoned, then recovering. "Compared to you, I was Little Goody Two-Shoes. Oh, yes, you've got religion!" She laughed bitterly. "You sit around like a passive coward, letting things happen to us. Mr. Early Saint, out of the gutter and into the hagiologies, all in one generation."

165

Blind fury! We had both become the beasts that lay within us, that, if we are honest, lie within all of us.

"Coward? Gutter?" I howled. "Oh, Jesus. But not a criminal. Not a criminal, Anne, like your old man. Oh, you're your father's daughter, all right!"

"Criminal!" I had done it, sent her berserk. "Criminal? Holy God! My father . . ." In another way at another time, I could have said almost the same thing about her father and she would have agreed. Now I only savored the hurt I had given her. "Yes!" I roared. "A fucking criminal and his daughter just like him!"

As soon as I said it, I realized its enormity. She swung at me, open-palmed. I grabbed her wrists. In our whole marriage, neither of us had ever struck the other. The bottom of the bag had burst and our civilization was pouring out.

Helpless physically, she spat. Wetness hit my face and lips. Disgusted, I hurled her wrist backward and she went with it, tottering up against a lamp that tumbled to the rug, its bowl and bulb bursting within the crumpled shade.

She did not fall, at least not to the floor, but slumped against the table before coming up rockily, confusion on the face that had a moment before been contorted with loathing. My anger was rising in me like a great vomit. I was dizzy with fury. I felt a rage that could make me strike her with my fist for what I had been driven to do and to be. It was almost as if her invocation of my heritage had made me regress to the violent me of those days.

I started for her and she must have seen the will

toward battery on my face for she scrambled up and ran for the stairs.

At the other end of the sofa, the second lamp still glowed. I snatched it from its table, ripping the cord from the wall. With both hands, I began to beat it on the table, hammering the wood until the lamp splintered and finally came apart in my bleeding hands.

For minutes, as my gasping subsided, I stared at the oozing blood. Then I bandaged my hands, cleaned up the room, and went to the guest room.

Alexa woke early. When she saw my bandages, I said merely that I'd lost my temper and broken the lamp. She opened her mouth to say something, then decided not to and went back upstairs with a distressed look. I set the table for Anne and me and listened to the familiar sounds of washbasin and shower as she prepared for work. When she came down, her face was phlegmatic, masking her feelings. I met her eyes briefly to give her a chance to speak if she wanted.

"By this evening," she said levelly, "we should each have a plan to deal with this. I don't want to talk about it this morning. Probably you don't either."

It was as carefully thought out as a tax opinion, and delivered as coldly. When she was gone, I went upstairs and lay in the unmade bed of the guest room, my stomach as sick as my spirit.

That evening, after a nervously polite supper, Alexa asked if there was anything she could do.

167

When we shook our heads, she hurried from the table, near to tears. Anne and I looked at each other in dismay over what we had done to Alexa. In that shared look, I felt the stirring of that old, deep liking. Anne, I sensed now, could bear to talk of our separating. But, unexpectedly, I could not. Yet that was what we were going to do over coffee.

"You go first," I said.

She took a deep, reluctant breath.

"It's time for us to get our lawyers," she said. "Please don't use Danny, George. I just couldn't stand it." She started to cry, and then pulled herself back into place.

"No," I said, "I won't. I can't ask you to reconsider. I'm not doing that when I tell you how sorry I am about last night."

"I'm as sorry," she said. "I didn't think it was in us."

"I thought you'd civilized it out of me," I said, trying to make it sound light. That drew a sad smile from her.

"Out of you? It was in us all the time, in all us nice little girls from Radnor, just like you—"

"Bad boys from Snyder Avenue," I finished. I waited for her to recommence. I was generally better at cross-examinations, but she was better at summations.

"There were just too many things," she said. "They overwhelmed us." I had seen my clients in these toils, had hardened myself so I would not have to share their confusion and pain. Now I knew.

"So we . . ." I said, trying to help her spring the

gallows flap.

She shrugged to cover up her inability to go on. I did it for her, resigned and miserable.

"So we get up an agreed list of assets and give the lawyers a rough idea of how we want it split." Well, I had pronounced the words. She struggled with her emotions a bit longer and finally got them sorted out.

"Can we stay in the same bedroom?" she said so unexpectedly it made me smile. "I would just rather not . . ." sever that last warm bond, she was trying to say and I was grateful. It didn't leave us much. But it was better than going out like morgue stiffs to cremation.

"Nor I," I said.

That night, we watched a revival of *Up in Central Park* on public TV. When Alexa ventured down, she saw two middle-aged people absorbing pleasant nothings in their family room. Alexa's face was puffy with crying. She went to her mother and put her arms around her.

"We are friends again," Anne said, very kind, very loving. "We aren't going to break anything anymore."

Alexa came and hugged me in her strong, honest arms. When she left, Anne smiled at me crookedly.

"Kids survive," she said.

"We all survive," I said, "until we stop surviving."

How crazy the French were to call sex the "little death." The "little death" was the end of a good marriage.

My days grew juiceless, but remained free of sharp anguish. I dropped the art classes and thought of taking literature courses, studying the stars, thought of taking a long trip somewhere. But I did almost nothing, stagnant in my failures: marriage, profession, sex.

We got up a list of assets, but instead of trying to divide them up ourselves, we left it to the lawyers to come up with draft ideas. We did not want to risk the pain of further explosions. I hoped Anne would keep the settlement solely in the hands of her divorce lawyer, not let it slop over to Brockman.

He had felt my disdain for him, I was sure. He would, subtly or perhaps not so subtly if he dared, urge on her a stiff settlement. And because the tax questions would be salient, he would know just what big guns to use against me, weaponry that Anne would tend to withhold if left to herself.

As the days passed, and with little else to do, I began to dwell obsessively on Anne, on how I, or she, could have done things differently so that it might have lasted.

When I wasn't dealing in those fantasies, I boiled up a pot of hate about Brockman. As I feared, he had been butting in. Anne's lawyer's first-draft settlement had Brockman's bludgeon markings all over it. Most assets would be prorated on our salaries during the last ten years, when Anne had made much more than I: Anne would get the house and everything in it with the exception of my office furniture and personal effects; she would get custody of Alexa, but I would pay for her education; the land willed her by her mother, where we had a great deal of appreciation, would go to her; I would take the losses on the barge deal (because it had been my idea); but the Delaware and Montgomery county land (which also had been my idea) would be held jointly and unloaded as tax considerations made it wise, the profits, which were substantial, to be split evenly.

Up to now, as we had planned in the interests of peace, we had left the actual money talk with the divorce lawyers. But this was too damned much.

"I saw that piece of junk you proposed," I growled at her that night after Alexa went upstairs to read and, to me contradictorily, listen to her rock'n'roll music.

"You've done enough business negotiating to know it's a first offer," she said, intimidated by my anger, especially as she had no ally at hand. "Why don't we let the lawyers talk about it."

"The real shyster in this thing is Brockman," I said, feeling calmer now I saw her embarrassment. She did not respond, looking upstairs instead to indicate Alexa would hear if we argued. I growled but let it go, knowing I was right.

Surrett called me and asked me to lunch. It was good to know someone gave a damn about whether I was alive or dead. Dylis, he said, was lying low as far as Philadelphia was concerned.

"Doesn't want to tangle with the Snyder Avenue gang again," said Surrett. Bernie had learned that Dylis was shifting his interest, using the money from Hellabilt for some unknown investments in Europe. "Illegal, no doubt, but not, at any rate, the assassin-export business."

"Not funny," I said. I still wasn't comfortable with shooting that little guy while he grimaced up at me. Surrett picked it up.

"They were trying to kill you, m'boy."

"I know. God, I hope it's over."

Surrett, thinking about the money he was going to get from the guns-for-narcotics deal, was more upbeat than I had seen him for a long time. Calvacadi was back in Italy "setting things up." Magliorocco had already begun using a contact in Algeria to approach the PLO. He had a Corsican mobster on retainer in Buenos Aires developing cocaine connections.

Danny's job was to find out about gun-export laws concerning various lands, to locate merchants here and abroad who would ship the weapons, and to set up contacts with purchasing agents who would serve as the middlemen.

It would be Bernie who arranged for the actual transshipments to the terrorists, committed, that is, the illegal act. Surrett was certain he had isolated himself legally from any criminal liability, and, with characteristic self-delusion, he had also isolated himself from any feeling of moral guilt.

"If it works with Calvacadi," he said, "it works everywhere."

"I thought maybe the thing at the airport and all this other stuff—"

"Bernie doesn't even think Calvacadi knows about it. And if he found out, so what? Everybody's so hungry for the guns, the dope, the big money." He shoveled some of the crab-stuffed flounder into his mouth.

"They're so greedy," he shook his head. And at that I scoffed. He saw the humor of it and perked up again. "At least for me, it's not just the money. I mean there's women, too."

"For a while yet," I said.

Surrett looked sour and speculative briefly, then stared at me earnestly and tried me again. "Why don't you come in with us on this thing. We're going to make money, so goddamned much of it."

"No," I said, more depressed than angry. "No more gangsters, Danny." Then I tried to cut into his self-satisfaction. "The whole thing is going to backfire anyway."

Danny smiled that wonderful blue-eyed cop smile he had smiled all those years ago when he was working on that first series of burglaries.

"Not so you can hear it," he said. "Sure you don't want in? Might pep you up."

"No."

"You got to stop vegetating," he said.

"I will when the settlement's done."

"Give her the goddamned money," he said.

"No. It's the only principle I've got left."

"It's only money," he said, poking fun at his own avarice.

Late summer burned out some of my flowers in the garden and dried the heavy foliage of Chestnut Hill. I court-plastered my ubiquitous aches. I went to movies, prowled the art galleries, sometimes crept out of our bed at night to work crossword puzzles or flip through old lightweight mysteries. In the mornings, I often slept late.

Finally, I knew I must make some compromise with Anne on the settlement, take control of the issue, so that I would be acting, not just acted upon. I wanted it clean: an accord with her, not with Brockman or her divorce lawyer. Almost formal, after all those years of companionability, I asked her at breakfast for a meeting.

She broke the lunch date she had with a banker and we met at La Panetière to discuss terms. With its Parisian-townhouse chic, the restaurant did not look like Appomattox Court House. Nor did Anne look like Ulysses S. Grant. She wore a black nubby suit by Halston and I my best preliberation garb, a hand-tailored suit that I had last worn a year ago at lunch with the chief defense attaché of Brazil. It was a suitable uniform for this sword-surrendering ceremony.

She made it as easy for me as she could, saying from the outset she wasn't looking for the full draft settlement. Still, I knew how the Japanese felt on the U.S.S. *Missouri*.

By the time we had finished the seven-dollar desserts made with umpteen kinds of chocolate, we were within a hundred thousand dollars of each other.

We lingered over coffee and liqueur, talking of Alexa, of how we would arrange the visitations. Once I was situated, she said, she wouldn't mind Alexa spending a month with me in the summer if she wanted to. No, she wouldn't mind long weekends for Alexa and me now. Something in her voice about the longer weekends, which would give her more time to herself, jarred me slightly. The money talk out of the way, I mentally stepped back and regarded her objectively.

It struck me that she had changed. Her dress was more feminine, her hair swirled less lawyerly. Rather she seemed today more like a successful executive in cosmetics, say, or women's fashion. Yet, conversely, she smoked — affected, it seemed to me — a cigarillo after our lunch. Her language, usually refined, occasionally was salty. Little things: but in them and other minor changes I felt a reckless quality, a headstrongness.

As we chatted, I let myself think this was simply her foretaste of the freedom she imagined she would have without me. But then I began to consider whether there might be another man in her life, a lover.

The suspicion grew and with it a terrible jealousy. For I saw in our sexual loyalty the last strong, vain evidence that something might remain of our marriage, an earnest that she still cared for me.

I had been jealous enough of her intellectual fan dancing with people like Schuyler Matthews. The greater my jealousy when I speculated she might find the bodies of other men attractive. Primitively, irrationally, I saw myself as the classic eunuch, justly rejected, but infuriated that she might take up with a real man.

Christ, I had seen these hobgoblin feelings so often in the lives of my clients. And here — both of us so civilized amid the faint smell of sweet distillates, perfume, and the smoke of good tobacco — that ugly, primitive syndrome was afflicting me.

When we left the restaurant and were out on Locust Street, we kissed on the lips and she pressed back hard as if to affix a seal to our expressed hopes. I knew she drew nothing sexual from the kiss. It was testimony to how asexual she found me, and added to my apprehension that she had a lover.

X.
PRIVATE EYE

In the following days, her phantom lover began to form in my imagination. I envisioned him as a banker, a man older than either of us, cut from Ivy League cloth, a rich, married WASP living on Long Island. At least, Anne, I thought bitterly, I have not endowed you with a four-flusher, a cheat, a tired libertine.

At times, I saw her affair in explicit terms: where they met and, drawn from the awful pornography of my calling, what they did.

I wanted to believe an affair was impossible. Yet I set little traps to catch her. When she was showering, on a morning after she had returned from New York, I quickly checked her purse for matches. I found nothing more suspicious than Windows on the World. After she had gone, I examined the suit she had worn the day before for short gray hairs.

We drank a bottle of lovely old Pomerol at supper one night. One of my former clients — I had saved him a million in alimony by catching his wife with a city judge—had sent us a case of it. After Alexa had gone upstairs, Anne and I chatted lightly over first one snifter, then another of Armagnac.

In bed, she reached over, touched my face with her fingers, and then turned to draw her body firmly up against mine while she kissed me. From the sudden fervency of it, I knew she must have been thinking of it all the way back, at least to the first Armagnac. There was no great love in her approach, simply a strong hunger that I met with flaccidity.

In the past, Anne would have sighed some word of forgiveness and settled into, at worst, mildly resentful frustration. Instead, she heaved her lower body against the top of my pelvis, put my hand instructively around her buttocks to where I could touch her clitoris and ground and manipulated her body to a deep, grunting orgasm. She had wanted something exact, by a means to which we were not accustomed, and she had gotten it. I held her in my arms, pleased despite my questions, unwilling to say anything that would end this hiatus of mutuality. Her body, no longer wracking against mine, seemed soft and gratified in my arms—our bellies and thighs snugly together.

But in that silence, I understood that my body had been all she had needed. The familiarity that had permitted her to demand of me something unfamiliar, yet something I would willingly give her, was the only thing that discriminated me from Body A or Body B in some Masters and Johnson field test.

In the last week of September, Hector asked me to testify in Chicago about some substantial debts owed to my old company by a supplier. I had not been out of town for weeks. I left after a supper with Alexa—Anne was working late. When I got to the airport, I heard myself paged. It was Hector. The opposing lawyer had been hurt in a minor traffic accident. The hearing was postponed.

I returned home; Alexa had finished her homework and was on the telephone with her libertarian. She covered the mouthpiece long enough to tell me that Anne had called to say she was stuck downtown until midnight, at least. Something in Alexa's tone told me she had a suspicion about her mother.

I dissembled my festering jealousy, anger, and curiosity behind the *Inquirer*'s sports pages. Then, unable to sit gullibly by any longer, I went to my own phone and called Anne's law firm.

"No, Mr. Fraser," said the receptionist, who always worked late when any of the partners worked late. "She's not in right now."

Right now? I wondered. Why "right now" instead of "not here"? Hadn't the receptionist also given me an unintentional signal?

"Let me talk to Mr. Brockman," I said. Suddenly anxious, I felt my hand like a vise on the telephone.

"He's gone for the evening." The careful distinction between Anne not there right now and Brockman gone for the evening! An effort to separate them! Of course the receptionist would know. Everyone down there would. Only I would not. The

179

receptionist, worried now, was asking me whether I wanted to speak with one of the partners still there.

"No," I said. "No thanks."

When I had hung up, I put my head in my hands and grunted like a man hit in the solar plexus. It was no tennis-playing banker who had taken the last bit of Anne from me. It was the Pied Piper of law groupies. It was Brockman.

I was not ready for the shock. Yet, veteran of a hundred cases, I knew I was not mistaken. I quickly grabbed up the clues:

The trips to New York — were they to visit bankers or had she gone with Brockman? Perhaps she had simply said she was going to New York but stayed overnight with him in Philadelphia. Her more frequent crudisms: words like *wimp* — out of his vocabulary. They cut my core like shrapnel. Yes, I could find a thousand clues if I wanted to make this case. Brockman smoked cigars, thus she emulated him with her cigarillos; her criticism of him lately, the classic means of putting off the spouse from the true spoor. Her sudden desire that night to make love with me and, when I was impotent, her knowledge of exactly what new way she wanted to be satisfied.

Brockman might learn tax law at her knee; he could teach her sex at his. Rage engulfed me. If Alexa had not been in the house, I would have hammered the phone to bits on my desk, obliterated it, as I had the lamp. My fury had come on me as swiftly as my revelation. I felt the same uncontrollable surges as I had all those years ago when my mother had slapped me in the face and I had gone near berserk with anger.

I must get out of the house, I thought wildly. So I could scream at the night. So I could puncture and drain the enormous sac of hot, bloody pus that had built up where my heart had been. I was breathing so deeply that I would soon be faint. I concentrated on getting my breath regular, trying to anesthetize myself. As I did, some of the dizziness passed. I began to see what I was going to do. The old coolness that had always helped me on investigations pushed out the mania. However much it hurt, I was going to know. I would make my case, then, oh dear revenge, I would dictate the terms of the settlement.

First, I must think as Anne thought. A good mother, she would call Alexa again sometime during the evening to see how she was, and to make sure I had gotten off to Chicago. Therefore, the telephones were my first concern. Alexa must not be able to tell her I had come back from the airport. Furtive as Polonius, I listened at the staircase until Alexa ended her tireless love call.

I took the plastic cover from the terminal box in Anne's study. Through it, all the phones were wired. Silently, with tried facility, I detached the leads to make dialing out impossible and to insure that incoming calls would get busy signals. I replaced the cover.

"Alexa," I called upstairs. "The phones are kaput." I was sure I sounded shaky. "I'll call it in from the shopping center. I'm going to catch a movie while I'm out."

"The phones?" she asked incredulously.

"The phones. Let in the telephone man if he

181

comes, okay?"

"Okay," she answered. I thought I noticed a fearful note in her voice. I grabbed up a tiny pocket recorder and an old Nikon I still used, with an instant-ready flash attachment.

At Hertz's downtown lot, I opened the Morgan's trunk and took my lockpicks out of the tool kit. I thought of the .38 in the glove compartment and left it there. I rented an unexceptional medium-sized Ford, told the clerk I would leave the keys in the drop box later tonight, and drove to Brockman's house on Society Hill.

Neither his Continental nor her Mercedes were in front. I parked catercornered and watched the house briefly. There were no moving shadows in the few lit rooms. Perhaps they were out to supper, lovers for so many weeks they no longer posted directly to bed when they met, but dawdled over good food and wine before they returned to make love. Again, tremors engulfed me. I closed my eyes, waiting for the fury to pass.

When it had, I drove to a pay phone and called an old police pal at home. I got him to telephone Brockman's number and ask for a fake name. I could have determined whether anyone was at home, but I did not want to spook Brockman with a telltale hanging-up.

"You're back in the business?" the cop asked.

"Just a case or two," I said.

When I called him back a few minutes later, he said no one had answered. He wanted to chat, but I put him off. I said I was doing some surveillance. That was true enough.

I drove the car back to Brockman's. The lights were the same and the Mercedes and Continental were still gone. Either they had met at a restaurant or she had put her car in a lot somewhere, I was sure. It was full night now. I parked the car well down the block and waited, lights out. How often in the past had I done this? How ironic it was that my career should bring me finally to this.

I considered picking the lock, hiding inside, and waiting for them. Or I could bug the bedroom, get my evidence on tape, as I had done so often. But something in me squirmed at the indirect, the seedy, the cowardly approaches.

My God! I thought, dizzying again. Anne had chosen Brockman! Not even a Matthews or someone else with a little class. Pulled a nobody out of her company supply closet! A lecher, an indiscriminate ass-chaser! A slob!

At nine-thirty, the Continental pulled up and parked down the block from me. I watched Brockman come around the car and hand her out. Rage washed over and into me. Up to now, everything had been circumstantial. Here was the confirmation.

Trembling at the change in mood over which I seemed to have no control now, I gripped the steering wheel to keep myself from lunging out of the auto. As I did, I cursed him, pouring out venomous, vile words I had not used since my army days. In seconds, the wheel was wet with my sweat.

Regal, tall, Anne walked ahead of Brockman up

183

the few steps to the stoop of his house and waited with a glance around, just to be sure, while he put the key in the lock. His arm came up and touched her back to ease her over the threshold. It was the familiarity, the customariness of their actions that enflamed me. The door closed.

My belly hurt with the strain. I shut my eyes, breathed deeply until things came clear in my head again. The lights in the front window dimmed. They had paused downstairs just long enough to grab a bottle of champagne from the refrigerator, or maybe some cognac.

Now they would be going upstairs. Brockman! He would reach up, touch her buttocks, run his hand up the inside of her nylon-clad thighs. Did Anne like that kind of thing in this prick, the kind of thing that in me she found uncouth? No more of that! I had probed myself too deeply. That way lay something awful: a rush back to the Morgan for the .38. Or some violent scene of crushed skulls and blood and heavy gasps.

While I waited the wait of experience, I imagined killing them both. Or just him and letting her go. But, juries convicted for crimes of passion nowadays. I cracked a death's-head smile. Surrett would plead me temporarily insane. I saw him in the courtroom, moving toward and away from the jury, the way he did, like a palm swaying, to lull them, or sometimes pacing back and forth, face angry and voice a growl—an aroused lion before an intimidated prosecution witness.

Don't be distracted, I told myself. You've blown one big case; don't blow this one. Pause and think, as Surrett had always done, as he had taught. But Surrett had never loved anyone much. He loved only motion, action, the excitement of making big money. Be circumspect like Surrett.

They'd have their clothes off now, I knew that from old experience as true as native instinct. The first kisses would have begun. I thought of Vivian Lambeth. I would time it, just as I had timed her and her Mafia boyfriend. I would get them in mid-stroke when they could no more come unstuck than a pair of copulating dogs: my sweet bitch-wife and Brockman, another dog.

I saw his lips on her lips, then their lips . . . where? Everywhere. I felt the pleasure of my fist sinking into his bare gut, folding him up on the floor. I cautiously let it go further: my shoe truncheoning his face and neck, the voice box, the temple. I banged the seat, uttering a muted cry. Again, I went through my routine, shutting my eyes, breathing deeply.

The lights dimmed upstairs. A digital clock of seconds and minutes began to run in my mind. The foreplay was over. I would let them kiss a little more, touch a little more. Now I did not see it, thank God, as Brockman and Anne, but simply as two mechanical dolls, doing things that took a certain amount of time. When, from my experience, I judged that enough time had passed, I would surprise them in their upstairs room.

I took off my necktie and put it in my left jacket pocket. The minirecorder was in the right. I put the Nikon strap over my head, the camera and flash inside my jacket. I loosened the car's dome light so it

185

would not go on when I opened the door of the car. I walked briskly across the street, surveying the neighbors' houses and the sidewalks. Using the necktie against the hotness, I unscrewed the low-wattage porch bulb. It darkened the stoop except for the soft light from the front windows and the erratic splinters that the streetlights made on the pavement as they filtered through the sidewalk trees.

I took out my picks. Brockman had not thrown any dead bolts. Why should he? In an hour or two, loyal mother Anne would have to go back out this door. I jigged a skinny blue steel pick in the keyhole, raking the pick's teeth on the tumblers until they fell into line. I cambered a plastic card into the crevice between jamb and door so that if my hand slipped or I turned the knob too far, the tongues would not click into the groove. Now I rotated the knob, felt the tongues withdraw.

Oh God, I thought, the idea almost unnerving me, the metaphor of locks and sex, of keys and brassy tongues. I dropped the pick in my inside pocket, where it would not touch coins or its fellow picks, entered the house, and closed the door part-way. There was no breeze. The door would stay quasi-shut, so that I could leave rapidly if I wanted to, and without any click of the lock.

I had been to Brockman's a couple of times for parties. It was not an intricately designed house. I paused in the hallway, listening, and looking up the stairs to sense whether they were waiting. I heard low voice sounds, a bed moving. I stopped, feeling control slip again. Did I want to confirm visually

186

and aurally a fact better left vague? I had made my case. Anything further was no better than masochism. But no, I would drink it fully, the sediment and all.

It was an old house. Ordinarily the stairs would squeak, even with the thick runner. I took the stairs on the side, not the middle. That would least bend the step, put the least torque on the nails in the risers. I climbed two at a time to cut the percentages of a squeak still further. At each step, I listened to see whether the sounds had stopped, whether they also were now listening. They were not.

In the hallway, on the carpet, I headed toward the bedroom. As I reached it, there was a tiny squeak from the flooring. I paused and listened, breathing noiselessly through my mouth, winded, but not from exertion. I flicked on the silent on-button of the recorder, thumbed the mike gain to "full."

Outside the room, I heard what I should never have ventured to hear, from him a murmured "oh, oh, oh," a young animal's grunts, from her, as if in soft counterpoint, a nearly silent "yes, yes" repeated in tentative and loving gratitude. I imagined Anne's lean body rearing up to meet the downrush of her swinish lover's flab and started to bolt into the room, tear him from her and destroy him. Instead, I stood paralyzed, a statue, a monument to my skill and my despair.

"Brock!" she whispered, her voice now louder than his. His "ohhs" continued, almost reflective, as if he were alone in some bliss of his own. Gradually, the grotesque trio of baritone, mezzosoprano, and the mechanical, expressive voice of the springs grew *forte*, increased tempo.

They were moving toward climax.

I heard, as I had heard before outside hotel rooms, the sound, like hands clapping, of their bellies acceleratingly slapping, reports as distinctive as machine-gun fire.

This was the moment when I had broken in on lovers. Was what I was suffering now some sort of hideous punishment for those days? For in what was left of my reasonable mind, I underwent the most egregious of sexual tortures: I knew this man was enrapturing her as I had never been able to do. And I was frozen, unable to rush in and fix them on film, frighten them asunder.

This was not the penultimate moment to one of those minor, moaning orgasms that had been sex for her during our twenty years. My rival was giving her pleasure, mighty pleasure. Still, I could not move.

Suddenly she burst out, "Brock! Oh my God!" and he, his voice distorted by sex into almost a noble tenor, cried, "Anne, oh, Anne darling!" From both of them, there issued guttural notes of strain, beastlike sounds that lasted . . .

In that moment, my ignoble passivity violently flip-flopped. Part of my brain flashed apart, an instant lobotomizing that regressed me wildly—far more profoundly than my blowup with Anne—to the most destructive days of my youth.

I banged the half-open door against the wall, clawed the wallpaper for the switch, and flashed on the ceiling light. In an epitome of all the naked tangled bodies I had surprised, I saw the squirming flesh of Anne and Brockman, the frightened open eyes and mouths of a hundred doorbusts. But with a ghastly difference—Anne's body was as familiar to me as my own.

How could she have preferred his fleshy body to mine, on which the years had told so much less. They unwound, crying out in inarticulate surprise. I swooped across the room and grabbed murderously at Brockman's throat. Clumsy as a girl, he tried to clutch my arms. This nude clown might perform better in the arts of love. He was a child in martial arts.

I gripped his throat with one hand, felt the pudgy give to it, and thrust him down on the bed. Cowed at the foot of the bed like a chained banshee, Anne shrilled:

"Don't kill him! Don't kill him!"

Almost robotized, I nevertheless registered her words. Don't kill him! I must not. I let go his spasming throat. I knew that if I killed him, I destroyed my future. Beyond this moment of fire, I had a life to live uncomplicated by criminal charges and newspaper luridness.

Desire still urged me to double up my fist, crush out his life with a massive, rupturing blow to his larynx or solar plexus. But, almost as if answering Anne, I grunted and began methodically to slap his face, bobbling his head one way and the other.

Anne, watching in terror, called, "No!" as if feeling her pummeled lover's pain. My wrathful glance at her cost me my advantage. Brockman caught me in the belly with his heel, and I crumpled off him, banging my head against the dresser.

Anne jumped up and grabbed a sheet to hide her nakedness; Brockman plopped off the bed and tried to make it into the hall. The head blow had hurt and angered me, but not stunned me. I caught him in the hall and grabbed him by his hair, stylishly — and now conveniently for me — cut long. As if he were a sheep or long-haired dog, I dragged him back into the bedroom. I put him up against the wall and smacked again at the puffy face.

He screamed and wriggled, then kneed at my testicles. The knee missed, but caught me agonizingly on the side of my groin. I buckled.

In a mindless effort to escape, he tried to roll over my bent shoulders. He had sensed the ferocity of my rage. I was ready to kill: he had bravoed my wife; he had tried to maim me, kneeing at my testicles. With what apt symbolism I might have crushed his! But I had not.

My control torched away, I bellowed and reared up. His desperate efforts had thrown him across my shoulders as if for a fireman's carry. I heaved his meaty frame higher on my shoulders and ran full tilt with him at the bedroom window.

Anne shrieked: he roared with fear, their voices dreadful burlesques of their love cries minutes before. At the window, I catapulted him from my shoulders. Panes shattered and fell into the street, but the metal sashing held and he dropped like a sack of fertilizer at my feet.

Still insane with rage, I dropped on him, pulled back my hand, tightened now into a fist. His nostrils flooded blood onto his gory face and throat. I wanted no blood on me, I thought, self-protection the only element still intact in my brain. But I wanted to strike where I would kill. I rose up, planning to stomp his solar plexus.

But as I unbent, a crushing explosion in my head blackened everything.

I do not know how I got down the stairs. When I came to, I was on the sidewalk and two cops were supporting me with practiced grips on either arm. At Brockman's front door, the light poured out. A third policeman was talking there with Anne, fully dressed now. I stank all over of brandy. Anne had hit me with the bottle.

"Come on," said one of the cops at my arm. "You're okay."

At the stationhouse, they led me past the wanted posters in the neat outer office and back to the booking desk. The clerk pulled out my wallet, my driver's license.

"This you?" he asked unnecessarily. My picture was on it.

I nodded while he booked me for drunkenness and disorderly conduct. Enough of my senses were coming back for me to shut up. With all the politeness and persuasion I could summon up out of my daze, I finally prevailed on the clerk to call Danny Surrett for me.

Subdued as a bull led from the arena by steers, I stumbled with the turnkey back to the cell block. Grateful to be able to close my eyes against the oppressive pain in my head, I lay on the thin, dirty mattress. I knew the place. Even the smell was familiar. As a kid, I had smelled it when I had lain in the reformatory, in the detention center. I had come back to where I began.

Thirty years older, but no less dapper than he had been when I was sixteen and he had rescued me the last time I was in jail, Surrett appeared at eight o'clock. He had been away from home all night, he apologized with a wry libertine's smile. The day clerk had gotten him only an hour before and he had already, as he said, "made a few calls."

The police told him a neighbor had heard the ruckus and summoned them. From Anne, he learned I had broken two of Brockman's ribs, two front teeth, and his nose. She said he wasn't going to prosecute on the destruction of private property, but might make a criminal complaint on the assault. It would depend, said Surrett, looking at the cops around us, who had their ears cocked.

On the way home, he told me the rest. Brockman's price for not filing criminal charges was an immediate settlement of the separation case and my departure from the city. Either a civil or criminal judgment along with the attendant publicity would pretty well destroy me in Philadelphia, not that there was much to destroy.

"They'd look awful, too. Particularly Anne," I said.

"They'd deny they were screwing." I thought of the taped proof I had. In my eagerness to maim Brockman, I had catapulted it out of my pocket, or else Anne had found it and taken it. The tape would be long erased by now. Brockman and Anne were that smart: they were no Nixons.

"The court would believe me," I said.

Danny looked at me harshly.

"Against both of them? C'mon. Anyway, for Christ's sake, Anne would be the worst hurt in this. You'd be second. Brockman would wipe you out with a civil suit and get your good name as well, what's left of it. Do you want that?"

"Why would she go through with something like that?"

"Why'd she go to bed with him? She's in love with him."

I thought about that for a while, and saw their two bodies, first with fury. Then I calmed. There was nothing I could do about that now. About anything.

I had thought earlier of traveling, going to Europe. Now I didn't have much choice but to leave. For somewhere. Italy, I thought, would be about right. I had wheeled and dealed through Rome over the years. Matriarchal homeland, I thought bitterly. I had enough street Italian to build on. I could get by there.

I would find some little coastal town, far from the Red Brigader and Mafia. I would not even tell Danny where I was. I could just disappear, become unfindable until I could stagger out of the mess of my life, assuming that was possible.

"What's the easiest you can get me off, assuming Brockman doesn't hit me with the assault, the heavy criminal stuff?"

"Drunk and disorderly," Surrett said.

"I can forfeit on that," I said. It was a minor misdemeanor.

Danny felt my misery and reached over and gripped my arm. When I left, he, too, would be losing his best, his only friend.

"I think I can get them to drop the disorderly," he said with just a vestige of that manipulative pride he had taken as a young cop all those years ago.

I would give him power of attorney, make him attorney-in-fact for me. God knows he would take better care of me than I could take of myself. When I bade him good-bye, we embraced. It wasn't something I ever did with men. But he was about all I had to hug.

I called Alexa from downtown, and then went out to see her. I knew Anne would be there. She would feel some kind of farewell, however unpleasant, was the ceremonial thing to do. Or maybe that was too unkind. She liked to close cases with a sign-off.

I wept when I said good-bye to Alexa and she went off blubbering, leaving Anne and me alone in the living room. Caught up in the tragedy of what had happened to us, neither of us could bear to be angry. Or maybe the anger was just wrung out of us.

"Danny is attorney-in-fact. I told him to tell the divorce lawyer to give you pretty much what you want," I said. "I won't be reachable. In Europe someplace."

I did not want Anne to be happy about my departure, though I knew she would be; it would leave her free to indulge her addiction. But I must bear it. I could no longer hurt her with my words. And what was the point? I had lost her.

Things I had done had made her stop loving me. And I had not been willing to do the things necessary to make her love me again. Indeed, I had not been able to do them.

"I'm sure it will work out," she said, meaning the money. This time, I knew there would be no disagreement. She was getting everything she and Brockman wanted. But I didn't care.

She saw that and the acid-etched lines on her face relaxed. Seeing it happen, her transformation into someone who looked like the person I had once loved, I thought of all the days and nights I would live without her voice, her body snuggled into the bed, our ordinary talk. Now would it be Brockman? I could not believe it.

"You could have done better," I said softly. "Even I'm a better man than he is. I don't mean that in a cruel way, Anne, I simply want the man who takes my place to be—"

"I know," she broke in quietly. We were in that vacuum before good-byes where only honesty is possible. We were at a place where we could do absolutely nothing more to injure each other. "I can't give him up," she said, shrugging.

"That bad?" I said without rancor, almost wonderingly.

"Yes," she answered, not meeting my eyes, glad maybe to be able to confess it to someone, even to me.

How little there was left to say.

"Is there anything else?" I asked her. I was emptied of everything but the pain of it all. Anne sat staring across the channel between us, feeling for my terrible awkwardness.

"God, I'm so sorry." she said. I knew it wasn't about my leaving, or about Brockman, certainly not about my pain. It was that our brave, good marriage had finally foundered.

Tears came to her eyes, though not to mine. She rose from the chair and I stood, too. Her tears rolled down. But I did not move to her. Pretty soon, she braced up, went to the cupboard, got a paper napkin, and wiped her eyes.

XI.
RAPALLO

I chose Rapallo more or less by chance. From the map, I could see it was more than a village and less than a city. It was in northern Italy, where I wanted to be, and it was on the sea.

The day I got there was out of character if one believed the travel folders: rainy, unseasonably chilly for the last days of September. I passed up the Excelsior, the town's fancy hotel.

Instead, I chose a hotel on the Corso Colombo with a lobby small enough to seem homey but large enough so I could pass the desk without saying hello to the clerk each time I came in. The Hotel Conconi was glad to get me at that time of year even on my vague basis: I told them I'd stay maybe three days, but it might be three months.

The energy that had gotten me out of Philadelphia and this far had run out of me as patently as sand out of an egg timer. Upstairs, I looked out from the small balcony at the gray rain slanting down into the Gulf of Rapallo. I stripped and climbed into the clean, cold bed. Soon, my body warmed the cavity in which I lay and I slept the jet-laggers' deep, exhausted sleep. I had come to ground.

I awoke. It was 3:00 A.M. I had slept ten hours. I turned and tossed for another hour, then slept two more. When I finally came to from my anesthetic slumber, the empty sky was backlighted by dawn.

I looked down at my naked body, seeming so whole. In fact, I was not. I thought of those signs in the Paris metro reserving seats for the mutilated of war. I, too, was mutilated: from the decay of my spirit that had led to my hideous failure on the Dylis case; from my reluctant but corrupting work for the Mafia; from the gaping wounds of battle with Anne that had left me impotent in several ways.

I was adrift, not happy, but free. I was free of Anne, free even of Surrett, and not without some relief. All my life he had been there, as she had been the last two decades. They had been around me, like the heavy air. The dependency I had come to feel for them was lifted, gone away.

Yet a free man is no better than a stray dog or cat if he has no self-respect, and no respect from people he loves, or if he has no duty or responsibility to himself or others. I was a free man, but I was a stray man.

In the next few days, I walked through the market with its stalls of foreign fish, meats, cheeses, its lush fruits and vegetables. I strolled in and near the town, lunching heavily, napping afterwards. I did listless sketches of the churches, the town's main monument, a mediocre tower commemorating some Genoan tyrant. At a bike shop, I bought a

198

used ten-speed. In the hillside public garden, I watched children playing.

I knew I was coming out of shock when my old compulsions for order and busyness led me to seek a new routine, one founded this time solely on my own wants. From the city tourist agency, I found a retired professor, a technician type with a genius for language teaching. For four hours a day, with a battery of recordings, tapes, and one-on-one pedagogy, he began turning my pidgin Italian into a blunt tool for verbal communication. To improve my vocabulary and grammar, he had me do rough translations of Leopardi.

That generally kept my mind from the extremes of remorse and grief. I practiced my Italian when I made my routine purchases, parsed out billboards, even began to cipher out the *Corriere della Sera*'s least difficult stories.

One of the elderly women at the hotel's desk sometimes chatted with me, giving me further chance to try out my new skills. We talked of the weather, inflation, the difference between Italian and American food. When she asked me what I did, I told her I had been in business.

"I have a small pension from an injury," I said, letting the image cover the literal lie. "Italy is more peaceful for me than America," I said.

"Ah, no," she said. "We have the Red Brigades."

Mention of them startled me, snapped me back uneasily to Philadelphia. I thought of Surrett, caught in the golden toils of Bernie Magliorocco's grand design. I felt a slap of guilt about the Rome massacre and a lesser blow about my work during

Calvacadi's visit. I felt apprehension about Dylis.

"Do they bother the poor and middle classes?" I asked neutrally. She must have thought I was mildly sympathetic with them.

"Oh, no," she said again. "Some of the people they kill are ripe to be killed." She used the word *maturo*, which also means "fully grown." From the way she savored it, I thought some relative might be connected with the Brigades.

Rapallo's diversions in October were not intense. Only a few busloads of German tourists, the poorer ones, were still in town. Some of the big hotels and restaurants were closed, but one could ramble around to places made famous by the famous. Sibelius, Petrarach, Freud, Ezra Pound, all had stayed by these blue Ligurian waters. The Treaties of Rapallo had been signed in a castle a few miles from town.

I chose a visit to Pound's old home not because I knew much about his poetry, but because my body, surfeited with pasta one day, needed such a long uphill ride as was provided by Sant' Ambrogio, where Pound had lived.

High above Rapallo, I looked down at the blue bay rimmed by hills of deep green olive trees. Here and there were deciduous trees splashing the green with yellow as they began to turn. Harbor hamlets, San Michele di Pagana and Santa Margherita, broke unevenly from the green, their towers faded to soft pastels. The beauty made me want to chime out in admiration for it, to tell someone about it. But I had no one beside me. Only the breeze on my perspiring body.

In the lot beside Pound's former house, workmen were putting up a second dwelling. Yes, the foreman said, this was where the American poet Pound had lived.

"Cook's tour?" he asked in English with a friendly smile. As he showed me through Pound's house, now owned by a rich lawyer who was putting up the second house for rental, he grew restive. Volubly and resentfully he told me he had taken a degree in literature and a helluva lot of good it had done him. Then he returned to Pound.

The poet had been visited here by d'Annunzio, like Pound, a Fascist, he said. But if they had been Communists, no one would have read them. The authorities had been quick to suppress Communist poets in those days, he said.

"All authorities are quick to suppress all poets," I said to mollify him.

"Good, good," he said aggressively. "Yes, that is certainly true." He himself wrote poetry and would have preferred to teach school. But in Italy a poet or teacher was lucky to be a construction foreman.

"And you foreigners wonder why there are Red Brigades," he said. Shit, I thought. Wasn't there any escape? Not even here? We parted with a strong handshake, poetic, if not political, comrades.

Walking the bike downhill on the cobblestone steps leading to the road, I peered back at Pound's balcony, which looked out on the Mediterranean. Day after day he had watched the sun go down into the sea. Then one day he had become a man of action, an anti-Semitic broadcaster for Mussolini. He had made worse than a fool of himself, had been a traitor and after the war had been put into an American mental hospital. A poet, he had left his element and been wrecked.

Conversely, I had begun as a man of action: a hinge cracker, a hired battering ram for corporate intriguers. Then, one day, I had climbed on a balcony to watch the sun go down. I had become a man of *in*action. In leaving my element, had I, too, wrecked myself?

Next morning, I felt not just alone but lonely. The days passed and I grew still lonelier.

I looked into the eyes of the remaining tourist women as if to magnetize them into chatting with me. They sat gossiping in the Gran Caffè Rapallo or promenaded by the sea. But none of my glances took. Did I send out some signal of failure that warned off women as a buoy's moans at night warn off ships?

I thought longingly of Alexa. How I would like to spend a day walking with her along the old roads I had seen from Sant' Ambrogio. We would pack a spectacular picnic basket of Rapallo's meats and cheeses, breads and fruits. Or with the same picnic basket, I would charter a local fishing boat and we would go out beyond the Gulf of Rapallo for rich-tasting *saraghi*.

In the evenings, to get out of the hotel, I ate in town. Afterward, over a final cappuccino or hot chocolate, I sat in the cafés reading books in English from the hotel's small, ravaged library. At night, I awoke at odd hours and could not go back to sleep. I was getting fidgety, bored with Rapallo.

At dawn one Saturday, a day when I had no language lesson, I left the hotel and rode to Camogli, a small fishing town around the cape. There, I shackled the bike to an iron railing and walked down the beach, saying good-mornings to the surf casters. I hoped to strike up a little talk about fishing, but they were angling in these depleted waters for meat, either for themselves or to sell at a restaurant. They had no time for me.

I kicked gloomily at the gray, disklike pebbles of the beach. The shore was littered with plastic cups, rotten shanks of rope, torn green vinyl sheeting, bottles — the common denominators of world trash. Flotsam and jetsam, like me.

Basta! I thought suddenly. Enough! What the hell was the matter with me? Instead of getting on with it, dealing with the problems at hand as I had done — and successfully — most of my life, I was whimpering down this littered beach like a divorce-court Hamlet.

Why wasn't I chatting with a beautiful woman, waterskiing on an Italian lake, strolling on a golf course? The reason, obviously, was because I *wanted* to wallow in my failures.

Why failures? Was it failure to decide I did not want to break down doors, sell bugging equipment to Arab despots, to peddle guns that fluked into massacres? My flop on the Dylis case: wasn't it a better me, in a devious way, telling me "Stop!"? I made a little "hunh" of reflective humor. By that token, I was lucky it was Brockman who put horns on me. At least with him, I knew I was the better man. Maybe that was a boon. It had tarnished Anne for me, dashed her from the pedestal. Now she was just another me, no better, no worse. I allowed myself an acid smile. Maybe she hadn't liked it on the pedestal.

Back at the quay, fishermen were unloading their pathetically small catch, joking despite the long night's work. A notice was posted on the quay with the departure times of a boat to the tiny settlement of San Fruttuoso down the coast. My guidebook contained some scant words about Doria family tombs, a statue of Christ erected beneath the sea, and the usual "long walks of great picturesqueness in nearby countryside."

Why not? The boat, no more than thirty feet long, was moored by the dock. Its captain and single crewman were loading it with wheat flour, fertilizer, fresh vegetables, demijohns of wine, and large wrapped boxes.

In a nearby store, I bought wine, bread, cheese, and salami. At a tobacconist's shop, I bought a postcard that I sent to Alexa, saying I was healthy, and thinking of her, and traveling a good deal—words to reassure but not to overinform.

Back at the boat landing, a skinny, distinguished German, by the looks of him, asked me in broken Italian when the boat left. I was flattered he thought me Italian, gave him the information in Italian, and pointed to the schedule. He caught my accent.

"You are? . . ." he asked, his English as broad as mine.

"American. From Philadelphia." We both laughed, instant empathy. Both of us had been trying to do the right thing by speaking Italian. We exchanged rudiments. He had run a county school system in New Jersey. His wife was dead. With retirement pay and a little inherited income, he spent early spring to late fall indulging a fascination with Romanesque chapels.

"You're content bounding around like this, nine months a year?" I asked.

He looked pensive, pursed his thin lips, which made him look more European than American, and said:

"Fairly. More than fairly."

We talked in the boat's stern as it putted toward the first stop, his goal, San Rocco. I could see the sandy gray church and monastery atop a cliff in the distance, relics of man's desire to flee even the simpler world of the quattrocento.

By the time we neared San Rocco's inlet, I felt comfortable enough to ask him whether he ever considered settling down, remarrying.

"No," he said. "At seventy-three . . ." He smiled.

"You don't get lonely?"

At that he looked down at the blue gray water. The boat chugged along, the bearded captain talking with a friend, the other three passengers, all local, holding bundles between their legs. He must have seen he had something I wanted. A reserved man, he wasn't sure he wanted to give it up. Then he decided and looked at me sharply:

"I'm married to my loneliness."

"And is it a happy marriage?"

"No. But it is not unhappy. Like most marriages of convenience, it works because one of the partners wants it to work very badly."

"And because it is less trouble than finding and living with another person?"

"Yes," he said, not particularly eager to go further, "that's it exactly."

We shook hands at the landing. He was going on northward that evening. I would have liked to have seen him again; one did not often get a chance to talk with a man married to loneliness. I was curious to know how it worked on a day-to-day basis.

At San Fruttuoso's pier, an elderly woman tugged and pulled a giant carton with rope handles from the bottom of the boat. I helped her heave it over the side, then to carry it to a small cluttered shop just off the beach.

"Thank you, thank you," she said. "German?" The race who had built the pillboxes now weathering like everything else on the cliffs of this soft, often-ravaged littoral, the race who had slain Italian partisan and American alike were now the master tourists.

"No. American."

"Oh, American." She smiled with surprise. Ten years ago, it was American tourists who swarmed over the Italian Riviera. Now our debased currency had made us the equals of the poorer European lands. A few more years, and dear old ladies like this would offer us small tips for such services as I had provided her.

The village was the quietest inhabited place I had ever been in. The ancient tombs of the Doria family, the tangled vineyards, and the rustic Romanesque church all dozed in silence.

Inside the chapel, I relished the cool and closed

206

my eyes. How little of my life I had spent in churches. My mother's Pentecostal beliefs, which had flamed over into our home life without hindrance from firewalls, had been repugnant. Anne's mild Episcopalianism had not taken root in me, and not much in Alexa.

If I were ever going to feel some presence, would it not be in this candle-lit chapel, and at this time of my life? But I waited in vain. The barrel-vaulted antiquity of the church made it even more a coffin of religion, a small, beautiful repository of superstition where God's absence was an injustice. I felt a lonely peace in the church, but the peace of resignation, not of God. Something might be happening to me, I thought, but it was not the Almighty.

Outside, a rusty metal sign pointed vaguely upward: Mt. della Bocche. From my map, I could see it was an upland path to Santa Margherita. There I could get a bus back to Camogli and my bicycle. The path gradually zigzagged up a valley, no threat to my acrophobia.

As I climbed, the olives gave way to chestnut, oak, and pine. Sweat drenched my shirt. I stuffed it in my day pack with the food and trudged on. A lizard rustled in the dry vegetation, startling me. Unidentifiable birds twittered where a gorge ran not water but rich ferns. Two kilometers along the trail, a broken-down house gazed out on the sea, empty windows latticed with the webs of huge spiders. If I wanted to marry loneliness, I thought, I could bring the bride here.

Near the top, huge pines, their needles eight inches long, thrust up from a shallow saddle on the mountainside. Beneath them were moss beds and an undisturbed quilt of needles. I made my way through a low wall of underbrush and put down my pack. I had seen no one in my hour-and-a-half climb. Heard no one. Here, save for butterflies and a small grasshopper or two, I was alone.

I ate my picnic and drank half the bottle of red wine, now warmed by the day. I spread my shirt and lay on my back, where I could turn my head and look seaward, or stare up where the pines filtered the sunlight. Their erratic shivering in the breeze from the sea had a psychedelic effect. The wine and the arduousness of the climb had already made me a little giddy. With the shimmering of the sun through the needles still playing on my lids, I dozed off.

I awoke feeling wonderfully refreshed, supremely isolated. Only the taste of the garlicky sausage and the slightly acid residue of the wine connected me with any past at all.

I breathed in extra deeply, drawing in far more of the clean air than my lungs needed, knowing in that aware part of my peacefulness that I was decreasing suddenly the carbon dioxide in my blood. I knew the hyperventilation, if I went on, would throw me into a dizzy, self-induced euphoria.

For many minutes, I luxuriated in that giddiness. It seemed to push out all my anxieties, my old hurts, all my cares. I stopped the forced heavy breathing and let myself simply inhale naturally. The fuzzy feeling gave way to clear serenity, as if I were a me-shaped jar empty of everything, empty and at peace.

"Son-of-a-bitch," I marveled.

I lay still, enjoying this strange peace until the pine needles beneath my shirt began to feel uncomfortable and the sunlight, refracted by the trees, hit my face. I sat up and took a swig of the wine. When I had decided to give up Fraser, Inc., on that day following the Roman massacre, I had been like a newly escaped prisoner standing at the edge of a field. Across that field lay freedom. The prisoner had no idea that the field was marshy, cored with quicksand and weed-covered ditches. Naively, I had set out. Now I had traversed that swampy nightmare. I was on the other side, peeling off the mud of the swamps and with it the detritus of a more distant past.

I was going to reenter life, and not as the spouse of loneliness. I would talk with people, eat with them, maybe even find a woman I could like, sleep with. I would no longer see myself as a half-made marionette slumped in a box waiting for a Geppetto to finish me and work my strings.

Musing on all this as I made my way down toward Santa Margherita, I got lost in a chestnut forest. At its far end, three women, stooped and busy, were picking up chestnuts and putting them in faded cloth bags. They did not seem to think odd a distracted American who chuckled to himself.

XII.
SILVIA SORGENTI

It was time to leave Rapallo. I took my final Italian lesson, bought a rack and saddlebags for my bike. I stored belongings I did not need at the hotel and took off southward down the coast for the Cinque Terre, chosen primarily for its appropriate distance of seventy-five kilometers.

The road wound uphill, making my chest ache, then curled circuitously down, giving me long thrilling runs to the sea. On the outskirts of little towns like Zoagli and Lavagna, workers stared curiously, some seeing my foreign clothes hailed me in German—"*Guten Tag.*" Only one old peasant, toothless and carrying a gunnysack, waved happily, "Hey, cowboy!" His cry made me unreasonably proud to be a middle-aged American cyclist remembered by some old veteran of World War II. I wished I had bought a small American flag to stitch on my saddlebag.

I spent the night at a *locanda* in Moneglia. Too exhausted for the heavy wine of the house, I drank mineral water, soaked my body in an old-fashioned tub, and slept like a corpse despite the putter of motor scooters on the road outside.

Next morning, as I pedaled, something self-defeating in me summoned up old dybbuk memories of Anne. I relived one episode after another from my life with her: those hopeful days on the Mid-National case, the birth of Alexa, the good and bad.

I knew I was testing myself: if the discovery of change I had made at San Fruttuoso were a delusion, then despite this sunny, cool Ligurian day, I would wrench toward gloom, depression. But no anguish came. I was getting well. I thrust down on the pedals.

"*Addio*," I said to my memories of Anne. Then, thinking of myself, I called out, "Hey, cowboy!"

The Cinque Terre—five lands—are five postcard villages isolated within a collar of the Apennines. The Italians consider the jewellike coastal enclave almost a country unto itself. But the Cinque Terre has never been treated as sacrosanct by other races. For a couple of milleniums, it has been occupied, threatened, or sacked not only by the usual Mediterranean raiders, but by such unlikely marauders as the Swiss, the Normans, and, more recently, the Germans as soldiers and now tourists.

Well before sunset, I rounded a curve into its largest town, Monterosso, and coasted along the arc of beach, past the tamarisks and pines of the promenade, then toward the harbor and medieval town center.

In the morning, I chose from the guidebook a mountainside hike from Monterosso to the tiny seaport of Vernazza. I had a twitch of trepidation over the path's heights. But the *padrona* of my inn assured me that mules managed it easily and gestured with her hands to indicate how much greater a mule's girth was than mine.

At first, the trail climbed slowly. I passed a fancy hotel on a hill, then cut inland through vineyards above the sea. I felt a tremor of panic. My last attack of acrophobia had been a couple of years ago when Anne and I had vacationed in Germany. At the Zugspitze, I had stood, all but paralyzed, in the middle of the uppermost platform, unable to go to the narrow railing and look down. This time, stubbornness made me push on.

In the next cove, I relaxed. The path eased landward into an unfenced vineyard. There it faded out. I walked, lost among the harvested vines, some still bearing bits of dried grapes. My lungs were full of the rich odors.

Higher up, through an opening in the vines, I saw a man and woman cutting dead twigs and cried out to them, "Where is the trail?" The answer, to my surprise, came from the opposite direction: a woman, out of sight, maybe eighty feet away, shouted, "Here it is!" or so I thought until I rearranged the nouns and verb and realized she, too, was lost. "Is it here?" she was actually asking. The man and woman uphill began shouting in rapid Italian over my head to the woman tourist below. My confusion was complete.

The conversation ceased and I brayed again, "Where is the trail?" There was further talk among the three, all at top lungpower. Finally, the tourist woman took over and, though she was still out of sight, shouted:

"English man. Here *sentiero*"—path.

I shouted thanks to the two vineyard workers and headed carefully across the rows to the vines from which the English words had come. Through the foliage, peering in my direction, I saw a chubby woman with gray-stranded hair, dressed in a neatly stylish cotton blouse and a light tweed skirt. I tramped through the stalks to her.

Once face to face with her, I was embarrassed at having lost my way and doubly embarrassed over not knowing what to do. Should I nod and go on at a fast pace, leaving her behind? Or let her go first, leaving me? Or did we go together?

"Is this the trail?" I asked in Italian.

She waved her finger no, then said, "No," and pointed downhill.

I saw in the woman's face a good deal of determination, but also confusion. She, too, apparently was wondering what was the protocol. We picked our way across the hillocks, she with a slight limp. In a minute, we were back on the considerably narrowed trail.

"You English?" she ventured.

"No, American." I could see her formulating words in her mind. I had at least gotten past that stage with Italian. I was sure she wanted to make English the lingua franca in our brief encounter, but at last she gave up and said in Italian:

"You are looking for the trail to Vernazza?"

"Yes."

"This is it."

"*Grazie*," I said smiling, and she smiled back.

"You are a tourist, too?" I asked. "From northern Italy?"

"Yes," she said. "Why northern Italy? You can tell from my accent?"

"No," I said. "You have blue eyes." She smiled again. Behind her wide but not full lips her teeth shone white and even. Except for her slight heaviness—I judged her about five seven and 145 pounds—she was an attractive fortyish woman.

"Would you like to go on together?" I asked, suddenly wanting it very much.

She tightened up her face and I thought disappointedly that she was going to say no. Instead she said, "I cannot walk too fast. You might—"

"No matter," I said. "I am frightened of heights."

She thought I was merely being nice. In any case, we struck off along the trail, she limping boldly now that she had announced her minor disability. The vineyards grew more unkempt, then disappeared as the path veered upward. I could not help seeing the swing of her buttocks within the blue and gray tweed. Sensing it, she smoothed her skirt with a down and outward motion as if wishing to add another layer of cloth. I saw no wedding ring on the stubby but tapered fingers.

At the top of the hill, the path opened again on the aquamarine sea. Far to the left, the little town of Vernazza was cupped by brown hills and red rocks. My companion looked out, leaning on the flimsy metal railing. I sat on a rock as far back from the brink as I could, scared of the height, scared to show it.

"Beautiful," she said, awed at her country's

magic.

I would have liked to second her, but was cringing.

She looked back. I stood and felt dizzy. The path from here corkscrewed downward and to the left, the kind of curve over sheer drops that most frightened me. Five hundred feet below I could see the white curls of foam around inshore rocks. She came a step closer to me.

"You really are frightened of heights?" she asked.

I tried to focus on the sweat on her upper lip. I looked up into the sea blue eyes and flinched.

"Yes," I said. "Very." She nodded, sympathetically considering. "Maybe you should go on without me," I said.

"No, don't be silly. We'll go together. Don't look out. Look only down at the path." She took the outside, shielding me though it meant she was closer to the edge. "*Avanti*," she said.

I looked dubiously at the path, still afraid. She took my hand securely. "Now, let's go," she said. "Look down, not out." She spoke firmly, but kindly, like a practical peasant with a skittish donkey.

We rounded the worst of the curves and headed down at a lesser incline inland where the cove leveled out. I sighed with relief. She dropped my hand.

"I'm sorry to be such a child," I said.

"No matter," she said amiably. She pondered the episode awhile. "No one is perfect. Only in books and movies. My ankle has not worked just right since I was five years old. Poliomyelitis," she said slowly so I would understand the complex word.

"We live with what we have."

What a nice lady, I thought. She is giving me this personal detail to make me feel better about myself. How wonderful is this simple thing of talking with another person even if she's going to be on her way in an hour or so.

"My father," I said, "both of his legs were paralyzed from polio."

"Then you understand," she said.

"Yes. I am sorry. There is no operation?"

"No."

"Then," I said with mock gallantry, which she recognized as such and began to smile even before I formed my sentence, "with your permission, if you will assist me around the high places, I will assist you on the steep places."

"The gentleman is very kind," she bantered. "The gentlewoman accepts." We smiled at each other and I ventured one more sally in courtly style.

"The gentleman's name is Giorgio Fraser," I said.

"The gentlewoman's name is Silvia Sorgenti." We shook hands, smiling. Hers was damp with sweat, the grip softer than when she had taken mine to get me around the curve.

As we walked, we chatted. She was, she said, staying in Monterosso, in the fancy hotel I had passed. She had two weeks off. She was a chemical engineer in Milan. I had to look that up in my dictionary to make sure she had not meant merely chemist. She had come originally from Ivrea in the Piedmont.

I told her I was a businessman from Philadelphia on an extended vacation and was staying in Rapallo. To her amusement and interest, I told her I had ridden "here" on my bicycle.

"To Italy?" she demanded humorously.

"No, no, to Monterosso."

We were almost in Vernazza, level now with the church spire, though still above the rooftops and the thirteenth century walls and watchtower of the old harbor. After so long a time with no friend, no human relationship, I wanted badly to hold on to Silvia Sorgenti.

"Do you have time for a glass of wine?" I asked.

"I must get the train back," she said.

In the town itself, I walked with her to the station amid the straggle of townpeople and the few tourists. She was less comfortable with me now, as if we were a black and white couple in America who functioned fine until they were reflected in society's eyes. Did my execrable Italian equate me, with similar prejudices, to a black man with a white woman? Or was Silvia simply being chary of a single man?

The next train to Monterosso was in twenty minutes. I tried to charm her into taking a later one.

"There is a local wine here" — or so the guidebook had said. "It is called 'sciacchetrà.' " I blundered the pronunciation. She corrected me. "You see, if you don't come with me, I won't be able to order it."

Ever since her initial rebuff, she had been considering what she would say when I asked again. That I knew. Yet when she answered me, it was with a Mediterranean sunburst of spontaneity.

"Then I had better come with you and order it for you." How little it took, in my loneliness, to make my heart chirp. And how naturally it went after

217

that: the coffee she had (she drank no alcohol, not liking its taste), my sciacchetrà (vastly overrated), the time stretching to one o'clock, my entreaties that she let me buy her lunch (and thus another train missed).

The hours had a peculiar quality of increasing transparency, as if we were in a bathysphere ascending toward the light. Gradually, she became accustomed to my mistakes in Italian, compensated for them. When a concept was beyond me, I sought out the Italian in the dictionary. When I failed to understand her, she found the English in the little book and rapidly enunciated the key words.

Primitive as it seemed, we adapted to it. She was a woman of great intelligence but no great patience. When I faltered, she interrupted to say it for me, then asked me if that was what I meant. Beneath her plumpness, which became more attractive as early afternoon turned to midafternoon, there was a sinewy personality.

What we told each other about ourselves also had a quality of expanding lucidity. First we put aside our small pretenses; my being in Italy as a businessman on vacation gave way to my revelation that my wife and I had broken up and I was trying to sort out my life. Her cautious admission that she was unmarried slowly enlightened into her confession that she was divorced and that she had never found anyone who both liked her and was intelligent enough for her to want to remarry.

Bit by bit, I learned that she was thirty-nine, was one of sixty-two women chemical engineers in Italy, had mastered bicycle riding and limited skiing de-

218

spite her bum ankle, was the daughter of an architect, had a sister who was a government physician in Rome, a brother who was a lawyer in her present home, Milan.

I went further with my own history, told her of my early life in South Philly, my trouble with the law. I added that I was now translating Leopardi (to sound as Byronic as possible) but told her my work was incompetent.

With a hint of a chill coming into the late afternoon, I felt again my hopes of seeing more of her were in jeopardy. She began to become wary, just as before when her train had been due to arrive. I felt she was capable of saying good-bye to me almost instinctively, like a once-burned animal might turn away from the very hearth fire that would warm it.

"I am only having a light supper," I said as we rose. "I would be happy if you wanted to have a quick bite this evening somewhere."

"Oh," she said. "I am on pension at the hotel."

"Could you not be convinced to eat in town, maybe just soup and fruit." I looked across the empty plates, bottle, and cups at her blue eyes and saw, in their profound caution, that they were about to signal no. Then they both lightened and hardened as if to challenge herself. Why not? they seemed to say.

"Why not?" she said. "But why not come to my hotel? We can both eat lightly there with less fuss than finding a place in town, where everything is off-season."

Back in Monterosso, on the way to my own hotel to shower and dress, I looked benignly on two lone male tourists I passed. I was not going to be alone at supper, as I had been for so many yearning days. Tonight I was spoken for.

That evening, the ascending bathysphere came more fully into light. She had been in psychotherapy during her divorce, had drifted from the Roman Catholic church, though not from belief in Christ, had thought herself in love twice since her divorce seven years ago, once with a weak, unpassionate man, once with a man who had been superficial but physically attractive.

"I was glad to learn I liked men," she said.

The bathysphere moved upward toward sunlight, clarity. Her husband's behavior had been "*sconveniénte*," she said. I scrambled in the dictionary, almost knocking over the mineral water bottle, knowing it was a crucial remark. And so it was. It meant "unseemly." "You mean?. . ." I asked, knowing it implied some sexual unpleasantness.

"Yes," she said, without specifying. "I was young, a graduate engineer, but on such matters, a frightened child."

I told her my discovery that there was another man. She clucked sympathetically and, I wanted to think, with the question in her mind: "How? A man like you. And she would seek another?"

After dinner, we walked through the medieval town, both of us acutely aware of how old the stones were, how young we were by comparison, and how rapidly time passed. On the rough cobblestones leading up the Hill of Capucins, I took her hand.

"I do not want you to fall," I told her. "I would rather have you think I am a libertine than for me to lose a friend to a broken leg."

She laughed and left her hand in mine.

"You appear anything but a libertine," she said.

"I am not." I silently searched my vocabulary for a way of saying what I wanted to say without sounding either like a braggart or childishly confessional. Failing, I said bluntly, "I was married twenty years and never was unfaithful. It is rare in America."

"In America? Everywhere," she laughed again.

On the walk back to her hotel, we paused beside that same heavy railing above the beach that I had passed alone that morning. She dropped my hand and put her elbows on the rail, her chin in her hands. Clearly, my talk of marriage had made her think of disclosing something more about her own. She turned now, leaned against the rail, facing not the sea but my face in the dim moonglow.

As if to clear the whole slate, she told it all: her husband, unsatisfied by her efforts to meet his odd tastes, had turned to hired women; furthermore, he had nagged her for not having a baby; she had gone to a gynecologist, who said it was not her fault; when she'd urged him to get checked out, he'd refused for fear of finding he was to blame. Her father, a womanizer himself, and her brother, hypocrite, had both tried to talk her out of the divorce even though the marriage had grown monstrous. No one but her sister had supported her. She had gotten the divorce only after threatening to reveal his adultery in court, an almost unthinkable step in Italy.

"You are a very tough lady," I said. There were tears of fury in her eyes. I saw them when she turned her head into the moonlight.

"Yes," she said. "I had to be. I do not want to be otherwise."

And I, too, stripped off the shame. I told her of my life as a private eye, a gun shipper, in all the worst details, except for the Mafia. I told her of my failure on the Dylis case and my ugly success in snooping on my wife and her lover, even to my standing in the hall. I told her of my brutal battering of Brockman.

We had shriven each other of awful elements of our past. We walked to the door of her hotel, but I did not kiss her there. In some curious way, that would have been to identify myself with her husband's "*sconveniènte*" behavior.

"Do you want to ride bicycles tomorrow?" I asked. "Perhaps to Manarola or a little past?" It was a hill town down the coast. "*Va bene*," she said. "I will find a bicycle." She took my hand again, both of us aware it was no longer needed to keep her from falling on any cobblestones. Star struck, not wanting to part, we looked up and then out to sea, where ships' lights mirrored the stars. The waves lapped; the small town to our right glowed ungarishly. With a sigh, she went inside, and I stood watching her through the thick glass door, bewitched.

Silvia rounded the corner and jauntily pulled up to my hotel next morning on a rented three-speed, her face full of smiles. Over my objections, she bought the picnic. I had bought lunch yesterday; we had split supper; it was her turn, she insisted.

On the rough road to Manarola, she was my match as a cyclist, her sturdy legs churning the pedals. We reached the village early and biked on to Riomaggiore, the easternmost of the Cinque Terre towns. At the final hill, we looked down at the town snuggled into a valley like a bean in a pod, an old church belfry soaring from the stucco houses. Fishing boats dancing in the light breeze by a jetty. It was as lovely as Vernazza. But by common feeling, we pushed through it without sightseeing, looking for seclusion.

We found it a kilometer past the town where a slope descended to a low bluff above the sea. Two decrepit pines kept out the noon sun. Flecks of brine, thrown high by the rocks and carried by gusts, touched our faces and tasted astringently of salt. I looked at Silvia's flushed cheeks and the curlicue of hair that the perspiration had made in front of her ear. But that seemed too personal.

The strain of the ride had left my stomach cramped. I took a sip of her mineral water, then a swallow of the warm wine and felt my belly unknot. I started to help her unwrap the parcels, but she pushed me aside gently. I sat, leaning against one of the pines, watching Silvia's deft hands move quickly among the lunch foods.

"This is contentment," I said to her. "If a person can make his mind empty of troubles, then it takes

223

such few natural things to make him content: wine, food, sea, sun, a friend."

She picked up on my thought. "And if there is no wine, sea, sun, then a friend will do nicely." A bit embarrassed, she went back busily to unfolding the paper wrappings from the meats and cheeses, passing the tub of unsalted butter under her nose: these simple competent gestures. "Maybe one should be a little cautious about talking of contentment," she said as if in afterthought. "It can make one self-conscious, and then contentment goes away."

On one of the pieces of oilpaper, Silvia brought me slices of Parma ham, salami, the cheeses. I took the cheap knife she had bought, broke off a piece of bread, and made her a luscious sandwich, which I handed back to her.

Hungry from the ride, we ate more heartily than we should have.

"We are a pair of pigs," she said. "If we had been wiser, we would have eaten lightly to make the ride back less hard." Her face fell. I knew she was thinking now about being overweight, of appearing gluttonous, middle-aged, and unpretty in the eyes of her new friend. I felt, even shared, her distress with all the emotion of one with a full file cabinet of his own spiritual aches.

I dropped down in front of her where she was kneeling over the remnants of food, wrapping them in oilpaper.

"Silvia," I said. "You are thinking of yourself the wrong way. You are thinking of yourself as I think of myself when I am being unjust to myself. If you are fair to yourself, you will think of yourself as a beautiful person who makes a lonely stranger happy. And why do you make me happy? Because you make me feel I am something special." I took her hand in mine.

She withdrew it, not wanting to give in to self-pity or to allow me to express pity in this way. Lest I feel a rejection in her gesture, she patted the back of my hand.

"I am a beautiful person," she mimicked me, "whose hands smell like garlic." Then not jesting, she said, "You are a nice man. I knew it right away when I saw you."

Then with that mock formality that we were both coming to employ when we wanted to make serious things sound less serious, I said:

"May the nice man ask the lady with garlicky hands to share another light supper and a walk this evening?"

"If the nice man will let the lady with garlicky hands take a nap and a bath, and if the supper is truly light, the answer is yes."

On the way back, a nail flattened her tire. She cursed mildly and began fiddling in the little saddlebag behind her seat.

"Let me," I said, spotting a small metal tool in the bag for taking tires off the rim. But she waved me off. In minutes she had the tire off the rim, the nail drawn, the tube neatly patched. Only on the coolie labor—pumping up the tire with her riding pump—did she let me perform. When we were done, she looked at me with an intelligent, skeptical smile, and said:

"If I could speak enough English or you could

speak enough Italian, you might find a mind a little more full of physics and chemical formulas and how to patch up bicycles and catalytic precipitators than you'd care for."

At supper, we chatted as easily as old friends. Afterward, we walked hand in hand in the darkened street, then stumbled upward to the ruins of an old monastery.

The talk turned to her friends and, inevitably, to her lack of a steady beau, a lover. I said, I thought soothingly, that "being lonely is no fun." But she took me up smartly:

"What you are saying is that the world's judgment is correct: that a woman—"

I interrupted her, "Or a man."

"—or a man," she conceded, "is incomplete without a mate."

"Yes," I said. "I do feel that. We, anyway I, am happy now because we have each other to talk with, to shut out the loneliness. Because we are together, loneliness has lain down and died." I felt rather proud of the poetic mastery of that sentence.

"Well, Mr. Philosopher," she replied, "You are romantic, but you are wrong. If loneliness were so repellent, you would be with your wife and I with my husband."

When, at almost midnight, we came back to her hotel door to bid good-night, I asked her whether she wanted to ride again next day. We discussed destinations and she suggested the Via Aurelia. It was a mountainous ride eastward.

"Perfect," I said. I would have answered the

same if she had asked whether we should sun-
bathe on nails. I had not let go of her hand. Holding it, I turned her to me to kiss her, but she
moved her lips away. I kissed her cheek. Again,
sensing I would fear rejection, she turned her own
lips to my cheek and kissed it softly, not a nip, but
for delicious seconds. Cheek to cheek, we hugged
each other. And when we parted, I knew that I
was, at least for this time and this place, in love.

XIII.
GEORGE IN LOVE

On the twisting road next morning, we were caught
in a cloudburst. Laughing wildly as the fat raindrops hit our overheated bodies, we ran our bikes
off the road and hurried to an old masonry wall sur-
rounding an olive grove. I helped her climb the
crumbling wall, feeling even as she wriggled, the
soft sweet flesh of her arm and then of her calf as I
boosted it over.

We stumbled toward a thick olive tree and threw
ourselves under it, protected from the rush of rain.
It pattered heavily into the leaves as we gasped for
breath, then just as the drops began to turn to small
streams along the branches, the heavy rain passed
on down toward Monterosso and we were left with
a chill, thin drizzle.

"Not even that bottle of wine to keep us warm," I
said to her. We sat, close together, leaning up
against the tree's rough trunk.

"To keep *you* warm," she said, reminding me that
she was a teetotaler. Lest it sound prudish, she said
in light self-mock: "Even in this damned drizzle, I

remain Saint Abstemious."

"The beloved patroness of families and the dairy industry," I said.

"Martyred in A.D. 276 by the Wine Growers Association of Italy," she joined in . "Her shrine in the charming Ligurian village of Acqua Minerale."

"Her relic, a healthy liver, preserved beneath the altar, uncorrupted by the years."

"She laughed, her white teeth showing, and touched my bare arm appreciatively. And that was all it took. I held her hand in mine and turned my body toward her. For an instant, I saw surprise in the brilliantly blue eyes, then I closed mine and kissed her. This time, her flinch was from astonishment, not caution, for after a tiny gasp she kissed me back.

When we broke, I started to try to find words, but dropped the idea, seeing her liking for me in her eyes, knowing she saw in mine that liking's reflection.

I kissed her again, the same way, and this time when we broke, she moved her other hand up to my cheek and moved her body closer to mine, pressing her breast hard against my chest.

"Bene," she said, and avoiding my lips as I turned to kiss her, she hugged me. *"Bene."* Then, though I would have stayed beneath the tree, she worked her way out of my grasp, came from under the olive tree, and stood up to brush off the dirt.

Before she could remonstrate, I kissed her still again. The touch of her lips had taken on heat. Senses all tingling, I felt the tiny pats of the drizzle, the wetness of the back of her blouse, the smooth flesh beneath it. Dizzily, I felt the walls of my repression fall over. I wanted her.

"For this time and place, I love you," I said, articulating what I had thought but not said the night before.

"And I, too," she replied but with a shade less joy. Was it the qualification I had put into my declaration? Or had she seen, even then, the end in our beginnings?

We might have commenced right there on the hill in that drizzle the kisses that would have led us to make love on the damp earth. But Silvia, by birth, and I, by conditioning, were bourgeois. Hand in hand, we walked to the bikes. The drizzle had lightened, but there was no sign it would lift.

Still, we were determined folk. In good spirits, we made up our minds to reach Via Aurelia, drizzle or no, if only because we had picked it the night before as our destination. On the wall, we snacked lightly from our picnic, pedaled to Via Aurelia, and got back to Monterosso in midafternoon.

Like bride and groom, we did not see each other the rest of the afternoon, but went to our rooms to rest and bathe. I slept the dead sleep of the honest weary as rain thumped outside the shutters. I awoke, aware of how good I felt, and realized it was in part because I had forgone wine and most of lunch and thus exempted myself from the logy awakenings of other afternoons.

On the way to Silvia's hotel, I stopped at a shop and bought an expensive tie. Despite its crispness, my clean wash-and-dry shirt, my comparatively wrinkle-free sport jacket, I was not the perfectly costumed groom, but I was as spruce as I could manage.

Silvia had also fallen into the matrimonial mode. In the lobby of her hotel, when she rose to kiss me lightly, I smelled the perfume, heavier than any Anne had ever worn. Her hair was combed delicately away from her full face, her makeup put on with great care. Her dress was a rich blue silk, falling so that it flattered her hips, her body. I wondered if, like me, she had gone shopping that afternoon.

The dining room's carpet, walls, and pillars were austerely rich in brown, tan, and pale blue fabrics and surfaces. The meal had a formal quality, too, spiced though it was by our liking for each other.

I toasted her with a split of French champagne. We touched hands sedately between the courses: fresh mussels with flecks of onion and herbs, tomato salad, broiled *orata* with fennel . . .

The headwaiter came and asked her how her meal was. She answered him in rapid Italian, and I joined in, finding the words of praise came trippingly off my tongue.

"Grazie, grazie, signori," he beamed. Showing that dignity with which only a truly fine headwaiter can retreat backward, he did so, looking both pleased and relieved, realizing, perhaps, ours was a supper of occasion.

"Your Italian is getting so good I am afraid you will practice such pretty phrases on others," she said. Then she added, with a lemon peel of acidity,

231

"How good my English would be now if . . ." She was an achiever, and it still smarted that I could speak Italian better than she could speak English.

"Would we have been happier if we had chosen English that day in the vineyard?" I interrupted. It seemed so long ago, now we had spent so much of these three days together.

"No," she said. "I could not be happier than I am now."

After supper, we walked in the town again. Lovers make their conventions, their traditions as they go along. This time, we clung together, pausing in darkened streets for swift kisses.

As we walked back slowly toward her hotel, we saw far up the coast the soft lights gradually growing dim as the small harbor villages went to bed. My arm around Silvia, I looked to westward, where two seas away I had lived all my life before I met her. I did not want to go back there. For now, I was happy here, a foreign wind on my face. I breathed it deeply, the salt taste strong, and kissed her.

"This afternoon," she said when we broke, "you said you loved me. But you qualified it with time and place."

"Yes," I said. "It was true."

"The love or the qualifications?"

"Both."

"All right, Giorgio. I feel the same way. But with much less qualification. So for me the risks are greater. Consider that, yes?"

"Yes, I have considered it."

By our parapet, I held her in my arms. I was ready to ask her if she would spend the night with me, and I felt she wanted me to ask. But I wanted some sure verbal sign, even now, that she would say yes. When she gave it, it was homey and natural.

"We'll catch cold out here," she said. "We ought to go in."

Once we were in her room, what savoir faire I had fell apart. I felt a panic fear of failure that even her kindness might not be able to overcome.

"I'm nervous as a new husband," I said, seeking a virtue in honesty.

"Giorgio," she said practically, "we have both been married before. Nothing is ever without flaw. If all I do is get from this chilly room into a warm bed and hold you in my arms, then I will consider it a night well spent."

That, surely, was as easy a condition as ever was put on an assignation. She went swiftly into the bathroom. I stripped off my clothes, put them in a chair, looked through the window at the town, whose lights were diminished even since we had been on the parapet, and climbed into bed.

She snuggled into my arms, naked, unreservedly, as if we had done it all the days of some past marriage to each other. I kissed the top of her head, smelling the perfume in her hair, then her nose, then her mouth, which tasted sweetly of toothpaste.

"I should have brushed my teeth," I said mindlessly.

The fears, myths, and taboos of a lifetime do not

drain all in a single hour. Silvia felt the physical evidence — or rather did not feel the physical evidence — of my problems. She made no mention of concern, not even an utterance that could have seemed a command to relax. Her touches were slow, friendly, as much to my face and hair as to my back and arms, her kisses less passionate then affectionate.

Gradually, her unthreatening flesh became familiar, exorcised my bedevilments. One last time, my mind tried to play the game of failure. It summoned up my final unsuccessful effort to couple with Anne, my fears of impotency. I began to go limp. But with quick grace, Silvia slid beneath me, touching my back lightly, undemandingly. With that reassurance, all other things went out of my mind. In an instant, Silvia sighed happily, her body relaxed now that it contained me. I thrust, and in instants more my body stiffened. She held me firmly until I lay upon her exhausted with relief, smiling to myself: it had been efficient, in a way, rather than beautiful. And for that very reason, because it had not challenged me to achieve beauty, it had been perfect. It had worked.

After a time, I said, "I never thought I'd be able to."

"That's crazy," she whispered. "There's nothing wrong with you."

We slept late. By noon, I had called Rapallo and told the hotel I would be in Monterosso *sine die* and please to keep my baggage safe until they heard from me. By four, after we had lunched in town, I had checked into her hotel and moved my scant belongings and bicycle there. Before five, we were back in bed.

As a boy in South Philly, my peers and I skipped school and bought the lewd caricatures of Blondie and Betty Boop and Popeye that did for pornography. Only in these salacious parodies did women enjoy sex. In real life, we came to believe, women got no pleasure from sex, even in, especially in, our lower-class milieu.

In no small measure, I had believed that lie. As had Anne until (and still I thought of it with hatred) her affair with Brockman. Now I also had found a liberation from that myth. And I was luckier than Anne, for I had found it with a human being of distinction.

Sylvia and I were as curious about the diverse machinery of our passion as if by examining the physical configurations of flesh and hair and tissue, we could ascertain why lovemaking created ecstasy. As well to explain Beethoven by studying the measurements of his manuscript staves and notes, or Shakespeare by the chemical formulas of the inks he used. Yet, the knowledge of the works and maps of each other's body seemed to heighten the feelings we had when, in endless, if minor, variations, we made love.

As transfixed, as investigative, as if she studied some rare filiform precipitation in her laboratory, she gently pulled to full length the few hairs on my chest, moved the patella on its sacs of bursa to see the action, examined the tautness of the skin when my scapula was distended.

Her body became a delightful museum for me,

full of unexpected and intriguing things: each small mole, the way her mouth went from seriousness to smile—I watched the tiny action of the musculature, touched her mouth's edges to feel it—the configuration of the hair of her brows, the wrinkles at her knuckles, the stiffness even of her ankle and the slight way her left hip had tipped to compensate, the microcontours of a dimple in one of her buttocks.

In the past, Anne's ideal face and body were the measure by which I judged other women. And if I placed on Silvia's body a cutout of my wife, Silvia would flair out at buttocks, stomach, and all Anne's leg would be contained in the perimeter of Silvia's.

Yet what Silvia's body did had shaped me new standards. Her thighs, hips, small breasts had become beautiful to me not because they satisfied any calipered rules of proportions, but because of their dearness, their delight. These things had made them not merely beautiful, but susceptible to worship.

Or was it always so? I had seen the unnamed Venuses of the Cyclades in an exhibit, and pictures of the little ivory goddess carved in European caves twenty-five thousand years ago. They were more Silvia by far than Anne. Had those inarticulate, unknown cave people known so early that such bodies encase women cut more to the cravings of men than the forms that were to become the ideal twenty-five milleniums later?

On our first day as lovers, I went into town to buy condoms after she told me how to say the word — *"preservativo."* She thought it amusing that she had contributed money and signed petitions to liberalize sale of birth control devices but had gotten so little personal return for her political crusading.

"Only now are my good deeds coming home to nest," she said.

During the next few days, the bed became the center of our universe. Proficient now in the formulas of each other's passion, we climaxed together time and time again. After one such encounter, I laughed in gratitude. She touched my face lightly.

"We women," she said, "know you see yourselves in the mirrors of our bodies. If we reflect back your passion, you are beautiful to yourselves. If we are dark when you search that mirror, you are desolated. Seeing no reflection, you are convinced there is no sexual you at all."

When our voraciousness subsided somewhat, we ventured out, almost astonished to be in the sunlight and temporarily unpossessed.

One day we took a trip down the coast to San Terenzo by train. We walked hand in hand along the seafront, then ate a huge platter of fried things from the sea and fresh salad, and strolled to the church, whose tall, square tower dominated the village like a gaunt schoolmaster over a class of motley-clad children.

Syliva was a bulletin-board reader. When she had turned away from the notices on the church's board, she commented, "The pope talks rubbish

237

about birth control and divorce and abortion. And people like me break with the Church. The Russians do the same. And you get crazies like the Red Brigadists."

I had told her nothing about Calvacadi or the mob. I pushed back the thought of them, of the old life in which they dwelled. It was easier now. All of it seemed more than a mere continent away.

"You're not comparing yourself with the Red Brigades?" I said.

"No. I would shoot you in the kneecaps only to keep you from running away from me." I would have preferred another jest.

Later, going back by train to Monterosso, I returned to her talk about the Church. Out of curiosity, and because it was easy to find in English, I had reread the New Testament in Rapallo. Jesus seemed to me a cranky, marvelous genius, but bullheaded to a fault, a male chauvinist, nuts on the subject of extramarital sex, and, like liberals today, more in love with people in general than in particular, with the exception of his own tiny coterie.

"You do not approach the New Testament as a scientist would," she said. I was intrigued. She went on knowledgeably about how the early churchmen rewrote Christ's words to their own liking and that was what had in fact come down to us. "They were as eager to control the actions of the people as Rome is today."

"How do you know that the good stuff in the New Testament, the really good parables, the humanity, isn't what's been added? How do you know the real Jesus wasn't a prude?"

"Not even the propagandists would have dared to meddle with the last words on the cross, the beautiful things you're talking about. It wasn't that they changed so much, but that they added —"

"You're saying that Christ believed we should make love?"

"Yes," and in the darkening train compartment, she took my hand. "If I didn't think so, I would not be able to . . ."

In that simplicity, there was for me awe. To argue about it just for the sake of talk was to dirty it.

"You are a very beautiful woman who believes in a very beautiful God," I said. "I wish I believed in the same God."

I could see her wondering whether to say what was on the tip of her wide lips. Finally she said quietly:

"When I think of how beautiful you are, I think you do believe in him." I was touched deeply, almost to where the tears were.

We put off talk of the future until four days before she was to go back to Milan. From the beginning, we had known how transitory our time together was. It gave our passion a gravity, a civilized desperation that we did not define. Silvia, I had sensed, had wanted to bring it up all along, to monitor our love's death as it died. She liked things sharp, uncompromising; I had been willing to slide over and past pain.

She dealt with our future, or lack of it, in the bathtub. It should have been in bed, or at a table with flowers and wine, or on a walk in the country-side.

"I don't want us to say good-bye when my vacation is over," she said. Nor did I. But I had vaguely accepted our breaking it off at the end of our time together, unless we could see some way to accommodate all the problems our affair would face in the outside world. Whatever the case, I thought we had agreed tacitly not to speak of it until the end.

"Can we talk about it later?" It sounded cruel, but I let it stand. I got out of the tub and began to dry myself.

She rose, taking my hand to help herself from the tub, and I began to rub her pink back. When she turned, she was crying.

"What do you think we should do?" I asked.

"What about you?"

Suddenly, I felt that old familiar clutch in my stomach: an argument with a woman I loved, a playback of my last months with Anne.

"I would like not to think of it for a few days," I said, trying again to buy time.

"On the face of it, that would be fine," she said. "But unfortunately for us both, I am in love with you. And so I don't want to abide by the rules." From my caution, she now sensed that I had subconsciously accepted an end to our romance. It hurt her and I could not bear that. I tried to console her.

"I am in love with you, too."

"Yes," she said. "But you said in the beginning, 'for this time and place.' And as I said, but was not sure I meant it then, I do not have those qualifications." With the rough towel, I tried gently to dry

240

her tears.

"Why?" I said, more harshly than I intended. "Why? It was so perfect."

"Giorgio, no one is more sorry than I."

Now the knowledge of the impossibility of things galled me. Surely she saw them. She was the scientist. Yet, she had let her emotions grow into dreams, not I. I knew what she was thinking: a small villa outside Milan where I would paint or sketch or fool with poetry. But that was absurd. How long could I stand being her appendage, a courtesan waiting for the weekend when she would visit me from the city? How long, really, could she stand that?

But all that was irrelevant, although I dared not tell her why. So long as Dylis was just across the Adriatic, I did not dare live permanently in Italy, no matter how I disguised myself.

Nor could she give up her life in Milan to come to America. To do what? To pick up enough English at Berlitz for her to hold down some low-level job with Dow? Compete with American-educated engineers fifteen years younger? She would be no better than the busywork consort of a dabbler. Wouldn't it all be a horrible reprise of my alienation from Anne, but with new, even more lethal complications?"

For with Anne, there were so many common interests: the law, art, books, Alexa. But Silvia was interested in the sciences, physics, the way things are put together. She was the consummate engineer. I, despite making so much money out of electronics, no longer had — if I ever had — any bent for the practical technology of it.

Slowly, or swiftly, the marriage would die, as my

marriage to Anne had died, the color going off it fleck by fleck until there was only the bare plaster where a fresco once had been. Better far for our love to die at the little station in Monterosso, where her train would pause to pick her up and she would disappear into a tunnel, literally swallowed up by the rocky earth.

"We could have separated as equals," I said.

She must have seen my torment, for now she smiled, lips compressed, and hugged me to her.

"You have said what my heart does not want to hear," she said. "I had wondered how to bring it up and then did so in this stupid way, but there is no way that would not be stupid. If you had loved me as much as I you, then maybe there was some way, even with all the problems."

But that, too, was delusion. Love was never enough. It does not conquer all. It wins no wars, only a few preliminary battles. Attrition conquers love. She knew that, so why did she let her heart do this to us? Perhaps never in my life would I have the chance to be so honest with anyone again. A quirk in our languages and a time in our lives had made it impossible for us to lie, to cheat. I could not do so, even to give her hope.

"This hotel room is not the world we would have to live in," I said.

"All right," she answered. Her love, as foolhardy and gallant as a cavalry charge into cannons, had made its attack and had been repulsed. "All right." She sighed, said nothing more, and kissed me passionately. I had given her an honest answer. She had left it open for me to say that somehow it would work out. And for better or worse, I had not told that lie.

We went to bed, more by rote than desire. Once under the covers, we began silently to make love. In our dumb act, we could ignore the refinements of who loved the most. We could briefly hold back the terminal nature of our affair.

Skilled in the uses of each other's flesh, we built toward a heady climax. Yet even amid the passion, a bit of my mind thought: from here on in, it's different. It is still loving, but it no longer has in it either the unspoken dream of permanence or the honorable presumption of equal forces.

I had read that Gypsies on the way to Hitler's gas ovens made love one last frantic time. In our intercourse that night, there was a quality of abandon we had not brought to the bed before.

We conducted the formal execution at breakfast just down the beach in Fegina on a café terrace overlooking the deserted shore. How much better if it had been gloomy with rains that now came from time to time in the mornings. But it was radiantly sunny and the sea smelled as fresh as if it had been spring.

"It's like the end of an experiment, a research paper, writing the abstract. The summing up," she said, finding some security in this simile drawn from a world where she was at home. She turned the coffee cup in her hand.

Yes, I thought, the experiment succeeded brilliantly, but the patient died. Listening, loving her, I broke in:

"Maybe I'm wrong. Why not try it a while?" But I

243

knew I was saying that because it was now safe to do so. I was saying it, in part, too, because I wanted her to have the option of saying no to me as I had said no to her the night before. My wish to defer was a repayment for the shattering compliment she had paid me of falling in love with me more than I had fallen in love with her.

"No," she said. "You weren't wrong. The world is *not* our hotel room. We know all the reasons it would not work." She poured more coffee, first for me, then for herself. "But what did work worked so beautifully . . ."

She began to tear up, but dabbed at her eye corner with the paper napkin, then pushed on, tearless again.

". . . what did work is that we gave each other splendid gifts. You showed me that I am a desirable woman, a beautiful woman, one whom a man I respect can love. You showed me that I need not compete with every man I meet, that a man can be my friend, and I his equal."

Of course, I thought with a shock: and Anne and I had not been equals! Anne had felt herself the goddess I had made of her, a superior who at last had come to despise me as an inferior. She and Brockman had been rutting goats, but with the reciprocity of coequal goats. My assaulting him had not altered that equality.

"You did everything for me, Silvia," I burst in on her emotionally. "You gave me back my self-respect."

"Yes," she said, sensing the direction of my thoughts, "your wife the famous tax lawyer let you go too soon. She could not accept the changed person, the person I love, and wait for him to change just a little so she could tolerate him. She stupidly pushed you out. But don't you think she won't want you back now I have helped make a new you of you." She was on the brink of sobbing. "I have made you into a fine man for somebody else."

I paid the bill and we got up and talked on the foam-sprayed beach. The salt tasted on our lips as it had what seemed an endless time ago at Riomaggiore. We held hands now, everything pretty well said, lovers without a future who had been perhaps too mature about something of evanescence, of colors that maturity dulled, polite people who had found a way to say good-bye with a minimum of hurt.

And yet, for all out pretty speeches, and perhaps precisely because we *were* grown-ups, we could not bear to give each other up until the last day. In those final days, we walked in the *campagna,* bused to Portovenere, an ancient town of old quays and good food, and fished one morning in the gulf off La Spezia.

On Sunday afternoon, I carried her bags to the station. We sat on a bench waiting for the train that would carry her to Milan: a thirty-nine-year-old with a slightly gimpy ankle who carried beneath her expensive, tailored traveling suit all the treasure of the worldly paradise; and a man changed by her love. Neither of us, not even Silvia, had been quite in love enough to forsake all. But both of us were plenty enough in love to ache. Even when the train came, a guillotine to the misery of parting, we sought a stay.

"So," she said. "We have been very adult about this. Yet, if you call me in Milan, I will want to see you, I would rather suffer a bit more than . . ."

"Yes," I said. "For all our wisdom . . ."

The bicycle ride back to Rapallo, thank God, was analgesic. Going uphill, I pumped to the limit of my energy while small cars and large trucks buzzed by. My downhill runs were slaloms past carts, people, pot-holes. My reckless speed made Sylvia less pervasive in my mind. But when I paused atop a hill and looked back toward the Cinque Terre, I missed her as a man might miss an amputated arm. If there was consolation in the simile, it was that I lost the arm in an honorable war, not the debased mix of humiliation, jealousy, and violence that was my terrorist combat with Anne.

That night, my right calf so knotted by cramping I could not go on, I stopped at Chiavari, ten kilometers south of Rapallo. When I dismounted my *locanda,* I fell under the streetlight like a drunk from the cramp and the stiffness.

I hobbled into my room, my weariness put me to sleep, but once my body was free of its physical tensions, my turbulent mind roused me. Like random snippets of a film, I resaw long bike rides with Silvia, walks on the beach, snatches of laughter, a movement of her hands at supper, moments of passion, her head tossing as she combed her hair, her sleeping face in the minutes before she awakened.

I could mull over convalescence, cure. But there

246

would always be turnings in roads, touches of chill in autumn by seas, smells of old pines, and the roughness of castle ruins to evoke her, undiminished. I groaned:

"You let her get away, the best thing that will ever happen to you. You've done it again." But even at this black hour of the night, my leg aching, my arms empty, I knew that was not true. What I had with Silvia was one of the great successes of my life. Why the hell shouldn't I pay for it with wakefulness, cramps, a bucket or two of sweat and longing?

XIV.
BACKFIRE

When I got back to the Hotel Conconi in Rapallo, there was a cable from Danny Surrett: "Urgently request you try to locate American tourist George Christian Fraser passport number G1228675. Important family matter. Notify him call undersigned his attorney who will compensate locator." Surrett ended with his name, his cable address, and his telephone number.

Surrett had probably used the power of attorney I had given him to get my traveler's check numbers from my bank, then cajoled a cop pal into asking American Express where they had been most frequently cashed. The Italian tourist people in New York would have told him which hotels were still open in Rapallo. He then had only to send out the twenty or thirty cables necessary to hit them all

The family matter had to be my father or Alexa. I tried to reach Surrett through the hotel switchboard, but couldn't. I rode my bike rapidly through the narrow streets to the post office and got a connection to Surrett's office in a couple of minutes.

He was out, his secretary in. The first thing she said, obviously at Surrett's instructions, was that it had nothing to do with my family: that this was the only way Surrett was sure I would call back at once. I was too relieved to resent the subterfuge. Beyond that, she only knew that he wanted me to stand by whatever phone I was near while she tried to get him. He called in fifteen minutes.

"How's the food over there," he said heartily. "I'm at Maureen's. You eating anything to match her duck and strawberries?"

"Danny, please," I said. "You scared the crap out of me. What in the hell?. . ."

"I can't tell you," he said. "You caught me just as I was leaving. I'm standing here with a lovely lady who. . ." He paused, said something to her I did not hear, then came back on with a heavy whisper.

"I sent her to the little girl's room," he explained. "I have to talk with you. In person."

"Why?" I said. Surely — even though, as we both knew, governments monitored at random all overseas calls — he could say more than that.

"Would I wire thirty-two hotels if I didn't *have* to talk?"

Even with the bad connection, there was something I had not heard before beneath Surrett's brash, familiar voice. It was panic, or something like it.

"You can't do it on the phone?" I asked, just to be sure.

"No. Can you come home?"

"No," I said. If he forced me to, I would. I owed him too many debts not to.

249

"Okay, where?" he readily assented. "Not Italy. Or Greece."

That meant it had to do with Dylis or the Red Brigades. And it meant, since he was so willing to come to Europe, that he was going to impose on me heavily. When I made no suggestion, he said:

"Paris? Lobby of the George the Fifth tomorrow at five?"

"Make it the day after."

"You got to wind something up?" he asked.

"Yes." I didn't want to explain that it was already wound up, that I wanted that extra day so I could go to Paris slowly, by train, to use its relative leisureliness as a sort of decompression chamber.

"I'm happy for you, or sad, depending."

"Be happy," I said.

I rode the bike slowly back to the hotel. Maybe it wasn't the mob. Maybe it was some thief he had not been able to save who thought Surrett had sold him out to a prosecutor. Maybe it was some African dictator, worried about what Surrett had learned when the despot was his client. With Surrett, as with me, there were no limits to the potential assassins.

Soberly, richly tailored, Danny was in the ornate lobby when I got to the George V. He seemed controlled: his old self.

"I called Alexa," he said. "She's glad for the cards."

"Anything else?"

"Anne called me. I hadn't expected to talk with her . . ."

"And? . . ."

"She said to give you her best and to say the financial things were working out. In other words, no problems."

"Nothing else?" I thought of Anne and tested her against Silvia's fresh memory. Silvia came through as nourishment, like a mature, sweet pear. For Anne, my feeling was stronger and sharper: a rush of anger and a stab of yearning that things might have worked.

"You mean her and Brockman?" he asked judiciously.

"Yes."

"Well, the talk is that it's still on. How about your girl friend over here?"

"Too many complications."

"Well. Be glad it happened. Be glad Anne happened. Being in love with two good women isn't a bad record. I wish it had happened to me." He headed us out of the hotel.

Paris was at its worst: the evening rush hour and rain threatening. We talked of Hector, who was doing fine. When he had walked in the direction of the Seine for a few blocks, cutting down two narrow streets where we could look back and see no one was following, he finally said, "I've picked a place to talk. The cops over here bug you for practice. There isn't even a word in French for 'civil liberties.' "

At the next corner, we stopped close to the buildings and looked back to make sure we were clear. Then he guided me down one last street and into a small Anglican church.

"We'll look like a pair of praying British fags," he

251

said. He was obviously a little embarrassed by his precautions.

"Why take chances," I reassured him.

With a last look around the empty church, he began:

"The fucking Red Brigade thing has blown up in my face."

To my horror, he began to shiver like a stricken man. I grabbed him by the arm and looked in his face. It was fixed, almost frozen as he tried to get control of himself. He had held it all in up to then. Now, he had given in to his fear.

"Come out of this!" I grated at him, staring at him still. How odd this reversal, an uninvolved part of my mind observed. It is I who am telling Danny what to do, ordering him to do it, not the other way around. It had never happened before and I felt helpful, almost fulfilled by it. I kept my grip on his arm until he stopped trembling. "Now, from the top," I said.

Still, it was a minute or two before he could handle the facts, and even then, they came out with long pauses.

Surrett said that Calvacadi, when he visited, had promised Bernie to deliver nine kilos of fine cocaine for $500,000, far under the standard F.O.B. rate. If everything worked out, there would be more such lucrative deals in the future.

Shortly after I had left for Italy, Calvacadi brought the drugs to Magliorocco in a variety of containers.

". . . three bars of soap hollowed out and patched up, a urine retention bag on each leg, a

252

foam shave can, even a big plastic cigar tube up his ass." Surrett gave a snort of black laughter. "A traveling junk man!"

The cocaine, all nine kilos of it, was pure. It weighed out fine, even a little over. Magliorocco and Calvacadi embraced Italian style, swore undying friendship. The don, who had been totally upfront during the entire time, even drove Calvacadi to the airport and saw him off to New York, where the terrorist had a connection to Zurich. Now Surrett picked nervously at a worn Book of Common Prayer in the pew box.

"Next day, Bernie had his two best guys taking the stuff to the lab to be cut. At a light, this Calvacadi steps up to the car, puts a pistol into the open window, which never should have been open, and jumps in. He has them stash the stuff—in coffee cans by now—in a suitcase, takes their guns, all this as polite as a wedding. Then he kicks them out on the expressway, where who the hell is going to pick them up, and ditches the car at Thirtieth Street, where I guess he caught the first train out to wherever."

"This lone guy kidnapped all the cocaine?" It was incredible.

"Fast as you can say Lindbergh."

Magliorocco immediately got in touch with his Mafia allies in Italy who made contact with the Red Brigades. The negotiations between the Italian mob and the Brigades had gone on for more than a week when the Brigades suddenly broke them off. Three days later, Magliorocco learned that they had sold the cocaine to a German consortium.

That was when Magliorocco called Surrett and furiously blamed him for the mess. Not only did Bernie owe the $500,000 to mob bankers, but he had lost face. Danny, he said, had guaranteed Calvacadi's integrity and must find a way out for Magliorocco.

Danny immediately began to try to find me.

"Why don't you just come up with the half million and give Bernie free legal advice for the rest of your life?"

"That'd be about thirty days," he said. It wasn't just a matter of loss of face. If Bernie didn't get the money back from the Brigades or make some dramatic symbolic gesture like deep-sixing Danny, he'd seem an old fool to every mobster in America. The ruling patriarchs nationally would *want* him out. As an aged bleeding shark, Magliorocco would be unprotected against an efficient coup de grace. And Dylis's position would be stronger than ever, particularly if he could solidify some new loyalties in the Philadelphia mob.

"So you've got to get the money from the Brigades."

"Right."

"How do you know it's intact?"

Surrett said the Red Brigades had just pulled off a bank robbery in Turin. That and the money they got from the Germans would pay for their operations for a while. They probably wouldn't dip into the Mafia money until it was badly needed. Even they must have some apprehensions about the Mafia unifying against them.

"But if the money isn't intact?" I persisted. "If it's

spent?"

Surrett, in the dull light of the church, looked like a sick, elderly man. From the dark cavities of his eyes, the fear glittered.

"Then good-bye Danny, unless . . ."

"Unless I kill him."

If the money had been spent, or if Calvacadi were cornered and put up a fuss about relinquishing it, then Magliorocco's face and ultimately his life could be saved by Calvacadi's being murdered. That would put the Red Brigade (and the internal rivals hungering for Bernie's position) on notice that Magliorocco was not to be trifled with.

Furthermore, if the execution were done by an outsider, it would be Magliorocco's way of saying that the Brigades must not construe it as a declaration of war. With Bernie's face saved and with Surrett the instrument of it, Surrett could then be let off with repayment of the half million. The only irony would be if the Brigades decided to tie up the package by killing Surrett.

And if it was learned that I had helped carry out the killing of Calvacadi? Then the Red Brigades, like Dylis, would become my hunters. Right now, as long as I lay low, both my family and I were safe, I because Dylis did not know where I was, Anne and Alexa because even Dylis would not kill them without also killing me. He would not want a vengeful, resourceful enemy stalking the world for his blood, a man with nothing more to lose.

And yet I could not entirely let down Surrett, perhaps could not let him down at all.

"I will try to find him and get back the money," I

255

said. "But if it's gone, you've got to get somebody else to kill him."

Surrett was suddenly cold. I sensed fluttering between us something hideous, batlike. Even this oldest friendship could die if the stakes were high enough.

"It's not as if you haven't done things like this before," he said icily.

For the first time in my life, I looked without warmth at this trapped, aging man. But he was right. In my shooting of Dylis's three assassins I had made a lethal judgment call. Vividly I saw the little driver, eyes bulging, cawing as I aimed the pistol at his head. Yet even there, I had killed hot on the heels of an atrocious attempt on my life.

"No," I said at last to Surrett. "I can't kill a person like that. There'd have to be some kind of provocation. You've got to leave me a way out."

"Okay," he said stiffly. "Would you hold him long enough for me to get somebody to come and take him off your hands?"

"Oh, shit," I sighed at last. "I'll go that far, yes."

"Georgie," he said, relieved. "God knows I hate calling in these chips. But my life is on the line."

I nodded, also relieved, but only because we had repaired the sudden yawning crack in our friendship. Danny, even more than I, was immune from tears. But he was moved.

"I could be noble and not ask you to help . . ." he began.

"No, I'd do the same. I did do the same. Thirty years ago," I said, turning it away from the unusual emotion between us.

But what kind of gunsel was Danny really getting? There had been San Fruttuoso and Silvia to make me feel whole, but this new whole me had not been tested, particularly not in the way that Surrett was demanding. Indeed, my last two investigative efforts had ended up in my bungling the Dylis case and my landing in jail with a busted pate from snooping on my wife.

"You're putting your faith in a pretty weak reed," I said.

"We all blow one or two," said Surrett.

We were getting nervous about being in the church so long. The vicar might come in and ask us to join in evening vespers. Not that we both couldn't use them.

Hurriedly, we got down to the planning. There were the films and photos that he had brought with him and passed to me now from his inner pockets. A mob man in Italy had heard that Calvacadi had popped up in Venice two weeks after the robbery. But he had not been sighted since. The Mafia in Italy was keeping a lookout for him and was using its police sources to try to locate him. Bernie thought that Calvacadi had an aunt somewhere in the United States. If she could be traced, a gentle visit might be paid her to discover his habits and his whereabouts. None of this really helped much: it still left me infinities of Europe to search for this lone man.

We talked about my needs. During my quest, I didn't want my real name on the hotel slips required by the Italian police. That meant a false passport. I would also need a fake driver's license and other

I.D. papers in case I were stopped by some law-enforcement type.

First thing in the morning, we decided, I would get the passport photos taken. I had no contacts here, so it would be easier for Danny to get my documents tricked up in Philadelphia and sent back via an airline's one-day packet service. As to ready cash, Surrett had, equitably, brought twenty thousand in cash for me, which he had in his hotel.

"I want a gun," I said unhappily. "Two." I didn't like to think about needing pistols. Even less did I want to think about being without one if I did need it.

"I thought of that," said Surrett. He had brought a name and address for me.

"Where'd you get it?"

"Bernie."

"He's been pretty damned helpful to you considering he may have to kill you."

"He likes me," said Surrett, some of the cockiness coming back now he had me in the bag. "He's just disappointed."

"How much time have I got?"

"A month. Two months. Unless somebody challenges Bernie's authority before then or something else unforeseen happens."

"In which case?"

"In which case, yours truly will be the victim of a permanent injunction."

Suddenly, I was weary, hating what I would soon be doing, the return to my old life on a case that I did not think I could make. And if I did? Why, though it would save Danny Surrett, it would be transfusing half a million bucks back into the Mafia's poisonous bloodstream. Surrett understood it all, even, as I did, the insane irony of his suggesting I kill a man whose life I had saved only a short time ago — and saved on behalf of Surrett.

"I'm sorry, Georgie. Life has gotten so awful . . ."

"If I get the money, you drop the mob," I said. I was a little surprised to hear myself as Georgie Fraser, moralist.

"You don't drop them. They drop you and if you're lucky, you don't land in wet concrete. Don't put any strings on it, Georgie. I need help bad, but not advice."

On the way back to the George V, I asked him about Dylis. Surrett said he'd heard nothing new, only that Dylis was working busily on some unknown project in Europe.

"He'll be thinking about reinvesting in America," Surrett said gloomily, unable to get the thought of his drug debacle from his mind.

"Assuming he ever stopped," I said.

Buying illegal pistols in the frumpy, and now somewhat worn, clothes in which I had lived the last month was as unthinkable as going to a white-tie dinner in overalls. I spent 475 of Surrett's dollars on a navy-colored nubby (fake) silk suit, a long-collared shirt, a subdued (genuine) silk tie, and dressy moccasins, what the middle-class, middle-aged hoodlum would wear on assignment.

The address Surrett gave me on rue Pertinax was

an arch leading into a dank courtyard blocked off by high battered metal gates. An enamel sign said . . . onnez, the initial S flaked off down to the rusty metal. I "onnezed," and heard a gurgling buzz inside, a door open, and shuffling steps. Through the crack in the gates, an old woman asked, "*Qui est lá?*" obviously who I was or who I wanted to see.

I gave her the name 'Dahboud." She must have caught the accent, because she muttered and repeated belligerently, "*Qui est lá?*" I had not thought to buy a dictionary. "*Ami,*" I said hopefully, almost the outer limit of my French. After more muttering and a long wait, a younger woman's voice asked from behind the gate, "*Anglais?*"

"No," I said. "American." Desperate for communication, I said, "*Parla Italiano?*" There was a pause and I saw I was not going to get any Italian but that it had an effect.

"Italian?"

"No. American. *Ami degli Italiani.*" If he assisted the mob, it might help to start on the premise that I was in with the mob, which, by extension, I was. More thought, then:

"*Revenuz dans une heure.*" Well that was easy enough. *Una hora*—one hour. I sensed the young woman eyeing me as I went out the arch.

I was near the flea market. It was in full fester with forged paintings, counterfeit Russian icons, and skimpy European-made sweat shirts with the names of American universities. I instinctively transferred my wallet from hip to coat pocket. I wandered around until I found a book stall. There I bought a used French-English pocket dictionary and began looking up words. I found *pistol* and *bullet* but not *silencer*.

When I got back to rue Pertinax, I sensed I was being watched, but not from inside. I rang and waited. The old woman came, heard my voice, said, "*Un moment*," and then shuffled away. I sighed. I was home again, in a world where people assessed you—from keyholes, across one-hundred-dollar lunches, and always on the basis of what you were trying to wring from them and what they could wring from you.

I heard steps on the cobblestone behind me without surprise, and turned to see a dark, intelligent Arab face, a worn suit, a sparkling white shirt.

"Dahboud," he said, putting out his hand.

"Tresco," I said.

"Italian?" he asked, still in French.

"Italian-American," I said, meeting his dark eyes. He was forty-five to fifty-five, his voice harsh, guttural. He led me up two flights of stairs to his apartment. The young French woman served coffee and left. Dahboud leaned over the table and looked at me fixedly. "Passport," he said.

I quickly looked up in my French dictionary the words for "secret" and "job" and said them in what I hoped sounded like French. Dahboud nodded impassively, thought again, and took the dictionary.

After consulting it, he pointed to himself and said, "all risks," and pointed to me, shaking his finger negatively, "no risks."

In reply, using the dictionary, I said my boss in America had in deepest secrecy given me his name. He seemed flattered but wary, as if he did not want his name in the hands of powerful men whom he did not know.

He took the dictionary, found "if," and, to emphasize he was undecided, pronounced it several times, and, in our verbal-lexicological language, asked me what, exactly, it was I wanted. "If . . . if . . . if . . ." he repeated, liking the sound of the word as well as its hypothetical weight.

I told him pistols, one small, one large, and drew him pictures on a piece of note paper of a Colt Cobra, a small Beretta-like automatic, each with a silencer attached, and hollow-nosed cartridges.

"*Artiste,*" he said humorously, admiring the sketches. He pointed to the Colt and shook his finger negatively, but took my golden ballpoint, the only material remembrance of Anne I had taken with me, and sketched a big automatic, the kind I had seen on the French police. "Unique 7.65," he wrote under it.

"Okay," I told him. I would have greatly preferred an American revolver, a weapon I felt comfortable with. But I knew that getting the silencers either barrel-threaded or with adapters was going to mean taking pretty much what I could get. I picked up the scraps of paper, tore them to pieces, and glanced up. Impressed, he pointed me to the toilet.

When I came back, he had the look on him of a doctor about to give a new father good news. He had a fresh sheet of cheap paper in front of him.

"15.000 fr.," he wrote—about $2200. I rolled my eyes. The French police pistols had to be available in every big city in Europe. All he would have to do was file off the serials. Little automatics were easy

262

to come by. The silencers would be harder, but the package shouldn't cost that much.

Besides, he'd be suspicious if I accepted his outrageous figure.

"$500," I wrote. He quickly converted it in his mind to francs and looked at me. I saw the deep humor in those knowing, brown-black eyes. Did he realize that we were like an American tourist and a rug merchant in some Casbah? Maybe. He waved off the five hundred as contemptibly low, so low that I should write a second figure. I heard the woman in the kitchen and glanced that way cautiously. My pantomime, I was sure, was as important as my words. I wrote "$800" and he waved it off. I raised, now with a bit of irritation, one finger — $1,000. Dahboud was satisfied we had a deal cooking. He raised one finger, then two more — $1200. I nodded yes, mimed unhappiness, and counted out the money.

That settled, we fixed a rendezvous two days hence at a café on rue Cicada, two metro stops away, at 5:00 P.M. Then, he gathered up the new scraps of paper and went to flush them.

On the day I was picking up the guns, Surrett called me at the hotel before dawn and told me a packet was arriving at noon by Pan Am. Inside on his legal stationery was a cunning covering letter telling me that "Mr. Orsini's passport and other identification have been replaced," wishing Mr. Orsini well and billing him $628.50 for the trouble. Just in case French Customs had checked.

That afternoon, I got dressed up for my rendezvous in my Mafia suit again, but with a different tie and a new light fuchsia shirt. I was sick at heart that I was back in the traces, but nauseously excited.

I came up from the metro into an early November street scene. The shops were open, their awnings shielding the late-season vegetables and a few melons, probably from North Africa.

I rounded the corner of rue Cicada and found it deserted. Instantly, totally surprised, I felt a hard object jammed into the small of my back. In fragmented English, an unfamiliar voice hissed, "He go this way." The nudge of the barrel directing me into an alleyway clarified the misguiding pronoun.

"Why—"

"No talk," said the voice, recognizably Arabic, though not Dahboud's. "No turn." The gun was steady, the grip on my arm firmly warning me with its vigor.

The alley stank of urine and garbage. I was angry more than frightened, conniving more than immobilized. This guy would be some Arab who had learned of my presence and wanted my money and maybe my life. Dahboud was too cagey to be involved in anything like this. He would not double-cross "*gli Italiani*," especially with his name known to them.

The gunman pressed the pistol even harder into my back as I tensely sought evidence of any fissure in his self-confidence, any flaw that would cue me to go for his gun. I would not die like some stockyard beast. He fumbled with something in his coat pocket. A blindfold? What the hell was going on?

A paper bag, from the sound of it, had come out of his pocket. Now would be the time to turn on him, but he was too close for me to maneuver. I felt him poke the bag at my left hand.

"Take," he said simultaneously. I felt my bladder give a bit with relief.

"Helluva way to make a delivery," I said. I took the bag in my fingers.

"No talk; no turn," said the gunman with a last jab, and fast as a squirrel darting at a tree, he was gone around the corner. I fingered the bag, felt the two main objects, plus other smaller things.

Dahboud was a quality merchant and a clever one. In waylaying me with his delivery, he insured that if I were a police plant or if the café were staked out, his man would not be in jeopardy. I was sure someone had followed me at a long distance from the subway to make sure I was not under surveillance by the police or anyone else. Thinking about how few of us in our common business did things that well anymore, I wished I had discovered a Dahboud or two in the days when I needed people like him.

I flew to Genoa, purposely avoiding Milan and thus the temptation of Silvia. When I got to my hotel in Rapallo, I found an express package from her at the desk. I opened it on the elevator.

It was a Morocco-bound collection of Leopardi's poems printed on thick, creamy paper. She had put the thin gold cloth page marker to a poem. In my room, without taking off my coat, I read it. She had underlined several verses in light pencil:

> . . . di piacer, quel tanto
> Che per mostro e miracolo talvolta

With the dictionary, I roughed it out: "Rapture, born by some freakish miracle from troubles, is life's great benefit . . ."

What was she saying? That we should go back together and reap those benefits again? Or was it a final statement of accounts? More likely she had chosen the equivocal poem precisely in order to leave the choice up to me. But I had no choices now. Surrett's mission had turned me to sterner things.

In the morning, I went into the hills above Sant' Ambrogio and checked out the French police pistol and the little automatic, a Beretta 950. Both silencers fit perfectly and hushed the muzzle noise to discreet "thwats." Both guns fired true.

I boxed my excess clothes, my sketches, and, reluctantly, the book Silvia had given me. I wanted nothing in Venice that I could not leave behind if I had to flee. When I had shipped the big box homeward to Surrett and thriftily sold my bike back to the shop, I returned to the hotel and dyed my hair dark brown. I would do the same with the beard I intended to grow. The passport's black-and-white photo would not be thrown off by the color change. If I had to face off with a bad guy in Venice, I did not want the real me fixed in his memory.

I took one last look southward from my balcony. The land toward the Cinque Terre was splashed with fall color. Far beyond the misty cape was Monterosso. I thought of Silvia. Even without this new burden, I would not have gone to her. Our bedroom was not the world and neither was Leopardi. I would have gone to Venice or Greece and on and on until the rhythms I had begun to hear in myself told me what to do.

In that sense, Surrett's assignment had simplified things for me. I was in no mood to chase a terrorist, but I knew I had damned well better get in the mood if I didn't want my kneecaps, or worse, shot off. The job gave me no choice but to get back into the game I had begun more than twenty-five years ago. It was a game where failure would cost my friend his life. And if I succeeded, it was in a line of work I now detested. Either way, it was as definite as a prison sentence.

XV.
SEARCH IN VENICE

On the way to Venice, I laboriously read articles in Geno's *I Secolo XIX* and the *Corriere* on a Red Brigades in *Panorama,* the Italian news magazine.

In Venice, I studied a map at the station and chose a hotel on Campo San Geremia. It was a square through which anyone walking between the station and northwest Venice's working-class district would be almost sure to pass.

The lobby, clean and Victorianly cheerful sported a pale gold plush chair and love seat, green and ivory wallpaper, a marble chip floor, and two English-looking horse pictures. Just the place for an unassuming gentleman to park himself and his two heaters while he hunted down a terrorist.

I did not venture a word to the clerk in Italian, lest it lead to conversation. I wanted only to be the unobtrusive American in a third-floor front room.

That first day, I rounded out my hunting gear: high-powered binoculars, an overpriced Japanese projector for the films Surrett had provided me, lead-shot weights and a heavy canvas remnant for a homemade sapper. I went through the few routine things I could do that might reduce my odds from two million to one to a million to one. Posing as a free-lance writer, I got a clerk at *Il Gazzettino,* the local paper, to let me read the morgue files on the Red Brigades.

There had been only two recent incidents in Venice, a good reason for Calvacadi to be here—a city where he would not be sought. On one of the two shootings, there had been an arrest. I checked the Venetian address of the suspect. The landlady at the cheap *locanda* said the young man had come from out of town, Bologna, she thought. No, he had never had visitors. I risked showing her a picture of Calvacadi. No, she said, she had never seen him before.

I could not check police records; I could not show my still shots to bank guards, post office clerks, hotel registrars, or others who might produce a clue. Any one of them might somehow alert my target.

I could not go to the right-wing terrorist enemies of the Red Brigade for help. They, too, might wonder why a middle-aged American with fast, but limited, Italian was looking for a Red Brigadist, and one whose name or picture might have a special meaning.

I looked at the movies of the terrorist until I had rememorized every motion of his body. A hundred times, I saw him walk toward me from the plane's exit. A hundred times, I saw his shoulders bobbing as he walked down the corridor with that odd bounce from ball of foot to toe. A hundred times, I saw him enter Surrett's bathroom and stare intently at his pimple before assaulting it.

I knew I would recognize his gait if I saw it on a seventy-year-old woman or on a man walking on the moon.

From the still photos and the movies, I sketched how his face would look with different kinds of face hair, no face hair, with dyed hair, with loss of weight, with almost everything but an eyebrow shave. I would know his face if the most ingenious makeup man in the world altered it.

I became in those first days of November a tourist little heeding the church façades and monuments, the vistas of canal and lagoon, the shop windows with their glass baubles, their rich gold-etched leather.

I looked only in the faces of young men—did they think me a lonely foreign homosexual? On a whim, I sought him in the archaeological museum. I saw his features in a statue of young Caracalla, lightly moustached, cruel, strong, and sensitive, the statue's hair, like Calvacadi's, close-curled to his head.

From dawn to nightfall, which came sooner and sooner with the approach of winter, I walked. I searched the Fondamente Nuove, which looked out into the lagoon, the nondescript samenesses of the Rio della Sense apartments, so much like a Camden housing project, the worker warrens, redolent of garlic and bad plumbing on the satellite islands of La Giudecca, Burano, and Murano.

On good days, clothes strung between houses flapped high above the cobbles: sheets, bright shirts, even washed plastic bags as colorful as yacht pennants spelling out messages. But none signaled me to Calvacadi.

I spent a day combing Chioggia — once a Venetian colony — surprised after the totality of my submersion in Venice to see cars and motorcycles again. I ate late at cheap restaurants, furtively scanning the patrons.

Other days, I sat at my window, binoculars to my eyes. When no men were passing I watched the girls in tight pants, the pigeons, the old women at the square's flower stall. As I gazed, I practiced my Italian aloud, finding words for the shades of the walls of buildings colored like the hides of ancient elephants. In that watchtower, I was like a hopeless explorer who waited for the Abominable Snowman or the Sasquatch to knock on his door and say, "Here I am."

I thought often of Sylvia, sometimes of Anne (with a mixture of desire and anguish). But when these images turned toward prurience, I banished them from my mind, shifted into neutral.

Sometimes my imagination built pipe dreams around Calvacadi. I endowed him with parents — a middle-class doctor and wife; with an education — prelaw; with a girl friend as hard as he. I imagined where he had been to school, near San Rocco; where he had vacationed as a youth, the Tyrol and San Remo; what he smoked, drank, even how he made love and whether he was true to his Stalinesque girl friend.

I practiced random encounters with him, saw myself meeting him, trapping him in his house, forcing him to take me where the money was. I urged him to be reasonable and to take back Magliorocco's message of peace to his colleagues, argued doctrine with him, parted peaceably with him, rancorously with him, even, in my darkest thoughts, parted murderously with him despite what I had insisted to Surrett I could not do.

Each day, after the mail reached the main post office, I checked to see whether a wire had reached me at *fermo posta* — general delivery — asking me to call Surrett, or a letter with some hint to aid my search or an instruction to seek Calvacadi in Parma, or Bari, or Sicily . . .

On the twelfth day, I got a cable from Surrett at general delivery, appropriately cryptic: "my exchange 4841. time your family census number. filly afternoon. no luck day. cheers. vitale." Most of it unscrambled easily.

He was telling me to call his telephone exchange plus 4821, probably a pay phone near his office. He wanted the call in the afternoon Philadelphia time. It was vital. The "family census" stalled me until I related them to a time, realized he meant our number: three. What day? "No luck day." Friday the thirteenth. But there was no Friday the thirteenth this month, ergo, this Friday.

I called him from the telephone room in the main post office on Fondaco dei Tedeschi. It was a busy, anonymous place, a little like a small, crowded bus station. Rucksacked kids chatted with the certainty of kids abroad — an American or two, some Swedes, a clutch of loud German youths.

"Any luck?" Surrett asked, not wasting any time

272

on small talk. I knew the National Security Agency had a system where certain words actuated their monitoring recorders. I'd never believed the damned things worked. But the Italians probably tuned in on overseas calls, too. All foreign intelligence services did. At least the Mafia and Red Brigades weren't into the automatic transatlantic telephone eavesdropping business. Not yet, anyway.

"Not a crumb," I answered. I thought of him by the pay phone, downcast as a losing bookie. But, no, his voice came back strongly, full of urgent hope.

"Okay, I have something. If what I say isn't clear, say so and I'll find another way of telling you." He went on, not waiting for any acknowledgment. "There's a son, about six, in the main kids' hospital there, on Fondamenta dei Riformati"—he started to spell it, but I cut him off. I'd passed it in my meanderings. "He's got leukemia," Surrett went on. "Our friend sends money to an aunt, rather an aunt-in-law, in Saint Louis, and she sends it to the hospital." So they'd located the aunt and bullied the information out of her.

"Will she tell him that your pals have visited her?"

"No." He paused. "You might say they put her on notice," he added dryly. So they'd threatened to kill her if she talked.

"I hate this," I said.

"I know." He sounded morose now. "Do I have to tell you what your doing this means to me?"

"No. What else?"

"He is sending her mostly fifties and twenties and she's sending it there in cash. It's not our money."

"At least not as acquired."

"Yes," he agreed.

"Is he seeing the kid?"

"I don't know."

"Don't those idiots have anybody over here I can work with?"

"They don't want to have anything to do with it over there."

"So I'm supposed to walk up to some guy and say, 'Hi, doctor, could I lay on you this wad in exchange for a little info?' "

"I know what you're up against," he said conciliatingly.

"Anything more?"

"Not much. The aunt thinks the mother's dead, doesn't know anything about her anyway except that they never got married."

"So there's nobody except him taking care of the kid?"

"Auntie thinks not but isn't sure."

"How long has she been sending money?"

"Eight months."

"So the kid—"

"Is crippled somehow, in other words—"

"He's dying slowly? . . ."

"It sounds like it."

"Anything more on our hero?"

"The local cops over there have told their counterparts here"—that would be the FBI—"that nobody in his family knows where he is. They don't disown him. Christ, it looks like some of the people over there think of these guys as Robin Hoods. The Italian locals have been sitting on the family, the father is a dentist."

Surrett had really shaken down his pals at the FBI for that kind of information. Passing on stuff from overseas police was genuinely verboten in the FBI, even for old-time contacts like Surrett.

"You'll be in the bag to our federal friends for the rest of your life."

"That may not be long," he observed unhappily.

"Is that it?"

"I think that's everything."

"Anything on anybody else?" I meant Anne, as he would know.

"She hasn't filed, if that's what you're asking. I'm having Wertleim"—my divorce lawyer—"stall with promises of sugarplums."

"But . . ." Were she and Brockman still lovers? It still bugged me.

"Yeah, it's sill on as far as the gossip goes." He dropped the subject. "Alexa called me. She wants to write you. Why anybody'd miss a—"

"What'd you tell her?"

"—an out-of-work failed gumshoe is more than I know. I told her I didn't know exactly where you were."

"Pop?"

"The same as he was. I go to see him every week or so."

"Bless you, Danny," I said, choking up.

At the hotel, I let the sunshine fall on the big

street map and studied the area around the hospital. Then I went by vaporetto to the stop nearest the hospital. As we passed it by sea, I saw high walls, a garden, the top of several buildings. Somewhere in that complex of old structures was Calvacadi's son.

The hospital itself was at the far end of the Fondamenta dei Riformati, a dead-end street beside which ran a modest canal. Next to the hospital was a chapel and monastery and next to these were old two- and three-story homes now broken up into apartments. On the other side of the canal, also commanding a view of the hospital entrance, was a five-story apartment building with small balconies.

The cluster of hospital, chapel, canal, the fading rusts and yellows of the mid-rise apartment, the houses' diverse mix of brickwork, iron balustrades, square and gothic windows, all backgrounded by the tower of Madonna dell' Orto, made a low-key but attractive composition. I brought my pastels to the Fondament dei Riformati and did three breezy, sun-brightened sketches, throwing in an imagined work gondola loaded with vegetables. Vintage Fraser kitsch!

Sketchbook under my arm, I went to the door of the house whose windows offered the most direct view of the hospital entrance. The brass bell plates showed there were six apartments in the dwelling.

I rang a first-floor apartment, got no answer, tried another. The door buzzed and I opened it. A suspicious-looking matron peered into the first-floor hallway at me. In my best Italian, trying to look like the mildly eccentric, well-to-do tourist which part of me still was, I told her I was seeking an apartment for two to six weeks. I was, I said, an American artist, an amateur, who had found the area among the most picturesque in Venice.

Who in Venice does not think that of their part of town? I flipped through my three sketches. As I expected, they caught her interest, particularly the one that showed her own house.

"Yes," she said. "Lovely. Here we are," she pointed to the house.

"Take it," I said. "It is only a sketch." I signed it "W.B. Orsini" with a dramatic swoop of my ballpoint and tore it from the sketchbook.

"I'm going to frame it," she said. Conquest: she invited me in.

My new friend, Signore Colpo, was sure there was no one in her building leaving for a week anytime soon. But she got on the telephone and, undaunted by failures in the next two best-located dwellings, finally found a friend in a third who had a friend . . .

With Signore Colpo paving the way ("Yes, very presentable . . . an American artist . . ." I heard her say), arrangements were made for me to have coffee that evening with a couple who were visiting their son and daugher-in-law in Switzerland soon. Their third-floor apartment was in one of the buildings across the canal.

The elderly husband was a retired accountant from a shipbuilding firm in Mestre, a Venetian suburb. They wanted $400 a week and a $200 deposit.

I paused, not wanting to appear suspiciously spendthrift, but they showed no hesitation whatsoever about appearing conspicuously greedy. They had originally arranged with a neighbor child to take care of their plants and their canary. So they were taking a profit not just on my lodging but on my horticultural and ornithological services. I struck the deal but out of justified spite did not give them one of my sketches.

In the morning, dressed in my spiv suit but with casual shoes and a soft conservative open shirt to make myself look less like an off-duty croupier. I visited the hospital and asked to see the administrator. I hoped my restrained manner, my American accent, and my air of unspent money would get me past the lower hired help, where most of those in the waiting room seemed stuck.

I waited among the pharmaceutical hustlers and the relatives of the ailing until a trim, handsomely bosomed woman of about thirty-five sashayed into the reception room. She introduced herself to me as Maria Tennaro, an assistant administrator, and ushered me down a hall and into her cubicle. It was tastefully decorated with posters and framed photographs of what looked like Byzantine illuminated manuscripts.

Signora Tennaro, for I spotted the wedding ring, might be the lowest-ranking assistant administrator or might not be. But I was sure she was the best looking. With confusion, I realized she had caught my glance at her ring.

"You are Italian-American, Mr. Burnham"—the name I had plucked up from an old friend. "You speak such good Italian."

"No, but thank you. You are busy. I will be brief."

"No, no," she said, meaning "yes, yes."

I was ready with my yarn. My father, I recounted, was a war-relief specialist in Venice with the U.S. Army after World War II. He and my mother had an apartment not far from the hospital. I often played in the playground near the hospital, and one day I foolishly climbed the hospital wall, fell off, and broke my leg.

Signora Tennaro looked mildly curious and sympathetic, but also ready for me to get on with it.

"There was much blood," I said, but did not know the word for "compound break," so indicated it with a snapping motion of my two hands. "My friends ran to the hospital. I was brought into these very buildings and a doctor stemmed the bleeding and treated me with sulfa. Such was the break that to wait until I could be taken to an American specialist at Leghorn might have meant I would be crippled. Your doctors set the bone carefully. When I was finally taken to Leghorn, the doctor told my father he had never seen such a fine setting of a bad break."

Somewhat to her surprise, I stamped my right leg on the floor.

"Solid as good wood," I said. "All these years! I played football in college." I had her hooked.

I told her I had picked up a good deal of Italian, as children do, while I was here and had made a study of it in school back in America. Thus, fortunately, I could tell her in my language of choice — she smiled appreciatively at that — why I was here. She smiled more broadly.

"I would like to make a small gift — a thousand dollars," I said, "but with complete anonymity."

279

"Che generosità!" she burst out, a break in the cool, if kind, reserve she had shown up to now. *"Che generosità."* Clearly, she had expected no more than a couple of hundred.

"It is nothing," I said. "The hospital gave me a leg and perhaps my life. That life has been far better to me than I have deserved. My gift is too little; would I could give more at this time."

I took from my pocket an envelope of twenties and fifties and gave it to her without now having the impertinence to look into her eyes.

"Veramente generoso," she reiterated, then in English: "Thank you! Thank you! Only an American would remember." Now I felt like a thoroughgoing skunk. At the same time, I had been moved myself by my story of the "Good American," and even by my, well, Surrett's generosity. When the gratitude level lowered slightly, I said: "I have only one tiny request if you are not too busy." My tone said it would not be hard to fulfill. I asked if she could give me a quick tour of the hospital, perhaps to where I had been taken that day, if the emergency room still existed.

"Of course," she said, other duties generously forgotten. She rose and I caught a whiff of her light, costly perfume. I pushed back my predatory thoughts.

The gravel path from the administrative offices to the patients' buildings wound under tall pines and poplars. The hedges' leaves were still glossy even this late in the year, and within their borders, fading ivy ran to the feet of rosebushes whose roses had long blown.

Inside the hospital proper, the green and white walls were spotlessly clean. But the repainted chipped doorframes, the repaired wheelchairs, the antiquity of the beds all were evidence of need.

I wished now I had donated $2,000 of Surrett's money. If I succeeded, it would benefit him many times over. If I failed, he wouldn't need it where he was going.

I followed the purposeful swing of Signora Tennaro. She stopped in a small curtainless room with built-in closet and a big round bulb on the high ceiling above the examination table.

"Here is where your leg was probably set," she said.

"It was so long ago. I can't remember," I said.

"You were not thinking then about decor," she finished, smiling.

I saw parents visiting children in several rooms. Yet the hours had said visiting only between 1500 and 1600 hours. When I asked her, she said visitors to the seriously ill were allowed in at any hour.

I tried to look impressed with the kindness and efficacy of this system. But my stomach fell. What it meant was that I would have to keep watch on the hospital entrance during virtually all the daylight hours and up until eight or nine at night.

Down the hall, there was a sudden silence and I felt before she said it that in these rooms were the dying. Through an open door, I could see the first bed. Sunlight streaked across an immaculately white sheet raised so slightly by the form beneath it that I could hardly believe even a child was there.

"This child," she whispered, trying to put it into

simple Italian, "has bones turning to calcium, like chalk." Calcification. I recalled from somewhere a picture of a wasted child whose eye sockets were calcifying, forcing the eyes to bug from his head. I did not want to see this child.

"It is those with such lingering illnesses who most touch one," I said.

"Would you rather not visit this wing?"

"No, it would be to such children that I would wish my small gift to go." She clucked noncommittally. The money, I knew, should go into the general fund where it belonged. "I had not intended to mention it," I said, measuring the lie out carefully, "but I had a nephew who died of leukemia. Part of the tragedy was that in the end, his friends avoided him, as if they might catch his death."

"Such a death is doubly sad," she said with a tremor in her voice.

I realized that Signore Tennaro was very much a pussycat. Feeling ever more the rat, I went on:

"It left him unable to walk at the last. He was in the hospital for his final three months. I yearned over his loneliness."

"Yes," she said. "We have similar cases." She swung her head to a partially open doorway to our left.

There, like an elongated rag doll beneath the sheets, lay a child. His closed lids were so much darker than his face. A large furry brown bear was beside him, its glass button eyes alertly staring as if guarding him while he slept.

The child was beautiful in his terrible dying. The slender fingers of one hand lay on the coverlet, their

282

tiny trembling the only evidence of life, for his chest scarcely moved, such small respiration was needed for that wasted body.

Did I see in this delicate near-death mask a juvenile tracing of the face I had put on paper when I imagined my target as emaciated? Was that nose a childish version of Calvacadi's, the wisp of bloodless lips the shadow once removed of Calvacadi's unexpectedly sensitive mouth, the cameo oval of this dying child's face the miniature of my quarry's well-shaped head, the fine, pink fragile hair simply too exhausted to generate the healthy red pigment of his father's thatch?

And then, more sharply, I saw in this pallor my father's serene whiteness. Like the child, part of him was already in the world of death and each day more of him slipped over the boundary. I felt the tears almost surge behind my eyes. I must see the old man again. What in Christ's name was I doing here?

I gasped, dizzied by the mystery of things. From my reaction, Signora Tennaro perceived a sympathy that I felt passionately, but whose complexities would have astonished and distressed her.

Outside the brick red building and in the garden again, she turned to me and spoke softly, her breath touched with garlic. The homely smell made her the more desirable, physically humanizing her just as the word *generoso* had done psychologically.

"The little boy . . ." she said. "The pale child . . ."

"Yes," I said, my heart throbbing. "He seemed so . . ." I looked for the perfect word that would unlock the child's secret.". . . *lontano*"—far away.

"Just so," she said. She started to name the disease, but with her perfect sensibility she said instead, ". . . the affliction of your nephew. We have had him ten months now." I gulped, steadied myself in the gravel path from a second moment of dizziness. The kind of treachery I was indulging in might not have shaken me a year ago. Now it did. Again she mistook—how could she not—the reason for my emotion. "We keep hoping that one of the new drugs . . ." We walked on past statues of Italian kings who had visited the old hospital. Beyond the wall were the sound of the lagoon, ship and gull.

"Could he not be treated at home?" I asked.

"He has no home. It is unusual." I could feel in her now some reticence. I plucked up my queasy guts and brazened.

"His mother?. . ."

I could see her about to risk it. After all, was I not a benefactor and one not likely to return? "No. But an aunt, another example," she blushed slightly, "of American generosity."

"Ah?" I said, pleased, interested, and sick with myself.

"His aunt in Missouri," she put the accent on the second syllable more emphatically than it belonged, "sends us money from time to time."

"But his parents?"

She shook her head.

"Who can say. The original note from the aunt simply said money would come. We know it is from

Missouri only by the postmark."

"How did he get here?" I asked.

"That is the unusual aspect. It must not be repeated, Signore Burnham."

"Who would I repeat — but if it makes you feel uncomfortable."

"No, no," she assured me. "With such a case in your family . . . At least the child had the consolation of his loved ones, but this boy was abandoned." I gasped and she nodded. "Literally. As in a book. He was carried in by a man, an old man. The child was in blankets and was put on a bench in our waiting room. The old man excused himself and never reappeared."

"He left a sick child? Disappeared?"

"Yes. We examined the child. He had the symptoms, you know, a very high white count, feverish. The tests were conclusive. We contacted the police, but what could they do? The child knew his name. Giuseppe Bruno." She shrugged, it would be like Joseph Brown in America. "He came from Milan. He did not know why he was in Venice. It was a case, pure and simple, of abandonment."

"But you admitted him. You care for him."

"Of course."

"As you would," I said, more passionately than I intended.

"Generous man," she said, the warmth breaking through.

"And the aunt's donations? . . ."

"Have come four times, with a note saying they were for the Bruno child."

"And never a visit, never a word from the old

man?" Had I played it right, understating? My apprehension that she would dodge the question must have made my real concern over the child seem all the more genuine. She looked quickly around her. We had stopped in our tour. On the horizon over the wall, there was, faintly in the blue sky, gray smoke from the glass furnaces of Murano.

"I should not tell you this." I held my breath. "Three times, the first time after three months, then in three more months, and then six weeks ago, a young man came to see the child."

"A young man? . . ."

Like so many officially reserved people, Signore Tennaro, now that she had captured a commiserative and harmless ear, gave discretion a rest.

"Feigning indifference, saying an aunt in the United States had sent him to see a cousin's child and to report to her."

"My God, it's like some terrible mystery. You say 'feigned.' Pretended?"

"I was not in the room, but the nurse notified me and I came and asked him if he could not tell us more about the child. He grew upset and irritable. He said if he had known he was going to be interrogated, he would not have obliged his aunt. It was unpleasant."

"But he came again?"

"Yes, bringing the teddy bear. I did not see him. We had thought of having the police question him. The aunt's money, of course, does not cover his care. But our chief administrator felt that if we called in the police, we would probably get no money and would only discourage the visitor from coming back." I breathed deep, and cut in:

"The visitor is the child's father," I said. "Is that not what you believe?" She gasped, then recovered.

"You are a perceptive man, Signor Burnham. Yes, that is precisely what I think. I will tell you why: I saw him in the room with the child on the third visit. He is in love with the child, the more so as the end draws near." I began to feel weepy. The imminence of the child's death would bring Calvacadi to me almost any day if the pattern of visits continued. I thought of the poor kid, a pallid pawn, oblivious as a chessman to the game I played.

"And the child? . . ."

Now, to my dismay, I saw tears in Maria Tennaro's eyes.

"Worships the man, lives for his visit. I know you will think it sounds melodramatic. The child obviously does not know the man is his father. We believe, he had been left with someone else in his early childhood, probably with a false name. The disease has brought them together. It is horrible and yet . . ."

She paused, unable to go on. And suddenly, I realized how close to the surface my own feelings had gotten these past ten, eleven months. I could not go on either. Oh shit, I thought. What am I doing in this mess?

I snatched out my wallet. I had $100 in lire and another $350 in fifties and twenties with me. This time it was going to be my money.

"Here's what I've got on me," I said impulsively, tremblingly jerking out the bills. "Spend it on the boy." I had been shattered by what I had seen and heard and what, in my deceit, I had done, and I knew the money would buy me only a limited relief from self-hate.

"I can't," she stammered, surprised by my vehemence. "You have already—"

"Please," I said. "Please don't argue. I cannot stand the pain anymore." What I really couldn't stand was further deceiving this good and beautiful woman whose silken blouse adequately hid neither her breasts nor her heart.

"Thank you," I said, "for the goodness of this hospital and yourself. Please excuse my . . ." I could not find the word I sought. "Rapture," I said, meaning to have said its cousin, "foolishness."

With that, I hurriedly shook her hand, looked anguishedly into her startled eyes, and ran from the garden and out of the hospital. The moment I was outside, I knew my outburst had gone against all wisdom. If Calvacadi visited his son, and if Signore Tennaro let drop that an American had singled out the child for that second gift, then it would alert him, would make my catching him impossible. He would find some back way out, through an old door in the real wall, or over it, for that matter.

Why had I done something so unprofessional? Because of the clash between my conscience and the case? When had my conscience begun to get a grip on me? It has surely been moribund while I peddled guns and private-eyed. Or had it been growing, benignly seeping into the amorality of those years? I grunted grimly. It was no compliment to me that I had only thought of morality after I had made a bundle.

I walked rapidly, paying no heed to the turnings I took, the bridges I crossed. Whatever the first cause of my conscience, it was giving me hell right now. Immovably, it told me that using the child to trap this man was monstrous. Calvacadi might be rotten. But the terrorist's unquenchable devotion to his son was unarguably good. And this singular good in him was my sole bait.

Danny Surrett was the rub. His fate was also a matter of conscience. Could I really say, "No, I will not use the child to catch the father"? To so indulge myself was to commit Surrett to execution, a default by me on a lifetime obligation.

I groaned as I walked. There was no moral course. There was only a course that was less immoral than the other. And that was the one I was unhappily taking.

Now that I believed Calvacadi would visit again, I dared not be away from sight of the hospital entrance between 7:00 A.M. and 9:00 P.M. I dared not even leave it unwatched during the three days before I moved into my new home.

There was no café where I could sit watching while I drank coffee and read all day, nor a park bench where I could laze and observe.

But men regularly fished the canal. I brought cheap worker's clothes, ran them through a Laundromat, purchased fishing gear, and then, at the hotel, cut off the right pant pocket. I shaved my right thigh and taped to its inside the small automatic, which I called "Little Frog." I kept the

289

French police pistol, "Big Frog," in my fishing gear bag. From steps that descended from the street to the canal, I could throw out my line and, more or less concealed, watch the hospital entrance.

At first, I felt optimistic about capturing Calvacadi. The feeling lasted even after I moved into the apartment. There I breakfasted at my window after shopping at dawn in the market. I no longer visited the post office, but the general delivery clerk obligingly went through the mail when I called once a day. There was nothing.

When no one was coming up the street, I read the *International Herald Tribune* and the Italian papers. I was getting long on vocabulary but remained short on grammar. At noon, I munched cheese, fruits, cold meats, bread, and drank mineral water. I did calisthenics, still watching.

Only in the evening did I relax. At 9:00 P.M. I untaped the automatic (which I retaped each morning) and sallied out to eat. Then I walked sometimes until midnight to augment my calisthenics and to unwind. When possible, I bought a ticket to La Fenice, the jewel-box Venetian concert hall, always missing the first part of the program.

Once, I took a late-night trip to Bologna to try to break the motonony, ate a midnight meal at the station, and sent a card to Alexa. On the way back from Bologna, obsessed again with the case, I looked at the faces on the dimly lit train.

As the days went by, I came to know the hospital's regulars. I fleshed out their lives, the ills of their children. The grandmotherly woman would have a pocketful of candy; the nurse would be in love with one of the doctors; the young couple with a child in a buggy were getting a checkup for his inflamed throat.

Several times, with an anxious mix of guilt and futile want, I saw Signora Tennaro. When she was out of sight, I was washed over by a sort of loathing for myself, of anger at Calvacadi.

I imagined Calvacadi in Venice, waiting, like me, his lean face absorbed in Mao or Lenin. I imagined him, too, nervously shopping, hastily eating during the day, daring to go freely only at night. Were his days, like mine, becoming a tedious and neurotic prison, each one another twenty-four hours stolen from our lives?

With little hope, I waited for a single figure to materialize from morning fog, or noon sun, or twilight drizzle. I fabricated in my mind a bouncy walk, a face that when magnified by my binoculars would be his.

On my seventeenth day by the hospital, heavy winds and black clouds rushed in from the lagoon at sunset. Soon the first raindrops hit my windows, making splashes big as tea saucers. In the canal, a commercial gondolier left his oar to pull a tarpaulin over his crates of chickens. Far down the street, a shopkeeper dragged in his baskets of fruit. Two women, one young, one old, stepped up their walks in the gloom like soldiers ordered into double time. Then, as suddenly, the deluge gave way to steady but lighter fall.

"Hup," I said aloud. Across the bridge a long block down from me, a figure in fisherman's yellow slicker and woolen watch hat came with familiar gait. I snapped up the field glasses. I could see no features except for a black beard. But the carriage of the head, the odd bounce were Calvacadi's. I watched him enter the hospital. The rough cylinders of the field glasses were wet with sweat.

I cursed the rain. In decent weather, people on the street would have provided cover for me to follow him to his home. Impossible now. But I had planned for any eventuality. I would force him down an alleyway at whose end was a lot cluttered with trash: a broken boat on a saw horse, discarded household appliances.

I threw on my trench coat with the Unique in one pocket, a nylon rope, heavy handkerchief, plastic merchandise bag in another. I paused a few seconds, checked the overcoat for the sapper, found it there, and left.

Running down the stairs, I felt my heart bump and I gasped for breath, not from the exertion, but the excitement. I took up a station in a doorway opposite the rear exit of my apartment. It gave me a view, if limited, of the hospital street. The rain pelted down, wetting my shoes, which I tried to edge into the doorway with the rest of me.

In my pocket, I clicked the larger pistol's safety off and on, then took it out furtively to make sure still another time. Through the pant pocket hole I checked the safety on Little Frog. I pulled my hat down. Wind was gusting the rain now and my lower legs were getting sopped.

I looked back at the hospital. What was this? The man was already coming out. What the hell had happened? I tensed against the wall. He was at the bridge.

After a quick look around, I slid into the oblique rain. There was no one else on the street.

The man was no more than twenty feet away. When I was just behind him, he turned. In the murk, I could not see his face well, only a beard, a certain roughness of feature, eyes open wide in surprise. No streetlight lit my deed. I clutched his wet slicker front and pulled his body to mine as if in some bizarre rape. I poked the big silenced gun under his chin.

"Your money!" I said in Italian. "Not a word!"

He grunted in fear, turning his head to look for help, but I pressed the pistol harder, feeling his bulk beneath the clutched slicker. This guy was too damned big. He wheeled his head, this time toward the faint light from the windows across the canal. I started with raw horror. The pistol dropped from his chin in my limpened hand, my left hand releasing his slicker as if it had burned me.

I had the wrong man. I saw the differences the darkness had concealed. The face was older, the cheekbones lower than those I had sketched so many times, the nose strong, yes, but irregular instead of straight. His face, riveleted by rain, twisted into anger. I ducked away from him, sick with self-repugnance, and thrust the gun into my pocket. I loped toward the bridge, where I could plunge into the mazes of Venice away from my dwelling, where I could get lost in rain and serpentine alleys.

My victim recovered his voice as I took the bridge steps two at a time.

"You are not even Italian!" he shouted.

293

I ran. He did not follow. The pistol, of course, would account for that. He also did not scream for police. Perhaps, like me or Calvacadi, he had reason not to seek them out. Or maybe he knew that at the best of times, police cases meant entanglements with courts and lawyers.

I slowed to a jog. The few passersby would assume I was running someplace for shelter. I was far from the hospital area now, fairly near the Riva degli Schiavoni. The rain, whipped by the northwest wind, was biting cold. My shoes and trouser legs below the coat were waterlogged. At last, breathless, I stopped, and stepped in under a church portico.

As soon as the discomfort of wind and rain had lifted slightly, the flood of shame swept in. "Uhhh," I grunted aloud, hit by the same shock of failure I had felt on the Dylis case. My God, how could I have let my obsession lead me to see Calvacadi in that stranger?

I plunged back into the rain and headed circuitously home. Shivering, shoes in hand to limit the mess, I went quickly to the bathroom and turned on the tub taps. While I waited, I sat in despair on the toilet cover. Now I could no longer put off self-flagellation.

When its flail struck me, the blow lacked potency, bite. Instead of the paralyzing lash I had felt when I knew I had blown the Dylis case, I seemed to be dealing with this setback sensibly.

"Son-of-a-bitch," I said, with something of the relief of a man who has been in a spectacular automobile crash and feels himself to see if he has been smashed with the car—and finds only some bad bruises. I smiled despite my dismay. I wasn't caved in.

And why should I be? I had made a whopper of a goof and confronted the wrong man. But suppose I hadn't grabbed him? Suppose, just suppose it *had* been Calvacadi on his one visit in six weeks and I had held back out of equivocation? How about that?

Besides, once I had committed myself to the error, I had done everything right. I reviewed my actions and tasted the rightness of them. My timing was perfect; I had been as good as a boxer in getting the guy immobilized and the gun under his chin; the words had been brief and ominous.

I eased into the hot water, feeling the warmth enter my chilled pores and penetrate the sinews and nerves that had tightened up first from nervousness, then shame.

"Damn it," I said to myself aloud. "Why are you so eager to torture yourself? Why do you want to see yourself as a flop?" The thought challenged me enough so I got out of the warm water, found a bottle of brandy, and took it back with a small glass to the tub.

Once again in the warm water, brandy in hand, I made a quantum jump: if I could forgive myself for this screw-up, why not for letting Dylis get away? Sure, that one was a failure of skills as well as failure of judgment. But what good did it do to keep tormenting myself over it? Besides, up to the point where I forgot the bullets, I had worked the case like a master.

"You are not God," I said. I held the brandy to the

light, saw its rich shimmerings, then took a sip and felt the luxury of its burn. Either I would capture Calvacadi or I would not. There was nothing I could do to speed it up.

XVI.
ERNESTO CALVACADI

For four more days, I watched in vain for Calvacadi. Sunday came, a lucent, blue-skyed day. The canal glittered in the sunlight; the last golden and brown leaves in the garden behind the hospital shuddered in the light wind, a final autumn show for kids who might not be around to see the next one.

As I peered from my balcony chair, my heart gave a thump that took my breath away. Calvacadi, no mistaking him this time, came briskly down the *fondamenta* toward the hospital entrance, carrying a big wrapped package in his arms. Stealthily, I slipped off the balcony and into the living room and watched him with the field glasses through the window.

The face could have come out of one of my sketches. He had dyed his bricktop to brown and had shaved. But his walk had that bounce, that movement from ball of foot to toe that made it so recognizable, so distinctive. I had been deceived in the rain. Today, I was sure.

He wore a knit sweater and corduroy trousers, like a young college professor on a weekend shopping trip. The professor image broke up when I looked at his eyes through the binoculars. They were wary even at this distance, roving from side to side as if he expected an enemy to dart at him any moment. Forty paces from the entrance, he took a slow look over his shoulder, then upward at the houses behind him and to his left. As he did, I drew back from the window. I was sure he did not know his hunter had found him.

Fevered with excitement, I readied as before. On such a temperate day, my trench coat was going to look slightly out of place. I tested the tape on the Beretta and thought with grim humor that if it went off by mistake pointed downward, the worst that would happen was a blasted kneecap or foot. Upward, it would be balls and all.

I hustled down the stairs. Once, I had considered forcing him at gunpoint to my apartment. But if anything miscarried, too many people knew my face here. Besides, on this perfect fall day, all Venice was in the streets. The crowds gave me the foils I needed to follow him.

In the downstairs hallway, one of the other tenants, a dowager-like woman of about two-hundred pounds, had just come in. I had encountered her before and been forced to admit I was an artist before I could get away.

"Has there ever been such a day, signore?" she asked, fat, friendly face beaming. "In America—"

"Never, signora," I said. "Never such weather."

"But you are in a coat. You have a cold . . ."

"Yes, a bit." I fidgeted, and began to cough. She stood her ground.

"Autumn colds," she said. "They are the most serious." I did not want, through rudeness, to bring any attention to myself. But, suppose, dear God, that the real Calvacadi, like the false one, went into the hospital and came right out. I hacked loudly, and lengthily until she began to look uncomfortable.

"Signora," I wheezed when I had stopped coughing, "in fairness to you. It is no mere cold. I am troubled with a terrible streptococci. I go even now for penicillin lest I infect my friends." I began to cough again. She looked sympathetic, but let me by. Coughing, I exited.

Outside, in my same vantage post, I waited. Calvacadi would now be with the kid. I envisioned the Nativity scene: the child, the beautiful Signora Tennaro, Calvacadi. I let myself think the worst. Suppose his visits, in the magic way of remissions, slowed or stemmed the fatal production of white blood cells, the mindless hyperactivity of spleen and lymph glands.

By forcing Calvacadi to relinquish his trove, I might be requiring him to flee some murderous kangaroo-court edict by the Red Brigade cannibals who were his colleagues. Was I destroying any future link between father and leukemic child?

Maybe. I could sympathize, but I must not wallow. Calvacadi had free will. I had not told him to throw his lot in with murderers. My task was to save

Surrett. The Beretta splinted my thigh uncomfortably. I twisted its silencer, then the Unique's. Both were already snug.

Calvacadi came from the hospital more briskly than he had gone in. As he walked up the *fondamenta*, his head again moved like a cobra's, his eyes catching and recording everyone in sight. I felt a twinge of admiration. How often I had done the same, forcing faces to register so that I saw them again I would know I was being trailed.

I moved along a half block behind him, urging the strolling crowds out of my wady with a *"permesso."* At the first turning, when I looked down where he should have been, he had disappeared. Forty feet away, though, was the side doorway of an ancient church. He must have entered. It could be the classic deception that fugitives use to insure they are not followed: a doubleback. If so, he would come out the front door or the side door of the church and head back in the direction he had come, surveying every face.

I buckled into the corner wall of the rough-faced old church. I heard the front door creak, thanked the Almighty for letting Venetian churches have creaky doors, and darted around to the side before he saw me.

"First doubleback," I said softly to myself as I waited for him to clear the narrow street. I was getting inside his head. He would vary his doublebacks, do them unexpectedly. I'd bet he was good for two more before he felt safe enough to head home.

By a bar with a windowful of bowling trophies,

he struck west, parallel to the hospital street, but deeper into nontourist Venice. I started around the corner, and saw him coming back my way, a second doubleback far sooner than I expected. But for his guarded glance at boatmen unloading boxes from a moored barge, he would have spotted me as I rounded the corner.

Still, I was in trouble. I could not get back down the street fast enough to avoid his seeing me, distinctive trench coat and all. Along the street were workers' row houses. I pushed at the nearest door. It was locked; at the next — locked. In a moment, he would round the corner and be upon me. The third door gave. I entered and shut it behind me, then turned to see a young man, his wife, and two children, all dressed up for a Sunday walk.

"Hey?" said the astonished man.

"Signor Tresco?" I asked as if as bewildered as he.

"No, no," he said. "Luigi Tizianel. You have the wrong house. You can't just — "

His wife picked it up, also outraged. "You must ring."

"He is a foreigner," said the husband. I was rolling my eyes around confoundedly.

"*Scusi, scusi,*" I said. I began to back out, bowing and apologetic.

"*Tedesco*" — German — said the wife, as if that somehow explained the intrusion.

I bowed again. "*Aufwiedersehen,*" I said.

Outside I picked up Calvacadi again, lost him briefly and — near frantic — found him heading for the Old Ghetto. Weaving after him among the Orthodox Jews, some in robes and yarmulke, I hurried across the main piazza with its ancient covered well and young sycamores.

Clever bastard: by going through the Ghetto — where almost everyone's clothing proclaimed Jewishness — he made sure that anybody following him from another part of the city would be as conspicuous as a red Maserati in a funeral cortege.

Calvacadi walked sinuously past peeling facades from whose yellow and red layers of plaster the brick of centuries poked. Behind a window, a man coughed and coughed as if his lungs were trying to leap from his body.

On a wall, one plaque praised Italian-Jewish soldiery. Another told of the two hundred Venetian Jews, the eight thousand Italian Jews, the six million European Jews killed by the Nazis. Calvacadi passed them both without a look. He did not see that his Brigades were the same as the Nazis: means justifying ends justifying means.

Suddenly, Calvacadi darted into an alley, reappeared, and approached me. It was an unexpected doubleback and he had caught me off guard. There were only the two of us. We would have to pass. I walked briskly as if with a definite destination, and as if preoccupied by my thoughts. Rapidly I debated whether, since we were alone in the street, I shouldn't put the gun on him and force him into a deserted alley. But I dismissed it. Better to let him see me, give up my margin for error.

We passed. His eyes were without expression but they observantly darted to my face and then away. Inside my trench coat, I sweated, my hand on the grip of the Unique. When I rounded the corner, I glanced back and saw him cutting through an archway. I did not know where it went, but suspected at last he was headed for his lair. I looked over a low, weathered stone wall, saw him skirt along a canal on a narrow walkway and then cut back through another arch toward the street where I stood.

As he emerged, I slid over the wall, then picked him up again. We moved down a tiny street canyoned by old tenements that might once have been fancy apartments or even town houses of nobles, but were now rundown lower-class dwellings.

With his detours, doublebacks, and false turns, he was the most cunning man I had ever followed. No wonder the Italian police had never caught him. In the little street, he paused and looked back. I pulled my eye away from the corner. After a few moments, I cocked my eye around again. He was at the door of one of the old tenements. I've got him! I thought triumphantly. He pulled out a key, put it efficiently in the front door, and slipped inside.

A minute or two after he entered the apartment building, I heard the rasp of ancient wood and saw a ground-floor shutter open slightly. This perfect day in Venice had betrayed its native son. It had provided me with strollers behind whom to hide. And its gentle autumn air and sunlight had been so dear to Calvacadi that in opening his shutters to it, he had shown me where he lived.

The rat was in his hole. That was where I was going to keep him. I watched the flutter of the tattered window curtain. Was it a remnant of Calvacadi's days with his girl friend?

In a few minutes the window closed. Whatever he

had come home for, it hadn't taken long. I had expected to wait for hours. Calvacadi opened the apartment building door. I held my cheek close to the rough stone, motionlessly watching him. He locked the door, and, still dressed as he had been, strode with that bouncy walk directly toward me.

I eased back my brow and cheekbone, drew the pistol, and held it just inside my open trench coat. Two people were a half block up the street to the right, a third and fourth, separately, a bit further to the left. One of the first pair, a woman, seemed to be looking at me curiously, but there was no time to worry about that.

Timing the moment when he would be less than five yards from the corner, I marched around it, bumped into him full chest, and jammed the gun into his side as I clutched his sweater.

"Not a word," I growled

Despite the gun in his side, he gave a huge wrench, but though wiry, he was no match for my strength. He tried again, with a choked sob of desperation. I dug the gun so deeply into his side that the pain subdued his panic.

"Back the other way," I rasped, gouging his side with the gun again and twisting his wrist emphatically.

He murmured in pain, but made no outcry. We were at the door to his building. I was so close behind him that unless someone were near, they would not see my grip on his arm, the gun in his side.

"Open it," I said. "No tricks or I will kill you here."

He fumbled for the key and I twisted the arm

higher. He grunted. I thought: Mr. Calvacadi, you are not so tough now that you are in pain. I wondered, as we slipped inside and I kicked the door shut, whether he had ever been exposed to torture. It would be easier for me if he had not, I thought with the beginnings of self-revulsion.

"Which apartment?" I said, jerking his arm up again.

"The fourth floor," he groaned. He had thought that one out, concocting for me a desperate shove on the stairway. I wrenched his arm upward viciously, forcing him into a sudden genuflect, and hit him in the face with my knuckles, weighted by the pistol butt they held.

"Ohh," he cried aloud, chin on his chest in pain.

"You lie. It's the first floor. We have been following you for two days." He might not believe the "we," might not think I had an accomplice. But he could not know. It was a useful ruse to stimulate paranoia and hopelessness. "Open the door!" He did. I pushed him in, bumped the door shut, and threw the bar lock with the gun butt to keep my prints off.

The shabby room's walls were covered with floral wallpaper streaked with moisture. The furniture was a worn sofa bed, a once-good heavy table, a sprung easy chair, and three straight-backed chairs. A window, one of its panes of cardboard, was in the tiny kitchen. I pushed it shut. In the bathroom, a ventilation hole went through the wall to the outside. Through it, I could hear the cheeps of a canary from a balcony or open window above us. That meant people outside could hear us. Still gripping

Calvacadi's arm, I thrust him into the bathroom.

"Stuff a towel in it," I said. With his free hand, he pulled a ragged towel from a nail and clogged the ventilation hole. Back in the living room, I forced him to lie face down, released his arm, and put the gun to the back of his head hard enough to hurt. He was so relieved at the end of the arm pressure that he sighed despite the silencer against his cranium.

He tensed again as, gun at his head, I patted him down. In his pant pocket he had a pistol, a seven-shot automatic not much bigger than Little Frog. I clicked the safety on and put it in my pocket. I was a walking arsenal.

I pulled out his wallet and put it on the table. When I gave his belt a squeeze, he squirmed violently, this time getting away. I hit him on the back of the head with the pistol butt, slowing him a moment, but he rolled on his back and grabbed for the silencer. As he did, I gave him a short jab to the solar plexus with my left fist and he doubled up, gasping.

I unbuckled his money belt and pulled it through the rungs. It was like a fat snake, a beautifully made folded job with no snaps. I put it on the table by the wallet.

I pulled out my rope, quickly tied a loop, made a slip noose, and put it over his head. He must have thought I was going to hang him on the spot, for he uttered a small bark of fear.

I shed the rope to his ankles, pressing them as far toward the back of his legs as I could. If he tried to relax his legs by stretching them, he would tighten the rope on his throat. I hoped he had no history of convulsions that might set him jerking and involuntarily garrote him. With the rest of the rope, I tied his hands together at the wrist behind his back. Then I put the pistol on the table and gagged him.

While he lay like a bound pig, I went through his wallet. There was about two-hundred dollars in lire in it — and a lovely set of forged documents, all in the name of Marcello Sabbioni. There was also a padlock key. To a money box? In the wallet there were no pictures of his kid or his family. He was wise not to endanger them by carrying around sentiments that the cops would find and use.

I cleared the money belt and counted the bills in honest amazement: more than twenty thousand dollars in Swiss francs. Not bad for an indigent Brigadist-ex-student. Was it his living expenses? The proceeds of some new robbery? Or maybe the money he was sending the kid came out of this cache? I folded the money back into the belt. It was too short for me to wear. I rolled it up and stuffed it and the wallet with its mysterious key into my coat pocket where the rope had been.

His face had contorted as I went through his money. For an extreme Marxist, he sure as hell had a bourgeois feeling for cash. Now he was trying to calm himself, breathing deeply to collect his strength and thoughts. I left him on the floor and turned over the single room, the kitchen and bathroom, digging at the kind of places I had looked in during my black-bag days: behind pictures for small wall cavities, under the stove for a floor hole, in the icebox, where the money might be wrapped up in foil like frozen fish.

I was satisfied that in hiding loot, Calvacadi's skills did not match mine in finding it. As I finished each area, I straightened up and wiped off any surface where I might have left prints. The search produced nothing at all. I returned to a straight chair, where I could talk down to Calvacadi's head. My Italian, I was sure, from hearing him at Surrett's, was better than his English.

"Signor Calvacadi," I said to him quietly. "I want you to listen very carefully to me. Your life and the lives of people you love, assuming you can love anything, are at stake here. When I ask you a question, it will be one you can answer yes or no. If the answer is yes, grunt once, if no, grunt twice. If you refuse to answer me, I will help you to do so. Do you understand?"

He made no sound. I kneeled and rough-wrenched the arm I had sensitized earlier. He grunted in pain.

"Are you saying yes, you understand?"

Again he was silent. I twisted the arm again and once more he snorted in pain. I began to feel nauseated. This was not my trade. Calvacadi had, no doubt, done unspeakable things in his narrow, cruel life. Red Brigade murders were numbering about twenty-five a year, shootings close to fifty. Yet I could not just regard his body as a thing, as my company-mates in Korea had regarded the dead Chinese whose teeth and eyes they had used as targets.

Was it too late to push all this off on Surrett? I had done my job in catching Calvacadi. I could march him to a telephone, gun concealed, called

Surrett, and get him or his torpedo over here to take delivery on this guy.

Shit, I thought. Ridiculous. Even if I could pull off the call, there wasn't time. During the day, I would have to hold Calvacadi. Any number of Red Brigadists might be dropping in. Or even if I took him elsewhere, he'd surely have some system of reporting in like a night watchman punching in on his clocks. When he didn't punch in, the red alert would flash.

On with it. I put a knee on his side and gave the arm a wrench damned near hard enough to tear loose a muscle. He tried to scream in pain, but the gag muzzled it to a gurgle.

Angered at him for forcing me to commit such indecencies, I hissed at him, "Answer! One or two!" I grabbed the arm again. Without my having to give it a jerk, he grunted once. I could have hugged him, so grateful was I that he had spared me.

"Now we can commence," I said. "In Philadelphia, you came into possession of $500,000. I need not review how you got it. I have learned you are still custodian of it. I want those funds. Do you understand so far?"

He grunted once. Again, I was relieved, impressed at how well I had said it all in Italian. The thought summoned up Silvia. Grotesque irony! Those sweet two weeks together had given me the facility with her language to do this dirty work. Momentarily out of kilter, I stopped my questioning. Then I went on.

"In exchange for the funds," I said, "I am offering you your life, Signor Calvacadi. If I killed you, few would be unhappy. The families of your victims, even the authorities, would applaud me. Or I could turn you over to the police. You have killed many of their brothers.

"The police would not handle you as kindly as I. I do not need to tell you about electric coils, which they are adept at attaching to one's genitals, one's eyelids . . ." I stopped to let him visualize it. "After they had wrung you out, you would be . . . impaired for life. Or more likely they would painfully extend your dying, killing you in the end. They would say you tried to escape or that you hanged yourself in your cell. You must know that the more excruciating the agony of your death, the happier many people would be.

"So my offer is not merely your life, but a life unaffected by pain that others would joyfully inflict on you. When I get the money, you will be free to go back to shooting people, if that is what you want to do. That is not my concern. I am not Italian. I would only suggest you be more cautious next time about double-crossing the Mafia."

From where I sat in the straight-backed chair, I gave him a disdainful kick in the side. I did not want him to feel we were equals. He must believe in my violence. For without having the skill and the time that the Soviets or Nazis or other institutional torturers have, I knew I must find a way both to degrade him and convince him there were no limits to how far I would go.

"You were a stupid child to betray those people. You thought you were a big shot taking their money and their drugs. If they were here instead of me, you

310

would be hanging from that wall"—I pointed—
"with a meat hook in your anus, as they have done
to other betrayers, keeping you conscious with ice
water and the shocks of an electric stick used to
prod cattle. Do you understand my offer?"

Again he was silent, testing me. I levered up his
arm and his legs jerked slightly, pulling the noose
tight on his throat.

"Answer!" He convulsed in panic. I did not
loosen the rope. Part of me writhed in horrible sympathy, begging him silently to answer. The other
part hated him for making me torture him, thus,
perversely making it easier for me to carry it out.

"Unh," he pronounced, the sound gone up a half
octave. He wriggled frantically and I hastily loosened the noose on his throat.

"That's better."

Choosing my Italian carefully, I explained that
the mob was aware I was after the money, would,
indeed, receive a share of it. But by letting me recover it, they were saying to the Red Brigades that
they wanted only to get what was theirs, not initiate
open warfare. In that light, he could see that I dare
not kill him if he gave me the money. Indeed, if I did
so, the mob would destroy me for provoking the
Red Brigades unnecessarily.

I had thought sweet reason was more compelling
than it apparently was. When I had finished, he
looked at me spitefully and, without my asking,
grunted twice: no.

"You are rejecting the offer?" I demanded. I was
furious. I had tried so hard. He had only used my
speech to gather together the moral and physical

311

strength to resist the torture, which he must sense I hated.

This time he did not bother to accord me an answer.

"There is one last thing," I said, holding myself in. "We saw you go into the Ospedale Pediatrico today with a big package. A colleague will now be checking out what you were doing there. While we would do nothing to a sick child, I am not sure whether the people in Philadelphia would be so scrupulous."

It was the cruelest thing I could say. I felt the beginnings of damnation on me. My stomach tied one more sickening knot. I had come three-quarters of the way. I could not turn back. I reached down and twisted his face to where I could look down into it. He came up on his abdomen enough to stare up at me from the corners of his eyes. I saw him curl his lips and he tried to spit on me through the gag, but it dribbled out the corner of his mouth and onto the floor.

I pulled the rope tighter and tighter and saw his eyes narrow and then close in anguish, heard a rattle in his windpipe as the blood rushed to his face. Terrified that he was dying, I loosened the rope. And then the horrendous thought that lay in me like a dormant monster came fully virulent.

Ricky! I had gone too far! How often in those first years I had imagined it: that bare two-person room that I had visited only twice in the year and a half Ricky was at West Chester; the ceiling pipes; the rope tightening against the largest one as Ricky's trachea constricted; the neck finally broken by Ricky's ghastly jig in the air; and, lastly, his limp, suspended body.

Pop and I had gone to the emergency room, which served as a morgue. The nurse had moved back the clinical shroud and we had seen Ricky's face, eyes closed mercifully, but the face still dark from the rush of engorging blood into his capillaries, the neck bruised and distended by the intractable rope. Pop had groaned and we had moved away.

On the way home, we had stopped at a bar. The stragglers on its stools, the weary barkeep, the plastic, mirrored walls had all stunk of unhappiness. But unhappy people, I could recall thinking, can at least choose between death and life. Choosing death had ended Ricky's options, forever. And so had I nearly done with Calvacadi. Only a split second had passed. I saw my brother in the gurgling man on the floor. Vomit rushed up from my stomach and I ran toward the toilet, my mouth bursting with the discharge, my legs stumbling. I vomited into the toilet, nose and mouth raw and sour before I could stop. I wanted to cry, but I could not. I washed out my mouth, cleansed my face.

When I got back into the room, I saw triumph in Calvacadi's eyes. As I steadied myself, his scorn vanquished the entreaties of Ricky's ghost. Calvacadi, I thought, you were a fool to let me see that look. I already abhor you for making me a torturer. Now your arrogance is baiting me. You make it easy for me to see you as a monster, myself as avenging angel. You make it easier for me to put my memories aside.

"My weakness and your stubbornness," I told

him quietly, "have forced me to show you I am a kind of man I did not wish to be. I want to know about the visit to the hospital. Is there a child there who interests you?"

He did not reply, testing me. Able now to do it, I tightened the noose, staring intently into his eyes until he shut them. He strained his throat against the rope. He shut his eyes and began to gag. I pulled more tightly. Blueness tinted his face as if from a filter put slowly over a stage light. With thumb and forefinger, I pulled up his eyelid and saw the hysterical-horsewhite eyeball roll. When I released the pressure on the rope, he was limp, his breath vibrating down the traumatized trachea into his lungs.

"You will answer now," I said.

"Unh," he said. He, too, now knew what his contempt had made of me. There was little defiance in his young face now. His eyes were closed, tears in their corners. He knew how death smelled and tasted.

I sat above him for a while, looked at my watch, and waited some more. Then I checked his knots carefully. "We will learn something more about your visit to the hospital."

I unlocked the door, relocked it, then opened the front door a crack and looked up and down the street. It gave me a chance both to fake a talk with my "accomplice" and to inspect the approaches to the apartment. Some kids kicked at a soccer ball in the afternoon sun. Two old men talked up the street. I saw no one suspicious and ducked back into the building.

Calvacadi had scooted himself toward the

kitchen. To try to rub the rope against something? He had made no progress with the knots. I kicked him in the side and thigh and dragged him back into the living room. When he was there, I tightened the bindings at his ankles, bringing him once more to the choking point.

"Paterfamilias Calvacadi," I sneered at him. "My colleague has determined that you are the father of a little boy with leukemia. He has been able to see the little boy and the teddy bear you brought him"—I hoped mention of the teddy bear would authenticate my companion's existence. "He says the little boy is much like you, with pinkish hair, but very pale. The nurse told him that the little boy lives for the few times when the man who brought him toys comes. My colleague is one of your countrymen, Signor Calvacadi. He believes we could find ways of taking the child out of the hospital. It would be my preference not to do this. It might endanger the child. It would surely upset the child to see you this way. But my companion is more eager to see some quick return on our long investment of time."

Calvacadi lay with his head averted. I got up from the chair and walked around to see how much discomfort he was suffering. I did not want him comfortable enough to recoup his resolve or to look into my heart and discover that evil as I was, I was still not sufficiently evil to do the job right. I let him strain for air awhile. Then, as he seemed to weaken, I said quietly:

"Are we ready for a rational two-way conversation?"

315

"Unh," he grunted weakly. Yes.

I took the rope from his neck. His legs, drained of blood, flopped uselessly to the floor. They would soon tingle into wakefulness. I tied them loosely to his wrists to hobble him.

"I am going to take the cloth out of your mouth," I said. I put Big Frog to his temple firmly. "If you shout and the police come, you will wish I was still your captor; if your friends come instead, I will kill you." When the gag was out, he waited for me to speak. "Are you ready for business?" I asked.

"Is this you Americans' way of negotiating — one party on the floor with a gun against his head and the other in a chair holding the gun?" His mouth was still numb from the gag. He sounded as if he talked through oatmeal.

"Yes," I said. "In this case."

He began by insisting he did not have the money, saying I had taken the only money he had with the wallet and the belt. The belt money was his own money, "From a long time ago," he said angrily. I believed him, suspected it was family money with which he had supported himself and — through his aunt-in-law — the child.

His arrogance, his look of a clever youth who has made up his mind unbendingly that he is right and that most of the world is wrong made him easy to dislike. It was the master-race mentality.

Like Marxist dialectic, each of us took the other's position, debated forcefully, and then went back to his own. God knows, logic not torture, was my weapon of choice. At one point, amid the shifting viewpoints, I said, "It is all very Kafkaesque." I had

316

read *The Trial* shortly after I dropped out and this reminded me of it.

Calvacadi's stiff mouth smiled up from the floor ever so slightly.

"Yes," he said. "We call it 'Pirandellian.' "

"One does not expect to find a murderer with any interest in literature," I said.

"One does not expect the handmaiden of the Mafia to read Kafka," he replied.

"Who better?"

"Touché." We were communicating, after a fashion.

"Perhaps we should reserve our literary evening for some other time," I said.

We were back in debate. He argued that I should know his colleagues would not let the money stay with him—the very man who took it. I argued they would do precisely that because he was trusted. He countered that even, for the sake of argument, if he had the money, he would do better to die so the Red Brigades would have it. I reasoned that his colleagues would not know where it was. As long as only he knew, the authorities could torture only one person into giving it up. Moreover, a single trusted custodian insured that some Brigadist, out of sync with the group or low on idealism, did not abscond with it and set up house on an island in the Pacific.

We argued whether I had an accomplice and whether if I did he would kidnap the child. If the child died, said Calvacadi reasonably, I would lose him as leverage. I conceded the truth of that, and further agreed with him that if the child died, Calvacadi might despair enough to die willingly.

317

Out of such concessions, I had learned the depth of his feeling for the child, had confirmed Calvacadi's own desire not to die if he could avoid it.

"I am not even sure you could kill me," he speculated.

"Reluctantly, I would kill you," I said almost reflectively. "First, I would inflict pain on you in order to learn about the money and thus be able to spare you, or rather myself, the indignity of your death. Eventually, I would find torturing you unbearable for me. So, with self-repugnance, I would kill you. I would rationalize it as best I could by reminding myself of the many comparatively innocent people in whose deaths you have had a part, and by my fear of identification if you lived."

A less able, less rational young ideologue would pander to his hate for the man who had hurt and degraded him and who now held his life and that of his son in chattel. Such a person would fume, make speeches, perhaps invite further torture and even death. I knew Calvacadi was thinking things out. When he spoke, he looked very much the pensive economist trying to be objective, as if he were forecasting trends in the tire or petroleum markets.

"Yes," he said. "I think on balance that if you do not get the money, you will kill me."

"Dying in itself is not entirely the issue," I suggested.

"No. You are not granting me the option of immediate suicide."

As the talk went on, I began to feel he was stalling. The night watchman with his clock key came into my mind again. Had Calvacadi's failure to "punch in" already sounded an alarm that would soon bring a fellow brigadist or several to his flat? The idea of his arguing while people were on their way to kill me infuriated me. I lost my temper.

"We have run out of time. Produce the money!"

He tried to argue the issues further. Now I was sure he was buying time. I grabbed up the gag and roughly started to bind it, but he flung his head from one side to the other.

"I don't have the money," he said loudly. Then, perhaps from dread of more torture, perhaps as a test of my resolve, he added in a hiss: "If you're going to kill me, kill me!" I tried to stuff the gag in his mouth, but he spat, hitting my sleeve.

I rolled him over on his back, twisting his arms and legs, and planted one knee on his chest. His face looked up at me defiantly. Proudly and hatingly, he puckered for another spit, but I slapped him across the mouth and, while it was open with surprise and hurt, forced the gun between his teeth.

"Now spit," I said. "People like you make it very easy for people like me to kill them. I cannot afford that luxury at this moment. I am not ready to write off the money for the pleasure of ridding myself and mankind of a murderer, a nasty, snarling little Nazi like you. We both know that."

I looked at his eyes, studying what I saw there, how much fear, as opposed to the hate. He closed them. I pushed the gun into his mouth, a ghastly forced oral sodomy that shamed me almost as much as if it had been the real thing. I will not soon be clean from this, I thought. I jammed the gun in harder. He grunted with the hurt to the back of his

319

throat.

"What a pleasure to simply squeeze the trigger and be done with you," I said. I held the gun in his mouth while he groaned. Still he strained defiantly, even as I increased the pressure. At last, he half screamed in agony, then began to gag on his own blood.

Carefully, in order not to break his teeth, I withdrew the gun. He painfully brought up the blood from his throat and spat it on the floor, but not insolently. I wiped it up with the gag. I did not want any evidence in this house of what had happened here. He started to spit again, but this time I told him to swallow it.

I could see him consider insubordination, but I grabbed his throat. "You want this again," I growled at him. "I am getting bored, Mr. Terrorist." He swallowed the blood. He could talk about death all he wanted. I was satisfied now he was a man who neither wanted to suffer or to die. Who did?

I put the noose across his neck but did not tie it. Beside the noose, I put the gag. I pressed the bloody silencer on his upper lip and stared into his eyes. "Okay, we have tried each other's limits. Do you need another test of mine? I am ready."

"No," he murmured, trying to sneer, but hampered by the pistol and the rasp in his voice. I pulled back the silencer a centimeter. "This is bestial," he said. There was measurable panic in his voice.

"You're fucking right it is," I said in English.

He closed his eyes. When he opened them, he said:

"Let me think a moment."

"Be my guest," I said. He closed his eyes again as if to blot out any reading of his thoughts. I looked at his prominent and vulnerable Adam's apple jutting upward. I hated him enough to kill him.

But I knew if I killed him, it would trouble me until I died. I would be like one of those cows, addicted to swallowing nails, hinges, bits of wire, who live on with this "hardware," as it is called, unable to eliminate their metallic bane from their guts. Calvacadi's death would be my "hardware."

How much simpler all this would have been if I were merely an efficient torpedo, a gunsel who could sit back, having done all in the way of argument and persuasion he could do, and await an answer. If it were one answer, then he would get the money. If another, he would kill.

The room was stuffy. Although the windows were closed, I could hear the shouts of the young soccer players outside. Who else was out there? I worried again about rescuers. Through the window, I could see the late sunlight hitting the clothes high up on lines across the street. Venice was getting on toward evening.

I sat there in the chair while Calvacadi's breathing became regular, his features relaxed. His swollen mouth, not unchildlike, parted slightly. In the darkening room, I aimed the gun at his head.

"Boom," I said quietly. How easy to squeeze and be done with it. The hollow-nosed slug would make no more than a quiet "thwat" as it left the muzzle, took away a chunk of brain and bone, flattened, and dropped from the plaster wall behind Calvacadi, spent by its killing.

"Boom," I said again, practicing another shot at Calvacadi. He opened his eyes, saw the gun pointing at him, and ducked, his face aghast at what he must have thought was my unexpected decision to kill him.

"Only practicing," I said, lowering the gun.

He smiled a silly smile of relief.

"At this distance, there is no practice necessary."

"Well? . . ."

"I don't suppose there is any way you would let me confer with my colleagues in my organization, by phone, from some place of your choosing." It was naive, almost as if he were saying if for the record, so at some future time he could tell them he had asked.

"No, of course not." I smelled capitulation, or rather a strategic retreat. The torture, the threats against his child, his correct understanding that my anger was making me less stable . . . whatever it was, perhaps even a conviction that this was the best way to destroy me, had led him to change tactics, seek a new position.

"Untie me, I will take you there."

"You've decided wisely," I said without jubilation, seeming to take him at his word. "But I am prepared to shoot you the instant I think there is trickery. Be smart, Signor Calvacadi, and avoid inviting me to kill you."

I scratched around in his closet, cluttered with dirty clothes, and found a respectable-looking Alitalia flight bag. I had figured during my long vigil that five thousand hundreds would take up about four hundred cubic inches. The flight bag would manage them nicely, and more safely than my plastic merchandise bag.

I untied his legs and watched him as he went to the bathroom to urinate. When he came out, he started for the kitchen. I recalled that attempt to scoot there when I left him momentarily two hours before. But now it seemed innocent. He wanted a glass of water, understandably. His hands still tied, his arms awkward, as if there were an elephant's trunk, he got a glass out of the cupboard and had a long drink. There was a small geranium on the counter. He watered it and put the glass back in the cupboard.

"I think I will never see this place again," he said.

He turned and pushed open the window.

I was on him in a minute, dashing him down. I was sure now what his plan was, to signal someone outside. He cringed on the floor while I stood flat against the wall, my eye on the open window. The curtain fluttered in the evening breeze. Outside the window, I could see the cage of bars.

"I wanted to give the plant a little of the last light, for God's sake," he hissed. "Jesus, is there nothing that doesn't tighten you up like a vise?" Against the wall, I crept around the side of the room until I could swing the window shut. When I did, the cardboard, loosened by his opening the window, fell to the floor.

Calvacadi picked it up.

"Here," he said, getting up with the cardboard in his hands. "Shoot me for patching up my window." I stood with my back to the wall beside the window, watching him as he reached up to put the cardboard back in. Only someone in a second floor across the way would be able to see his face, and that not easily. He gave the cardboard a practiced rap to make it fall between the retaining nails.

The incident made me nervous. I marched him back into the living room.

"I'd like to wait until dark," he said. "I can get it better then." Maybe he was telling the truth. But now that I had his agreement, suspicious as it made me, I wanted out of this cell-like apartment. I was a little stir crazy, for one thing. For another, some instinct told me to get on with it, not to linger, that my clock-punch theory had merit to it.

"Shut up awhile," I said. He started to argue and I grabbed his sweater and looked him in the eye, seeking a clue to his duplicity, or whether I was imagining it. I saw nothing but disdain. "Talk some more so I can break your teeth for you," I said.

I tied him hurriedly to the chair again and pulled from his closet a worn sports coat. With my jackknife, I cut holes from the inside of the sports coat into the left- and right-hand pockets. Without untying his legs, I took the rope off his wrists and made him remove his sweater and put on the sports coat.

I threaded the rope through the hole in the right side of the jacket and tied his wrist to his belt so he could not get his hand out of his pocket. I made a loop of the shank and let it dangle slightly out of his left pocket. That left him with only his left hand free and a loop on that side for me to grab if I wanted to restrain him or if he tried to flee. Then I unbound the other piece of rope from his legs and put it in my trench coat pocket.

"You do a professional job," he said.

"That is why I am where I am and you are where you are," I replied.

"I want to rest," he said. "I'm dizzy. We've got a long way to go." It wasn't unreasonable. He did look sick. Instinct again told me to get the hell out of this apartment.

He went slack and leaned against the wall. I smacked him sharply across the cheek with my hand and he jerked back like a good steel spring. Dizzy my ass, I thought.

"You little bastard, you've got something going in that crazy head of yours. I am telling you. If you ever want to see that kid again, or if you ever want to get through this day without a bullet in you, don't fool with me."

I jammed him up against the wall, squeezed his jaws between my thumb and forefingers until he opened his mouth. I rammed the pistol into his throat until he gagged.

"You want to stay here? This is the fucking way we'll stay here, with you choking to death and slowly on that goddamned piece of steel."

He began to flop against the wall and I pulled the pistol out. He fell to the floor, hacking from the injury to his throat. I let him catch his breath, then jerked him up to his feet again.

"Now, where are we going? Talk quick! And be right! I've just about used up my share of that money in patience. When that's done, you can offer up your prayers to Trotsky, shithead, because you are going to die."

Twisted as it might seem, I felt that in resisting my

impulses to shoot him, I was treating him decently, even humanely, and that he had cozened me. So my hatred now had the additional classic element of he whose trust is betrayed. My anger transmitted itself to him undiluted. He believed now I would kill him. He was right.

"Torcello," he said, gurgling a little blood on the soft *c*. It was an island off Venice. I'd seen it on my maps.

"Put that goddamned flight bag on your shoulder," I said. "Let's get going."

XVII.
LAST BOAT FROM TORCELLO

With December newly here, the street was in shadow. I held the gun next to my jacket and gripped the loop of his "leash" from slightly behind him. Any sniper out there was going to hit him first. My heart thudded heavily with fear. I was as intent on avoiding a "tail" as Calvacadi had been all those hours ago. The vaporetto was only five blocks from where he lived. By our circumbendibus, it took fourteen.

As we walked, I informed him I wanted nothing but English spoken from now on, unless I told him differently. I said my accomplice would be at the hospital. The kid inside was his hostage against any funny business by Calvacadi while we went for the money. Calvacadi did not, I thought, really believe in the accomplice. But could he be sure?

Once out of the dense blocks of workers' apartments, we were beside the lagoon, which was coppered with the sun's final rays. I smelled frying fish from a restaurant. I was hungry. Perhaps at another time, this cruel, idealistic young man and I might have argued politics over food and wine. Now we considered each other's deaths.

In the near darkness, Calvacadi's skinny face was impassive, inturned as a young saint's from some smoky old Spanish masterpiece. We moved to the vaporetto schedule. The last boat came back from Torcello at 11:25, the first in the morning at 5:55.

"Can we make it back tonight?" I asked him in English.

"I hope," he replied.

We boarded the boat peaceably, my gun in my pocket.

"To the rear," I said. "Outside." We walked through the inside section, rows of wooden seats. It smelled of holiday travelling: garlic and cheese. The small outside section was a semicircle of benches under a canopy, a private place. I thought with our English we would pass as a couple of tourists on the way to the good restaurant on Torcello, though I was not sure it was open.

I kept a grip at seat level on the loop coming out of his left-hand pocket. The boat bumped and churned away from the pier and then toward open water. We passed the cemetery island, its cypresses spearing the dusk. Farther on were the lights of Murano, another island, then glimmering faintly across the water was San Erasmo, and beyond that, out of sight, Torcello, fifty minutes by boat.

I would not wager much that the money was there. More likely, Calvacadi had somehow triggered an ambush for me at one of the islands where we stopped, or at Torcello itself. But I could only take precautions; I could prevent nothing. I could deal only with what I had.

Between stops, we both dared to relax slightly.

"Why cannot you give me back the money belt?" he said. "Since you know that the money is going in part to the child? . . ."

"I will make your case to the Mafia that your own money should be returned. It is possible they will agree as a sort of gesture if a general truce can be worked out in this regrettable business. Admit that is more than others would do."

"Probably," he said.

A young man and woman who had gotten on at Murano moved out to the fantail. They were speaking Italian too fast for me to catch it all: something about someone named Filippo.

"These things aren't exactly speedboats," I said to Calvacadi. I had let go the rope again, but kept my hand by the pocket. I didn't think he would jump overboard. It would risk bringing in police.

"Vaporetti are the speedboats of the people," he said self-mockingly.

Soon the young people, chilled by the night breeze off the water, got up to go into the cabin. The boy nodded politely to us.

"Good evening," he said in accented English.

"Buona sera," I said in worse Italian, giving Calvacadi a cautionary glance to remain silent. We were alone again. The boat rumbled on, its propeller shaft reverberating as unevenly and unreassuringly as a faulty heart.

We were headed in toward Mazzorbo, the last island before Torcello. I sat erect, tensing as the conductor came out. But he only reached for the tickets I held out to him.

From the channel, I could see the immense tower of Torcello and the lower hulk of the cathedral in the dim light. Gulls, white as cotton puffs in the moonlight, sat atop Mazzorbo's seawall so close together they looked like a cornice.

The crossing to Torcello took only a few minutes. We moved gently into the pier. The deckhand twirled his heavy rope over a stanchion and drew the boat to the dock, then plopped down the short gangplank. Here, as with so many places, was a time and a spot where I could die.

"No mistakes," I said to Calvacadi in English. I nudged him through the doors to keep the flight bag from catching. He walked slowly and I stayed close behind him up the aisle and out onto the pier. On the walk into the island's interior, I would be exposed, as never before, to a sniper. Paranoia was on me.

Some of the passengers peeled off at the first turning toward farms or houses whose window gleam I could see through the silhouettes of orchards. Now it was dark except for the moonglow and widely spaced lights on the path. We walked, still close together, past fences covered with berry brambles and twisted old fig trees.

"Where are we going?" I hissed at him. I had the pistol in my right hand now and walked behind him, holding the loop in my left.

"Straight ahead," he finally replied, making me sweat for that inadequate answer. I couldn't bully him into being more explicit. We would soon be coming to a small clump of buildings around the cathedral, and I didn't fancy marching him through with a pistol sticking out of his mouth and me on the other end of it.

Suddenly, gigantic by the pale moon, was the cathedral and the tower. Dwarfted in the foreground was Cipriani's, the restaurant. The lights on its sign and the menu were out. Clearly, it was closed officially. But through its windows I could see a private party of some kind going on: one last night of good food and wine and light before the winter fogs blew over the lagoon and enwrapped the island.

We passed the restaurant like ghosts. In the moonlight, the basilica and tower sides were cratered as if the stones had suffered smallpox many centuries ago and the scars had now softened with age. Buttresses, like old men's knees, pushed at the massive walls to keep them from sinking further into the island's mud.

In the shadow of the tower, I heard the chittering of bats, then we passed again into moonlight, where old columns and wall stones rotted in weeds behind the edifices. The path cut under tall cypresses and poplars. Through a break in their gnarled trunks, I saw the lagoon on the far side of the island, lighted by cold silver light. Christ, suppose a batch of Brigadists arrived from out there by boat and cut me off along the path. I poked the gun into Calvacadi's spine.

"Signor Brigadist," I said, "if anything happens to me, my finger is going to contract on the trigger and the bullet, which is hollow nosed, will take away your backbone like a shovel digs into soft dirt.

331

If it misses your backbone, it may just paralyze you from the waist down, making you piss and shit in a bag for the rest of your life."

He said nothing. But when I stumbled slightly, he said, "I am not eager to be killed. So walk carefully. I am going to where the money is and so you can worry more about carrying out your part of the bargain and less about your threats." He said it soberly and not without dignity. I almost believed him.

The path narrowed as it crossed high ground between marsh on one side and a degenerated canal on the other. Rushes brushed our thighs. Calvacadi held the flight bag in front of him to prow out spiderwebs and twigs. He cursed when one or the other ticked his face, and more loudly when a rotten limb wrapped in briars snagged him as he stepped over. A signal? I wondered neurotically.

"Shut up," I hissed. We were at a rickety bridge crossing a stagnant canal.

"Watch the boards," he warned. "Be so kind as to point the pistol elsewhere when you cross, so that if you stumble, you do not kill me for the wrong reason."

I edged over the bridge, felt a decayed plank give, and stepped over it. We skirted a deserted orchard and I smelled, heavy on the wet fall air, the rotting fruit. The trees had long since blotted out the tower, my landmark. But I did fixes on the orchard, the bridge, the raised walk, a farmhouse. If he escaped—or, for whatever reason, I had to flee back this trail alone—I wanted to know where I was going.

We walked a half hour before we came to a small

farmhouse with shuttered windows. Its front yard was comparatively clear of brush. I suspected it was occasionally occupied.

Calvacadi stopped as if thinking or listening, then turned toward a weedy canal that ran into the property. It had once been an outlet into the lagoon. Now it was clogged with bushes. Far off to westward, a few lights on the mainland twinkled.

"Okay," he said, his voice loud in the silence of this isolated place. "We are here. Where the money is. I want to talk about the arrangements for my release. That's fair enough, isn't it?"

On the face of it, that was reasonable. Indeed, I had made detailed plans: back in Venice I would truss and gag him under the broken boat in the trash lot in a way that would give me a half hour or forty-five minutes to grab a motorboat taxi to Chioggia, the beginning of an unlikely route by boat and bus to Switzerland.

But an instinct strong as fact told me not to trust Calvacadi, that I had overlooked something. And suddenly I was nauseated as I rapidly replayed how and when Calvacadi might have signaled. He had twice headed for the kitchen. The cardboard had been knocked from the window. He, not I, had put it back. And he had put it in upside down, like a flag signaling distress.

I nearly retched, the saliva rushing to my mouth. My heart began to pump wildly. I was about to be murdered by some ambusher. Calvacadi still waited, seemingly docile for my promises of how he would be freed once I got the money.

"Fuck that," I said. I jammed the gun into his

back. "Let's go. Not another damned minute!" He started to protest. Frantic, I kicked his legs from under him. He dropped awkwardly to the ground, his bound right hand making his fall worse. I crouched over him and put the gun into his mouth, against his clenched teeth.

"Man, I am on the brink of killing you, money or no money. My life is more valuable to me than all that lousy money, and my nerves are frayed. I know why you're stalling. You think Garibaldi and Cavour are going to come riding in on white horses and save you. Right."

I grabbed him by the throat and growled at him, momentarily wild with terror: "The goddamned cardboard patch! Signor Murderer, do you understand me? You are within seconds of being a dead man!" He choked. Sotto voce, I ordered, "The money, man! Now!" I snatched him up from the ground. "Where is it!"

Frightened by my loss of control, he first tried to calm me, then quickly said, "By the pier. Over there."

"I don't see a goddamned pier," I snarled. Intimidated, he pointed and I pushed him toward the weedy canal at a half run. "Baby, there had better be a pier or you're going into that canal alive with the busted backbone I promised you. Turtle feed! Understand!"

Through a mesh of briars and underbrush, I saw the skeleton of a pier. Son-of-a-bitch, I thought, the exultation breaking through my fear, I'm going to get the money! It's here! Some chemistry in him, catalyzed by the dark night and his terror of me,

334

had made him solidly decide his life was worth saving, that he would not die for the money. Whether aid was coming was another thing.

Small trees vaulted the blocked canal like low Gothic arches. The exposed ribs of a hull-less rowboat jutted up from the muddy banks. Beneath the pier, I could see black water.

"Wherever it is, get it!" I said, shoving him hard. After every word, every action I paused to listen. If I missed a snapped twig, a dry footfall, I would be xed out by a bullet or club or knife without ever even hearing or seeing my attacker. My nerves were as frazzled as Calvacadi's, and he knew it. He could more or less deal with the predictable torturer. With this irrational me, he was terrified.

I cut the rope at his wrist and snatched the flight bag off his shoulder. I shoved him again toward the pier. These Red Brigade bastards weren't all that smart. They were newcomers. Hiding objects in watertight containers lashed to pier struts below the waterline was an old stunt. Years ago, a Cuban bunch in Florida had hired me to find some money stolen by anti-Castro Cubans from CIA funds at the time of the Bay of Pigs. I'd traced the money to a rifle container at the base of a pier. Instead of the $300,000 they'd expected, it was $25,000 in tens about a third of my fee.

"Be careful," Calvacadi said as I pushed him into the water. "If I stumble, for God's sake, I'm not running, it's—"

"Shut up!" I said. "Get the goddamned money!"

He had waded in up to his knees, clutching the uprights of the dilapidated old pier. In a moment, he was chest deep. He dove down, and popped up with a rope in his hand. Wet and muddy, he struggled up the shore, dragging the rope. At its end, I saw what looked like a two-gallon paint bucket. I pulled out my Swiss knife and handed it to him.

"Cut it. Then use the screwdriver to open it up."

I kept the gun on him as he sawed the rope through and then pried at the bucket top. Finally, the top came off. It had been sealed with something tarry. Inside, I could see by the moonlight the glisten of plastic.

"Cut the plastic." Dripping muddy water, he slashed the plastic bag. There was the tightly packed money, like prime-quality tuna. I had it!

Now dear God, to get back with it. First, though, I wanted to make sure I had real money, not just a layer of cash on top of cutup newspapers, the old Murphy game.

"Lie on your face," I said.

As if I'd hit him with a red-hot poker, be began to run. I was after him, caught him only two strides away, and knocked him down with a cuff to the head. He lay on the ground, groaning with fear, his body tense with fright. Shit, I said to myself, he thought I was going to shoot him.

"I'm not going to kill you," I said. "Just lie there while I check out this money." I wiped the tar of my hands with the gag and carefully began taking the money out of the can bit by bit.

Calvacadi still lay pressed to the ground. I would have to loan him my overcoat to cover his bedraggled clothes on the trip back. I wondered why he had not at least come up on his elbows to watch. I looked around nervously.

Simultaneously, I saw a man with a gun not ten yards away. His pistol spurted fire. I heard the blast as I dropped and recognized in the defiantly cognitive part of my mind that Calvacadi had heard the approach of his cohort and was lying low where the bullets wouldn't be.

I rolled over and over into the underbrush. The pistol powwed two more times. I raked my coat pocket for the Unique as I rolled, finally got a grip on it, and shot once where I saw the dark figure crouching against the lighter backdrop of the sky. I knew I had missed him, and felt a gush of frustration and fear. But the dismay had no time to resolve itself into new action. From behind and above me, my gun was wrenched forcefully from my hand.

For a split instant, I thought it was a second new assailant, but even as I twisted to grab at his forearm, I knew it was Calvacadi. The gun dropped into the underbrush, but quick as a mongoose, he was on it. I rose enough to bump him to the ground, then caromed into another series of rolls, clutching frantically for the Beretta.

Now the other man was on me. I flailed back at him, but he had caught me from behind, his powerful arm locked around my neck. I tried to kick upward, tried to roll him, but the iron muscles were unrelenting. My breath caught in my throat. Suddenly, I saw Calvacadi, in front of me. He had found the Unique and I saw it go up in the moonlight and then plummet in his fist toward my head. I was stabbed with pain and went blank.

I could not have been out long. When, head aching and groggy, I came to, they had tied my hands in front and were lashing my feet with rope. They had dragged me the few yards to the side of the canal. My back was to it. Neither said a word as they worked at my ankles. But there was something familiar about the newcomer, a man in a dapper topcoat with a build like college halfbacks used to have. His head was bent over as he tied the last knot.

When he was done, he looked up and in the pale silver light I saw his face and the long welt of a scar down his left cheek. It was Baxter Dylis, né Bassio di Lessandro of South Philly, late of Athens.

There was a moment of frozen time after I gasped at the recognition. He continued to stare at me, triumph blended with hate I could see dimly on his face. Calvacadi held his own weapon on me now. They had taken it from my coat pocket. I could still feel the metal lump of the Baretta on my thigh, but how to get it?

"Benvenuto a Torcello," said Dylis, his deeply southern dialect so much in contrast with Calvacadi's, so reminiscent of the voices of my youth. I made no reply. Raw fear and rushing thoughts on how to find a way out commingled in my jumbled mind. Above all, I had to buy a little time, I knew, find a way to delay their killing me. They would not want to waste many minutes.

"I am astonished to find you with a man who tried to kill you at the airport," I finally mustered to

338

Calvacadi. Odds were he knew about it by now, but I wanted to be sure. Any old frictions I could stir up. I was speaking in English now.

"We have accommodated ourselves to that, Mr. Private Detective," said Calvacadi, liking the way *private detective* sounded. Obviously, in the minutes I was unconscious, Dylis had identified me. Except for the throb in my head, I was alert now, or alert as I could be with the dumbfounding burden of Dylis's presence in my mind.

"How? He tried to assassinate you."

"Don't waste time on him," snarled Dylis. "I want to do some business with him and then go." Despite my near panic, I could feel that they had not done that good a job tying my hands. If I could get something slick on my wrists, maybe mud — but Dylis crouched over me, a knife, blade glistening under the moon, at my chin.

"Georgie," he said. "You were Georgie over on Snyder Avenue, right?" I tried to sound as gutsy as I could. Buy time!

"Whatever I did to you then, I'd have thought the statute of limitations would've run."

Dylis uttered a nasty laugh, but a laugh.

"I got plenty that the statute hasn't run on."

He pricked my chin with the knife, just enough to break the skin. "I want to know two quick things, Georgie," he said. "Tell me, and dying will be easy. Don't, and" — he pricked me again — "dying won't be easy."

"You ask, I answer," I said, unable to hide the fright in my voice.

Dylis moved the knife to my throat to where he

could hold it steadily against me while I spoke.

"Who put you on me and the woman?"

"Vivian?"

"Yeah."

Why lie, I thought. A vague, near hopeless plan began to form to my mind.

"I waited in the bushes, picked up the car plate, traced it to her." I began to spit it out then, but he poked by throat, this time going into the skin.

"Cut it short. You followed her. She didn't tell?"

"Yes. No," I said. "She didn't, I mean."

He grunted with satisfaction.

"And how'd you manage to kill Niko and the other two? You were tipped, right?"

Niko was the Greek who had tried to kill me. And now I lay here as helpless as the third one that night, the little driver I had shot.

"Wrong," I said. "They were clowns, botch artists."

He though about it a moment, weighing whether I had told him the truth.

"They're all clowns," he said at last, almost reflectively.

Calvacadi, silent and gun on me, was getting restless. Why hadn't he been more eager to revenge himself on me in some way? Then, I knew. When Dylis got what he wanted out of me, I would not die easy at all. The thought terrified me.

"How about telling me how you two got together," I said huskily. Then added, and it sounded like a whine in my ears, "I won't be around to testify."

"Q and A is over," said Dylis. I noticed that he did

not close his knife.

"You," I said to Dylis, "figured you'd take over the gun-and-dope idea if you took over from Bernie, right?" I said, desperately trying to reengage him to talk. "And you knew he"—I nodded at Calvacadi—"was the key to it. All you had to do was let bygones be bygones, you two. Smart. Just establish a little trust. And you," I said to Calvacadi, "were eager to be back in business, getting the guns, the money for the dope, just like it was supposed to be with Magliorocco. Only this time, you'd go through with it. Because you wouldn't dare monkey with him"—Dylis—"the way you did with Bernie. Honestly among"—I started but shifted clichés—"equals."

"*Via,*" Calvacadi said to Dylis, ignoring me. "Let's go." But he didn't mean "depart," he meant "begin." Dylis was irritated. He must have thought a good while about how he would deal with me if he ever got me in this position. He wanted to do things his way. But he couldn't be short with Calvacadi.

"I'd like to drag it out," he said.

"You said you'd make it quick," I said, my mind fixed on a desperate maneuver if it could be managed.

"I lied," Dylis said, evil and exultant. "I lied to you Georgie. You ought to know never to trust a South Philly boy. Pull'em down," he said to Calvacadi, nodding his head at my trousers. I saw the shock on the Italian's face even as I went numb with terror. Dylis, who got his pleasure with women in an unusual way, who in his obscene calls talked of sexual mutilations, was going to take his pleasure with me by castrating me, leaving me to bleed to death or drown in this clogged canal.

"No," I gasped, the urine running hotly into my pants.

"Some other way," said Calvacadi in Italian. "I'll help you to strangle him. But there are some things—"

"Fuck ya," Dylis said crudely to Calvacadi. "Keep the gun on him." His knife in his right hand, he reached down with his left hand and shoved my bound hands aside so he could get to my belt buckle.

"No," I said, panicked. "No." I looked wildly at Calvacadi, who was shaken by the scene, almost unaware of the automatic he held in his hand. "Don't let him!"

"Fuck ya," repeated Dylis with ugly determination, more at Calvacadi in disgust at his reticence than at me, his victim. He undid the buckle and then the button at the top. With a quick pull, he drew down the zipper.

The knife still in his right hand, he pulled at the pants to try to get them over my hips. Unable to do it with one hand, he looked up momentarily at Calvacadi to insist that he hold me while he jerked at the pants.

In that instant, I swung my arms, tied at the writs, like a bludgeon, knocking the squatting Dylis off-balance, and with the strength of mania tightened my calves and flung myself over the bank with a backward somersault. I hit the water as the pistol went off. I sank to the bottom and, though bound at hands and ankles, jerked my way under the water to the dock like a crippled shrimp.

There, I wrapped my knees around one of the old dock supports underwater, holding my breath while I clutched in the encumbrance of my trousers to get my right hand on the Beretta. Once it was in my grip, I shot my hands out of the water and pulled the trigger, thanking God I had taken such care in its greasing and cleaning.

It went off. I submerged again, this time working my wrist and the rope against the slimy stanchions until the poorly tied noose came off my left wrist, taking a layer of skin with it.

Again I came up, fired again. This time, I crouched behind one of the uprights and peered around. The two shots had driven them to cover. All I could see were banks and weeds. I was still as helpless as trout in a bucket. They would find some clear spot where they could see my form if I stayed above water. If I submerged and surfaced firing, they would soon know I had exhausted the automatic's magazine. There was no sound from them. They were not such fools as to urge me to come out in exchange for any promises. What I had won, I knew with a fierce pride, was a decent death instead of mutilation while I was alive. Ah, I thought, if I could just get one of those bastards. Just one!

I saw the fire from a muzzle and simultaneously heard the blast at the end of the muzzle. The slug thudded into the wooden pile behind which I hid. A splinter caught me on the neck. I yelled out in pain and ducked into the water, but came up instantly, Beretta aimed at the shore end of the dock.

The cry and my thrashing had led an overeager

gunman to peer into the canal, pistol out. I recognized the dark face of Dylis, saw his surprise and then intensity as he brought the gun around to where my head protruded from the water only four feet away. But my Beretta had less distance to traverse than his pistol. I shot him full in the face, knowing with vast joy and satisfaction that I had killed him.

Now, it was Calvacadi and me, he with the advantage of terrain and of firepower, for I had only three—or was it only two?—shots left. I had no time to count. He would have both the Unique and his own partially discharged automatic. In order to unhobble myself, I worked off my shores against the piling underwater and tried to push off the ropes. But they were tightly bound. Despite my exertions, I dared not breathe hard, for fear of giving away my exact position. With gun and eyes above the water behind the piling, I waited like an old-time photograph I remembered seeing of an ape of some sort in a lake during a fire.

Of a sudden, there was a rustling in the weeds and I swiveled my head, thinking Calvacadi somehow had gotten in behind me. But it was only a rat. One, I thought, who will eat his fill before the night is out.

In the still, the chirping of night birds and the rasp of late season insects, like katydids and crickets at home, sounded amplified in my straining ears. Somewhere on the bank, Calvacadi was listening, too, suitably warned by the fate of the man who inadvertently had liberated me. Dylis, stone silent, seemed to be peering into the canal's depth, his black hair toward me, his eyes fixed on the water.

As I listened, I heard the tiny clink of metal on rock. My God, why hadn't I thought of it! So intent had the two men been on my death, that any less than their morbid attention was unimaginable. Yet what had Calvacadi to gain from my death now? It was the money that would have precedence for him over his personal revenge.

Then I would live! I felt a tremendous surge of joy. When he left, I could hide and in the morning turn myself over to the authorities, buy whatever protection I needed to get home alive. Alive!

And Surrett would die. But what could I do?

The water chilled me. I could not stop Calvacadi except at great risk to myself, so newly brought back from the dead. Well, suppose I tried? Suppose I tried to capture Calvacadi again, or to kill him, if that's what it took now to get the money and thereby to save Surrett. Why scruple? Calvacadi had certainly been eager enough to strangle me.

Eyes and gun hand above the water, I eased my still-disabled lower body toward the shore and worked my way up the bank directly behind Dylis's convenient corpse. Two shots. Was that all, I had? When I got my eyes at ground level, I saw no one. Then I heard movement in the weeds. It would be Calvacadi, putting the last of the loot into the can or transferring it from can to Alitalia bag.

The methodical rustling, a man stuffing money into a container, came from behind a tree. Calvacadi would be there, one eye around the tree at the dock, one on the money. In a moment, he would have his stash ready for traveling.

345

Like a giant mudworm measuring out distance on his side, I crept silently along the mucky, caved-in bank of the canal. Upstream from him, I oozed up the bank and saw him clearly in the moonlight — thinking the tree was still between us — closing up the can. I was halfway up the bank, coming over its top and therefore most vulnerable, when his head came up from his engrossing job like a surprised deer waist high in weeds.

He spotted me and threw himself against the tree. Shadowed as he was, I saw him bring the Unique down in my direction. Even as I saw it flash, heard the minor crump of its silenced report, I squeezed off a shot from Little Frog. I fired again, knowing I had missed the second time before I realized I had gotten him with the first one.

I crab-scuttled across the weeds to him, unsure whether I had put him out of action permanently, and grabbed at his gun hand. Nothing. In the moonlight, I saw the hollow-nosed little slug had struck him on or near the chin. The bullet and splintering bone had torn the lower part of his face away. Yet despite — or was it because of? — its ghastliness, I thought suddenly, surprisingly, and perturbedly of the child. I had forever severed the link between Calvacadi and his dying son.

Amid so much horror, I had not time for the luxury of pity, or self-pity. I searched for the Unique, which the shock of death had catapulted from his grasp, and found it by the tree.

Nervous and sorely chilled, fearing still another attacker, I lay still by Calvacadi's body. In his coat pocket, I found my jackknife, my extra cartridges, his wallet. He had put on his money belt while I was knocked out.

I cut my ankle ropes and reloaded the Unique, which had served two masters this night. As I waited, I felt an ache in my left forearm. Only then did I realize I had been hit. I reached up the sleeve and felt blood.

For the next fifteen minutes, I knew I must not shift my location. Other Red Bigadists or gangsters might be hard on Dylis's heels. Yet I had to know how badly I was hit. I rolled quietly on my sides to squirm out of the trench coat and sports coat. Blood had stained both.

My wound was running but not pumping. With Big Frog on the ground by my hands, I tied the gag over the wound and strapped my belt above my elbow.

I thought about the unsilenced shots. The amateur bastards! Both of them, particularly Dylis, should have known better than to use pistols without silencers. Yet even if the gunfire did summon constables or police, I might still keep the money hidden, still perserve a chance for Surrett. The minutes passed.

Soundlessly, I pressed on the bucket lid with all my might. I crept to the canal with the bucket and fished what was left of the rope from where it had sunk near the shore. I tied the rope hank, still attached to the pier, to the bucket handle and eased it into the water.

Again, I waited. When, after fifteen minutes, no one came, I pocketed Dylis's wallet and passport. Even if the passport was phony, his picture in it

347

would be a sure proof he was dead as a bounty wolf's head. Besides, taking it would stall identification by the Italian cops. I took the pistol from his stiffened fingers, removed his topcoat, and brushed the mud from it. My own coat was like a muddy mop. When the time came, I would wear his. I pulled off his shoes. They looked a size or two too large and were too pointy for my taste, but would fit better than Calvacadi's.

Then I stripped. I rolled the bodies into the stinking canal. The breeze had died and mosquitoes, ravenous last-of-the-season monsters, found me. I climbed gingerly into the water and shoved the dead men under the crossed branches and brambles that grew in the passageway to the lagoon. I hoped the lagoon's small tide would not wash the corpses out by the pier where they could be seen.

That done, I dragged the bucket from the water again, wrung out my clothes, and dressed. From the bucket, I carefully removed the plastic bag with the money and transferred the whole packet to the Alitalia bag. On the ground, I found six cartridge cases shining dully in the moonglow.

I carried them, the bucket, its top, the cut rope to the lagoon a hundred yards away. I heaved out the bucket and the rope and sailed the top. I threw in the cartridges one by one. Their whistling sounded eerie in the quiet night.

Back by the pier, I looked around. Except for the blood, which a single drizzle would take care of, there was no evidence of foul play. I donned Dylis's handsome coat. I put my own across the Alitalia bag, wondering whether it would be less conspicuous if I wore it under Dylis's.

So now I could go. But was the money intact? I had only begun looking at it when Dylis fired at me. True, Calvacadi had been stuffing it back into the bucket. Still, was it all there? I'd better make sure. But now the moon was blotted by clouds.

I carried matches, from habit, for I no longer smoked. They were wet and there were none in Dylis's coat pocket. In the cabin there would be matches. The windows were shuttered. It would be safe to light them there, or maybe even a candle.

Calvacadi must have trusted the tenant or he would not have stashed the money by the old pier. Indeed, assuming the cash wasn't all in the bucket, some of it might be inside.

The door was padlocked. I considered smashing the hasp. But the sound . . . My God, I thought, where are my wits. The key: it would be the one I had found in Calvacadi's wallet.

Once inside, I closed the door tightly and felt my way to the kitchen. I touched an iron stove, felt around it until I found a big box of matches on a ledge. I lighted one and cupped it briefly in my hands before blowing it out. The cabin was made up of the kitchen, a room with a heating stove in the center and a few old chairs, a dark bedroom.

I worked my way back to the Alitalia bag, which I had put down by the door. In the dark, I rapidly counted five hundred of the bills. I lighted another match and riffled them with one hand. They looked fine. I quickly riffled through the remainder; they looked okay. The match was down so I lighted another and measured the first five hundred off against the bulk. The whole $500,000 or something close to it looked to be there.

My arm was throbbing. I loosened up the belt, still in the darkness. I thought about the way my trench coat bulged on the top of the airline bag. There had been a kerosene can by the stove. I felt inside the old-fashioned stove and discovered, as I thought I would, a screen across the stovepipe's mouth. It was there to block sparks from getting up the chimney and igniting the dry underbrush outside. I could burn the coat.

But wouldn't a good police chemist be able to identify the American cloth among the remains, raising odd suspicions? I decided to take the coat back to Venice, where I could safely get rid of it. I tried to jam it into the airline bag, but the money took up too much space.

Soon Danny Surrett, my once proud friend, would be presenting, hat in hand, the cash to Magliorocco. The old man would be pleased, but stern to Surrett, an emperor forgiving a valued courtier.

There was something damned unseemly about that. From there on, the scenario didn't get any better. Magliorocco would lay off the killings on us, making it clear, however, that Calvacadi never would have been shot if he had not tried to kill Bernie's surrogate, who was only trying to recover the money.

Then, peace overtures with the Red Brigades begun, the Don would put his newly recovered investment capital to work with less adventurous and more trustworthy narcotics dealers. The half million might go this time into heroin, the drug of choice of the disadvantaged, rather than cocaine.

I felt the bag. The ten pounds or so of money would buy at wholesale six pounds of heroin, eighteen pounds of cocaine, several million pep pills of one kind or another.

And goddamn it, when all was said and done, it would buy me. I had been able to rationalize my jobs for the mob up to now: the first unwitting, because Danny hadn't informed me; the second, bugging and following Calvacadi, to help Surrett; the next couple to protect me and my family; this one to help Surrett one last time. But I had run my string. One more and I was their man as surely as Surrett was. I was Buttonman Georgie Fraser, benefactor of the drug traffickers and users of America, Magliorocco's man on Torcello.

I stood there, the minutes ticking away, knowing that much more delay and I would miss the last boat to the mainland. At last, I sighed and dropped the bag. The hell with it. Bernie wasn't going to get the money. And Surrett?

Well, was Bernie sure to kill Surrett if the $500,000 didn't come back? Maybe not. Hadn't Surrett himself said that if the Red Brigades spent the money, then killing the thief and Surrett's paying the $500,000 out of his own pocket would satisfy Bernie?

And hadn't I also killed Bernie's archthreat, a two-for-one bargain? Surely, all that would keep the remaining wolves away from Bernie's door. Surrett saved, all the rest was bullshit.

But what would I do with the goddamned money? I couldn't steal it or give it to charity. I'd be suicidal to do that, a sure bet for martyrdom. Or maybe Anne and Alexa if I wasn't immediately on hand to take my medicine.

I'd have to destroy if, prove it was destroyed, and blame it on Dylis or on Calvacadi, come up with a Grade A lie. My life would hang on whether it was credible. I thought it out: I would say I followed Calvacadi to Torcello; that he heard me from the farmhouse door, thought I was a police team and burned the money. Dylis, I would say, came on me in the dark, disarmed me. It was too late for them to save the money. Then I turned the tables on them.

I tested the tale for holes. It passed first muster.

"Oh shit," I said aloud. "Well, here goes."

I pulled a handful of bills from the flight bag, put them in the stove, and groped on the floor for the kerosene can. I dribbled in some kerosene and set them afire. Maybe ten thousand dollars and it wasn't much more to-do than burning newspapers.

Apprehensive that despite the screen, sparks might escape and be seen, I stoked steadily rather than all at once. As the money, fueled by the kerosene, burned, I prayed no one would appear. After the final batch had scorched, I doused the bills with water from a saucepan I filled in the kitchen.

When every ember was out, I opened the door to give myself a little light. Move out fast now, I thought. A charcoaly puddle had formed on the worn wood floor. It would dry and be one more clue for the Italian police to ponder after the bodies were discovered, if they were. I scooped out the residue, a saucepanful at a time, squeezed the money juice out in the sink, and packed each gooey panful into the plastic bag. No more than twenty or thirty bills were whole enough to be redeemed. Surrett could turn the whole mess over to Bernie as an evidence of good faith. Bernie's chemists could estimate how many bills had been burned, even if not what denomination.

My heart beating with exhilaration and fear but not a smidgin of regret, I packed the plastic sack with its contents in the Alitalia bag and crammed in my overcoat. The bag wouldn't zip shut. At least, I thought grimly, burning the money had almost solved the overcoat problem.

In the kitchen, I cleaned up the sink and the pan. I used some kitchen toweling to wipe my fingerprints from everything I could remember I'd touched, and locked the house. Then I took off briskly down the trail. Three men had passed that way tonight. And only one was going back.

At 11:10 I plunged into the shadows of the cathedral. Relics of ancient days stood in its yard, lighted eerily now by the risen moon. An eroded stone chair, a marble capital, remnants of an ancient Torcello stood as if on midnight auction. Each could make a hiding place for an assassin.

I swept widely past both them and the restaurant, where, in the doorway, a few hangers-on stood with final glasses of grappa or wine in their hands. As I moved up the path toward the vaporetto stop, I paused frequently to listen for an unseen step. When the boat came, I waited in the shadows until the partyers from the restaurant had boarded, and quickly stepped on last. Again, I sat on the fantail, alone.

The boat moved toward Venice; the partygoers dozed off in the glassed-in cabin, shared by two working men and a peasant, all going to Venice or Murano. When the conductor came to be paid, I held the arm of Dylis's coat against a stanchion to hide any mud.

Off the little island of San Francesco del Deserto, I surveyed my fellow passengers, all asleep or preoccupied, and the crew, who stood smoking, talking in low voices by the skipper's station. From what had become damned near a used-gun repository, I pulled out Calvacadi's pistol and dropped it over. A minute later, I did the same with Dylis's gun, then Big Frog and, separately, the two silencers.

I kept the Beretta. I might be able to explain one pistol, what with all the publicity about the Red Brigades in Italy. I smiled grimly. Easier to explain it than half a million in former dollars.

I looked back at the wake. Soon my armaments would be sunk safely within the mud of the lagoon's bottom. As I raised my eyes, I saw, black on dark gray, the tower of Torcello, monstrous in its immutable massiveness. In front of me, the lights of Venice rose from the lagoon, making a soft luminescent path to me on the water. I was alive; I must turn my thoughts to remaining alive.

For openers, at least I did not have to rush from Venice that night, fixing in a motorboat-taxi-man's memory an unusual post-midnight trip to Chioggia. Nor would I have to flee circuitously south, then hook on my way north to Switzerland. There was no Calvacadi or Dylis to describe my looks to interception teams.

354

As I ran my plans through my weary mind, I put my hand on the rail, my head on my hand. I felt the wind in my hair, thought of how snug Dylis's coat was, and fell asleep. I awoke when the boat nudged into the pier, started wildly, clutching at the flight bag, at my gun. I was at Fondamente Nuovo, deserted now, five blocks from Calvacadi's apartment, ten minutes from mine, a light-year from where I had been thirteen hours ago.

In Venice's dark streets, I doublebacked until I was certain I was not being followed, then made for my apartment fast. There I cut up my bloody undershirt, shirt, and sports coat, also the films, sketches of Calvacadi, and soft parts of the Alitalia bag. The toilet clogged on the tatters of my trench coat. I would have to take an arm and Dylis's topcoat with me. I bathed and dressed my oozy wound, which now hurt like hell. Leaving the green plastic bag open in hopes its contents would dry a bit, I packed everything else and dozed off in an easy chair.

XVIII.
THE FUGITIVE

Before dawn, I woke and wrote, in English, a short note thanking my landlords, explaining my son had taken ill and that I was leaving today, gracefully forfeiting my deposit, and telling them I had watered the plants, fed the canary, and clogged the toilet. Early as it was, I awoke Signora Colpo, told her the same story, and gave her my defingerprinted movie projector. She was foggy and a little unnerved, but sympathetic.

"It's too cold for you," she said, feeling my light Windbreaker, which I had on in lieu of my trench coat — most of it now floating seaward in pieces — or Dylis's topcoat.

"Don't worry," I said, masking my uneasiness. "I'm fine. I wonder if you could feed the canary."

To avoid going near the station, I hired a motorboat taxi for the short hop to Mestre, where I caught a bus to Padua, a second one to Verona. There, I put the hard parts of the Alitalia bag and my trench coat sleeve in a trash bin.

The slow local buses had delayed me, but kept me

away from where the Red Brigade searchers might be. It was now almost 3:00 P.M. I called Surrett from Verona's post office, grateful that in Italy all you did was give the number and pay the tab, no questions asked.

He wasn't in. I told his secretary I'd call him tomorrow at this time on the number I'd reached him before. Knowing he would be on tenterhooks, I told her to tell him I had done the job well enough to satisfy him. In fact, I was more and more gnawed by my worry that the mob would not believe me, that my sally into virtue might kill me. And I still had to get out of Italy.

My arm ached, I hoped from healing, not infection, and my baggage was heavy. I was one sad sack. But I didn't want to take my big risk, the train out of Milan north, until late at night. For now, Verona was safer. At a trattoria across the Adige, far from the tourist area, I bought a bottle of their best red wine and drank it with pasta and then spicy liver. It helped.

I could not leave Italy without calling Silvia. Her secretary clicked me onto hold for a moment, then the familiar voice came on breathless, excited, asking me why? how? when?

"Slowly, slowly, *cara*," I said. "I can't understand." Only hearing her voice made me want to stay. Just one more night. It was a siren voice that could shipwreck me.

"Where, first?" she asked.

"I don't even want to say. I got a call from home, fulfilled an obligation for a friend. It has made it hazardous to stay."

357

"Something . . ." she looked for a kinder word than "illegal," and said, ". . . outside the law?" I laughed hollowly: only double homicide, mayhem, kidnapping, housebreaking, grand larceny, disposing of two bodies without a permit, flight to avoid arrest, not to mention various gun violations.

"More or less. But not, well, reprehensible. It may be that one day you will read something in the paper and say, 'Ah, this is what it was,' and that will be that. But I am not calling for that reason, Silvia." I stopped. How to say it? How to explain that I was afraid my Torcello story would not pass muster, that Magliorocco would have me killed, and that, therefore, I must speak to her once more?

"I am calling you because to leave Italy without calling you just wasn't thinkable. We bound it up in a neat package at Monterosso. But I can't let it stay that way."

I felt her discomfort.

"Be careful," she said. "Giorgio, I do not want to go through again what I have been through these five weeks. *You* have been occupied — I do not know in what, but occupied. *I* was healing and unless —" She stopped, and said bluntly, "And I want to go on healing."

"I don't want to break open your healing," I said gently. "But if I hadn't called, wouldn't you, a little of you, have thought, 'for him it was just an episode?'"

"Ah, no. I knew —"

"Be more honest, Silvia."

"Go on," she said, a half concession.

"So I called to let you know that whether we ever

358

see each other again, it was, in a certain way, the most important time in my life. We talked that morning at Fegina about how we had remade each other. But the remade me had not been tested to see whether all the welds would hold. And so I am calling to thank you for making a me that stayed together when I had to stay together."

"You make me sound like an auto body repairman," she laughed. And for a moment, we were back where we were in those intervals when we were friends and not lovers.

But that comfortable mode was more than I could maintain.

"I love you, Silvia," I said. "I—" But she had built herself into a fortress against such words and cut me off.

"No. I don't want to hear about your love. I am starving for you, but I don't want to hear—"

"I only want—"

"*You* want? I wanted and you could not give . . ." She quickly realized how cruel that sounded and made amends. "But you were right to call. We told each other *addio* in Monterosso. But we are not characters in a tragic love play. We should have said *arrivederci*. It would be stupid to avoid seeing each other again if fate should take us that way, if only as comrades, as people who—"

"At one time meant everything to each other."

The line went silent. I knew she was bringing it all under control. *"Bene,"* she said at last, unwilling to enter into my emotion, not knowing, nor would I tell her, that behind my sudden want of her was fear of death. *"Bene,"* she repeated thoughtfully. "Or not *bene*. We will see."

So once again we had brought it to a closing. But this time without the finalities of farewell.

"Then, as you allow me, *arrivederci,* Silvia."

"Yes," she said, plucky and warm. "Yes, that."

I took a cab to Brescia. It cost me a fortune. I spoke Italian to the driver, telling him I was a Swede. It would hide my identity and explain my extravagance. In Brescia, I bought a train ticket from Milan to Brussels to avoid going to the ticket counter in Milan. There, just before the train pulled out, I sprinted for it, feeling like a moving duck in a shooting gallery. But no shot came. I caught at the carriage door, opened it, and was on my way out of Italy, the last aboard.

Sleepless, but uninspected by the lenient Customs along the way, I stepped from the train as it pulled out of Luxembourg, taking with it to Brussels, I hoped, any spoor a pursuer might be following.

Still practicing my doublebacks, I found a hotel away from the station. I bought an attaché case, some leather gloves to keep my fingerprints to myself, and packed the case with the money ash in the original plastic bag, the money belt, the two passports, and two wallets. Then, lugging the attaché-case with me, I called Surrett from a booth in the central telephone office.

He must have been standing guard on the pay phone, for he picked up before the first ring ended.

"Jesus, I'm glad to hear from you," he said.

"Didn't dare sooner."

"You got it?"

"No . . ." I heard him gasp. "Wait. He burned the stuff. Thought the cops were after him. But I have the ashes; I saved maybe two thousand of it." The old security worries got to me and I went euphemistic. "He and a certain Greek friend who came to help him got unpleasant. One of the friends you set me up with in Paris solved the problem." Surrett gasped, then was dumbstruck a moment.

"D?"

"Yes."

"Holy shit!" He let it sink in. "Solved permanently?"

"Yes. Both of them. My guess is that they won't surface for a few days." Surrett had been a cop long enough to think of bodies popping to the surface from gas after spring weather set in. He was silent, assessing what all this meant to his chances of survival.

"Can you prove that the two guys destroyed the stuff and that you had to, uh, solve the problem in self-defense? That's vital."

"Yes. My word. Jesus, why else would I lug a batch of wet ashes across half of Europe?" Surrett thought some more.

"Wasn't there *any* way you could have prevented the fire?"

"No," I said. I was getting irritated. I had rehearsed my story so often that I had come to believe it on one level. I resented Surrett's questioning me about it. "You told me in Paris that if something like this happened and you made up the loss, you'd be home safe."

361

"Can you bring the remains—of the stuff, I mean—home?"

"No, I'm not crossing any more borders with it."

He thought some more.

"Nobody's followed—"

"No, I'd be . . . solved permanently myself if they had. Look, Danny. I have to know. It's important to me. Is this thing going to do the trick?"

"My chances are up from a million to one to better than fifty-fifty," he said. I thought they'd be better and felt a grab at my heart. But he was encouraging. "How's that? And by your work with D, we're all safe on that score. At least I'll be"—he tried to sound cocky—"only be permanently solved from one direction."

I wanted to get down to details. But suddenly the emotion he'd dammed up so long swept over the top.

"I hate myself for putting you through this." He paused a long time. "You gave me a shot at living, and you didn't even want the case." Over the telephone, I heard the unimaginable. Surrett was weeping.

"Get a hold on yourself," I said. "Your blubbering is going to start up every monitoring device in fourteen countries." He tried to laugh at that, but recovery came hard. "Come on," I pleaded. Where was his old pizzazz? Maybe all those weeks of wondering whether the Mafia was going to trash him and put him in the trunk of some stolen car would have gutted my courage, too.

Finally he came around. I glanced behind me. A goatish-looking little man in a worn black suit was waiting for the phone. I still had to tell Surrett where I was, and make arrangements for him to meet me. Using a code he, but no monitor, would get, I began with the place. Its first letter, I told him, was the second letter of my daughter's first name, its second letter was the second letter of his last name, its third the fourth letter of my daughter's.

"I'm too nervous to get it," he said. "Another clue." Then it registered. "Oh yeah, oh yeah."

"Can you be here tomorrow?" I said. "The time the same as the number of my kids?"

We agreed I would call him back in two hours to give him a detailed spot for the rendezvous and to let him pass on the news to his "clients." Laboriously, using our codes, we worked out a new pay phone number where I could call him.

While I waited, I bought a tweed coat and then wandered around the town looking for a rendezvous site. I found it in the rambling municipal park, acres of elm, oak, sycamore sheltering statuary, benches, playgrounds. I picked a statue that looked like Abraham Lincoln but proved on inspection to be Victor Hugo.

When I called back, the odds had fallen away from fifty-fifty. I could tell by Surrett's voice that something had gone wrong.

"It's not going to be me coming over. "It'll be the client's son." That would be Magliorocco's eldest, an oily ewer bearer who, Surrett had suggested, was something of a disappointment to his old man. He had, like Dylis, gotten an education before he joined the family business. My guess was that he wouldn't come alone.

"Why not you?"

"They don't want you and me to hoke up anything. Maybe they don't want me out of the country. They don't fully believe your story," he added with a heavy wad of fear beneath the stiff upper lip. "They're worried you may have taken the stuff."

I began to sweat as the implications of their disbelief struck me. Dylis, my enemy, was dead. Had he been replaced by Bernie Magliorocco, my enemy?

"Ouch!" I said.

"You're sure your story will stand up?" Now even Danny was doubting me. Small wonder, since my story was a lie. And lies, as opposed to dissembling, had never been my strong suit.

"Of course," I said firmly. "When's he due here?"

"Thursday. He's coming all the way from Hong Kong." He'd be there, I knew, on the guns-drug thing. Weevils in the flour: they never rested. Thursday was two days away.

But Bernie would not worry that I would cut and run. Anne and Alexa were his hostages in Philadelphia. He would not hesitate to injure of even kill one of them if he thought I had stolen his money and fled. The death or maiming of one would guarantee that I would return to face the music and save the other. On that kind of thing, the mob seldom makes mistakes.

Gloomily, using codes with base words from our long friendship, I told Surrett where I'd meet young Magliorocco. And whoever.

"A statue. My ex-deputy's first name, but with a *V*"—that would be *Vector*, but it was close enough.

Using the same kind of name code, I spelled out *Hugo*.

"You misspelled the statue's first name, stupido," he said when he had gotten it. At least some of the spirit was coming back in him. "Where is it?"

"Their embassy will tell you. Or a librarian maybe."

"I'd have been better off as a librarian," he said.

"Listen," I said. "If you get desperate, you can get me at the hotel . . ." I coded out the name of the Cravat. "I'll be eating my last supper there."

He did not laugh. I had a final thought.

"Tell Anne the family doesn't have to worry about D, and tell her—" and I gulped, the tears starting, thinking of her calling me a wimp, a coward—"that I'm over here arranging things so that she won't have to worry about the rest of them either."

If it came to saving my own ass or theirs, I didn't have much choice. Surely, I thought, that says something decent about me. I wanted Anne to know about that if the worst happened and I wound up doing the dead man's float in the Alzette.

"I forgot to tell you," Surrett said, now both anxious and abashed. "I got so upset I forgot to tell you that she and fatso are finito."

"She told you?"

"I saw him at a disco-restaurant with one of his legal teenyboppers." Danny, like me, would know that meant Anne and Brockman were finished. She might demean herself with a man like Brockman, but not unless he were hers exclusively.

"Is she seeing anybody else?"

"I don't know." He paused. "Maybe you should call her." That had too much of the death-bed portent for my tastes. I wanted her to know what I had done, but I didn't want to call her.

"How about the settlement?"

"It's stalled again. She's got a new lawyer. She's going to be easy on you."

"Look," I said. "Don't fool around. Tell my guy to give her everything she wants. Tell her that, too, when you call. That I said that." I was feeling teary all over again. Last will and testament. Surrett tried to rally us both, with graveyard humor.

"I'll put it in writing," he said. "The executor"— Surrett himself—"may not be around to handle the estate."

I thought of how I would like to see Alexa before anything happened to me. I thought of seeing pop one last time, too. But when I imagined his face, empty of everything but the all-embracing kindness of his blue gaze, the fragility of it, I remembered wrenchingly Calvacadi's child, just as I had seen pop in the boy.

If I were there with pop, I thought, I would tell him about Silvia. "She is one of only sixty-two women chemical engineers in Italy," I would have said, knowing that was the sort of thing that would once have interested him.

At the hotel, as dusk came, I tore Dylis's topcoat until it looked worthy of the trash can. I ditched it in a bin near the go-go district of the Americanized little duchy.

In the morning I skulked out and bought the *Corriere* and the *International Herald-Trib* to see if there was anything possibly about Dylis and Calvacadi. I also bought a paperback of Camus's essays, the only book in English I could find at the store besides the Bible that reflected the solemnity of my mood. As I read in my room, I sweated, occasionally staring out at the late fall traffic on boulevard Roosevelt.

In one of the essays, a couple of lines jumped out at me that I read over and over: "If all experiences are indifferent, that of duty is as legitimate as any other. One can be virtuous through a whim."

I thought about that for a while. It was too barren. In not taking the money back to Bernie, in risking my ass now for my family, I was being virtuous. Virtue was different from simply doing good. Virtue was doing good when doing evil or nothing was safer and simpler. Virtue had been a long time coming to me. And now, as part of the universal foolishness, I might be going to die for it.

XIX.
A BRIEF REUNION

The same day, a little after noon, the room phone rang. At first, I was sure it was the wrong number. I picked up the receiver; but it would be Surrett. Maybe tomorrow's meeting with Bernie's son-en-voy-executioner was put off. Or put forward. Maybe this was Magliorocco junior himself. Maybe they'd decided to believe me. Not likely. No, it could only be bad, bad, bad news.

I was dumbfounded to hear Anne's voice, a little tentative but, from such long practice, crisp and controlled.

"George, I'm at the airport. Here in Luxembourg." I pressed the earpiece to into my head. It was impossible.

"Anne?" I asked, still not fully believing. "What the hell—?"

"Yes, me," she said, cutting in on me. "I've found your hotel on the city map. I've rented a car. I want to talk with you ."

"You came this far?"

"I'll come by. Would it be good to take a drive?"

She spoke rapidly to make sure I did not say no, even had I wanted to.

I saw her bewilderment when she pulled up to the hotel and spotted me, a man with unfamiliar brown hair, a beard, and a moustache, in a European-style coat, striding toward her car. On her face was a moment's fright. Did she see me as a Mafia killer come to wipe her out after murdering her husband?

Then she recognized me and her face relaxed. She leaned over the seat of the new, rented Ford, pushed open the door, and we drove off.

"I'm stunned," I said. "What? . . ."

"Okay," she said, maneuvering the car carefully up to an unfamiliar cluster of traffic lights. "Okay, just let me . . ." She crossed the serpentine river and said, "I picked a town called Echternach. It's supposed to have a restaurant in an old castle. I thought maybe . . ."

"Fine, fine," I said, still amazed. "Why? . . ."

She took a deep breath and explained that Danny had called her and given her my messages: That she need no longer worry about Dylis or the rest, and that she could dictate the settlement.

"It sounded like he was reading me your will," she said. "He said it all a little bitterly, as if you are putting your head in the noose." Her next words came less confidently. "In a noose for us."

"So you—"

"I asked him for details. You know Danny. No go. I asked whether it would hurt things if I flew over there."

"He said, 'No, it wouldn't,' " I interrupted.

"Yes." I smiled and her tenseness lifted a little. "In

369

effect, he said, 'Go.' He gave me your hotel and your phony name." Usually so glib, she looked for words. "Whatever you think, I'm not an ingrate. You are taking a risk with your life for me, us — that was what Danny was saying — I wanted a hand in the decision regardless of what's happened between us."

"You needn't have." In my heart, I was pleased. There was nothing I could do other than stiff it through, hope that fear did not conquer my audacity and my ingeniousness, hope that I was smarter than the Magliaroccos. But it was good having this once-pal, once-wife caring about me. I was grateful and she must have felt it. She went on:

"I, since Alexa doesn't even know, am indebted, no, am damned moved over what you are doing." She paused, her hands tightening and relaxing on the wheel. "I sound like I'm giving you the gold watch on the twenty-fifth anniversary."

Damned if she wasn't getting worked up about me. Me now, and not just her own self-interest in coming.

"So I had to say this to you: about the things that angered you most, my talk of cowardice, my throwing South Philly in your face. The first wasn't true and the second wasn't fair. I said them because I knew how much they would hurt you. I know you, George. And I knew you feared cowardice in yourself and that I had always made you feel so bad about South Philly, maybe even unconsciously. I would have felt guilty all the days of my life if I had not explained, apologized . . ."

If I got killed. The thought plunged me into one

of those bottomless gulches, like stock market panics. They seem to have no floor. Then I turned to agate, like I wanted to do. They were not going to kill me, I thought silently. I am going to make it through. Now I interrupted, echoing her.

"We said awful things to injure each other, not because they were true." I yearned to touch her, to make physical in some way my feelings of forgiveness. But I did not.

She sighed, her important piece said, not looking at me. The suburbs, not much different from those in America, had given way to little hamlets with Germanic churches and shops. We slipped through fall-covered fields and woods. In the bright sunlight, I saw how surely the lines had creased Anne's face. She was almost forty-five, six years older than Silvia. Silvia was less beautiful; but she would also be younger longer. Anne had been thinking other thoughts.

"How much can you tell me?" she said. "Do you have to be like Danny? This masculine stiff-upper-lip thing?"

"Dylis is going to pop up dead one of these days in the company of a guy from the Red Brigades," I said.

"God," she said. "You did do—"

"Deponent sayeth not," I stopped her with lame humor.

"But Dylis was Magliorocco's worst enemy, right? Then why are you still on the skillet?"

Ah. God, it was all so complicated. Why was I on the skillet? Because I had shipped those guns to Monrovia. Because I had taken on Danny as a lawyer when I was sixteen. Because I was born where I was born.

"Because I was supposed to recover some money for Surrett that belonged to the mob," I said. "The money got burned and all I have to show them is the ashes. And they're so goddamned itchy now that they think I salted the money somewhere."

"But Dylis . . . surely that should outweigh . . ."

"Right. You'd think so. Bernie is rid of his nemesis. And Surrett is willing to make up for the money loss. But they don't think that way. So his son and heir is coming over." I grimaced. "Maybe not alone."

I could feel her distress. It had a familiar, secure tingle to it, the feeling of her caring about me, as she had long ago when I had a high fever, or a heartburn that seemed like a coronary, or a bad kink in my back.

"I am going to stay over here until it's settled," she said so abruptly that I laughed in spite of everything.

"The hell you are. You're getting on a plane tonight. It's flattering as hell, honest, but — "

"Danny should be here," she went on.

"No, they wouldn't let him. It doesn't work that way."

I had told her what she needed to know, maybe more. It had cleansed me, shriven me in a way. My anxieties were lifted enough for me to be hungry for talk of the familiar, to want to get away from the subject that led nowhere.

"How about Alexa? Pop?"

She was as glad as I was for a break in the intensity.

"Alexa's fine. All A's, as usual." She hesitated. "A new boyfriend, equally poor. From Chester." She looked at me to see how I was responding. "Would you believe a philosophy major on an indigency scholarship at Penn?"

"These kids from the wrong side of the tracks just keep cropping up generation after generation," I said. Even as lightly as I had said it, it still would have been sparks in tinder when I was at home. Now she smiled, indulging me.

Alexa, she said, had a weekend job and was earning enough to make a down payment on a new car next summer. She was an orderly at Methodist. It was a downtown hospital a half dozen blocks from my old neighborhood. I smiled, pleased almost beyond words, and glanced at Anne. She looked up from the road long enough to meet my gaze with mutual pride. It was the sort of things we expected from Alexa, decent, difficult. The look between us said, "We did something right."

"Alexa had checked out my postcards on a big National Geographic map of Italy to trace where I had been. Anne said she, too, had been curious. I liked that.

Once into talk of home, the words came easy for both of us, as if there were nothing ominous in our being together: just two friends, perhaps not as close as they once had been, driving on an autumn day through a picturesque part of the world.

"Pop?"

She had gone to see him every two weeks. I felt that same moment of—damn it, what else to call it—love, indebtedness, that I had felt toward Surrett when he told me about his own visits. Anne, though, would be the one person besides myself whose presence might transmit itself through the semiconductor of the old man's brain.

"I had a long talk with the head nurse last week," said Anne. The nurse was a woman in her sixties with the polished manners, the ritual kindness of someone who has a piece of the corporate action. She'd be at the nursing home herself one day, using up her equity. Anne mimicked the nurse perfectly:

" 'We're feeling fine, maybe just a little weaker. There just comes a time when we begin to fade.' " That was the way the nurse talked about her patients, always in the first person plural.

As considerate as Anne had been, shielding me with the mimicry from what she was saying, I felt an ice-pick pang. Pop was fading, she had said.

"I want to see him," I said softly. I began to choke up. You will see him, if you lie well enough, I thought.

"They'll believe you," Anne said sturdily. "The one thing. You never lied. You never really knew how very well." She had no way of knowing how nervous that made me.

Echternach was at the foot of a mountain scaled down to the size of the little country. A river separated it from Germany, and the town had fine old merchant houses, narrow streets, broken, futile ramparts, and an ancient church. It was a Teutonic Monterosso.

We lunched in style. The inn was in a chalet, not a castle—as advertised—but it was requisitely antique. They gave us a table beside the fireplace. Under the rafters, darkened by the candle smoke of centuries, there was a special intimacy, something out of Vermeer. They had oysters, shipped in wicker baskets from the coast, and I got them to put two dozen by the fire so they would pop open as they had when we were happy in Chestnut Hill.

"Still life with oysters, wine and ex-husband," I said.

She started to say something. I was not sure what. But she slipped past it, turning safely to talk of the house, to my mixed relief and disappointment.

The downspouts were going and she couldn't remember who it was we called to fix downspouts.

"I looked for the bills . . ." she said.

"It's slipped my mind. I'll call . . ." then I remembered that I would not be anywhere I could call anybody unless I was lucky. I picked at the paper-thin Ardennes ham and tried to look hungry over the calf's liver quenelles. Talk was coming hard again.

"It should be easier than this," she said. "What are you going to do about your hair?"

I smiled, feeling some of the tension go, pleased by her curiosity about something personal. I dug into the food.

"You don't like the brown?" I asked.

"Not much, hardly any. I liked the gray. I didn't think it was your style to follow the TV ads, you know, 'Take a few years off every day.' God," she laughed, "you look young enough anyway . . ."

It was the most intimate thing she had said. The complexity of its meaning was important to me. Was she saying she found me physically attractive? That older men had an easier time finding women than older women had finding men? She saw me dissecting her comment. Now it was I who shifted gears.

"Whatever else, that disaster with Dylis this summer was reversed, so I feel . . ." I looked for a non-boastful word for it.

". . . a little smug," she finished for me and broke into rich laughter, the heartiest of the day. But it was laughter at my expense. She stopped and, though still smiling, added, "I'm sorry. I'm trying so hard . . ."

"It's okay. I *am* feeling pretty good about myself." I imagined young Magliorocco about to make his way to Europe. "In spite of everything." She looked at me thoughtfully.

"Goddamn it," she said, with no heat or rancor. "You may just have pulled it off." There was no joy in it either. I waited for her to go on. "Danny probably told you that it's all done with Brockman."

"He said he thought it was over," I said circumspectly, not trying to fake sympathy, for I felt none.

"He's going to leave the firm," she continued, "open his own."

I wanted to say who broke it off so that I could relish her telling me it was he. But what satisfaction was there in hearing what I knew: that a prick like that had ditched my beautiful wife? The contrariness of my thoughts made me want to chuckle, if bitterly. Instead, I said, as I had that night we made our good-byes:

"You can do better than him."

"Yes," she said with asperity. "If I want to." Her lips were stiff, unrelaxed. She thought I was going to press her to acknowledge Brockman had left her, that I was going to rub it in. I poured her the last of the wine.

"Drink up," I said. "I don't bite anymore."

"I'd like to believe that."

"Believe it," I said.

She studied me seriously. If she had suspected that I had fallen in love while I was away, now I think she knew it. There was an opening to say something, to touch the vulnerability sprung from Brockman's desertion. The moment passed. I felt a schizy mix again of disappointment and deliverance.

"We should get some business stuff out of the way, Anne," I said. Then, wanting to cement some fragment of what almost had happened, I added: "Thank God we aren't fighting, hunh?"

There was a little tightness in her when she said, "Why should we? We were both nice people before we turned cannibal."

We talked — leaving it unspoken as to whether the eventuality was divorce or death — about how to unmeld melded funds, how best from Alexa's point of view we could dissolve joint tenancies and our shareholderships in common.

On the way back to the capital, we discussed how we would handle Christmas: one big, wonderful meal for all three of us — just as if it were sure there'd be three of us around to eat it.

She asked me again as we approached the town, dusk setting in now, if I were sure I didn't want her to stay over, to be here to counsel with if there were some new decisions to be made.

I didn't want that. If my story didn't hold up tomorrow, they would kill me here and I didn't want her around. I thought to myself: being killed is such a personal thing, like going to the bathroom. It is not the sort of thing normal people want to have anybody around for.

And in this world I had gotten myself into, it was as casual as going to the bathroom. Magliorocco's torpedo would dispatch me in the park, or later as I walked the street, with no malice, as simply and satisfyingly as a wrecker knocks down an old wall.

But I could not fly, could not save myself and thereby endanger this woman who did not love me, and my daughter, who did. I had to take my chances, was helpless not to.

Anne sensed my thoughts. The gray dusk of December in a small, industrialized European capital lay cold and drab on the city. The rush-hour cars poured past in the opposite direction.

At other times, her strength and her defenses would have worked to spare us both any great pain. But I had seen in her today, perhaps for both the first and last times, a mirror of myself when I first began to think of dropping out. Something in her, too, was saying, if faintly, "Do I want to do this anymore?" Tax law and brilliant parties weren't going to be enough pretty soon.

We were downtown. Simultaneously, we thought of tomorrow. She reached over and clutched my hand and I held hers as tightly, both of us silent. She broke our grip only to turn.

At the hotel, she hugged me, crying . . . as I knew she would. Leave-takings had always been tough for her. They would have been difficult enough if we were saying a final good-bye to our marriage. But we both knew it might be a final good-bye, period.

I held her, hoping to comfort her, feeling the slender, once-cherished body through her light coat. When she stopped weeping, I broke away and looked into her tear-stained face. Under the yellow light from the street, her eyes were unpretty from running makeup. Yet it was her face, familiar, even beloved.

"You know, I guess that I would have offered to spend the night with you if I had thought you would say yes," she said.

"I know," I said, and I began to cry, too, turning my lips to hers, tasting saltiness from our tears in that long, desperate kiss.

I could not read Camus that night, nor could I sleep. Almost until dawn, I rehearsed my talk with young Magliorocco. I was mad to do that: the repetitions would cost me freshness and authenticity. But how could I think of anything else?

At last, my groggy mind said, "No more," my wakeful nightmare clicked off like a switch. In that limbo between fear and exhausted sleep, I felt at peace, able to indulge myself. I thought of Anne winging back toward Chestnut Hill. She would soon be lying cozily in our bed, her long legs drawn up. If I were with her. I would make love to her and then, all night, I would curl around her, warm in that chrysalis of sheets and blankets.

I thought of what Silvia had said that morning over breakfast at Fegina: "Don't think she won't want you back now I have helped make a new you of you."

Did Anne want me back? I thought I'd had a hint of that. Maybe it was no more than her wanting some man of her own now that Brockman had flushed her. I grunted. Did I want her back?

Despite Anne's sudden dazzling appearance *in extremis,* the divorce was all but at the decree stage now. And as she had been diminished in her own eyes by her affair with Brockman, so she had diminished in mine.

She might be wiser, even kinder now. But she was battered, a goddess without a pedestal or shrine. I was no longer a worshipper. My love for Silvia, my accomplishments in Venice, murderous as they were, had freed me of the religion in which she was the idol. We were, after so many years, equals.

The traumas of the past month had freed me not just from Anne. I believed I could feel it was worthwhile to put in a day's work that would hurt no one, rather, would help them.

I could now take a case like that of the householders on Darby Creek fighting off the industrial poisoners. Or I could form a company to market small electronic medical aids at a decent price. It would be the sort of thing I'd be good at. Jesus, the big hearing-aid companies were robbing the deaf blind.

I was my own boss. I had bought that independence on the installment plan and at a high cost, part of which was that I was alone. Yet I could live with my loneliness, if I lived.

The old man at Camogli had married it. Being married to loneliness was, when all was said and done, better than nothing at all. It was far better than other terminal diseases, infinitely preferable to summary execution.

XX.
LAST RITES

At one, I went to the park and sat on the bench beneath the author of *Les Miserables,* and finished up the latest *Corriere.* Little Frog was in my pocket. I was reluctantly willing to die if I had to. But if it came to it and I had the chance, I was going to take at least one of my killers along.

I saw young Magliorocco at the same time he saw me. He was a nervous, balding man who looked like he should be running a dry cleaning shop. Except around the eyes—they were flat, almost oriental, and cunning as a monkey's. There was no one with him. His accomplice, if any, would be among the trees, where he could pop me off if this twerp gave a signal. I imagined it would be hidden and private like the bid of a millionaire at an art auction.

"I saw the statue from across the street," he murmured after we had shaken hands and sat down. "It looked more like Lincoln."

"Funny, I thought the same thing." We both laughed uneasily.

"Mr. Orsini," he said, "I don't want to be rude,

but I wonder if I could see your passport?" He knew, of course, that was not my name. But his business accustomed him to maintaining certain pretenses.

Still, his question further heated up my paranoia, which was already simmering at about 210 Fahrenheit. How the hell, really, did I know this was the don's son? I gripped the Beretta in my pocket.

"Look, I don't want to be rude either," I said. "But I have been sitting on hot nails for more than a month on behalf of your lawyer and your family and I am one jumpy son-of-a-bitch. I have got a small pistol pointing at your nuts right now, in fact. So maybe *you* had better produce *your* passport first, and then we can get down to business."

He looked shocked, then gave me a sallow smile. He had put himself in my shoes. "Of course," he said. He pulled out his passport and there it was, Bernard Lucian Magliorocco, Jr., the photo a cut above your average mug shot.

"Fine," I said, "fine." I pointedly took my hand out of my gun pocket and opened my fake passport.

"We have big problems, Mr. Orsini," he said.

"Well," I said, "Surrett said to tell you everything, so ask away." He looked at the attaché case.

"The, uh, remains are in there?"

"Yep. All I could dig out of the stove and I dug out all there was, I think. When we leave, it's all yours. There's also about twenty thousand in Swiss francs in a money belt and maybe two hundred in lire in his wallet. Also Dylis's wallet. With about a thousand in it."

"What happened to the half million?" he asked.

As planned, I blamed the burned money on Calvacadi, saying I had picked him up at the hospital and followed him for hours. At the farmhouse on Torcello, he had heard me and thought police had found him. He had burned the money. Dylis had bushwhacked me, but when the two tried to kill me, I had turned the tables and killed them.

As I talked, I tried to read the man. His appearance was so unprepossessing, the son sent out by the father to try to make the best of an unpleasant and complicated glitch in the family business. His fingernails were chewed to frayed stubs. I wondered if this generation of Mafia heirs went to shrinks to get rid of anxieties like other businessmen did.

This one might be fine at extortion, narcotics, and payoffs to police, but he was no logician, no long-term thinker. In this foreign land, with this offbeat job, he was a dinosaur, lacking real ability to adapt. Still, he was quick and had a feeling for relationships and nuances. Maybe America was lucky that's all it took to be a top hood. If they were strategists, they might own even more of the country than they already did.

When I finished, he pursed his lips and tried to look thoughtful. What he was weighing was whether to believe my basic story or not. That was spooky. I might look down on him, but he was my judge and jury with power over my life.

"You knew the Red Brigade man was burning the money when you saw the smoke?" he began his cross-examination. On your toes now, I thought.

"He knew I was out in the clearing, heard me as he went in the house. He didn't know how many I was. I saw the smoke. There was plenty of moon. But I could see the smoke."

Watch out, I told myself. Not so damned much talk.

"And you knew it was the money?"

"What else would be burning if he thought I was the cops? He wouldn't be fixing me a veal parmigiana."

He smiled wanly.

"You could not rush the house?" he asked.

"No," I said. "I wanted the money. But it would've been suicide. If you want to understand it thoroughly, you can go there, and walk into that goddamned jungle at night to see whether you would try to rush the house." I began to sweat beneath my new tweed coat.

"Why didn't he come out of the house as soon as Mr. Dylis captured you?" He said the name with contempt. He must have suspected daddy had considered disinheriting him in favor of Dylis.

"He did come out. Dylis called to him. He had me down by the canal. Calvacadi told him to hold me and went back and put out the fire."

More thought. Then:

"You don't mind my questions?"

"Surrett said to tell you everything."

"How come Calvacadi heard you in the brush? You couldn't hear Dylis?"

"Who knows? For one thing, he was farther behind me. I came on Calvacadi right there at the farm house, you know."

"Dylis was maybe ten minutes behind you, far enough back so you couldn't hear him even if the wind had been blowing your way?"

"Yeah," I said. "About that." What was he trying to do?

"So you had Calvacadi cooped up for ten minutes."

Sure, I thought, if Dylis was ten minutes behind, then I would have had Calvacadi cooped up for ten minutes.

"And Dylis—"

"Came up on me from behind. Knocked down my gun. Got his in my back. I felt like a goddamned fool."

"I'd think. Why didn't he just kill you? Avoid the risk?"

"I can't read his mind. Maybe to find out what the hell I was up to . What kind of manpower I had with me in Venice. You know, my appearance must have been pretty—"

"Upsetting for them, too," he agreed.

He had me describe the encounter again and how I had turned the tables. Maybe he had sensed the ad hoc quality of my recitation. I told it flatly, without any emotion over killing the two men.

"There was no avoiding that? About Dylis we are, of course, pleased. But about the Red Brigade man. There could be problems."

"No. I had no choices."

"Why was Calvacadi going to the island for the money, anyway?"

"I don't know. To turn it over to the Brigades? To change its hiding place?"

"And he heard you on the path as you came into the clearing?"

"No, within the clearing itself. After he'd gone and gotten the money, wherever it was hidden." He had tried to mousetrap me on a detail about my position. Jesus, what other little land mines had he laid down? "I saw him at the door. Not long enough to get a shot at him."

"Pity," he said. The greed was in his voice.

"I thought killing him was a problem."

"Yes, but not having the money is a bigger problem." He said it evenly, the malice and power in the words, not the voice.

"Well, there was no chance to shoot him at the door. Besides, killing is not my ordinary *mestiere*"—trade.

"You changed to that *mestiere* pretty well when you had to," he smiled that wan little grin again. "What made him think you were the police?"

"Perhaps he didn't. He'd have done the same if he thought I was your people, I suppose." Son of Don nodded. I wondered whether I was passing. He was winding down on the questioning, but still went back through the whole story again, hoping to come up with a new question, worried, no doubt, that his father would think of something he hadn't asked. He hit on a new one:

"Was there gasoline or something in there to burn the money with?"

And suddenly I saw that this question that he had stumbled on could be my sentence to death. And Surrett's too. I had said Calvacadi was only inside for ten minutes because Magliorocco had approached it from another angle: how far Dylis was behind me. It had taken me at least twenty minutes

387

to burn the money. Calvacadi could never have done it in ten even if he lit the fire the moment he closed the door.

This small, not terribly bright man could begin a process ending in my death because of this unexpected pop quiz question. I was frightened to the core.

"Kerosene," I said. It was still smoldering when I got in there." Oh blessed little lies, I prayed, be believed and let me live!

"He could burn up five hundred thousand dollars in hundreds in ten minutes? That's how long you said he was in there." Gentle as a cat playing with a dead mouse, he had hit me with the crucial question.

"There's a little of it left," I said. My mouth went dry as sand. I hoped there was no change in my expression. "It must smolder pretty fast even with water on it."

"Ten minutes?"

"Look," I said, affecting a long-suffering tone. "I did not have a stopwatch on him." His eyes were flat, unrevealing. I stared into them and said softly, "Have you ever waited in the dark outside a house where there's a man with a gun, and in a country where you can't half speak the language?" He blinked from my gaze. "No, you grew up on the fucking pretty-boy side of the business."

"I've done what I had to do," he said, a bit defensively.

"Then next time you do what you have to do with the piss all but running down your leg from fright, you tell me the difference between ten and twenty or

388

thirty, even, minutes."

He stopped, feeding the answer into his head, the possibility of whether he had caught me in a lie or whether a mistake on the ten minutes was a natural one, of whether my lashing out at him was genuine scorn or desperate camouflage. He would be thinking how his father would judge the same answers. With no change in tone, he went on.

"Why did you take chances, bringing back this money belt, and these wallets. You could have kept them and how would we have known?"

"I earn my money," I said. "Besides, you guys are scary bastards."

"You overestimate us," he said, not meaning it. "You could have gotten away with that much."

"You might have learned about the francs. You maintain your liaisons with the Brigades."

"We would be fools not to," he allowed himself a small self-congratulation. Again, he tracked back and forth across my story. At the end of another half hour, I thought he was pretty well done. If I sensed anything, it was that I had passed, by a hair. But I wasn't betting on it.

"Could we take a short walk?" he said. "I want to open the attaché case. Even more privately."

Privately? I thought, in panic. Further into the park! They are going to kill me! Magliorocco saw me reach into my pocket and grip the pistol. But I didn't care. He found a bench and signaled me to it. Taut with fright, I gave him the combination of the three-cylinder lock and he opened the case and peered into the green plastic bag at the ashes.

"That's the works," I said lamely.

"Jesus," he said, poking at the now dry gray mass, "all that money." He unfolded an edge of the money belt but did not count the francs. Then he glanced at the lire and fake identification in Calvacadi's wallet and, intently, at Dylis's passport.

When he'd finished, he shut the attaché case. I pulled out a handkerchief and wiped off the case and the combination dial, feeling at the same time my palm wet with sweat.

"You ought to be careful about your fingerprints," I said.

"Yes," he said, looking nervous. "Yes. You're right." He held the attaché case gingerly.

"Sorry I couldn't deliver this to you in Philadelphia," I said.

"I understand. You've done your share," he said, unfailingly polite.

"I'm sure you know a good lab that can give you a money count. And there looked like a few thousand could be salvaged." He only half bought the appeal.

"Yes," he said, playing the efficient businessman, one whose company has been down on its luck, but who knows how to handle things. "We have connections here for such things. We won't even have to take it back home." Then he looked at me, more sharply than usual. "The problem is that with burned money, one cannot tell the denominations, only whether it is, in fact, money." I felt my apprehensions deepen. But it was only an observation. He added:

"We sometimes have jobs we like to farm out." I could have hugged him. I had passed. I felt faint, dizzy.

"I would like not to think about jobs for a while," I said.

"Yes," he said, even sympathetically. "We can reach you through the lawyer friend?" He did not like to say the word *Surrett.* I felt they still blamed Surrett for their troubles, even though they had, in an adequate if not entirely satisfactory way, been solved.

"Probably," I said. I felt steady enough to make the pitch I had not not found an opening for or dared to make up now. I suggested that he return the money in the money belt to the Red Brigades as a gift to the kid, along with the $200 in lire from Calvacadi's wallet.

"With Calvacadi dead, there isn't going to be any money going to the kid," I said. "From what I gather, you guys don't want any more trouble with the Red Brigades. It would be a sort of peace gesture." And peace would mean no revenge on Calvacadi's killer.

"Yeah, but twenty thousand dollars?"

"Surrett? . . ." I suggested. They were already into him for the half million. And the extra $20,000 would be the best kind of life insurance that Surrett could buy for himself, and for me.

"I'll think about it," Magliorocco said. "Keep quiet about that. If we go for it, it'll be just yours and my idea."

I could see him coming around. It was the kind of thing his old man might like and think him wise for coming up with. After all, it was the old man who was most hot for peace.

"I wouldn't have thought of it if you hadn't

kept asking me about the francs and the kid and so on," I said, kissing his ass because he was not now going to kill me.

"Let's not bullshit each other," he said, seeing what I was doing, not displeased with it, but wanting me to know he wasn't such a fool that I could con him. I began to see something in this little criminal. It was a bad habit: I was not a good hater. He must have sensed me warming to him.

"You've had a tough go, hunh, paisano?" he said.

We got up and walked the rest of the way through the park and gardens. At the end of the gardens, there was an old people's home and then an outlook on the Alzette River, far below us.

"You'll be going home?" he asked.

"I don't know," I said. "I don't know what I'll do."

"But not this anymore?"

"No," I said. "You?"

"We do what we have to do."

The little man was trying to sound gallant about it, but it didn't work. Far away as he was at this moment from where he did what he had to do, he allowed a wistful note into his voice. "It's not exactly what I learned at Rutgers," he said.

"It's a fine school," I said. We shook hands at the big street that ran by the gardens. He walked up to the corner to hail a cab and a second man, taller, beefier, moved from the park and joined him, my would-be executioner. Be satisfied, I told them silently, my body shaking uncontrollably. You got a free vacation in picturesque Luxembourg.

Both looked behind them, sharp as Calvacadi,

sharp as I would have been, sharp as cops and private eyes and shyster lawyers, our whole brotherhood, all of us wanting to make sure no one is following.

After they caught their cab, I walked back to the hotel, still shivering. I bought some hair dye on the way. At the hotel, I called Surrett. I told him I thought we were going to get by.

As elliptically as I could, I described what had happened.

"It will be okay," he sighed. "I know the way they work. From what he said, from what they did, it's going to be okay, Georgie." He talked about it excitedly, then gratefully. I told him I was coming home, was ready for work.

Surret suggested big cases he would get me: another utilities case, like the one I had started on, *Mid-National v. Purpose-Richman;* an aluminum rivalry between two giants . . .

I told him I didn't want that anymore. I wanted cases that I could feel clean about. I told him about the polluted creek.

"Robin Hood stuff," he said, with no sarcasm. He was eager to talk about my future. "Shall I get it around you're in the market for David-and-Goliath cases?"

"No," I said. "I don't want you to do a thing. Please, Danny." It was the kindest way I could think of to let him know that things weren't the same. He waited for me to say more. My silence was as eloquent as if I had slapped him. Quickly, he hid his emotions.

"Okay," he said. Then, wanting to make it as easy

for me as he could, he added, "I understand." Now it hurt me. But there wasn't anything more for us to say about what had changed, at least nothing that would make it any better.

I called Anne at the office.

"Fraser and Associates," the secretary said. I grinned: bye-bye Brockman. Anne came on, her usual calm shattered by nervousness.

"It's okay?" she asked.

"Yes."

Ah, Anne. She wept, great marvelous sobs on the phone. I waited until she stopped.

'Don't make the mistake of thinking that I am weeping for anything other than relief," she said. She broke down again for a moment. I did not argue the point. I told her I would be coming back to Philadelphia.

I would get a small house on an acre with a garden, but I did not tell her that. I wanted to see Alexa as often as I could, but I did not go into that either.

"We ought to think of seeing each other from time to time," I said. She would know I did not mean merely to work out details of the separation. But I was unwilling to say more than that. For there was Silvia, too. I would see her again. And although I was neither fickle, nor, God knew, promiscuous, I knew there would be other women I would meet and like before I chose to remarry.

"I would like that," Anne replied perkily, making me feel good, wanted. But she could never just let it go. "It would all have to be structured differently, wouldn't it?" she added. How quickly she was able to desert emotion for abstraction.

But why argue it: Of course it would be different. We were different.

I sat on the side of the tub and cut up my fake passport and identification papers and flushed them. I broke down the Beretta and put it in an envelope. That evening I would sow the parts in various stretches of the Alzette. The snake was shedding his old skin.

I dyed the brown out of my hair, trying to turn it back to it's natural gray black. Then I shaved off the beard and the moustache, carefully washing the severed hair down the drain. I had left quite a record of this unwanted case in the sewers of Italy and Luxembourg. How much of a record, I wondered, had it left on me? Soon, I would find out.

More Adventure in
THEY CALL ME THE MERCENARY
by Axel Kilgore

TRIVIA MANIA
by Xavier Einstein

TRIVIA MANIA has arrived! With enough questions to answer every trivia buff's dreams, TRIVIA MANIA covers it all—from the delightfully obscure to the <u>seemingly obvious</u>. Tickle your fancy, and test your memory!